Betting On PARADISE

Other Titles By Lizbeth Selvig

Seven Brides for Seven Cowboys:
The Bride Wore Denim
The Bride Wore Red Boots
The Bride Wore Starlight
Betting On Paradise

Love From Kennison Falls:
The Rancher and the Rock Star
Rescued by a Stranger
Beauty and the Brit
Good Guys Wear Black

Novellas and Shorts:
Going Out on a Limb
Clockwork Whalers - with Naomi Stone

Betting On PARADISE

A Seven Brides For Seven Cowboys Novel

LIZBETH SELVIG

Webster Publishing

Betting On Paradise

Copyright 2017 by Lizbeth Selvig

Editing: Kelli Collins
and
Jennifer Selvig Van Vranken

Cover Design: Dana Lamothe-Designs By Dana

ISBN: 978-0-9988564-1-4

To Riley David ...
... my freshest inspiration, my latest crush, my newest little hero. May you grow to learn that the most important things in life are your family, your character, and your heart.
And that all you EVER need is love.

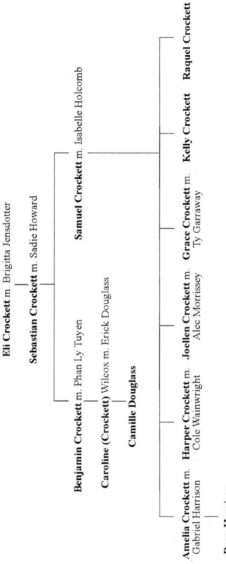

The Crockett Family Tree

Eli Crockett m. Brigitta Jensdotter

Sebastian Crockett m. Sadie Howard

Benjamin Crockett m. Phan Ly Tuyen

Caroline (Crockett) Wilcox m. Erick Douglass

Camille Douglass

Samuel Crockett m. Isabelle Holcomb

Amelia Crockett m. Gabriel Harrison

Harper Crockett m. Cole Wainwright

Joellen Crockett m. Alec Morrissey

Grace Crockett m. Ty Garraway

Kelly Crockett

Raquel Crockett

Rory Harrison
Sadie Isabelle Harrison

Prologue

TY GARRAWAY HADN'T had a windfall in the past six months of Wednesday night poker games, but this week he had a good feeling. Whether he'd finally made room for Lady Luck by mucking out his apartment in order to host the game, or perfectly aligned stars simply graced the sky, for the first time in ages the old magic zipped through his veins.

Ty knew not to depend on poker-night winnings for his financial well-being, although a great night could yield up to five or six hundred bucks. Tonight, however, his finances were more dire than usual. His ancient F-250 had blown a head gasket, and where the hell he was going to get sixteen hundred dollars to fix it was beyond him. If he *didn't* get it fixed he had no way to get to his job, and if he didn't work, he didn't pay his rent.

He was not a big fan of homelessness.

So he coveted the five hundred bucks amassed in the center of his worn, secondhand table. Unfortunately, as well things had been going, at the moment he held his worst hand of the night: a ridiculous three of a kind with fours.

"What's your pleasure, Garraway?" Carl Wagner's brows arched in impatience.

"Yeah, time's up, Ty-rone." Pete Hagen at least added a grin to his prodding.

Ty scowled. They were only giving him shit, but he had been contemplating for too long.

"I call," he said finally.

An explosion of pounding on the door made all five men around the table jump and rendered Ty's decision moot. Pete dropped a card from his hand. Bryce Holloway, balanced on the back legs of his chair, windmilled his arms barely in time to right himself. Ty stood and stared at the white metal, low-rent district, standard-issue apartment door.

The pummeling came again.

"What the hell, Garraway, did you forget to pay your rent?" Bryce asked.

"Oh, keep your girlie drawers on. It's probably Girl Scouts selling cookies." Ty reached the door and cut off a third round of pounding.

"Hey, wanna tell me what's going on?" he asked before his words lodged in his throat.

The woman looked vastly different than she had three years before, but Ty recognized her immediately. What had been wavy, shoulder-length hair the color of russet ale, was now short and spiky and dyed candy-apple red. She'd put on about twenty pounds, which, honestly, looked good on her, and she held her lips in a thin, determined line. The only thing that hadn't changed was the wild-assed brightness in her eyes that hinted at the unpredictable time bomb of crazy buried deep inside.

"Good God. Carrie?" he asked.

Her eyes calmed by a degree.

He hadn't figured out the crazy until well into their two-month relationship, but once Ty had broken off the affair, he hadn't mourned.

"Long time no see, huh?" The words tumbled from her mouth in a slightly breathless rush, as if she'd run the five flights of stairs to stand at apartment 501.

"What are you doing here?" He stared, still incredulous.

That's when he saw the child.

She stood beside Carrie, steel-blue eyes wide and innocent as a fawn's, three and half feet tall, with wind-blown strawberry-blonde hair that framed her face like a pastel sunset. A field of freckles decorated her cheeks and the bridge of her nose, making her a pink angel of a little girl—complete with a pink backpack and miniature pink rolling suitcase. Ty's mouth went dry with the blossoming of confusion.

"What's going on?" he asked.

"Tag," Carrie replied simply. "You're it."

With no further explanation, she unslung a larger canvas bag from her shoulder and set it on the floor.

"Now hold on—"

"Surprise. You're a daddy."

Emotion punched into his chest, real as a fist, and would have sent him staggering backward, but he clung to the door handle while shock burgeoned into full-on fear. He knew the woman was mistaken and that her crazy was in control, but for the moment she believed what she was saying and had the luggage to back it up.

"I don't know what you think you're pulling here or what kind of trouble you're in, but this is not funny."

"Dang right it's not funny." Her lips tightened further. "I let you off the hook for three years by telling my husband she was his. Now he knows she's not, and I can keep him or keep her. My parents, who watched her most of the time, died earlier this year, and I'm not losing Curt too. That means it's your turn."

"She is *not* my child."

Crap on a Cheez-It, he sounded like Michael Jackson.

"Oh, honey, that's where you're wrong."

He liked women, he couldn't deny it. But he wasn't callous, and he didn't sow his oats without protection. Ever. He'd learned that lesson from his old man, who'd been anything but careful his entire miserable life.

"Carrie, you can't do this to a child."

"Give her to her father? Watch me. I'm about to." She turned to the girl, who hadn't made a peep, and tilted her face upward. "Teagan, this is your dad. See? He's real."

Teagan? If that wasn't the trendiest name. Who saddled a baby with a moniker like that?

"Say hello," Carrie continued.

The girl switched her gaze calmly to him. "Hello, Daddy."

The punch this time was different—deeper, harder, less expected, and much scarier. Ty sensed the incredulous stares of his poker mates, glanced over his shoulder, and saw the four men gaping as if they'd spotted Bigfoot, Nessie, and Santa Claus rolled into one. He couldn't blame them. Flying reindeer were more believable than the idea of Ty Garraway as a father.

He didn't know what made him squat in front of the little girl named Teagan, but when he did, prepared to let her down gently, something snared the words in his throat. She looked back at him, quizzical and baby-faced but with a perception far beyond what he thought a three-year-old should have had. Then her tiny tongue poked from between her lips and twisted sideways before she bit down on it thoughtfully.

Ty's heart skipped a beat. Any number of people bit their tongues when they were thinking, but that added tongue twist

... how many times had he been teased about that very habit as a kid?

He still did it when he was tired.

A freaking coincidence.

"Look ..." What did you call a miniature human? Honey, sweetheart, kid? He shook his head. "Look, uh, Teagan? I'm not—"

Her little body launched itself at his, and she wrapped her arms around his neck, snuggling in tightly as if to ward off a rejection.

"Aw ..." He bit off a mild curse and tried to heed the voice in his brain warning him to peel the child off and hand her back to her mother.

"I wanted for you to be real," she said.

The earlier sensation of a boxer's fisted knuckles slamming into his chest returned, morphing into fingers that grabbed his heart and squeezed. Not knowing what else to do, he supported her by her tiny little butt and stood. Teagan laid her head on his shoulder, and something inside heated and melted. The sensation terrified him.

"Looks like the bonding happened in record time." Carrie gave a quick, satisfied nod. She pulled the girl's tiny suitcase through the door and propped it against the wall. Reaching into the bag she'd set down earlier, she pulled out a thick manila envelope. "Everything you need is in here, Ty. She's a good kid. Take care of her." She held out the packet, and when he didn't take it, she set it on Teagan's suitcase. With a shrug, she turned to leave.

"Oh no you don't. Hold on a go—ol dang minute." Again he narrowly avoided cursing and pulled Teagan from their embrace to set her on the floor. "You cannot walk out and leave me with a kid who doesn't have a clue who I am. I have no way of taking care of her. What do you mean, your husband knows she's not his?"

"When he needed some medical tests done, there was a reason to do a DNA match. It was pretty obvious I'd lied about her being his daughter. If I'm going to stay with him, you're the only choice there is for Teagan." She nodded coolly at the child pressed to the side of his leg.

"Carrie, for crying out loud! How do I get in touch with you if she needs you?"

Carrie's eyes betrayed nothing, no regret, no sadness, not even the light indicating crazy. "Oh she won't. Will you, baby?" She regarded Teagan as if the child were a stray she was leaving at the pound. "I'm not the warm, maternal mommy type, anyway. She's spent most of her time with my parents, and they're gone now. Good-bye, Ty."

Every instinct told him to run after her. Teagan's face stopped him. Like her mother, she didn't cry, but was the poster child for utter sadness. Good God in heaven, what must she be thinking? What did a three-year-old even understand? Weren't they temper tantrums waiting to happen? Or was that a two-year-old?

Another wave of panic crashed him into rocks of uncertainty and froze him in place with no clue what to do or say.

"Daddy?" she asked.

"Don't call—"

He halted. He'd just been worrying about her feelings. How could he crush her further? This wasn't her fault.

"Hey," he said. "I'm sorry about your mom leaving you here like this. Are you okay?"

He didn't know if she understood what he was saying, but

to his shock, she took the pointer finger of his left hand and gripped it as if it brought her comfort. "Mommy and Daddy Curt don't want any little girls. If you do, I'm okay."

She had the face of an angel, the stature of a small child, and the diction and vocabulary of a ten-year-old. Or a six-year-old. Or maybe all three-year-olds talked like this. He had no freakin' clue. But her eyes bored into his asking for his answer, and when he couldn't turn away, she smiled as if to encourage him. It was tentative, questioning. And there were those enormous, blue, baby deer eyes again.

A fresh new swell, big as a surfer's dream wave, rose up and crashed over him—but this time it was protectiveness. He couldn't keep this helpless creature for any length of time. He'd find out who she really was and locate her true relatives. But until then he could try, despite the four gamblers, two cigar butts, and ten empty beer bottles that made up most of his décor, to keep her safe.

"You know what? Tonight I do want at least one little girl. And I promise—we'll find a way to get you back with your mom where you belong."

"I could belong here," she said. "That would be easier." She pronounced it "easy-oh," the first sign of baby talk he'd heard.

Panic reared its ugly head again. It would *not* be "easy-oh" to have her there. It was the furthest thing from easy he could imagine. He didn't know where she was going to sleep tonight—forget about forever.

"Hey, pops." Pete was the first to break the awkward silence. "Are you going to introduce us?"

His four fellow Hold 'Em partners converged, and more protectiveness spurred Ty to help the child take off her backpack, which sported Hello Kitty—the only child toy thing he recognized. Then he lifted her into his arms again.

"What's your whole name?" he asked.

"Teagan Ann Garraway."

He nearly dropped her. "Garraway?" he asked. "When did you get that name?"

"It was Miller. Mommy said I have a new last name now."

His friends slapped him on the back with raucous congratulations and prepared to abandon ship.

"I think it's time for us to head out," Pete said.

"Yeah, you'll be busy now," Carl added. "Besides, you won the hand with a damn, uh, dang three of a kind. Looks like your lucky charm showed up just in time."

He patted Teagan's back, and then made for the door. The others gathered their belongings and followed Carl out with good-byes that were far too cheerful and way too sudden.

Once he was alone, Ty patted the little girl's back awkwardly while a fog of confusion and despair settled firmly over him. Even the windfall of bills in the middle of the table didn't help.

Lucky? This was lucky? What in the name of all that was holy was he supposed to do now?

Chapter One

Two years later

SERVING TRANQUILITY WITHIN Your Turmoil.

Grace Crockett focused on lacy, ecru-colored script hand lettered on the coffee-bean brown walls around her. She'd come up with the motto herself and believed fully in the power of her cozy café to deliver on the promise. Today, however, tranquility had called in sick, leaving turmoil, and its minions annoyance and agitation, to do the serving.

She loved Triple Bean Café—the restaurant she owned with her two sisters. She played her part in their successful business as hostess and customer service rep, and she lived in the shop eighty percent of the time.

Grace had designed more than Triple Bean's catch phrase. The entire physical space, from burnished oak floors to European lace valances, was her creation, and it was sometimes hard not to feel an out-of-balance pride, although her sisters Raquel and Kelly were equally responsible for the café's phenomenal success.

And Triple Bean was a Denver phenomenon—popular beyond any of the Crockett triplets' wildest hopes—begun as a coffee shop experiment for one of Raquel's college business classes. That it had grown into much more was a testament to the sisters' determination and collective talent.

She glided a cloth along the pretty, antique buffet that served as a condiment counter, straightening a pile of napkins along the way, turning the cream and milk carafes so the labels faced out and were perfectly readable, and squaring up the lids and cup sleeves in their holder with the corner of the counter. Such tweaking normally soothed her.

Not today. Her genuine love for what she and her sisters had created made the bombshell she was planning to drop on them hard to understand even for her. Leave it all? She'd been practicing a speech in her mind for weeks to tell them she was about to do exactly that, and she still had no idea what she was going to say.

Turmoil.

From behind her, a manicured hand attached to its owner's toned and tanned arm snaked past her waist and twisted the cream pitcher to the right, throwing off both symmetry and practicality.

Grace sighed at the mini-prank her sisters had been pulling on her since they'd been old enough to know she liked her life more orderly than they did.

"Raquel," she warned. "Go back to your Excel spreadsheet and take a pill."

Her sister, eldest by fifteen minutes, wrapped her in a hug and then let her go with the husky, attractive laugh all three girls shared.

"Gracie, quit reliving last night's perfect date and come work your magic on the espresso machine. The hunk at the window table is waiting for his cappuccino."

Grace didn't need to look. The "hunk" was Emil Sully, a

widower in his early seventies, and a Triple Bean regular.

"Perfect date my butt." She addressed the first comment. "Perfect the way dinner with a family of Neanderthals would have been perfect."

Grace fixed the cream pitcher and slapped Raquel's hand out of the way when she reached to twist it again. "Don't touch my half-and-half or Mr. Sully will wait longer for his cappuccino."

"Aww." Raquel chided her as they headed for the kitchen and their youngest sister Kelly. "Where's all my Gracie's benevolent Christian charity today?"

Grace whirled on her. "I left it at church last night with the latest Mr. Perfect you sicced on me. You guys are driving me insane with the whole Grace-is-full-of-Christian-charity thing."

The date, which had honestly been awful, wasn't what angered her this morning, but the subject handily served as a cover for her agitation.

Raquel grinned, unfazed by the outburst. Kelly looked up from her industrial mixer, where fresh gingerbread dough filled the air with sharp molasses and sweet cinnamon. "We're driving you insane again?"

They stood in a lopsided circle like three legs on a stool— the movie stars: Raquel, Grace, and Kelly. Three identical girls named for their father's two favorite actresses. They'd stopped trying to live up to either the Princess of Monaco or the ageless Miss Welch years before, but they hadn't ever stopped trying to live up to one another—pushing and encouraging, succeeding and failing, laughing and crying, always together, making their unique relationship the talk of Denver. "Attached at the hip," according to local news features. Which, truthfully, is what they'd been for twenty-six years.

"Yeah. Insane enough to punch a saint," Grace agreed. And that broke the ice.

Grace laughed along with her sisters, but the hollowness that filled her chest more and more often lately remained. For the first time in their lives, unbeknownst to Raquel or Kelly, there was an odd triplet out.

Raquel draped an arm around Grace's shoulders and gave a squeeze. "You've been in this mood since you got home last night. Was it really so bad? He seemed like a genuinely good guy. The total spiritual man package."

Grace's stomach clenched. "He was a sanctimonious prick."

In the brief second of shocked silence, she didn't miss her sisters' wide-eyed exchange before they burst into laughter.

"Gracie!" Kelly crowed like Peter Pan. "I didn't know you had it in you. We've *never* heard you bad-mouth a fellow human being."

Then you've never heard me talk about *you*." The flippant reply cooled Grace's ill humor, and she faced the machine to make a cappuccino for the ever-patient Emil Sully.

"I'm sorry the date didn't go well," Raquel said, and Grace halted.

"Why didn't you know before it happened that it would be a disaster?"

"Huh?" Raquel frowned in confusion.

Grace crossed her arms although she didn't turn around. "I'm serious. You both should have known. It's like after all these years neither of you has a clue. You think what I'm looking for in life is a big joke."

The words hung between them, their hot, accusatorial tone too out of character to ignore. Frustration bubbled up again, bringing Grace to the brink of the confrontation she'd meant to save for after closing. Her unhappiness after their business meeting three days before had clearly been forgotten, not that it surprised her. Her sisters knew mild-mannered, slightly OCD, prone-to-over-sensitivity Grace was always placated with gentle words.

After the stinging barbs she'd just slung, however, Grace knew she wouldn't get away without explaining herself. Carefully, while her sisters' eyes bored holes into the space between her shoulder blades, Grace made the cappuccino and swirled a perfect leaf into the foam. Her best culinary talent: putting artwork on the foamy surface of expensive coffee.

"Nice," Raquel said mildly, looking over her shoulder. She motioned to Em, their favorite waitress, who took the cup for delivery. "Now. Care to explain why you're angry at us?"

At the direct question, Grace faltered. Did she *really* want this? They'd never messed with their trinity. They'd always been all for one and one for all.

Yes. She did want it.

"Fine." She drew in a bolstering breath and spun. "I am different from you two—this is not news. I make my decisions emotionally, and I don't know how to make them sound logical enough for you, so they get ignored. I've lived with that because I know we each have our gifts. You two are the brains and soul; I'm the heart. Because I am, I've also lived with the 'Grace is the perfect good girl' jokes, too. But you know what? I'm tired of them. So I'm a little OCD about guys, too. So I want one who isn't a jerk. Who ticks off a few important boxes. Who'll *wait* if I want him to. So it's how I've chosen to live my beliefs in this way for now. How you turned that into me wanting to date holier-than-thou, boring-as-gray-paint men who learned about women from reruns of fifties television shows, I don't know. You keep setting me up with zealots when all I really want is a decent guy."

Raquel hauled her in gently for a hug.

"Gracie. I'm sorry about the date. We take a chance when we hear of somebody we think would respect you the way you dream about. We know you don't want runaround goofballs. And we respect your no-sex decision. Truly. Neither of us hangs out in the right places to meet your dream man."

"Because *you* don't hang around men at all. And you," she pointed at Kelly, "haven't found a guy you *won't* hang out with."

"Hey now."

Her youngest triplet looked stung. Grace hung her head.

"I'm sorry. Oh, Kel, truly. I am sorry. That didn't come out anything like I intended—it was uncalled for. You're right. I'm in a foul mood."

This was becoming a complaint about the date—she was wimping out on the real issue. Again.

"Ummmm …" Kelly straightened and nudged her. "I hate to say it, but speak of the self-righteous."

Grace lifted her head and took two shocked steps backward, immediately wishing she could teleport to the sanctuary of their office. Unfortunately Micah Stensrud caught her eye and headed across the dark oak floor, cutting off any hope of escape.

He was a nice-looking man, with a sharply defined jaw, and dark brown hair and eyes. After their date—a rollicking night at a quiet family diner followed by a surprise trip to his church's Friday night Bible-praise-worship-testimonial gathering, and a long discussion afterward—she knew his looks were the only thing attractive about him.

He'd been "so pleased to find a good Christian girl to date," but he'd soon discovered her views on faith didn't match his—skirts too short, shirt too revealing, politics too lax. Still, she loved the old hymns and wasn't looking for sex, so there was hope. The date had followed a slightly judgmental path after that. Grace had shoehorned in a ten-minute chat about the Colorado Rockies and less time on the Denver Broncos, but Micah wasn't a sports fan. Nor was he a horse fan. Or a camping fan. He didn't seem to be a fan of much that was fun.

"Hello again, Grace," he said when he reached her. "I hope you'll forgive me for stopping by, but you left this in my car last night. I thought you might miss it."

He held out a small white zippered case. It contained her iPod and earphones, which she hadn't yet noticed were gone.

"Oh my gosh, thank you, Micah. They must have slipped out of my purse, and I might not have known where I'd lost them."

"I took the liberty of looking inside to make sure there wasn't something you needed immediately. I hope it's all right that I waited until this morning."

"Aw c'mon," Kelly whispered, barely audibly, in her ear. "He's like a little puppy begging for a pat."

Grace kicked her in the ankle, eliciting a snort and giggle.

"It's fine. Thanks again. This was a long drive for you."

"It was not a problem. I …" He shuffled closer to the counter where, fortunately, there were no other customers. "I feel called to be honest about one other thing."

"Oh?"

"I saw that this is a music player. I admit I took the liberty of scrolling through your list of songs. Curiosity is really the only reason, although I believe I was led."

A hot flush crawled from Grace's constricted throat and up her cheeks. "You looked through my iPod?" It wasn't as if he'd memorized credit card numbers or seen anything particularly personal, but something felt wrong. Invaded. "I'm not sure how I feel about that."

"That's exactly what I think the Lord wanted me to talk about with you."

"Excuse me?"

Kelly choked behind her, and Grace kicked her again but more softly this time.

"You have some rather inappropriate choices here," Micah said. "I understand why you'd be embarrassed to have someone find this."

"Are you kidding?" Too dumbfounded to let actual anger show, she could only splutter, "You're telling me God sent you to let me know he doesn't like, who? Green Day? Bruno Mars? Oh—must be John Denver."

"John Denver is fine."

It took a fair amount of effort to stop the twitching muscles in her fingers from reaching straight over the counter for his pious neck.

"Know what? Thank you, Micah, for returning my iPod. I think maybe I'll say good-bye now."

He looked surprised, proving he literally had no idea how awful he sounded. "Sorry to hear that. I did enjoy our time last night. I hoped, perhaps, you'd consider accompanying me to church tomorrow."

"I … don't think so. I'm not sure our music will ever be compatible."

Behind her, Kelly gave up and walked away, disappearing into the office with Raquel, stifling coughs that sounded for all the world like she was choking to death.

"I'm sorry you feel that way, but it was nice to meet you," Micah said amicably. "I do believe we were meant to cross paths. Perhaps some things we talked about will influence you as you go forward in your walk."

Once again he nearly had her dumbfounded. This time her voice came back with light but uncharitable laughter.

"I've learned a great deal," she said. "First of all, I think maybe this is a sign for you to go forward and get yourself some Pink and Bruno Mars CDs to find out what fun music you're missing. Second, I'm more certain than ever the God my grandmother taught me to believe in isn't anywhere near as big a stick in the mud as you think he is. Thanks for dinner last night; it was nice meeting you, too."

She very rudely left him standing at the counter looking confused as a lost foreigner, and hurried to the office door. Kelly and Raquel dragged her into safety, and while her sisters fought paroxysms of laughter, tears seeped from Grace's eyes. She dashed them away in anger.

"Oh my gosh, how much more right about Neanderthals could you have been?"

Kelly tried to close in for a hug, but Grace shrugged her away, basking in a harsh epiphany. This wasn't her sisters' fault; she'd allowed her own false politeness to turn her into a doormat.

"Do you know what, though?" she asked. "He's also the perfect embodiment of how the world—how you all—look at me. I'm exactly that crazy in your eyes."

"For crying out loud," Kelly said. "You know our network of idiot friends try to set us all up with men at every chance. Jo down at the library sent this guy your way."

"So he was on the judgmental, let-me-show-you-the-way-of-the-Lord end of the spectrum and thinks you have heretical taste in music," Raquel added. "All that means is you don't have to go out with him again. Laugh it off, Gracie. You're taking this way too seriously."

She was not. Micah wasn't the problem, but he was the spotlight showing her what was. She knew people, friends included, who thought she'd adopted a touch of fanaticism herself. In this day and age, focusing more on the spiritual than the physical side of life made everyone look at you funny, or at least want to set you up with iPod invaders like Micah Stensrud. Kelly and Raquel, the two people she knew and loved better than anyone else in the world, thought she knew nothing about men, or sex, and only wanted to date guys who thought holding hands meant they'd gotten to third base and touching tongues would be grounds for visiting hell in a handbasket.

But she knew plenty about sex—they all did. She also knew every woman deserved the best in respect, in commitment—in romance. If getting it all meant waiting for marriage to have sex or simply waiting for the perfect guy, she didn't mind waiting. But that translated to others as "Gracie is such a good girl. We need to find her a good boy."

What she wouldn't give for a nice guy willing to wait for sex but who'd still kiss her silly like a teenager in a dark, parked car. Not that the few guys she'd found all by her lonesome had been winners either. In fact, on her own, she was the worst judge of character on the planet.

But that was all beside the point.

The point was, Grace's nice, naïve girl rep also translated into being seen as the last person on Earth to be an astute businesswoman. She wasn't sure *how* one followed into the other—but it did.

"I'm not taking it too seriously at all," she said. "Lately I've begun to realize how serious this is. Bad date set-ups are no different than business ideas brushed aside. 'Gracie will understand.' Well, Gracie doesn't understand."

Raquel, always the most practical, let loose a long sigh. "Honestly? *I* don't understand. This dude pissed you off last night, and the date was a bust. It's *maybe* the third date you got roped into in a year. We do not do this all the time. Why are you suddenly so angry and hurt?"

The advantage, and sometimes disadvantage, of growing up seeing her own face perfectly reflected in her sisters' was that she could read their every expression and feel the emotions behind them almost as if they were her own. Each of them understood exactly how rare they were as identical triplets— literally one in a million. Their mother called them her three miracles. Their father had treated them like a trio of golden princesses, alternately enchanted and bemused by them. He'd been lost in a sea of estrogen from day one since, at their birth, he'd already had three older daughters. For their parts, the three older sisters had made it their collective mission to watch over the triplet babies like second parents. And they had.

Grace, Kelly, and Raquel had been inseparable from birth. Nowadays they were bored to tears with stories of how they'd spoken their own secret language, finished each other's sentences, and delighted in tricking people into thinking they were each other. And they rarely fought—never pitted one against the other. Never felt the "three's a crowd" curse despite having three completely different personalities. For twenty-six years they'd never needed any other best friends.

What she was about to do—tell them that after a lifetime of perfection, she wanted to be more than her one-third of a whole—felt like the highest form of mutiny. But having to fake happiness, to avoid revealing how *un*happy the past few months had been, was the painful answer to why everything had suddenly come to a head.

"What's really wrong, Grace?" Kelly asked gently.

She could start with the joke that was her important-sounding title of HR director. Ostensibly she hired people, but rarely did she have much of a say on the final choice of any candidate. On the other hand, when it came to firing people neither of her sisters cared to share the awful job. Greeting customers and always being cheerful got exhausting, no matter how adept she made herself seem. Having zero input about the kitchen or menu because Kelly ran her area with military meticulousness left Grace with no outlet for her own culinary ideas. And since Raquel had been freakishly good with numbers since grade school, and managing a restaurant came like second nature to her, Grace's business ideas were routinely overlooked.

In truth, her job at Triple Bean was largely serving as chairwoman of the decorating committee. She looked around the cozy, three-person office that she had, as with all other spaces, decorated. Trendy, modern, comfortably functional, the browns, caramels, and ecrus seemed, lately, to be blander than cold oatmeal.

"I … I need to leave. At least for a while."

Confusion flooded her sisters' features.

"Leave? You mean take a vacation?" Kelly grabbed Grace's hand and pulled her to the loveseat beneath the official portrait of the three of them in front of the Triple Bean sign, taken six years before, when they'd looked even less like successful businesswomen than they did today. "I totally get that. We haven't rotated time off for a long time now. It got so busy with the second store closing and all the reorganizing."

Grace braced against a stab of pain as Kelly touched her other wounded spot. The second branch of the restaurant, Triple Bean Too, had been Grace's idea, and the one huge business brainchild she'd stubbornly pushed through. Once opened, however, nothing had gone smoothly for the satellite location—and in two years, almost none of Grace's original vision had been implemented. Compromise had been the key element in the new space's designs. Grace had strong theories as to why the new café had failed, but since she was the sweet, emotional sister, not the financial wizard or the trained chef, she couldn't possibly understand real business.

"I don't need a vacation," she said quietly. "I've been thinking about firing myself."

"Grace!" Kelly squealed her disapproval.

"Because of the men?" Raquel asked.

"Of course it's not the *men*."

"Then …" Raquel stared as if trying to decipher a foreign language. "Quit? Aside from the fact that it makes no sense, what on Earth would we do without you?"

"You'd do fine." Grace rubbed her tired eyes. "Anyone can greet the customers. Anyone can make work schedules."

"I wouldn't trust 'anyone' with those jobs." Raquel perched on the edge of her desk. "Look, whatever's going on is because of stress. Like Kel said, you haven't been off in a long time. Why don't you take a couple of weeks and travel? Time for you."

"Don't either of you ever get tired of us always being

together?"

Grace's frustration stopped boiling and simmered more slowly below her heart like indigestion. The uncomfortable truth in what she wanted to say warred with love for the two women beside her. The very last thing she wanted was to hurt them.

"We get sick of each other all the time," Kelly said with a twisty, humor-filled smile. "What's new about that?"

"Don't you ever want to know if we could live without each other?"

"Sure," said Raquel. "And I have no doubt someday we *will* live apart. But not until someone way more gorgeous and hot-bodied than you two takes your places."

"Amen," Kelly replied.

This was what always happened when Grace tried to get serious. Kelly, who if she ever became an animal would be a rainbow-spewing unicorn, would make a joke, and Raquel, who would be a tireless dam-building beaver, would logic-solve any problems away. Grace was the group puppy, begging for pats and approval and looking to make everyone happy.

Even now guilt tried to topple the moment. She shouldn't be thinking about making herself happy. It was all for one …

She reined in the urge to waffle. "This is not about waiting for Prince Charming. You two are supposed to be liberated women."

"Hey. Do you see any males making this place run?" asked Kelly. "No, it's one hundred percent woman power, but that doesn't mean I wouldn't move in with Mr. Handsome if he came along. A successful woman likes a pretty man by her side."

Raquel nudged Grace. "Some things never change."

Grace didn't respond to the call for good-natured ribbing. The trouble was, Kelly was serious. She liked men and they liked her. She didn't sleep around, but she'd had several "great loves" and would not stop until she found the final one. Outdoorsy, no-time-for-great-loves Raquel, had followed up a very bad boyfriend with one not-quite-perfect relationship. Since college, Grace had had no long-term boyfriends.

It had been a mistake to start this out using dating and a man as the catalyst for her discontent. They were nowhere near the real issue.

"I want you to find your pretty man, Kel," she said. "But I also have to start finding out what I need." She paused. "It isn't finding Mr. Perfect or making moose on the tops of mochas either."

"Moose on mochas?" Raquel and Kelly exchanged a look of confusion.

"That's my biggest job around here these days—coffee-top art. I want more."

The confusion between her sisters changed to the first glimmer of understanding.

"Oh my gosh. This is about closing Triple Bean Too, isn't it?" Raquel asked.

"It's a little about that." Grace took a breath before jumping off the cliff she'd never be able to climb back up. "It's about a lot of vetoed ideas and dreams. Triple Bean is far too established for me to be experimenting with new ideas; we've proven that. Or, at least, it's been made clear."

"Come on," Raquel said. "We talked about this. You know why we had to close TB Too, and you agreed."

"Of course I agreed." She kept her voice surprisingly calm. "I'm not the important vote."

"Hey now—" The first hint of heat tinged Raquel's voice, but Grace held up a hand.

"I'm not angry. I'm not. Frustrated maybe, but this isn't only about closing the restaurant. It's about the ideas I still had for it that you weren't willing to try. It's about the kids' café in the corner, it's about an update in the logo, it's about trying a new supplier. I've decided I'd really *like* to try those things. I want to start my own café, but I want to do it without putting you two at risk."

"Start your own …? Jeez, Grace, this is crazy. You can't actually have a plan," Raquel said.

"Oh? And why would you think that?" Grace narrowed her eyes, but the calm in her voice remained.

"I …" Raquel stared at her before throwing up her hands. "I don't believe this. You haven't said one word to us until you're ready to quit and go into competition with us?"

"I'm not quitting tomorrow. I will work this out with both of you and give you plenty of time. And I'm not planning to compete with you."

"Gosh, thank you for that." This time Kelly's normally bright voice held the note of anger.

"I'm sorry," Grace said. "I had planned a much better way to tell you."

She accepted responsibility for the disappointment and hurt she saw in their eyes. She couldn't blame them for it; she'd ripped apart the unbreakable circle, threatened the symbiotic relationship they shared. Still she couldn't find more than a spark of regret. Mostly she felt slightly more hopeful than she had in months.

"I love you both. You can't possibly doubt that."

"I know you," Raquel said. "You love your cosmic or

heavenly or whatever signs that you believe tell you what to do. Is something like that responsible for this insane plan? How are they telling you to go about avoiding competition with Triple Bean?"

"I'm not staying in Denver." With effort, she ignored the "insane plan" remark and the slight sarcasm. "I'm either going back home to Wyoming or trying Colorado Springs. And, yes, I have no doubt I'll know which one when I need to know."

The landline phone on Raquel's desk postponed any response, and she stood to answer it. Her eyes cleared of anger and annoyance. "Mia!"

Their oldest sister calling from Wyoming. For the moment, the pain in the room was set aside. Calls from home were a huge treat, especially now, when every call held news about how eight-months-pregnant Dr. Mia was progressing.

"Hang on, let me put you on speaker," Raquel said.

"Did I get lucky and catch most of you there at one time?" Mia's voice, familiar and bright, filled the room.

"You did! Hi, sis!" Kelly called.

"Hey, you," Grace added.

"What's up, Doc?" Raquel asked. "Did you finally change your mind about letting us know whether we're having a niece or a nephew?"

Mia, a pediatric and general surgeon at the VA medical center near their family's huge cattle ranch south of Jackson, Wyoming, had once been a no-nonsense New York doctor. Two and a half years after marrying the love of her life and moving to Paradise Ranch with her husband, Gabe, she was not just a brilliant doctor, but a ranch wife and already a mother to their adopted son, Rory. She was always a treasure box of wonderful stories.

"Nope, gender is still unknown." Mia chuckled.

"Then what could possibly be of any importance?" Kelly teased.

Mia hesitated. "Other than the good news that we finally hired a new ranch hand—and seriously, can I get a hallelujah on that?"

"Hallelujah!" the triplets chorused.

The busy family ranch always needed a good hand.

"I do have less-than-great news," Mia continued. "I swear everything's okay with the baby. I uh, had a really stupid accident."

"Mia! What happened? Are *you* okay?" Grace's skin prickled in a flush of beginning panic.

"I'm fine. I'm fine. But I broke my foot."

"Oh no!" Raquel cried. "Did you fall? Are you *sure* Baby is okay?"

"I'm a doctor, Rocky, Baby was the first person I had checked out. Everything is fine. I tripped over—"

"Your own feet?" Kelly laughed.

"A dead mouse."

Silence fell again but broke seconds later with four voices cackling in simultaneous laughter.

"How is that even a thing?" Kelly asked.

"Jack made it a thing. He brought the corpse in as an offering."

Jack was Mia's son Rory's huge ragdoll cat, who'd taken to ranch living like a miniature mountain lion. He was a better mouser than all the barn cats combined.

"Jack brought you a mouse, and you tripped on it. That takes true talent," Kelly said.

"You can't do anything but laugh," Mia agreed. "I stepped

on the stupid thing in my bare foot three steps out of bed. I completely freaked out when I saw what it was. I tried to turn, lost my balance and fell back against the bed. My foot didn't go where the rest of me did. Broke the first and fifth metatarsal bones—a toe on each side of the foot. They had to put the pinky toe back in place with surgery. It'll be fine, although it may not be out of the cast before this child comes. Do you want to see funny? Imagine a beluga whale on crutches."

"Oh, Mia, I'm so sorry." Grace felt her sister's pain acutely. "What can we do?"

"I can't lie," Mia said. "I was really hoping you'd ask. Harper and Cole are threatening to cancel work to stay home with me. Joely and Alec are out of town." She named their other two sisters and their husbands. "It seems like ever since Dad's funeral, for the past two years, all we've done up here is call you three with the latest disaster, but I wondered if there was a chance in the world one of you might have a week to come and take up a little slack until Joely comes back. I really hate to ask."

Supernatural shivers popped up all over Grace's skin, and she turned triumphantly to Kelly and Raquel. "How's *that* for a sign?"

"What?" Mia asked.

"Sis?" Grace said. "I have a longer-term proposition for you. How would you like a live-in, pre-baby nanny?"

Chapter Two

THE VISTAS OF Paradise Ranch never failed to take her breath away. Grace closed her eyes to shut out the mesmerizing view of Grand Teton in the distance and drew in the spring scents—rain-soaked lawn, fragrant lilac, gentle clematis and freesia—that enveloped her thanks to her mother's incomparable master gardening skills. An early May breeze hugged her, cool and fresh as an apple blossom yet mild with the promise of true warmth around the corner. After eight years, Denver was more or less home for her body. But this, Paradise Ranch, her family's home for three generations, was where Grace's heart belonged and where her soul felt freedom.

"I'm so grateful you're here."

Mia hobbled onto the deck, her extended baby belly awkward between aluminum crutches, her right foot swathed in four inches of immobilizing purple bandaging.

"It's wonderful to be here." Grace plumped a deck chair cushion and patted it. "C'mon. Sit down. You're supposed to have your foot up, but you're fussing like Mom."

"I hate this." Mia sank into the rattan chair. "If only it had been a sexy accident, like skiing Everest or falling off a circus high wire."

"I don't know. Not many people can brag they fell over a

half-gnawed mouse. It's a cool story."

"You're twisted."

"About time someone noticed."

Mia didn't treat her like a sensitive little butterfly. On the other hand, she'd been studying Grace with surgical intensity since she'd arrived twelve hours earlier.

"Tell me what's going on, Gracie," she said. "Kel and Rocky sounded a little strange when I talked to them after you left. Are you three having problems?"

Grace shifted uncomfortably from foot to foot and finally forced herself to sit. There was no point in pretending Mia's instincts weren't on track, but nobody knew about Grace's plans to leave Triple Bean. She wasn't quite ready to tell all. Not until the first part of her plan was set. "The restaurant is fine—doing great, in fact. And Raquel and Kelly are fine; they were just surprised by my decision to spend longer than the week you requested. But I think I need the time. I've hit some burnout, I guess."

Mia reached for Grace's hands.

"This sounds serious. Honestly, are you all right? Is my asking you to come causing trouble?"

"I'm fine, Doc." Grace smiled, honestly grateful for her big sister's caring. "And no, of course it's not causing trouble—they're happy to send me to help. I'm just going to do a little chilling out and thinking while I'm here. I'm positive I'll need advice."

"Fair enough." Mia studied her, and then her features firmed until she turned into Grace's tough big sister. "Okay, no. I want details now. Mom and Grandma Sadie and I have been analyzing our gossip about you ever since you agreed to come home."

Grace pulled her gaze from Mia's. Lifting her head to stare out over the deck railing, she looked to the mountains. A little over eighty miles away, the Grand Teton massif tipped its cockeyed peak as it had for thousands of years—a very national mountain that had always felt like her personal natural wonder, watching over her home.

Her mother, Bella, and grandmother, Sadie, were the family's Grand Tetons.

Bella, newly sixty years old, could still be cast as a romantic movie leading lady. Nothing escaped her maternal eagle eye. Grandma Sadie, their late father's ninety-six-year-old mother, was on her way to never dying. She still held the keys to all things wise. The pair of matriarchs always knew the instant something wasn't right, yet Grace was safe at Paradise Ranch. She could say anything and still be unconditionally loved.

"I think being burned out started when we made the decision to close the second store. I wasn't ready to give up on it, but I was the minority vote. I'm not really part of the business decision-making branch of the operation." She held up a hand to stop Mia's protest. "We each   developed our area of expertise based on individual strengths. I'm not the business brain Raquel is. But I need to regroup a little. I have some ideas I want to flesh out."

"The other two are resistant to change?"

"Why shouldn't they be? Who wants to mess with success?"

"You sure you aren't angry with each other?"

Grace shook her head emphatically, mostly to convince herself. "We aren't."

"Sweetie, believe me, I know what it's like to be at a crossroads, which is where it sounds like you are."

Her sister's sincerity wrapped her in comfort like one of

Grandma Sadie's handmade quilts. Mia's decision two years before to give up on her dreams of a high-profile surgical practice in New York City had been beyond difficult. And yet, Mia's life had turned out like a fairy tale—broken foot aside.

"It's fair to call it a crossroads," Grace allowed.

For a long, thoughtful moment, silence reigned. Grace drew in the clear mountain air once more and nodded toward the house. "When Mom and Grandma get back from town, I'm planning to ask for help learning to make Great-Grandma's chocolate whiskey cake."

"What? You *want* to cook? What have you done with Grace Crockett?" Mia widened her eyes, not bothering to hide the teasing light behind the mock surprise.

"I know. Cue the defibrillator. Call it part of testing new ideas. I rarely get a chance to play in the kitchen since Kelly is a hundred percent in charge of the menu. And this isn't cooking, it's baking. I've always liked to bake. If I'm to test this new restaurant idea, I'll have to find a cook to work with me, of course, since I'm no Kelly. But I want to have some ideas to share with him or her. Plus—this will get me in the mood."

"Good enough answer for me. I know several big, strapping men who'll mob the kitchen for that test cake."

Grace grinned. "It's good to have big, strapping men around."

"That it is."

"But …" Grace stood and reached out to wrap Mia in a hug. "Despite appreciating the chance to dump my issues at your broken foot, that's enough of that. And dessert is a long way away, so what can I get you right now, sis?"

The sound of children giggling—with the kind of laughter that drives spikes of fear into a parent's heart—interrupted the conversation. The voices carried on the breeze from well beyond the deck where they sat.

"Rory?" Grace asked.

"Sounds like all three kids," Mia replied. "You should go meet them; make sure they haven't dug up a skeleton. Or buried one of their own. I haven't decided yet whether they're the Three Musketeers, the Three Stooges, or Bonnie, Clyde and Al Capone."

"Wait. Three kids? And you have a potential Bonnie?"

"That would be Lucky. She has Rory, along with Aiden Thorson, wrapped around her brilliant little five-year-old finger."

"Lucky?"

"Ty Garraway's daughter. Ty's that new hand we hired two weeks ago."

Ty Garraway.

"There's a cowboy name if ever I heard one," Grace said.

"He's not, although he says his grandmother had a small farm with horses he visited when he was young. He's a truly amazing handyman and carpenter. Cole says he asks great questions and picks up everything fast. He reminds us of Cole, with his mechanical and problem-solving skill set."

"How'd you find him?"

"He was working at Morgan's Conoco station in Wolf Paw and Cole found him. He had to do some fast talking, I guess, to convince Ty he should come and work here. But once he found out what a strong background Ty has in construction, Cole was convinced he'd found the hand he's been looking for."

"And this Ty person has a family?"

"An unusual one. A literal genius of a little girl and a girlfriend Lucky calls Lil. They're a friendly couple, very nice, but hardly what you'd call publicly demonstrative." Mia shrugged. "You should go find out what the kids are doing and meet Lucky. Tell me what you think."

The intrigue of a band of mischievous little ones roaming Paradise Ranch was too good to ignore. Memories of her childhood summers, when she and her sisters had stashed the movie star princesses status bestowed upon them by their father and explored Paradise like wild Mowglis from *The Jungle Book*, surfaced and made her smile.

"Okay. I haven't seen my little Rory yet anyway. Good excuse to sneak up on him."

"Wish I could watch it. Go. Take 'em out if they're breaking the law."

Mia laughed. Grace loved seeing her so relaxed about the kids and their antics. Dr. Amelia Crockett from New York had been much less easygoing than the very pregnant Dr. Mia Harrison she was now.

Grace reached the bottom of the deck steps and listened for the small humans' voices. She reached the quarter-mile-long driveway leading from the ranch house to the main ranch yard with its sprawling barns, corrals, and sheds. At the top of the driveway's descent, she stopped to gaze. It had been a long time since she'd really appreciated the beautifully laid out, perfectly organized heart of Paradise Ranch.

When she heard laughter again, she followed it gleefully and finally found the children ten yards off the driveway in a small copse of mountain ash trees starting to flower. The tableau they presented was the opposite of innocent baby fun. They weren't burying a skeleton or killing anything, but they also weren't picking dandelion bouquets for their mommies.

They sat in a triangle around a two-foot rectangle of

plywood: Rory, the biggest and oldest at nine, Aiden Thorson, the ranch foreman's son at eight, and a petite girl child with gorgeous, pale rose-colored locks pulled into a wildly fraying ponytail. All three wore jeans and various colored T-shirts along with scuffed, well-worn tennis shoes.

They didn't hear Grace or her quiet gasp at the sight of playing cards and a small collection of quarters in the middle of the board.

"I call," the girl said. "Show me what you got."

"I'm gonna win this time," Aiden replied. "I have a full house."

Grace bit down on her bottom lip, shocked.

"I only have a pair of kings," said Rory, and slapped his cards down.

"But *I* have four eights," the little girl, Lucky, said. "So …" She gathered in the quarters—maybe five of them—without smiling. "I win."

"Wait? Four of a kind *beats* a full house?" Aiden asked. "That doesn't seem right."

"It is. We can go ask my dad. He's an expert."

Grace wanted to stop the crazy game instantly, but a morbid fascination with the bizarre scene stopped her. The girl spoke with the erudition of a physics professor. "Literal genius," Mia had said.

"Aw, I'm not gonna ask your dad," Aiden said. "But I can't play anymore. I'm out of quarters."

"Just one more hand?" Lucky asked and turned to Rory.

"No. If I have no money left my mom will notice. Let's do something else. You always win poker anyway."

Funnily enough, although they complained, there wasn't a shred of animosity between them.

"We could have a spitting contest," Lucky suggested.

"Cool!"

"Yeah!"

The boys gathered up the cards as if she'd promised them frogs and candy bars for helping.

"But I'm not teaching you how to spit anymore," she said.

"No, show us one more time, Lucky," Rory said. "You spit farther than anyone I know."

"Crap on a Cheez-It you guys are lame." The little girl pushed the board and cards to the side and stood. She was maybe four feet tall. "I've shown you a million times."

How old was this child really?

"Okay, watch one more time."

She bent slightly from the waist and presumably collected a mouthful of saliva. The next thing Grace knew, she watched a long, disgustingly neat arch of spit travel three feet through the trees. The OCD in her didn't know whether to gag or clap.

The boys dropped to the grass and rolled around like puppies, laughing so hard they couldn't breathe. The girl turned and saw Grace first. She didn't startle but cocked a quizzical, strawberry-blonde brow. She was the most angelic child Grace had ever seen in her life. The rounded cheeks were spattered with truly pretty freckles, and the big blue eyes held a sapphire glow that came from deep within. She didn't look more than four although Mia had said five, and she spoke like an adult.

"Hello," Lucky said. "Who are you?"

Not the countenance or demeanor of a freakishly talented poker player-slash-spitter.

"Hello back. I'm Grace Crockett. Who are you?"

The two boys calmed their maniacal laughter and scrambled

to their feet.

"Aunt Grace!" Rory sped toward her and threw himself into her spread arms. A warm rush of love swept her.

"Hi there, handsome. You're turning into a grown man without asking my permission. You're almost as tall as I am."

It was true. The nine-year-old came nearly to her chin, which made him a couple inches shy of five feet. He was a stunning child in his own right. His mother had been a friend of Mia's, whom they'd lost to breast cancer nearly three years before. Rory was half black, and growing up proud to study the culture of his mother's Jamaican heritage. Mia was doing a great job helping him to know himself. But his continuing hug was proof he now belonged heart and soul to the Crocketts.

He finally let her go, and she draped an arm around his shoulders as she faced the other two kids. Aiden Thorson was a miniature version of his father, Bjorn, who in turn was the son of Leif, the Norwegian immigrant who'd become Paradise's first hired foreman in the 1960s. The Thorson family was now as much a part of Paradise Ranch as the Crocketts.

"Hey, Mr. Aiden Thorson," Grace said. "You're not exactly staying little either."

"Hi, Miss Grace. I'm in third grade. My mom graduated me."

Melanie Thorson was homemaker, ranch wife, and homeschool teacher extraordinaire.

"Congratulations. That's pretty darn awesome."

"And this is Lucky." Rory escaped Grace's hold and pointed at the girl. "She's new. Her dad works for Cole now."

Cole Wainwright was her sister Harper's husband. Although all six Crockett daughters had officially inherited the ranch when their father died, Cole and Harper had taken on the official role of Paradise's managers, and worked the ranch full time with Leif and his family. Mia and her husband Gabe worked away from the ranch at the nearby VA medical center, but lived in half of the huge ranch house with Harper and Cole. Their third sister Joely and her husband Alec owned a home in the tiny neighboring town of Wolf Paw Pass, but spent the school year in Colorado while Joely finished vet school. They'd braided together a close-knit family Grace truly missed, and all of them worked to keep Paradise Ranch one of the top cattle spreads in the region. If Cole had hired Lucky's father to be part of the team, the man had to be what Mia said he was, a decent guy and a hard worker.

"Hey, Lucky. So … are you the poker champ or the spitting champ?"

Grace tried to add slight displeasure to her words. Lucky, however, paid no attention if she even noticed.

"My dad taught me how to play poker. I can beat almost anybody."

"I see." She couldn't quite wrap her mind around the thought of a father teaching his five-year-old to gamble, much less do it competitively.

"And he says spitting can come in handy for all kinds of things. Like if a bug flies in your mouth, or your nose is stuffy and you don't have a tissue, or if you're bored."

Once again Grace couldn't decide whether to laugh or let her slight disgust color her words. She chose neutrality.

"Is Lucky your real name?"

"It's my real name. It's not my given name," she said.

"What *is* your given name?" Rory asked.

"Teagan Ann Garraway."

"Teeeeeeegan?" Aiden hooted.

"That's a beautiful name!" Grace squatted in front of her. "I'd think your daddy would brag that name all over the place."

Teagan Ann "Lucky" Garraway simply shrugged. "It's more like my old name. Daddy says my real first name is Lucky and my middle name is Break. Because I always bring him luck."

"Lucky?" The deep, resonant call came from the driveway, as if the girl had conjured it by talking about her father.

Grace turned toward the voice, along with all three kids, and might as well have walked face first into a high-voltage fence. The living embodiment of a clichéd cowboy was making his way through the trees. In the space of one gasped breath, Grace went from conversation with three kids to hyperventilating over sex appeal in boots. Her mind reeled at the highly inappropriate thoughts racing into her head, and she blushed as if the children could see them.

"Daddy!"

The word came out in such squealy excitement it gave the first indication, aside from her height, that Lucky was actually her advertised age. Grace calmed her internal, all-feminine-parts-involved reaction and got a grip as the man drew closer. Not that proximity revealed a single flaw in what she'd imagined she'd seen.

He glanced at her, his eyes widening momentarily with surprise, but said nothing before squatting in front of his daughter. Lucky threw her arms around his neck. He pried them free, took hold of the child's upper arms gently but firmly, and Grace caught the firm set of his amazing jaw. Even pressed together, his lips were full and defined—inviting as all get out.

"What are you doing up here?" Lucky's father asked his daughter. "You had Lil worried to death. Not to mention me."

He glanced around the copse, caught sight of the cards, and

although he had stormy green eyes that made him appear as though yelling might come easily to him, he didn't yell. Lucky, for her part, looked him straight in the eye, uncowed and smiling. "Sorry, Dad. We were playing."

"Lucky, were you playing poker for money? Boys? Did you give her any money?"

Aiden and Rory hung their heads, nodding.

"Aw, Daddy, I just won a little."

"That is one hundred percent against the rules. You know that. Believe me, I'll get back to you on that one, but worse, you were supposed to tell Lil if you went anywhere."

"I left her a note."

"A note?" He looked at Grace again, a helpless question in his eyes. "What five-year-old leaves a note? We didn't look for a *note*."

"Looks like they were playing for quarters." Grace shrugged. "I wouldn't have told my folks either."

His brows, thick, beetled, and Sean Connery-worthy, hooded his eyes. He turned back to Lucky.

"New clarification on the rules. If you're going out of sight of the house, you have to make a verbal check-in, okay? But, if you really left a note, I'll cut some slack this time."

"I did."

He stood, sighed, and offered Grace a shrug. "Some days I'm only the referee who keeps her in bounds." He turned back. "Now, about the poker game. What have I told you over and over is what you can play for?"

She curled her little lip. "Buttons, gum, or rocks. But I don't need any of those."

"Too bad. I'm the dad; I make the rules. I know you're a great poker player, but you can't play for money. Not until you're eighteen. Show me the money you won."

Lucky only frowned. For a long moment she didn't comply.

"I assume you won. Come on," Ty said.

"She won." Grace couldn't help confirming his guess.

A hint of pride touched the upturned corners of this mouth. "Must be genetic."

Wait? This was a talent of which he was proud? Still, her stomach reacted to his smile with happy flips.

"Oh? So you taught her to play poker?"

"You give your kids what you can."

A merry light danced behind his eyes and, despite his rule on gambling, Grace's attraction to him hiccupped for the first time.

"Some parents might try for something a little less ... adult."

He didn't seem to hear the minor censure in her voice because he laughed.

"She's a little advanced in math. It's a good way to engage her. There are worse vices." He assessed Grace for the first time, a toe-to-head sweep with interested eyes. "I'm thinking you must be Bella's daughter up from Denver. I heard another Crockett was coming. Should have known she'd be a ten like her sisters."

Her natural attraction took another nosedive. A *ten*? Really? The man was the walking-talking embodiment of a good-looking guy possessed of the belief that he could say anything he liked and be considered charming.

"I'm *Grace*." She emphasized the name. "You must be the hand Cole recently hired. Do *you* have a number or can I assign you one?"

Not a flicker of discomfiture crossed his features. He grinned wider on his way to offering a handshake. "If I have one it's pretty dang low." His hand engulfed hers in a strong, nonsexist grip—a point for him. "Yeah, I'm Ty Garraway. Cole's a decent guy—took a chance when he found out I know my way around tools and fixing things."

"Good to meet you, Ty." She crossed her arms and inclined her head toward the three children with a mildly disapproving frown. "Since you're in discipline mode, you should also know they were about to start a spitting contest. I'd think a guy's guy who's so good with *numbers* would find such an unhygienic activity unsettling. I'm sure you could suggest a better use of playtime?"

For the first time since he'd pushed through the trees and into Grace's world, Ty's handsome features darkened. "I don't know about that, Miss Crockett. I'm sorry if the idea of spitting offended you, but I can't truly say I have a problem with it. Lucky knows where it's not appropriate to spit."

"A girl won the spitting contest at the county fair last year." Lucky turned her anime-wide eyes away from her friends and stared at Grace.

Grace's cheeks heated slightly. She'd always found the spitting contest disgusting. She reminded herself Ty had at least begun this by telling his daughter she couldn't gamble for money. That was something.

"You couldn't have steered her toward 4-H or making fudge or something?"

Any amusement left in his features turned to annoyance. "For someone so adamant about not being a number, I'd think *you'd* believe it's a no-no to stereotype girls. Cooking versus spitting? Sounds hypocritical."

His eyes smoldered protectively—the dangerous, impenetrable green of a primeval forest.

She was saved from having to backpedal—and rightfully so, she had to admit— by another call from behind them, this one feminine and slightly southern, but definitely not gentle.

"Lucky Garraway! You little instigator, I oughta drag you home by your brilliant earlobes and make you paint the fence like Tom Sawyer."

The woman, a little older than Grace, strode to their gathering on model-perfect legs that went halfway to her throat. Aside from that, voluptuous was barely a big enough word to describe the bustline straining her navy-blue, scoop-necked T-shirt, and her hair flowed like molten copper waves, dark and rich, past her shoulders.

"Hi, Lil." Lucky called.

Ah, the somewhat mysterious girlfriend.

"I've been looking to the moon and back for you, young lady."

Lil's accent thickened slightly with admonishment, but the scolding clearly rolled off Lucky's shoulders, and she threw her arms around the woman's waist with a smile.

"I didn't go to the moon," Lucky said.

Lil peeled the child off of her with firm hands just as Ty had done, but Grace didn't miss the smile she gave above Lucky's head. "The moon, the main house—all the same to me if I can't find you. It's time for you to come back." She nodded to Aiden and Rory. "You can come to our house, too, but you might have to help her paint that fence."

"Huh?" Aiden stared at her as if she had four eyes.

"I don't want to paint any old fences," Rory added.

Lil allowed a hearty laugh. "I'll explain to you on the way back about Tom Sawyer and fences. You'll *love* the metaphorical story."

Grace stared. Who were these people? One taught his five-year-old to play poker and spit, the other used the word 'metaphorical' with young children.

"Hi," Lil said, surprising Grace out of her contemplations and holding out a hand. "Lil Wagner. You must be Grace. I'm sorry the kids got away from me. Little barbarians." She gave Aiden a quick noogie, and he laughed. "Take my eyes off of 'em for two seconds and Miss Ringleader-Thing here marches them off nearly to the big house."

"Big house?" Rory said. "Isn't that prison?"

"Yup. You go farther up this road and you find yourself in Mrs. Crockett's Big House. She'll imprison you there if I ask her to. This lady here is her girl, Grace. She'll tell you." Lil winked at her. "Go ahead. Tell them what happens to kids who don't follow their rules."

Grace couldn't stop the rush of amusement and kinship that welled up at the ruse. Lil made herself easily likeable.

"I know Mrs. Crockett pretty well," she agreed. "She loves to take children and put them to work either in her slave kitchen or her wild garden. If you don't behave, she could have you working on baking bread for her three giant sons, or pulling the weeds from around her dark, blood-red roses."

Lucky turned her full attention to Grace for the first time, and Aiden's big baby blues turned as skeptical as a seven-year-old's could. But Rory started to laugh.

"Aunt Grace, you're weird. Don't believe her. Grandma doesn't have three giant sons."

"She does," Grace said, and grabbed him to her for another hug. "One of them is your daddy, along with your uncle Cole and uncle Alec."

"There you have it," Lil replied. "Now what needs to be

cleaned up here, anything?"

"Yes." Ty held out his hand. "Give me the money." Lucky reluctantly dug in her pocket and handed him the quarters. "Thank you. Now, how much did you boys lose?"

When they told him, he redistributed the cash. Aiden and Rory were ecstatic.

"Thanks, Mr. Garraway!" Rory said.

"Next time, you're in charge. No gambling for money. No personal property. No clothing."

"Yes, sir."

Lil set a familiar hand on Ty's arm and smiled. "I'm sorry I called you away from work. Tell Cole I'm sorry, too. I panicked."

"Bah." Ty reached down and swung Lucky into his arms, cradling her like a babe until she giggled with high-pitched indignation. He kissed her tummy and then her cheek before setting her back down. "Anything for my girls. But, gotta go back to work. You—" He pointed at his daughter. "We'll talk tonight. Until then, you follow the rules."

"Bah," she replied, her tone saucy as a mynah bird's. "Anything for my guy."

She absolutely was no ordinary kid.

"Nice meeting you, Grace from Denver." Ty faced her, every ounce of male heat and sunny charm back in place. To her dismay, all her irritation curled up like a submissive puppy and rolled over on its back. "Are you here for a vacation or staying a while?" he asked.

"Ah … staying. At least until Mia's baby comes."

"The baby," he said. "Get your bets in soon—the pool's getting richer."

"Pool?"

"Five dollars a pop. Winner takes all. Your grandma is

holding the pot." Ty kissed his pointer and middle fingers, touched them to Lucky's nose, and winked at Grace, who no longer had a voice. Everything about this man stunned her, from his looks to his nonchalance. He'd just lectured his daughter about gambling for money, then turned around and told her about a betting pool. He turned and sauntered back toward the barns and sheds, presenting her with a backside nearly as perfect as the front.

"I can tell you the simple rules." Lil touched her upper arm to get her attention. "Gamblin' Man there thinks he has a lock on the outcome." She raised her voice as Ty sauntered away. "But he's wrong because it's a *girl*."

Ty lifted his hand in salute without looking back.

"All right you guys," Lil said. "Let's go. Rory, I called and asked your mom if you could come until dinner. Aiden, we'll stop at your place on the way if you want."

"We don't really have to paint fences?"

Lil laughed, her Dolly Parton figure shaking. Grace hunched her shoulders, feeling like a lumpy sack of apples. Ty's woman—she assumed, since she clearly lived with him—was a cowboy's dream.

"No fences. You start off. I'll catch up." She turned to Grace. "Hope the kids weren't in your way."

"Not at all," she said. "Kids are great. The poker took me aback. I'm not used to seeing a five-year-old card sharp."

"Ty thinks it's funny even though he's fairly strict about it. He's such a guy. But he does love his daughter and, in reality, he's doing all he can to raise her right."

Grace furrowed her brow. "I'm sure he is. You two haven't been here long, right?"

"A little over two weeks. It sure seems like a great place. We all feel welcome already. Come on down and visit. We're in the second rental property. I'll tell you all about how we found our way from Las Vegas to Wyoming."

"I will. I look forward to it."

That was the truth. Lil's had all the promise of being a great story.

Chapter Three

'DID YOU FIND her?"

Ty entered the workshop, where Cole Wainwright looked up from a hand plane he was using to shave the last inches off a new door for the barn tack room. It was the first of a set of two, and had nearly been finished before Ty had run off to search out Lucky.

"I did. She was up the driveway with Rory and Aiden."

"There's not usually a lot to worry about around here, especially if she was with the two boys—they know their way around. But I don't blame you. All it takes is a walk too long in the wrong direction. She'll learn the ropes."

"Yeah." Ty buried the cheerful carelessness from earlier with the kids and pulled on his work gloves. "I'm more afraid she'll learn them too fast, twist them to suit herself, and corrupt the others."

"You dads." Cole laughed. "Always something to worry about. I'm not there yet, but I'm taking notes. You're doing okay by her, don't worry. This place'll keep her in line. Paradise is pretty, but she's a stern taskmaster."

A wave of guilt washed over Ty, as it had begun doing ever since Cole had insisted Ty, Lucky, and Lil move onto the ranch, and Ty's lawyer had insisted it would be a good idea. That hadn't been his desire—he'd have preferred getting to know Cole from a distance. He wasn't surprised that he respected the man, but he was starting to like him. There was no room in his plans for sentimentality.

"Yeah, I guess I've seen a little of that already." He took a deep breath and changed the subject. "How's this coming?"

"Nearly done. Ready to tackle the second? If you are, we should be able to get them hung before dinner."

"Let's go."

He dove into the work, relieved to be past the talk of Paradise Ranch's virtues and happy to be using his hands for something immediately gratifying. He'd always been good with tools and had enjoyed his jobs in construction—as he'd bragged to Grace Crockett. Grace of the sultry eyes and judgmental attitude. He hadn't quite figured out how she'd managed to annoy him at the same time he found her mesmerizingly attractive.

"I, ah, met your wife's sister," he said.

"Gracie?" Cole straightened. "It was generous of her to take time off and come to help Mia. Grace is one of the nicest people you'll ever meet. You maybe already saw a little of that."

I'd think a guy's guy who's so good with numbers would find such an unattractive activity unsettling.

He heard her voice in his head. Remembered the censure in her eyes. He laughed humorlessly. "Oh yeah. I could see she's a sweetheart."

If Cole heard the sarcastic tinge in the words, he didn't say. Ty doubled down on the work, placing the door's hinges on marks he'd made earlier.

Miss Grace Crockett didn't qualify as a sweetheart in his book. He bristled at anyone who criticized his child or his ability to raise her. He needed to forget about her and concentrate on his plans. His most important job was to stay focused on looking ahead to the things that were going to secure his future, keep his little girl safe, and give her back the legacy she deserved.

Grace Crockett would play a part in all of that. She wouldn't feel as smug then.

Three hours later, Ty stood at the front door of the house he now lived in on Paradise Ranch property. After two and a half weeks, he still wasn't comfortable with the arrangements, amazing though they were. Once Cole had offered him this job, Ty had had every intention of living in town and minimizing the chance that his purpose would be discovered. Yes, he wanted to scout the land, learn the ropes, and absorb the ranching lifestyle, but he had no desire to get entrenched with or attached to the Crockett family.

Cole, however, had insisted. The house was part of what Ty earned as a Paradise hand—the ranch's version of a bunk house. Long ago, Cole had explained, his late father-in-law, Sam Crockett, had set aside forty acres and built four modest houses for his hands and their families. Each house sat on ten acres, and an employee could live in one for the cost of utilities. Ty had tried to turn it down, but as Cole told him—everyone on Paradise was family, and it was important Ty be available whenever help was needed.

Lil was ecstatic. Ty was nervous. But it was a good deal, especially for Lucky, who'd already made good friends.

The house also saved him money, which was a good thing. But Ty was after his own land and a legacy for his daughter. It would take some time to work things properly through the courts, but in the end he would get back the parcel of land his great-grandfather had lost—the original homestead he'd been duped by Eli Crockett into losing in a poker game nearly eighty years before. A game Ty was certain had been fixed, and as illegal as a three-dollar bill.

***

"What do you really know about the new hand Cole hired?"

While Mia took a forced nap to elevate her foot, Grace stirred milk into one cup of hot Irish breakfast tea and sugar into another, and lifted the pair of pretty china cups by their delicate handles. It was another thing she loved about being home: Bella and Sadie Crockett had been collecting cups together for forty years, and Grace loved them. She'd often thought about a potential restaurant of hers offering tea in lovely, one-of-a-kind cups like these.

"Thank you, sweetheart," her mother said. "You're spoiling us. I'm awfully glad you're home."

"It's wonderful to *be* home." Grace sat, her own plain herbal tea already steeping.

"Ty seems like a nice young man," her mother said. "He's quiet. Keeps to himself, and does his job well. Cole and Bjorn like him."

"What's the scoop with Lil?"

"She's also very private, but friendly," her mother said. "Ty told us she's just a friend who watches his daughter, but they seem quite close. Like old busy bodies, we assume they're a couple and figure Ty just thinks we'd frown on them living together, but we haven't forced the issue. As for Lucky, she's such a gifted child—not six yet but already reading *Harry Potter*. She has a high affinity for numbers and patterns, and she's extremely verbal."

"I noticed. And she spits like a baseball player and plays poker like a Vegas high roller."

"Poker?" Grandma Sadie's blue eyes shone more brightly than normal.

"Her father sounded downright proud."

"Oh, my dear." Sadie chuckled. "I used to beat my brothers at poker all the time."

"Grandma! You?"

"When I was young? I surely did. Once they got older, they played more and could best me. But until then, I won a ton of money off of them."

"I'm disillusioned." Grace shook her head, purposely hiding her smile. "Here I was lecturing Lucky and her father about it being inappropriate. Good grief, my own grandmother."

Sadie laughed fully, her voice strong in her slightly shrinking body. For being ninety-six, she was surprisingly strong and sturdy. Although she'd walked with a cane for extra balance for years, she could move quickly and had refused to let advanced age stoop her body.

"Your dad taught you all how to play poker," Bella said.

"I know. But when were teenagers. To his credit, Ty did tell her she wasn't to play for money, but still … It's not that she knows how to win actual cash from other kids; it's that she knows at age *five* that it's possible."

"I'm sure he doesn't *want* her gambling with other children."

"I supposed I should forgive you, Grandma. You turned out to be a lady."

"It depends entirely on the standard by which you're measuring ladies," her grandmother replied. "I would make quite a disaster out of high tea at Buckingham Palace. Or the occasional church ladies' circle meeting." Again her eyes reflected a bright sparkle of fun.

"You were always a rebel, Sadie," Bella said. "The years you led the church ladies were the best."

"I was almost impeached, wasn't I?"

"Over what?" Grace asked, thoroughly intrigued.

Grandma Sadie was one of the most spiritually serene people she'd ever met, and the idea of her causing an uproar at church didn't compute.

"Over a homosexual couple." Grandma Sadie made the statement with such nonchalance, Grace found herself staring while their family matriarch took a casual sip of her tea. When she set the cup down, she cocked a white eyebrow. "Why is your mouth open?"

Grace snapped her jaw shut. She'd been caught in a cliché, thinking her elderly grandparent would be appalled by the idea of same-sex relationships.

"Sorry," Grace said. "I can't believe we've never really discussed anything like this, and I wouldn't have a single idea how you felt or feel about a gay couple."

"When your dad was alive, we didn't discuss controversial subjects," Bella said, nodding. "But in recent years, with a few new faces around the table, a lot of things come up."

A small wave of homesickness slipped through her at what she'd missed by staying away from Paradise for so many years. "I guess I don't know what anyone around here believes anymore, do I?"

"We're all over the board on some things," her mother said. "Mostly the economics of ranch living. But we're cohesive on most social things. Sadie was ahead of her time."

Grace leaned forward. "Well? What happened with the gay couple?"

"They wanted to join the church. Can you imagine that back in the early seventies?" Sadie shook her head. "There was not simply opposition but a frenzy of plotting, from how to convert them back to being heterosexual, to how to get them to move from town."

"Until Sadie told everyone to sit down and shut up." Her mother placed a youthful hand over Grandma's veined and wrinkled one. "Didn't win her a lot of new fans, but after Sadie's liberal bible thumping, the couple was allowed to join and stayed members for nearly fifteen years until they moved away. Had the most darling pair of adopted kids. A wonderful family."

"Way to go, Grams!"

"So you'd have agreed with me?" Grandma Sadie winked.

"A hundred percent."

"Then I guess we've managed to raise you right."

Grace's homesickness intensified. "I wish I'd been home for some of these family discussions," she said. "Maybe that's one reason I'm happy to be back. To be in on this kind of thing— my vision of faith gets a little stick-in-the-mud when I don't hear from the wise ones."

"That's *a* reason—and a very kind one." Her mother transferred her hand from Grandma Sadie's to Grace's. "Now I want to hear the main reason you're back."

All of Bella's sincere motherly concern triggered an avalanche of jumbled emotions Grace prayed neither woman would decipher. Disloyalty, impatience, fear, selfishness, pride, shame, and the homesickness … they all coexisted in her heart.

She'd skirted the truth with Mia, mostly because she could hear their late father's voice, strong and firm, exhorting to all his children that Crocketts picked themselves up and finished their commitments no matter what hardships they faced, and she didn't want to admit she'd given up on her life in Denver.

But in the face of her mother's unconditional love, she couldn't hold the emotions back.

"I'm in the process of selling my third of the restaurant back to Kelly and Raquel."

The blurted words hit the air like hail on a new car roof. For long seconds, Grace could have heard a flea sneeze.

"I love this kitchen," Grandma Sadie said, her mouth lifted in amusement. "It's a place where you never know what topic will pop up next."

Her mother's fingers curled more tightly around Grace's hand, and she took a long, thoughtful breath. "Before anything else, are you okay?"

That was her mother—always the gentle counterpoint to their rigid, tough-minded father. It was still easy to forget that no stern inquisition from Sam Crockett was going to force her to justify her actions. For one flash of a moment she missed her towering figure of a father. Sam had never abused a soul in his life, but not very many souls had dared cross his iron will. Except Bella.

"I'm fine, Mom. I truly am." Grace squeezed her mother's hand back. "I can't say I'm not a little freaked out, but this is a change, not a disaster."

"And we want to hear every detail."

Before Grace had to start the story, Mia crutched her way into the kitchen, beautiful and awkward, her cheeks filled with a little more color after her nap, her thick brown hair falling in rumpled waves past her shoulders. Behind her, their sister Harper followed, carrying an overstuffed purple pillow.

"Look who I found gimping around the living room," Harper said. "I told her she could only come to the party if she let me put her leg up. She whined about it but agreed. Doctors make the worst patients."

"Don't I know it?" Grace wrinkled her nose at Mia and stood to pull out a chair. "It took the threat of a locked door and bed without supper to get her to lie down in the first place."

Harper reached Grace for a warm hug while Mia swung herself to the chair with a scowl aimed at both of them. "You two are horrible at listening to what the doctor knows is best."

"Bah, save the lectures for your babe," Harper replied. "We'll be the bosses of you."

Mia couldn't quite hide the sneak of a smile that crept onto her lips as she reached for a cookie in the middle of the table.

"How did the studio treat you today?" Grace gave Harper one last squeeze and stepped back, happy to talk about anything but herself.

Two years earlier, Harper, an amazing artist, had started a community art center and studio on property once owned by her husband's family. Several miles away by car, the Double Diamond Community Art Center was Harper's haven, where she created her successful paintings, and facilitated art and music programs for kids and adults. In truth, she was Grace's inspiration for striking out on her own—a living example of how successful one person could be if she used a little imagination.

"I brought my most recent finished painting home," Harper said with a modest shrug. "It's a little different—not my usual landscape, but one of a series of scenes from Wolf Paw Pass. They want to hang them in the Jackson airport."

"That's awesome!" Grace gave a little shimmy of excitement. "I'm proud of you, Harpo. Where's the painting? Let's see it."

"All in good time." Harper squinted in admonition. "I heard something when I walked in about needing to hear every detail from you. Time for you to dish first, and then we can critique the picture."

Grace's excitement deflated, and she flopped onto her chair. The last thing she wanted in the midst of cheerful good will was to talk about her discontent. She hadn't been raised to be negative.

"I'd like a change," she began, as brightly as she could. "I think I'd be good at a few things I don't get to do very often."

"Change is good," Mia said. "What things?"

"Creating a menu. Changing up the focus on the restaurant atmosphere to include more family-friendly spaces. It's nothing against Rocky and Kel at all. The current Triple Bean has a definite vibe that I don't want to mess with."

"I thought that's what the second restaurant was going to be." Her mother gave a thoughtful scowl. "Is that why it didn't work out?"

Grace knew she stood on a shaky precipice. She didn't want to blame her sisters for the restaurant closing, and yet she really wanted her family to understand that she didn't feel she'd had a fair chance to make her vision work. "We didn't have a completely unified vision for Triple Bean Too. I think we got the concept a little muddied, and it was financially risky to take the time to straighten it out. Raquel and Kelly believed it was better to cut our losses. They were probably right."

"You wanted to keep it open." Harper placed a hand on her shoulder.

Grace shrugged. "I did."

"And that caused a rift?"

"No, no. I understood. But …" Again Grace hesitated. "I don't think Rocky believes I know enough about finances to have much input. And, the longer I've thought about it, the more I know I have to try out my vision. The only way I can do that is to try it on my own."

For the first time a well of tears filled her eyes, but with effort she kept them from spilling over. Tears wouldn't make her case any stronger or make her look more competent.

"I get it," Harper said. "It's like when I had to decide after Dad died whether to let the oil company come in and explore the way they wanted or go with something really weird here in Wyoming. Putting up the wind farm in the south quarter of the ranch wasn't a popular decision at first, but it turned out all right. I think you need to go with your dreams sometimes."

Gratitude washed over Grace at Harper's acceptance. She hadn't expected her family to fully embrace the idea of abandoning a sure and successful thing like Triple Bean.

"I know it seems rash."

"This entire ranch was built on rash, honey." Grandma Sadie straightened in her chair. "You know all stories. This place was built on everything from homesteading, to snapping up foreclosures, to winning seven thousand acres in a poker game. Sometimes you lay down your hand and walk away, but sometimes you pick up the chips and make another bet."

"Grandma, I swear I'm not sure I can handle Sadie the wild rebel." Grace shook her head.

"She's always been here," Grandma replied. "You haven't needed her until now. If you want to try something new, we're all for it."

"I'm not sure Raquel and Kelly are as understanding," Grace said honestly. "They're a little wounded."

"And that's understandable, too," Bella said. "You pulled away and changed their lives. That doesn't make this a bad idea—if you think it through carefully before burning bridges."

"And that's why we have a mom." Harper grinned.

"You got that right." Bella took a sip from her tea, exchanging brow raises with Grandma Sadie.

"*Not* burning bridges is why I'm no further along in this process," Grace said. "Making a decision to jump ship is hard."

"You three girls have been attached for twenty-six years," her mother said. "Nobody should expect this to be easy, least of all you. My only advice would be to keep Kelly and Raquel in your loop as you go. Make them excited and don't let them feel like you no longer need them. Then again," she ran a gentle finger down Grace's cheek, "you know far more about being an identical sibling than I do. And of the three of you, you're the one who'll care for the relationship best. You and your strong moral compass. You have that in common with your grandma here."

Grace smiled at her grandmother. "I'll never measure that tall."

"Cockamamie," Sadie replied. "What moral compass? I spit when I was a child, remember?"

"Spit?" Harper asked.

"You don't want to know," Grace replied. "Now go get that painting. I promise I'll ask for lots of advice as I need it. It's enough to know you all might support me."

Harper stood and disappeared into the living room. When she returned with a canvas—smaller than most of her paintings at twenty-by-twenty-four —and set it on the table, the reaction of the five women was swift and unanimous.

"Oh, Harper." Bella's words emerged in a near whisper. "This is stunning."

She'd painted a woodsy scene infused with what had become her signature burst of rainbow backlight behind the main subject. The magical halo surrounded a cottage. In real life the building stood half a mile behind the main street of Wolf Paw Pass. Although charming, the cottage had never looked this enchanted in person. The walls were made of weathered planking—sturdy, long boards of thick pine, faded to a smoky, rich gray. The foundation and a huge chimney were formed from large, classic fieldstones, and the long front porch was bedecked with climbing vines and their mother's favorite blue morning glories. The wooden front door was a friendly, worn, windswept aqua blue. Under Harper's amazing touch, it had been turned into a fairy cottage, or maybe a forgotten wizard's hideaway. It called to Grace with a siren's insistence.

"I think I've fallen in love," she said. "I could live there."

"You could," Harper laughed. "It's been empty for several years. I don't even know who owns it."

"We do." Once again, Grandma Sadie's voice cut solemnly through the room.

Stunned silence followed her announcement. "Say what?" Harper asked at last. "We who?"

"Your great-grandfather, your grandfather, your father, now you six girls. The building has been many things since Eli built it, including my home for a short time. It was once rented out to a trapper."

"I sort of remember him," Mia said. "He always had creepy dead skins."

Sadie laughed. "The house did a year as a makeshift library while the one we have now was being built. Then it did the same for the visitor's center. Your father rented to various groups like the local Lions and the little Boy Scout troop in town for storage. But it's been empty since a year before he died. I often forget it's there."

"Unbelievable," Mia said. "Mom, did you know this?"

"I did." Bella peered at the painting. "But I never spent any time in the house."

"Sebastian and I lived there for about two years when we were first married," Grandma Sadie added. "Eli and Brigitta built it as their winter home in town for those first years when there was no heat here at the homestead, and no roads to get them in or out during the worst of the season."

Grace let herself be drawn more deeply into Harper's painting. She could almost smell the deep woods and feel the protective crowding of the pines surrounding the cottage. Images flashed through her mind of a flower-lined path leading to the door, of a crackling fireplace, the scent of wine and clink of silverware. Of voices filling an old, old space that longed for life.

"Do you remember when we all sat in the dining room the night of Dad's funeral, trying to decide what to do with the ranch now that it was ours?" Grace looked at each woman around her in turn. "You all have rebuilt the dream—pulled it out of financial troubles. You're the ones who have done all the work, and still you tell me, Raquel and Kelly every time we're home that we can each have our little piece of Paradise wherever we choose? Is that still true?"

Harper blinked, and then lifted her chin almost as if she followed Grace's thoughts. "Of course it is. Always …" she said, her brow knotted.

Grace pointed at the painting. "Do you think I could have that?"

Chapter Four

LUCKY POUTED ALL the way up the drive to the main house, her arms crossed in front of her as if Ty were forcing her to a punishment more horrible than eating worms. He smiled at her yardstick-straight back.

"I don't see why I should have to apologize for spitting or for playing poker."

"You don't have to apologize to Miss Crockett for the poker. Only for not spitting in your own yard."

"I was spitting in Rory's yard. Isn't he allowed to spit on his own property? And how could we have had a spitting contest if he was in one yard and I was in another? That's just stupid."

Ty knew most five year olds didn't reason like his daughter did, and her logic no longer threw him off balance as it had when she'd been three and four. Most of the time he managed to answer in kind while trying to parent. What he worried about was effectively refereeing interactions with others, as he'd had to do today. The same way he'd done Lucky's first day of school, when it had been like sending a lawyer to kindergarten.

"This is about being polite," he said. "There's no logic—it's to make people feel better. We're new here, we want to make a good impression."

"I have to say it even if I don't mean it?"

"You'll mean it. You're not all that bad a kid."

She giggled and her backbone loosened a notch.

It was true Ty did want to keep the nice-guy reputation he was carefully cultivating. Not that he was normally a jerk—at least he didn't think he was—but having a good guy rep wouldn't hurt when it came time to tell the Crocketts why he was really here.

And then there was the condescending Grace Crockett. He couldn't get her critical reactions to Lucky's spitting and the inadvertently chauvinistic "ten" comment out of his mind. Nor could he erase the image of laser-sharp blue eyes and her, well damn it, her "ten" body. Something about her made him determined to prove he wasn't raising a rude street hooligan. More importantly, however, he was doing the best he could by Lucky. If, in the end, people didn't like *him*, he could take it. But he wanted them to like his very cool kid.

"We'll get this over with and then head into town," he said.

"We can still eat at Dottie's, right?"

"I promised."

"And I still get to go over to Dr. Ackerman's and play with the puppies at the clinic while you have your meeting."

"Lucky, I haven't changed the plan. I know looking at the rescue animals is sacrosanct."

Amazingly, he knew *she* knew that word. "It *is*." She finally glanced over her shoulder to throw him warning sparks. "Since you won't let me rescue one of them."

"There are tons of animals on this ranch. You can play with dogs anytime you want."

"But they aren't mine."

"You *are* mistreated, I'll give you that." Ty grinned and Lucky flounced her head and shoulders back to the front, rolling her eyes along the way. "Yeah, because I have a weird daddy."

Warmth washed over him like the spring sunshine. He loved being Teagan Ann Garraway's "weird daddy." More than he could have ever dreamed. How a child he'd not known existed until she was three years old could burrow her way into his life, heart, and plans so unalterably and turn a wayward bachelor into a father who only wanted the best for her was still a mystery after two years. But she had. And here he was, telling her to be honest and kind when he was being the ultimate in deceptive. He hardened his thoughts. It was only temporary, and only because he wanted only to give Teagan Ann Garraway a family legacy every bit as strong and lasting as the Crocketts'.

They mounted the steps to Rosecroft, as the main house was known, and on the massive front porch Ty handed a small bouquet of daisies and pink carnations to Lucky.

"Go ahead. Ring the bell," he said.

Lucky shrugged, done with her scowling now that the task was inevitable. She was nothing if not a realist.

To his surprise, Mia answered the door, balancing on her crutches and unable to hide her surprise at the visitors.

"Ty! Hello."

"Howdy, Mia," he replied with a grin. After only two and a half weeks, he'd already chosen Amelia Crockett Harrison as one of his favorite people. She managed to combine genuine friendliness with an air of no-nonsense, and he admired the way she spoke to her son, Rory. A person could learn a lot from a calm and collected mom like that.

"I'm pretty sure your family shouldn't be making you and that baby answer the door."

She laughed. "Well, if you could see the state of the rest of the women in the house, you'd know why I got this job. Come on in. Hey, Lucky, you look as fresh as that pretty bouquet. Are you going on a date tonight?"

"With my daddy. I'm going to Dr. Ackerman's to see the new rescue puppies in her clinic."

"Now there's a dad who knows how to treat his daughter." Mia wrinkled her nose in a smile. "To what do we owe this pleasure?"

Ty nudged Lucky gently on her shoulder.

"I came to talk to Miss Grace. I have to say I'm sorry."

Ty nodded when Mia frowned with incomprehension. "We kind of got off on the wrong foot with your sister," he said. "Unintentionally."

"Goodness. I can't imagine Grace thinking she needs an apology, but I'll get her." She started to pivot on her crutches. "Better yet, follow me into the kitchen. You might forget all about saying you're sorry when you smell what's been going on there."

The first misgivings plopped into Ty's stomach. He'd never been into the intimate areas of the huge house, and he didn't want this much contact with the members of the family that didn't concern him or his job. When Ty had first agreed to hire on, Cole had ushered him through the high-ceilinged living room, warm with wooden beams and colors of a southwest sunset—blues, golds, pale yellows and vivid splashes of red—to the office, where Ty had signed papers and made his employment official. He could make peace with what he was doing when it came to business. Being in the kitchen, from where he could already hear laughter, was way too personal.

"Look who rang the doorbell!"

Mia's announcement cut off the chatter in the room, and four beautiful faces turned in unison to study him. One by one, each woman smiled, but only one sent his stomach into a tailspin.

She literally had a smudge of flour on her nose and a curl of damp hair hanging in front of one eye, which she brushed aside with the back of a wrist. With her caramel-brown hair pulled back, her face looked more cherubic than it had that afternoon. He hadn't noticed the height of her cheekbones or how their rounded curves softened her eyes when she smiled. Where was the opinionated sex goddess he'd remembered? This was a wholesome family girl who happened to have the most winning grin he'd ever seen.

Okay. He was clearly unhinged. Or allergic to flour and it was affecting his brain.

He shook his head and cleared his throat. "I'm sorry to bust in on you. Hello, Mrs. Crockett. Miss Sadie."

So much estrogen filled the kitchen, along with the mouth-watering scent of chocolate, that Ty—who suddenly remembered his cigar-smoking, poker-playing nights with more than a little nostalgia—almost feared he was about to be lectured by five clones of his mama. He'd learned the first week at Paradise Ranch that the women here wielded the power. How had he forgotten and let that "ten" remark slip?

Because he'd never before had to apologize for complimenting a beautiful woman.

"Everything all right, Ty?" Bella asked, and he knew he'd been staring.

"Sorry. Yup, everything's fine. Lucky has something for Grace."

Looking directly at her didn't help his non-functioning

brain one bit. She knotted her brows and turned to Lucky. When his daughter held out the flowers, Grace's features softened.

"I'm sorry I was spitting in your yard, Miss Grace," Lucky told her dutifully. "We should have gone to my yard or behind a barn or something."

The uber-sincere apology impressed even Ty.

"These are beautiful, thank you." Grace took them and gave them a deep sniff. "You didn't have to do this."

"My daddy said it was necessary politeness."

Once more Grace lifted her eyes to Ty. Amusement passed between them, and beneath he saw the look of surprise shared by everyone experiencing Lucky's vocabulary for the first time.

"And he made you come even though you didn't want to?"

Lucky took her turn being surprised. "Yes." She nodded.

"I did." Ty jumped in before any more honesty popped from his daughter's mouth and made things worse instead of better. "I figure a good first impression is important, and we probably didn't do a great job this morning. I apologize, too. For the number comment."

Grace made skepticism adorable. "Well thanks."

"You know the men will all be here in a few minutes," Bella said. "Why don't you and Lucky stay for dinner? Grace tried out a new dessert recipe and she needs guinea pigs. If you're willing to suffer through some sloppy joes first—there's a chocolate whiskey cake that has us all considering skipping dinner."

The being-smothered-by-mother feeling returned, along with a zip of nerves. He did not know these people that well. He didn't want to interact on the intimate stage of a family dinner.

"Oh thanks, Mrs. Crockett, but we have plans in town already."

"Daddy, you said your meeting isn't until seven. I like sloppy joes."

He stared at his daughter's about face. "Uh, what about Ina's and the puppy rescue?"

"Well ..." She considered thoughtfully. "Lil is gone tomorrow night, too. We could go then. And there *is* chocolate."

A touch of panic rose in Ty's chest as his extroverted child dragged control of the situation from his grasp.

"Oh stay." Grace's chiding invitation didn't help. "She's got great taste."

One man, regardless of the fact that he was The Dad, was no match for the super power of multiple Crockett women, but then the back door opened and Cole sauntered in. For a short moment, Ty's hope flared. His boss wouldn't want the hired help sharing family supper.

"Man, does it smell good in here," Cole said, setting a direct course for his wife but reaching for Ty's hand along the way. "Here for dinner?" he asked.

Ty had no words. Again—what was with this group of people?

Fortunately Cole didn't wait for an answer before he pulled Harper into his arms. "Hello, painter woman. How's the art world today?"

Harper giggled while they kissed, and Lucky clapped her hands over her eyes. "Eeeww."

"No. It's romantic." Grace patted her on the head. "Someday you'll get it. You'll marry a handsome cowboy like Harper did and you won't think it's 'eeww.'"

"She's five," Ty said, sighing. "Don't be marrying her off

already."

"Don't worry." Sadie appeared in front of Lucky, a cane-toting fairy godmother, and held out her hand. "You have a very long time to wait until some special boy impresses you by beating you at a spitting contest. Come with me and we'll set the table. Ty, you help Cole pick out a bottle of wine. Since we have guests for dinner, we might as well celebrate right.

Lucky skipped happily off beside the elderly matriarch, who moved with plenty of vigor despite the use of a distinctive black lacquered cane covered in bright red poppy flowers. "Let's use the fun china," Sadie said. "It's got butterflies and rabbits on it."

"I'll help, too." Bella followed, and the three disappeared into the dining room.

"She's a little bit scary smart, isn't she?"

He swung his head to find Grace staring after his daughter, too.

"She takes some getting used to," he replied. "About the time you think she's turning into a normal kid, she opens her mouth. I'm barely smart enough to deal with her."

"It was good of you to have her apologize. It honestly wasn't necessary, but it's nice."

For another second, camaraderie joined them—two bemused adults left in Lucky Garraway's wake.

"Has she been this way since birth? I mean, did she do everything early?"

"No idea."

That sent confusion into her eyes. "Okay ..." She crossed her arms and leaned against a counter to wait for his explanation.

"I had no idea Lucky existed until she showed up at my door when she was three. All I can tell you is that she was like this then, and hasn't gotten any more normal."

"You've only had her two years? Wait. What? Of course she's normal."

There was the censure. He grinned all the harder.

"Yes; her mother left her with me. Yes, I'm her real father. And she's *not* normal. She's perfect, but she ain't normal."

"Well I hope you never tell her that."

"Don't have to; she knows she looks at the world differently than most people. She also knows she's perfect the way she is. But I have learned in two years that she needs to be shown how to fit in with those who don't see things her way." He held up a hand to stave off whatever critique was headed his way. "I don't tell her she's better than anyone. I just tell her that before her friends can understand her, she has to understand *them*. She gets it."

"What can I say?" The light of skepticism didn't fully leave Grace's eyes, but she uncrossed her arms and eyed the stove, where a large Dutch oven simmered on one burner. "Sounds like you have it figured out."

A laugh caught in his throat. He'd never have this gig figured out, but he wasn't going to say that out loud to Grace Crockett. From the first, she'd immediately decided Ty knew nothing about parenting. Instead he took the bone she'd already offered with her earlier compliment and let himself be content.

"I have it figured out up to today," he agreed.

"Glad to hear you say that." Harper passed him and patted his arm. "Most days I feel the same way."

"Come on and check out the wine cellar." Cole said++. "We built it last summer. You won't be impressed, but it's all we've got."

Ty snorted. What did the Crocketts ever build that would

fail to impress?

And yet, there wasn't anything grand about the small room built off the back porch that was not much bigger than a walk-in closet. Ty guessed the wooden racks might hold two hundred bottles, were they filled, but at the moment only twenty-five or thirty bottles took up random spaces in the attractive but small "cellar."

"Know anything about wine?" Cole asked.

"There are red ones and white ones. Some come from California." Ty shrugged.

"Brother, welcome to the club. Harper and Mia want us to start keeping good wines on hand, but not a person here knows what those would be except Kelly down in Denver. We all like different kinds. So, at this point, this is the extent of our collection."

"German beer. Southern states craft beers. I could help you there."

"We have a local beer that's pretty good." Cole nodded. "I'm with you. But, Sadie rules so we're here to deplete the wine stock by a bottle or two. What pairs well with sloppy joes?"

Ty had to laugh; it sounded ridiculous.

"Uhh, red goes with hoity toity food; white goes with anything that tastes like chicken?" Ty shrugged.

Cole sputtered appreciatively. "Sounds 'bout right to me. Okay since I have no clue either

, we'll take one of each. I'll pick red, you pick white."

"Why, so they'll blame me if it stinks?" Ty wrinkled his nose.

"Exactly. Watch this." Cole closed his eyes and turned around once. With no thought, he reached for a bottle and pulled it out. "Yellow Tail Shiraz," he said. "Sounds perfect to me."

Ty shook his head and pointed left. "I like it. Whites over here?"

"Yup."

"Let's go low." He bent and pulled a lone bottle from the bottom row. "Oh, hell, look. Horses on the label, surprise-surprise." He laughed at the wine name: *14 Hands Hot to Trot White Blend.*

"Bought by my wife precisely *because* of the horses. Come on. If the girls don't like these, they can send us for beer next time."

"I'm all over that decision."

The meal went off without a hitch. Lucky devoured two sloppy joe buns, scarfing up the saucy meat along with an accompanying fruit salad and roasted asparagus like a starving prisoner. Conversation and laughter flowed like the two bottles of wine, which garnered no complaints. Lucky drove part of the chatter, asking detailed questions about the ranch horses she was quickly falling in love with and the four dogs she loved even more. The idea of rounding up cattle on horseback fascinated her, but when she learned that kind of classic cattle gathering only happened once or twice a year and the rest of the time cattle got moved with four-wheelers and even a helicopter, she went thoughtful rather than excited.

"Doesn't that scare them?" she asked.

Watching the reactions around the table gave Ty insight into the family dynamics. Grace and Harper exchanged raised brows. Mia shook her head and Cole shrugged, along with Mia's husband Gabe. Clearly opinions on the subject varied.

"We get the babies used to the four-wheelers when they're

pretty young," Cole said. "They aren't any more afraid than they are of the horses. The helicopter is mostly used for finding the herds when they're far from the ranch yard. We don't get too close."

"I saw pictures of people flying airplanes and helicopters close to the cows until they stampeded," Lucky said somberly. "I didn't like that."

"Hear, hear." Harper, seated beside Lucky, held up her palm for a high five. "I don't either, but since Cole and I started managing Paradise, we've made sure everything we do is kind to the animals. We learned when we were kids that the ranch is way too big for old-fashioned round-ups every time we have to herd the cattle. We'd never get done with all the work on time. So, we have to use machines to help."

Lucky nodded, apparently satisfied. Ty tried to catch Harper's eye to thank her for her patience. Instead, he caught Grace assessing him like a confused pup eyeing a snake she wasn't sure was a potential playmate or a thing she needed to attack. For the first time, she unnerved him. It was as if she saw something in him that nobody else noticed, and whatever she saw gave her the ability to read his mind.

"It's nice to have you all here." Bella broke the tension growing in Ty's stomach. "Joely and Alec will be coming home from Colorado in less than two weeks. Ty, you and Lucky will have to come on back when we fill up this table."

They were ten at the dining room table already, but there was room for six or eight more.

"Don't threaten him with that." Grace raised her eyebrows in amusement. "You wouldn't want him to quit."

"Don't be silly." Bella laughed. "We're fun."

"We're loud and crazy," Harper added.

"Especially when all three of her are here." Mia pointed at Grace. "The actual Three Musketeers had zip and nada compared with *our* triplets."

Ty couldn't stop his gaze from drifting back to Grace, and what he found in her expression—aimed at the tabletop and not him—set him back in his seat. All at once her face was filled with uncomfortable guilt. Interesting. Grace Crockett had her own little secrets.

"Even the Musketeers took time apart for relaxation. We're blessed to have you home to help, Grace," Sadie said.

Grace leaned to the side to give her grandmother a hug. "You're the best, you know that right?"

"I'm simply the oldest," Sadie replied.

Never in his life had Ty experienced anything like the give and take, the support and teasing, and solidarity this family displayed. He, Lucky, and Lil had perfectly pleasant meals together now, but dinner when he'd been a child had consisted of complaints from his father about his wife being a lousy cook, silence between him and his brother for fear of being sent away without any supper, and tirades about how difficult his father's day at work had been. He barely remembered his mother's voice, but his father, a master of verbal cruelty, was still apt to take over Ty's memory at unwelcome moments.

"Aunt Grace, are you really going into Wolf Paw Pass after we eat?" Rory spoke and, just as they had when Lucky had asked questions, all the adults turned to him.

"I am," Grace said. "I have to pick up some things for breakfast, and I have a super-secret mission I'll tell you about tomorrow."

"What is it?" Rory nearly jumped up from his seat.

Gabe put a hand on his shoulder and laughed. "She said

'tomorrow.' I think we have to wait to find out."

"Can't I come along?" Rory asked. "Please?"

"Come *with us*." Lucky blurted the request, and every eye turned to her. Ty himself nearly stood from his chair.

"Uh, Lucky, that's not a great idea. It's going to get late, and Rory's parents don't know us well enough yet."

"That's right, you two are going into town," Harper said as if she hadn't heard him. "Why *don't* you all go together? We're all about being as efficient as possible here. Save a little gas. Go your separate ways once you're in town, and then meet to come on back."

"I like it," Mia said. "I'll let Rory go if Lucky's going to be there, too. They can keep each other company while their grown-ups are busy."

The big, friendly family suddenly felt like a suffocating pillow over Ty's face. They'd come up with the worst idea in the history of bad ideas, and panic rose in his chest while he waited for somebody else to shoot down the terrible plan. To his relief, Grace came to his rescue.

"Mine's a quick errand," she said. "Ty won't want to be on my schedule, or vice versa."

"Sweetie, you're going to look at the little cottage," Bella said. "When you're done, you can sit at Ina's with the kids if Ty needs longer. Go. Rory and Lucky will have a good time, and you'll help save the planet by carpooling."

"For crying out loud, Mom," Grace said. "What part of super-secret mission did everybody not understand? And how did I get one of the rare families in Wyoming that drives hybrids and uses windmills?"

It was a great question, Ty thought. But he could already see The Family was going to win this argument unless he plain refused. He should. Thirty minutes in a car with Grace Crockett didn't seem like a good idea at all, and from the way her narrowed eyes refused to meet his, he could tell she agreed. But he still needed to build up the good will, and if the only person he pissed off by taking Grace into town was Grace, then he'd make the sacrifice.

"I'd be happy to drive," he said.

She nailed him with a glare that proved he'd guessed right: Grace was one pissed-off Crockett.

Chapter Five

TO SAY TY Garraway's twelve-year-old Ford F-250 crew cab had seen better days was an understatement. The kids didn't care about the patches of rust on the bumper or the flakes of formerly bright-red paint missing from the doors, but Grace couldn't miss the dusty, threadbare floor mats and scuffed dashboard, or several tears in the back seat upholstery. It was also hard to miss the scent of citrus covering up traces of old cigarette smoke. She wrinkled her nose as she climbed into the front seat and turned to make sure Rory was buckling his seatbelt.

"Old girl has seen finer days." Ty slid behind the wheel, his long legs easily taking up the distance between his seat and the accelerator. Grace could have fit a European vacation's worth of luggage at her feet.

"Time flies." She brushed a small clump of dried mud out the door with her boot toe.

"Sorry about the air freshener." He continued reading her mind as he pulled his own belt across his chest and lap. "I was a smoker before Lucky came along. Hard to get the smell out."

"You quit for her?"

"Seemed like the thing to do at the time."

A person had to be impressed by that, she supposed.

She had no clue what it was about him that put her senses on alert. Her first impression that he was a bad parent had clearly been wrong; he was polite; he'd used his napkin at dinner and given all the right compliments; he'd said thank-you ten times. She could have blamed her edginess on the way her pulse misbehaved around him, but in reality that was like a private little treat she didn't need to tell anyone about.

There was something else. Something a little too smooth, too practiced, too perfect about his actions that she couldn't quite identify.

"Tell me again where it is you're heading." She pulled the door closed and winced at the loud squeak of its hinges.

"Meeting an old friend."

He turned the key and the truck roared to surprisingly quick life. However rickety the body was, the engine at least sounded capable of getting them to Wolf Paw Pass.

He backed away from the house, made a deft backward turn in the driveway, and headed for the county road that bordered Paradise land. At least the man was no wimpy city driver—he'd earned the right to wheel around a pickup. Another distractingly sexy trait. He had, however, dropped the dinner act and, strangely, his curt, male-typical sentences quieted Grace's alarm bells slightly. Maybe the man simply knew how to be polite at a dinner table. She didn't need to chatter with him all the way into town—this was better.

Only it wasn't. There were reasons Grace had been the designated hostess and all-round customer wrangler at Triple Bean. You didn't let people stand, sit, or eat in awkward silence. It had always been her job to banish discomfiture—and she was usually good at it.

"Do you like it here?" she asked.

He turned his head slowly and scanned her with unhidden skepticism. "Can you define 'here'?"

She frowned, her mind blanking on the question's meaning. "Define *here*?"

"The truck? The road? The ranch? The state?"

"Good grief." She let her breath out in a long huff. "Here. In Wyoming. After such a long move." Was he seriously trying to be obtuse?

"Wyoming's fine. Nice people. Nice views. It's a good place to put down roots."

"What made you choose it?"

There was no mistaking the sharpened definition of his knuckles as he put a choke hold on the steering wheel, or the tightness in his voice when he answered. "I remember visiting as a kid. When I needed a new job and decided I wasn't tied to Nevada, I, ah, remembered the Grand Tetons. I'd read about this little town and I came—found a job and then a job found me."

The tautness in his voice made her study him for long seconds. His profile reinforced the pure male beauty of his face with its classically straight nose, wide, full lips, and long, enviable black lashes that softened his brooding eyes. She forced aside the attraction, which was highly inappropriate anyway, given Lil. At last Ty's hands loosened on the wheel and he gave a small yawn.

"Cole working you too hard?"

He glanced at her again. "You don't have to force a conversation, you know."

"I never have to force a conversation." She flicked her hair with mock haughtiness. "I can get the life story of a brick wall if I want to. Extroverts have crazy skills."

"Like my kid. Although I admit talking a brick wall to death definitely shows rare talent." The hint of a smile played on his lips.

"Hey. If you don't like conversation, all you have to do is say so. I can also be perfectly quiet."

"For how long?"

She scowled for the first time. "Are you *looking* for buttons to push or are you always sexist and sarcastic?"

"I'd love to push your buttons." His barely there smile turned into a full-fledged grin. "And that answers your question about my sexist tendencies pretty well, I'd say."

"You're proud of that? And here I was thinking what a good role model you seemed to be for your daughter."

She might as well have physically wiped the smile from his face herself. "All right, look here." A warning, parental tiger growl formed in his voice—low and aimed at her alone. "I was simply teasing a pretty woman I thought seemed perfectly able to take it. Don't *start* making this about my daughter."

Normally, any anger turned on her people-pleaser self sent Grace's insides coiling up with wounded feelings. This, however, was such an impressive and immediate display of protectiveness that she could only stare back at him thoughtfully. Whatever else he was or wasn't, she was learning quickly his love for Lucky was pure and instinctual.

"You're right," she said. "That isn't what I meant, but I shouldn't have said it at all. I can tell you're great with your daughter." He stared straight ahead for long seconds as if deciding whether or not the apology had been enough. "You sounded so serious, and I'm not used to guys who know how to joke like that. My sisters would say that I don't know how to take a compliment, but—"

"Hey, your apology is accepted, okay?"

He didn't exactly smile—it was more like he rolled his eyes in amusement—but his spine relaxed back into his seat.

"Thank you. I've always had a need to explain myself when people misunderstand. When *I* misunderstand."

"Like now?" He laughed. "You're explaining why you're explaining."

She'd never been good at letting people's opinions of her slide. She sighed. "Yeah. One of my crazy mad skills."

He didn't reply, and Grace craned her neck to look in the back seat. This wasn't the scene she'd have chosen to play in front of the kids.

"You two settled back there?" she asked.

She needn't have worried about the pair overhearing her and Ty. Rory had a new electronic tablet with two earbud jacks, and he was engrossed in showing Lucky the intricacies of the game his mother and Ty had approved before leaving. They sat with heads mere inches apart, Lucky absorbing every word. Grace smiled. The pair made a little map of the world: Rory with his rich, deep-toned complexion and dark, wide eyes, Lucky all strawberries and freckles. Yin and Yang. Friends who would, thankfully, never stop to analyze the beauty of their new friendship.

Satisfied, she faced front again. The two-lane road sped by beneath the truck's tires, and Ty drove casually, one hand atop the steering wheel, the other in his lap with his index finger extended to rest on the wheel's bottom curve. That long finger fascinated her. Straight, well-formed, with balanced knuckles and just the right amount of roughness. Her eyes traveled the back of his hand to his wrist. She'd never paid so much attention to a man's hand before. In her unpretentious and unimpressive dating career, she couldn't say she'd ever spent time with a truly sexy man. Attractive. Kind. Devout. Sweet. Judgmental. But never a man who'd made her want to take his hand in hers and trace the veins or stroke his skin.

She shivered and looked away. Lil, if she and Ty were together as her mother and grandmother suspected, was a lucky woman.

She hadn't been back to Wolf Paw Pass yet this trip home, and Grace found herself leaning forward as they entered the small town, looking for the familiar and for the changes. Her great-grandfather Eli had founded the foothill settlement with a handful of hearty trappers in the first years of the twentieth century, and in the town that had grown to twelve hundred, there were still a few buildings that bore the Crockett name. Since the town had always bordered Paradise land, and the family had been an institution in the area since before Grace or any of her sisters had been born, coming back into Wolf Paw Pass was always like coming home.

"I love this little town." She spoke aloud for the first time in ten minutes.

"It is little," Ty agreed. "I've only been here a couple of times to run errands for Cole. I've done my big shopping in Jackson."

Jackson was thirty miles farther north.

"We grew up mostly supporting local." She laughed. "But there are some things that definitely require a trip to the big city."

They drove slowly down Mountain View, the town's main street, and quietness greeted them, since they were still three weeks away from the opening of tourist season, Wolf Paw Pass's bread and butter. It wasn't yet seven o'clock and most stores were still open—Dottie's Bistro, Ina's Ice Cream Emporium, the hardware store, the little bookstore and the veterinary clinic. Grace had always loved that her little town didn't totally roll up its streets at five. Everyone believed that leaving the shop fronts open would keep the place vital and homey for the locals.

"What's your timetable?" Ty asked. "I'll drop you off and pick you up wherever you want."

"We're going to Ina's!" Rory had the earbuds out of his ears and leaned forward as far as his seatbelt allowed.

"After the boring stuff, when everyone's done," Grace agreed. "Not that you need ice cream after eating chocolate cake at home."

"Excellent chocolate cake," Ty added.

Her cheeks heated in pleasure at the compliment.

"What boring things do you have to do, Miss Crockett?" Lucky asked.

"You can call me Grace, sweetie," she said. "And I'm going to meet an old school friend who's a real estate agent. She's taking me to see a very old house that belongs to my family."

"What are you going to do there?"

"I'd like to see if it could be used for something other than a house." Grace turned to Ty. "I need about an hour. How about you? What's your super-secret mission?"

He shrugged a little too quickly and furrowed his brow as he searched for a parking spot. "I have a meeting as well. Some … family business that followed me here."

The nagging sense that he hadn't told her the entire truth returned, but family business was exactly that—for families. Whether she totally believed Ty or not, Grace knew from long experience with her high-profile relatives that you didn't talk about private matters with others.

"Fine. Rory and I can meet you at Ina's when you're finished," she said. "Or we're finished. Whoever gets to the shop first can save seats." She smiled at Lucky.

"I'd rather go with Rory." Lucky's little mouth settled into a thoughtful line. "Your meeting sounds boring, Daddy."

"It is, but it's something I have to do," Ty replied. "And it's like Grace said. You have to do the boring stuff before the fun stuff."

"I'd still rather do Rory's boring stuff."

Grace bit her lip to keep her smile from showing.

"Grace and Rory have their own business to take care of." Ty finished parking the car in an angled spot a block from the ice cream shop.

"I don't care if she comes along." Rory held up his game. "We can play this while we wait for you. Then nobody will be bored."

"That's the best idea ever!" Lucky unsnapped her seatbelt. "Hard to argue with that, Dad. You don't want a whining, bored kid on your hands, do you?"

"That is totally beside the point." Ty squeezed his eyes shut and rubbed them with one hand as if trying to ward off a headache.

When he opened his eyes again, the hazel-green irises shone with helplessness and the weariness of a father who'd fielded one too many logic questions today.

"Sorry," he said. "She'll be fine once we're on our way."

Without planning to, Grace touched his arm. Her fingers jumped at the slender tautness of his biceps, and she had to quell the ridiculous urge to stroke it. She pushed aside the errant thought and lowered her voice. "You know, I don't care if they come with me. I'm not conducting any business. It's up to you, of course, but she's welcome."

There was no doubt at all what emotion registered on his face this time. Relief. She almost laughed.

"Are you sure?" he asked. "It's not necessary—"

"I'm sure. I might be able to use the pair of them as guinea pigs." Her evil grin made him squint one eye skeptically.

"Guinea pigs? For what exactly?"

"I'll tell you if my plan works." She whispered with intentionally dark innuendo. He narrowed his second eye and she laughed. "If I let anything happen to the kid in my charge, my sister would tear me limb from limb. I imagine you'd do the same. They'll be safe."

"As if I worried."

"You were. For a second."

He snorted and opened his door. "All right, everyone out. Lucky, Grace said you can go with her. I'd better hear what a delightful and charming child you were."

"Lil says I'm always delightful and charming."

"Yeah. That's the main reason I keep her around, isn't it?"

Again Grace thought what a lucky woman Lil was. These two clearly adored her.

When they all stood on the sidewalk, she put a hand on each child's shoulder. "We'll meet you back there at Ina's in about an hour."

He nodded and squatted in front of Lucky. Tall, muscular, and gorgeous with slight cheek and chin scruff, the usual skepticism in his eye disappeared, and he suddenly looked soft as a teddy bear. "I know you're the perfect kid. Show it off a little for me, okay? I need the PR."

Lucky threw her arms around him. "I will," she said. "I know you need all the help you can get. And she's pretty."

Ty pushed her gently away and stood, pinching the bridge of his nose. In the spring evening light, Grace couldn't miss the heightened color on his cheeks—like an instant suntan. He cleared his throat and skated his gaze across Grace's face with another apologetic shake of his head.

"They didn't warn me about this when the storks brought her."

She had to laugh—the man was utterly attractive at the moment, discomfited and searching for a little bluster to hide it. "I don't have any experience of my own, but I've heard they never remember to leave the manual. She'll be fine."

He nodded, gave Lucky a narrow-eyed, pointed-finger warning and turning away. "See you in an hour."

***

There was no denying the relief. As he made his way down the sidewalk, putting more distance between himself, his daughter and Grace Crockett, Ty's shoulders dropped six inches, and he could breathe normally for the first time since Grace had slid into the truck. From their first meeting, he hadn't admitted his true reaction to her even in his deepest thoughts, but he had to admit it now. "Ten" he'd kept repeating to himself—she was simply another ten. Knowing he annoyed her had kept his attraction at bay. So, too, had her original arrogance.

Now, however, he'd seen the woman behind the arrogance, and she was smart, quick-tongued and funny, and great with kids. Highly sexy in far more than a ten kind of way. One minute she was cute as a tomboy, the next pretty as a prom queen, the next sexy as the movie star Cole had told him she'd been named for. How was he supposed to keep his mind on shallow things when in the space of an hour, she'd chattered her way into being precisely what everyone had described—a very nice person?

He felt like a genuine cad. For all intents and purposes, he'd driven her to the scene of the future crime that would make her family his enemy—no matter how much he wanted to pretend they might understand. He gripped a pocket folder containing the secret plans he wasn't about to abandon more tightly.

At the next corner he turned left and headed for the home office of a lawyer his attorney back in Las Vegas—an old, in both the time and the age sense, poker buddy named Nate Winter—had found for him. This meeting would be the first with Andrew Metcalf who, if fortune could just give Ty one more little nod, would help see to it that he and Lucky could have their home and future.

The house belonging to Andrew Metcalf, Attorney-at-Law was modest by big-town Jackson standards, but pretty posh by Wolf Paw Pass standards. The slate-gray structure was two stories tall with full front porches on both levels and pristine white trim that glistened in the evening sun just starting its drop toward the horizon. Its perfect, lush landscaping, tidy edged walks, and lack of a single stick out of place was the opposite of Paradise's wild beauty. The austerity was slightly intimidating. Ty's hand hesitated briefly before he reached for the doorbell. Once he rang it, the die was cast.

Metcalf was not what Ty had expected. The picture in his mind of a middle-aged family man exuding wise calm gave way to a man not much older than Ty himself, who greeted him with a smile and an eager handshake. Almost cliché, with dark-rimmed glasses and neatly styled hair brushed back from his forehead, the lawyer looked too wet behind the ears to take on a family like the Crocketts.

"Ty, I assume?" he asked.

"That's right."

"Drew Metcalf. Come on in. I'm glad you could make this unusual timing work."

"Wasn't a problem. It's better for me, too."

The foyer presented the same pristine picture as the front garden. Classy striped wallpaper above mahogany-colored wainscoting showed that someone had done a lot of good restoration on this part of the house—the craftsmanship was obvious.

"Let's go into my office," Metcalf said. "Sorry we have to go through the house. I lock up the back entrance at night."

"Not disturbing your family I hope."

He chuckled. "Not at all; we just finished dinner upstairs in my mother's apartment. It's her seventieth birthday and a couple of my siblings are here."

"I'm sorry. We could have done this another night."

Ty took in the living and dining rooms as they made their way to a wide hallway. Less formal, heavy furnishings gave this part of the house a masculine feel that sat more comfortably with Ty, and he relaxed slightly.

"No, this is great. I'm the one who's been too booked in court to meet with you, and now I'm leaving town tomorrow and won't be back for a week. Taking mother to her sister in California—birthday trip."

A leather sectional sat on a bare oak floor in the living room in front of a flat-screen television that had a measurement at least equal to Metcalf's mother's age. Ty relaxed further. At the end of a long, undecorated hall, behind a closed door, a spacious office took up the entire back of the house.

Several diplomas and certificates hung on the cream-colored walls. Both ends of the room were taken up with built-in bookcases, and a large, worn mahogany desk stood at an angle in the left corner. Sparse and unfussy.

Two upholstered blue armchairs stood in front of the desk, a couch and coffee table stood against the opposite wall. In the right corner, four wooden chairs surrounded a small pedestal table. A perfect place for a poker game. Ty banished that thought.

"Have a seat, please." Metcalf indicated one of the armchairs. "I have my notes from our phone conversation a few weeks ago, and I see you have a folder with you. I assume that's the correspondence you mentioned to me?"

"It's all the information I have on what happened back in 1935." Ty handed him the folder.

"I'm eager to see the letters. I'm sure they'll shed more light on what you've told me."

Metcalf's words struck the right mix of friendliness and professionalism. Ty's hopes rose incrementally as the lawyer took the letter Ty hoped would change history.

"This is definitely interesting," Metcalf said, after reading carefully for several minutes. "The Crockett family doesn't know about this?"

"Not as far as I know. I found the letters in an old ledger among some of my father's papers that got buried in my brother's basement. Nobody seems to know how they got there or when. Neither my father nor brother have seen this before either, and they have no interest. When I decided to pursue the matter, my lawyer counseled me to keep the information close to the chest until everything was certain. I told him I wanted to come out here and see how much of the story I could verify before opening the can of worms. The job at Paradise Ranch was not planned, but it's been helpful to learn firsthand about the life style. I am starting to have second thoughts about the wisdom of lying to them ..."

"I agree with your lawyer—Mr. Winter?"

Ty nodded.

"The Crocketts are powerful. If you were to decide not to move forward with any kind of action, there's no sense alerting them and getting the town in an uproar—which would happen because the family is also extremely well thought of. If we find there are grounds for a law suit, there'll be time to tell them. I would suggest, however, keeping your relationship with them purely business."

Ty swallowed. The man had just touched on the problem—the very reason for Ty's burgeoning guilt. But ... He straightened in his chair. It was more important to him to take care of the future than to be fair to the Crocketts. At least for the short time this should all take.

"I know there are issues after this many years," he said, pushing his guilt aside. "But I'm ready to get working on this. I'm looking forward to having you help get back the land Eli Crockett stole from my family."

Chapter Six

"LOOK AT THIS, Aunt Grace."

Rory, who'd at first hung behind when Marni, the real estate agent, had led them into the old house, had slowly braved his way to a tiny room off the side of the main living space. He stood in the doorway pointing, and Grace moved in behind him, placing her hands on his shoulders.

"Whatcha got, Mr. Harrison?"

"The tiniest bedroom in the world and there's still a bed in it."

"This looks like someone divided a larger room, maybe a dining room, into two small ones." Marni Dressler, Grace's former classmate and now an agent in her father's local real estate company, stepped into the closet-sized space.

"I don't remember much about this house," Grace said.

"I'll ask my dad if he knows anything specific about changing or adding walls," Marni added. "He's the one who always dealt with the rentals and leases of this place. I've never been in here before either. It's kind of a neat place."

The house had been fancy in its time. Built in 1918, it had been, as her grandmother said, Eli and Brigitta Crockett's home in town. The exterior was hearty oak planking that had been chinked with mud originally but redone at some point with cement. A long, deep porch ran across the twenty-five feet of front wall, and a half second story created more space for bedrooms. The house's most impressive feature, however, was the huge fieldstone chimney that ran up the west end of the building. Best of all, the stonework had been carried through to the interior, and the fireplace in the living area was original.

"Our ancestors knew how to build things right," Marni said. "The original care shows through despite the changes over the years. I definitely think the bones look like they could stand up to remodeling. What do you think of the layout?"

Grace turned in place, taking in the whole main room. Floor, ceiling, window sills and mantel all bore thick coats of dust, but the original wood flooring and the grandeur of the massive fireplace did shine through. In addition to the divided room off one side, two other much bigger bedrooms stood off the other side, along with an ancient bathroom.

"I see lots of potential," she said. "Let's find the kitchen."

Once they stood in the medium-sized room at the back of the house, surrounded by a forty-year-old stove and even older sink, plain shelving and only two cupboards, Grace knew that if she chose to take on this project, the most money by far would have to go toward making a restaurant-worthy kitchen. The existing room would barely function for a small family.

"Walls would have to be knocked out big time to expand this," she said. "I can only imagine what that would cost."

"Turning this into a restaurant would be no small feat," Marni agreed. "It's not just converting a house—it's converting a very old house."

For a moment Grace's heart fell.

This was too much—she had no financing. Her sisters didn't

have the cash flow to allow them to buy her out immediately, nor had she insisted she needed them to do it at all. On the other hand, she had the Crockett name and Paradise Ranch behind her. That would count for some collateral. Maybe ...

"But boy would it be awesome if it happened." Marni continued searching with her eyes. "Imagine if that wall was gone and you moved the restrooms toward the entrance. You could add ten feet easily. You don't need bedrooms down here ..."

"Maybe for storage and an office?" Grace mused.

"Offices could be upstairs. We haven't checked up there yet."

Marni's renewed enthusiasm buoyed Grace again. "Sounds like you'd be a great idea person if the time came."

"Aunt Grace, Aunt Grace!"

It wasn't until Rory came dashing into the room with Lucky on his heels that Grace realized the kids had been gone. Kicking herself for her carelessness at losing track of them, she rested her hands on her thighs and bent forward as the pair of kids nearly slid to a stop in front of her.

"What's wrong?"

"Nothing. But you should see all the cool stuff out back."

"There's a shed," Rory said.

"And a boat and a pond! And swans!" Lucky added.

"A pond?"

"A big pond. With swans," she repeated. "And ducks."

"Okay. This I have to see."

The backyard and its idyllic setting sold Grace on the entire place and project the instant she laid eyes on it. Overgrown and tangled with dandelion-dotted grass, shrubs, and wildly out-of-control trees, the spacious back lot was still green and delightful with potential. Ideas flooded her imagination: an outdoor eating space, a duck-feeding station for kids, a craft or consignment shop if the huge shed was in any kind of decent shape. Crazy ideas went even further. She could offer a wedding venue, or a place where senior pictures could be taken, or birthday tea parties for little girls …

"Couldn't you imagine having a birthday party here with your friends? We could bake tea cakes and have place settings for your dolls or stuffed animals?" Grace turned to Lucky with a conspiratorial wink.

Lucky's brow furrowed. "Why would I ever bring a doll to a birthday party?"

Grace bit her lip and studied the girl, whose inner professor had returned. With her neat, shoulder-length bob and jeans rolled up to mid-calf, the child looked and sounded a little like a strawberry sundae-haired Scout from *To Kill A Mockingbird*. She *didn't* look like a kid who played with dolls or tea sets.

"Tea parties can be pretty awesome." Grace said.

"I'd rather use that boat out on the pond and have a pirate party."

Grace added a mental note about pirate parties.

The pond was every bit as impressive as Lucky had claimed. It sat nestled in a thick ring of trees, maybe an acre or two in size, making it plenty big enough for canoeing or rowing.

"This is lovely," Marni said.

"There they are!" Lucky pointed as the advertised pair of swans floated into view and put on unseen brakes to halt mid-glide at the sight of the humans watching them. One flapped its wings, beating ripples into the water, but neither flew or swam off.

"I want it. I want it all!" Grace lifted her eyes to the treetops and turned in a circle, stopping when she faced Marni. "Can't you see this as a boutique kind of restaurant? Something that wouldn't compete with Dottie's Bistro because it wouldn't serve that kind of traditional food. And it wouldn't be a supper club like the Basecamp. I think it could fill a niche—for tourists and special occasions."

Marni's cheerful laugh buoyed her enthusiasm higher.

"Fortunately this is the easiest sale I'll ever have in my life. I'll hand you the keys tonight if you want them. We looked into all the old leases and there is nothing still active. If you decide you want to take it over, I'll make sure we take down any advertisements online that the space is available. My only advice is to get some serious financing commitments. You're not talking an inexpensive undertaking."

Grace pushed the counsel temporarily out of mind. She didn't want to spoil her first flush of excitement and freedom. Too many things had happened in auspicious order for this to be anything but the kind of sign she looked for in every decision. This was meant to be; she was sure of it. Panic could come later.

Forty-five minutes after leaving the cottage, Grace shushed her two charges, who were laughing almost to the point of screeching. Ina's Ice Cream Emporium was a summertime gold mine in Wolf Paw Pass but far from a beehive during the winter and early spring. Nonetheless, an elderly couple sharing a milkshake and some fries occupied one other table, and the pointed glances from the woman every time Rory let loose with a hearty little-boy's shriek made it clear she considered her date night ruined.

Lucky had brought along a backpack filled with activities, and the current choice was reading riddles from a book of jokes for kids. Once again the girl astounded Grace with her advanced comprehension. It was hard not to fall in love with her. The mix of normal child and PhD candidate made her endlessly fascinating.

"You guys are having way too much fun," Grace said. "I think we need to tone down the laughter a bit."

"Knock, knock," Lucky said in response.

"Who's there?" Grace asked, unable to resist.

"Interrupting, squawking parrot."

Grace laughed at the old joke, hesitating long enough for Rory to jump in.

"Interrupting, squawking par—"

"SQUAWWWWWWKKKKK!"

Lucky's gleeful leap into the punchline at the top of her lungs sounded like a parrot being beaten over the head with a kazoo. Rory fell to his side on the padded bench seat, holding his gut with both hands. Lucky looked so pleased that Grace couldn't keep her own bubbling laughter inside.

A moment later, the woman from the milkshake table stood beside theirs.

"We'd like to ask you to please keep the noise level down," she said. "We came for a quiet moment away from home. Can you control them, please?"

The shock of how much the woman's complaint angered her struck Grace momentarily dumb. Lucky and Rory literally straightened in their seats like little soldiers being reprimanded by their commanding officer. Slowly Grace gathered her cool. The woman was a stick in the mud, but she wasn't wrong. Disruptive children in a public place were aggravating. But before she could speak up, Lucky opened her mouth again.

"Where do pencils go for vacation?" she asked, staring the

lady directly in the eyes.

The woman's jaw popped open. "Excuse me?"

"Where do pencils go for vacation?"

"Lucky, that's not polite." Grace attempted to cut off the joke and apologize at the same time. "We need to think about other people's feelings, too."

"But maybe if she laughs, she'll feel better."

The woman's mouth twitched slightly and Grace wanted to sink into the floor. The kid was at her adorable best, but how did you make someone else's child understand inappropriate behavior?

"I'm so sorry—"

"Where?" the woman asked. "Where do they go?"

"Pencil-vania!"

From across the aisle, a deep chuckle reached them all, and the woman looked to her husband and then shook her head with a smile. "So you're telling jokes, are you?"

"Yes." Lucky nodded for emphasis." She held up the little book she'd carried in her backpack. "I memorized them all."

Grace rubbed the furrows from between her brows and let out a slow breath of relief. Maybe the older woman would let this all pass.

"I understand your laughter, then," she said. "Do you think you could do it a little more quietly?"

"Sure. Why did the girl spread peanut butter on the road?"

"Lucky!" Grace admonished. Pushing their luck was bound to backfire.

"Why?" asked the woman.

"To go with the traffic jam."

The rumbling laughter came again from the woman's husband, and she shook her head. "All right. I admit you know some funny jokes." She turned to Grace. "Your children are delightful. They're just quite loud."

She didn't have the will to explain they weren't her children. "We will keep it down, I promise. Thanks for understanding."

"I sometimes forget how much I miss my grandchildren."

With that, she turned and went back to her table. Grace turned on the children with a fierce whisper. "You two dodged a bullet. You know that, right?"

"She didn't have a gun, did she?" Rory asked.

"She means we almost got in trouble," Lucky explained. "Sorry, Miss Grace."

The girl and her limitless charm had won over their angry neighbor with guileless ease by being herself. Grace let out a long breath. This little chickie was going to give her daddy a run for his money.

"You weren't doing anything wrong. Like the lady said, you were just doing it very loudly."

"Okay." Lucky turned to Rory with a theatrical whisper. "How do you make a tissue dance?" Rory's eyes widened in anticipation of the answer and Lucky leaned closer. "You put a little boogie in it."

For a split second Rory processed. When he got the pun, there was nothing quiet about his explosive response.

"Boogie. Booger!"

Grace closed her eyes in resignation. She was destined to be toast in this matter. "Come on," she said, sliding from the booth. "We're going up to order now. Your dad can catch up whenever he gets here. You guys are impossible."

She urged them from the table, leaving jackets and backpack behind, shot an apologetic grimace to the woman and her husband, and herded the kids to the front of the store. She'd always prided herself on being pretty confident with kids, but these two had her over a joke barrel.

The pair skipped to the front counter, where Ina had her winter selection of ice creams available, along with her bright overhead menu of fall-to-spring favorites. She didn't have a lunch or dinner menu exactly—just a handful of comfort foods like French fries and basic hamburgers or hot dogs. Ina's true specialties were breakfast waffles with ice cream and decadent frozen desserts.

She was also a saint with the kids, laughing with cheerful patience as they changed their minds again and again. Grace noted her treatment of them with admiration and relief. The night had gone exactly as she'd hoped as far as the old Crockett building was concerned, and yet her nerves jangled like Christmas sleigh bells. She hadn't reached panic mode over what she planned, but excitement was turning into reality and her stomach flopped and flipped to the point where even ice cream didn't sound good. When she wasn't willing to eat a dessert at Ina's, earlier chocolate cake or not, it could only mean something dreadful, something wonderful, or the zombie apocalypse was imminent.

When the shop's front door crashed open she screeched, believing it was the apocalypse.

With a tsunami of wind and cool night in her face, Grace turned in perfect time for the figure that flew through the door to hit her like a six-foot wave. He'd entered at a trot, looking back toward the street and paying no attention to who was in front of him until his body collided with hers.

She grunted and two strong hands grabbed her to him as she stumbled backward, and a familiar scent of spice, now laced with an attractive hint of adrenaline-fueled, masculine perspiration, enveloped her along with his arms. Grace tried to brace herself, fully believing Ty's tackle was about to take her all the way to the floor. Instead, he managed to shore them both up against the firm, blessed strength of the entrance wall.

"Daddy!" Lucky cried, but her voice faded into nothingness.

He breathed like a sprinter at the finish of a race. Each hot puff brushed her cheeks with feathers of pleasure and killed off brain cells that would have helped her push him away. Ty took another quick look over his shoulder and scooted her roughly around the entry wall and up against the other side inside the seating area. Instead of letting her go, he pressed closer, placed one hand on either side of her cheeks, and spoke into her ear.

"You're a godsend."

Hot sparks raced down the side of her neck, zipped across her shoulders and joined the twitching that already plagued her nerves.

"What are you doing?"

"I think I'm escaping my past."

He pulled back enough to look her in the eye, and the sparks between them set off a bomb of electrical shocks that reverberated to her toes. She struggled slightly to indicate he should let her go, but he only held her more firmly against the wall. With his eyes boring into hers as if he searched for the meaning of life, her struggle ended before it had really begun. He mesmerized her, confused her, sent her pulse into the stratosphere, and made her want to stand, in his arms forever. Heavy heat she hadn't felt in so long, dropped low into her groin, startling and thrilling her.

"Let me go."

"In a minute. Honest, I need you."

In that second she needed him, too, but she didn't know

what on the Lord's green Earth she needed a sweet-spice-smelling stranger on the lam from his past *for*.

"Daddy?"

"Hang on, Luckster."

Ty turned his head to check out a window behind him. The movement pressed his length against Grace's, and he moved his hold to her upper arms, grasping desperately.

"Ow!" she said, involuntarily.

His hands flew away even though the rest of him didn't move. "I'm sorry. Grace. I truly am sorry."

She swallowed and forced herself to think beyond the sensations. "Tell me what's going on."

A figure, bulkier and shorter than Ty, passed by the window, walking slowly but confidently past Ina's shop. After one last heat-filled moment, Ty finally relaxed and released her. With a shaky step, he moved back.

"I'm sorry again."

She stared, still gathering her wits.

"Daddy, why did you almost kiss Miss Grace?"

Heat rushed up Grace's neck and, she was sure, flushed her face red.

"I would never kiss Miss Grace without her permission." He smiled at his daughter and ran a finger down her nose.

So why didn't you give him permission?

Grace slammed a lid on the thought and straightened. First, Ty had a woman in his life. Second, why would she ever contemplate the thought of kissing any man who blew in like Bigfoot, captured her, and held her against her will?

So not true.

The only thing Ty had held her against had been the wall and, although the admission embarrassed her, she hadn't tried very hard to get away. She could claim shock or blame it on his strength, but the fact was, something deep inside of her while he'd pressed his weight against her, had wanted to see what would happen.

Maybe that last terrible date with Micah before leaving Denver had killed off a few brain cells, too.

"Would you care to explain what just occurred?" She forced herself back to the present and stared at him, finding no remorse in his face or the smoky sage-green of his eyes. "Am I suddenly harboring a fugitive? What's so awful in your past that you have to burst into a public place and hide in a woman's arms?"

His eye went a little wide and a smile tugged at his mouth. "Darlin', I can't think of a better place to hide than a woman's arms, awful past or not."

His eyes shone with irreverence, and the words flowed with a boisterous confidence she hadn't seen when he'd worn his perfect table manners. The man was a modern-day rake. He *was* the sauntering cowboy who'd first come up the drive and assigned her that number.

"Smooth talk me all you like. Who were you hiding from?"

"An old man who's been stalking me for the past two months."

She almost laughed. "Why would he do that?"

His jovial demeanor faded, and he glanced one more time out the shop's plate-glass window.

"He's part of that family business that followed me here. He wants something I have, but I'm not ready to speak to him."

"Daddy, you never told me we were in stranger danger."

Ty's enigmatic features broke out of their concern like sun from behind a storm cloud. He took to a knee in front of Lucky and placed his hands on her shoulders. "Look at me. Teagan?"

The child's big eyes went bigger at the use of her real name. She copied him by placing her hands on his shoulders, and leaning forward until her forehead nearly touched his. In the now-familiar, wise-beyond-her-years voice she asked, "What's wrong, Daddy?"

"There is *nothing* wrong. Baby, this man is one hundred percent not dangerous, I promise."

"Okay." Lucky hugged him with the absolute faith of a child.

"So he's a relative you refuse to speak to. And for that you needed to burst in here like the grim reaper was after you and upset the kids?"

And me.

He smiled, the rake's light returning to his eyes. "You aren't upset, are you kids? Especially if I say it's way past time to get our ice cream."

"*I'm* not upset." Rory turned toward the ice cream case.

Ty swept Lucky into his arms so she could see down into the tubs. "Look at 'em all."

"Grace said this is nothing compared to what they have in the summer."

"Holy Rocky Road, Batgirl. Guess we'll have to be sure and hang around to see *that*," he said. "Now what can I get y'all? This is on me."

"You don't have—"

He silenced Grace with a shake of his head. "You babysit. I treat. It's a law."

"My dad has a lot of weird laws." Lucky burst into sudden peals of laughter as Ty dug his fingers into her side.

Yeah, Grace thought. Like it seemed to be illegal in Ty World to give a straight answer.

Chapter Seven

"YOU LOOK LIKE your trip to hell was a success."

Cole's grinning commentary on Ty's bedraggled form from behind his oak desk only drew a scowl as Ty dragged himself into the log building that served as Paradise Ranch's business office. He prided himself on resilience. Late nights, even after a few beers, normally had no power over him. There'd been no beer last night. Only a sleepless night born of nerves, a hot fudge sundae the size of Wolf Paw Peak, all in addition to Grace Crockett and that danged Trampas Manterville.

He still didn't know who rattled him more, the beautiful goody-two-shoes woman who made him feel like the scout leader from the den of iniquity or Trampas, his maddening—or maybe simply mad—great-uncle who refused to die and leave him alone. Making yet one more person he had to face sooner rather than later with the truth.

For a while, staring at the shadowy ceiling in his bedroom overnight, he'd considered giving up this quest and returning to Vegas. He was scaling a slick, treacherous wall, and even if he succeeded in getting to the top against all odds, he would not win any medals or friends. But he'd just promised his daughter she was in no danger. If he suddenly hauled them back to Las Vegas, even Lucky's overdeveloped cool would fail her. She craved security as everyone did—more so because of being abandoned by the first parental unit she'd had in her life. God knew, Ty understood rejection all too well. No way was he really going to give up on providing his child the love, the sanctuary, the heritage that he'd never known.

But all that soul-searching had led to this bleak and very early morning.

"Damn coyotes," he finally said in response to Cole's ribbing.

"They were pretty vocal last night, weren't they?"

Ty almost laughed. The gods of morning apparently pitied him. He hadn't really heard a single coyote during his unwelcome vigil.

"What's on my docket today?" he asked.

Cole grinned as if he had great news. "Didn't you tell me back when you hired on you wanted to get the lay of the land—see what fifty thousand acres really looks like? And you wanted to know the truth about rumors you'd heard of a nefarious poker game. Today's Tour of Paradise day, my friend. I need to fix a breach in some mountain fencing we can only reach on horseback. It's a long ride, but you did all right the half day we spent on the flat last week. I think that will fill up your schedule pretty nicely."

Ty liked horses well enough. He'd ridden on his grandmother's small farm as a kid. Still, he might have done "all right" that first morning, but he'd walked for two days afterward like a man who'd gotten a serious ass-whuppin'.

"Yeah, okay. But don't expect me to take anyone dancing for the next week."

A friendly rumble of laughter told him Cole understood. "We have a pretty good track record turning tenderfeet into cowboys around here. Mia's Gabe wasn't a rider before they started the veterans' wild mustang program a couple of years ago. We've had a lot of city-slicker vets spend summers here working after they learned to stick in a saddle. You already have the know-how—you just have to put in some hours slapping the leather."

Ty winced. "That sounds bad on a lot of levels, boss."

"Welcome to cowboy double-entendre, man. Somehow I don't think you'll have a problem picking it up." Cole grinned again and pulled open a drawer. He withdrew a rolled-up tube of paper. "Let me show you where we're going today. We'll trailer some horses about twenty miles up into the hills, and then ride about fifteen miles into the higher elevations where it's hard to navigate with a four-wheeler. There are very few sections we can't reach with the motorized vehicles; this is one. A local chopper pilot, who checks in if he spots an anomaly while he happens to be flying over, says he saw cattle on both sides of a fence line. It's not a catastrophe, but if we don't keep track of where the beasts are, it makes 'em hard to get at gathering time. You might as well keep getting more familiar with this place."

He unrolled the tube and spread it over the top of his desk. A detailed topographical map of the ranch's fifty-thousand acres appeared, and Ty swallowed guiltily. Cole had no idea how very well Ty already knew this map, or how many hours he'd spent poring over a particular seven-thousand-acre section of it in the middle of the northwest corner.

"Here's the area." Cole set his finger on a spot.

The breath left Ty's chest with a rush. Cole pointed right in the middle of—

"This section is filled with a lot of scrub pine and tough terrain," Cole said. "But it's also got some of the most beautiful views on the ranch. You're geographically closer to Grand Teton here than anywhere else on the property, and the cattle like it because the only things that compete with them for forage are elk and a few mountain goats. Wild horses don't bother that much with the higher ground back here, so we use it every other year or so."

Ty barely heard. His pulse climbed knowing he was about to see this bit of land in person. The closest he'd come was Google Earth maps—and in this remote part of the country, the satellite images weren't great. He'd been plotting ways to wheedle a trip into the area by asking about the "legend" of the poker game—now he was being handed the opportunity without the need to chance blowing his cover. What more proof did he need that not only the gods of morning, but fate and fairy godmothers, and whoever else was out there thought his cause was righteous?

"It sounds like a good trip."

"I've got three more invoices to write up, and then I'll meet you at the barn. Bjorn should be there now, so go on up and help him start loading the trailer. I'm trying to talk him into coming along. He knows the land even better than I do."

"I have a better idea. Take me."

Ty's head snapped around at the husky-sweet voice coming from the door.

"Gracie!" Cole stood from his chair, his face genuinely joy-filled. "What a treat!"

How Ty's heartbeat could choke him and sink into his stomach at the same time, he had no idea, but all at once he couldn't swallow past the boulder of dread in his gut.

Please, God, do not let him say yes.

Grace Crockett was, without a doubt, the main reason he'd

lost so much sleep last night, and the vision she presented now, slender legs encased in yet another pair of faded jeans and lengthened by the heels of scuffed cowboy boots, wasn't helping chase away the memory of what a fool he'd made out of himself at the ice cream shop.

"Morning, Ty," she said, her smile a bit north of shy and just south of cocky.

"Grace."

She didn't look like any city chick visiting the ranch that was for sure. Today she stood there, a born-and-bred cattleman's daughter ready to ride for days. He had no doubt she'd look as sexy and fresh after a weeklong ride as she did standing in the doorway today.

He didn't want her, first of all, to watch him "slapping leather" like the newbie he was or, second, to be anywhere near when he crossed into the territory he planned to take back for his family. Cole he could face—that was man to man. But Grace was sensitive, probably smarter than he was, and his nervous system's Kryptonite. He'd already figured out he would fold like an origami mouse if she figured out his secret before he was ready to tell.

"You *want* to ride fences?" Cole asked.

"Harper told me that was your plan for today. Mia has a doc's appointment and then is going to work for a while to finish up some paperwork. Harpo's going to the community center to paint and then set up arrangements for some big surprise guest artist she's trying to get later this year. The kids are all in school, so I might as well get some riding in while I have a chance. I miss it, and there won't be much time once Mia really needs help. So—I'm volunteering. I haven't been up to the mountains for a long time."

"I'm all for extra hands," Cole said. "And Bjorn really doesn't want to go, so he'll love the idea. Welcome to the crew!" He winked at Ty and stepped around the desk to wrap Grace in a hug.

The rock in Ty's stomach grew larger and harder.

His new boss stepped back, eyes dancing. "Hey. Long as I have you, how'd you like to do some horse training along the way?"

Excitement rose in her eyes. "Really? That would be *awesome*. Who needs training?"

Cole laughed. "I can always count on you Crockett girls and horses. We picked up a new mare a month ago when we were at the BLM holding facility," he said. "She's on the big side for a mustang—just over fifteen hands—and man, is she pretty, and smart as can be. Harper's worked with her. She does well in the ring, but she's had limited time on the trail. I'd love to have her on hand as another cow horse and also to be available for vets in the program. But until Joely is back from school for the summer and can help, this little girl doesn't get as much attention as I'd like. She's about five; I think she'd be right up your alley."

Grace did a fast little football-player jog in place and threw her arms around Cole's neck. Ty swallowed, remembering the long, painfully exquisite exchange the night before when she'd been squeezed against him. It hadn't been his finest moment— but the moment had been way more than fine.

"I would love to ride her," Grace said. "Is she down at the barn?"

"Probably in the pasture because I didn't know she'd be coming along. Bjorn can tell you all about her and fetch her for you."

Grace waved her hand in dismissal. "I'll get her. What's she look like?"

"She's a chestnut." Cole took his turn holding up his hand and grinning when Grace wrinkled her nose. "Let me finish. I don't know what it is you girls have against chestnut mares, but we're talking a dark chocolate-colored, liver chestnut with the purtiest auburn mane you've ever seen. Streaks of lighter flax in her tail. Really rare coloring. And built! I'm saying 'built' like an Arab stallion got mixed up in the herd for a night and lent his genes to the pool built. Go. See her. I guarantee you'll change your mind about redheaded girls."

Ty didn't understand most of the exchange. He'd learned elementary horse-speak as a kid, but the nuances were missing all these years later. The gist to him seemed to be that if you were a Crockett female, you went a little nuts over horses unless they were chestnut colored.

"C'mon, Ty. Let's go get the trailer ready!"

She'd lost all the reserve she'd shown upon entering the office, and the childlike energy he'd seen a few times yesterday engulfed her. For a moment he feared she was going to grab him by the hand and drag him out of the office, but she turned and simply held the oak door open for him.

"Be there in a few minutes," Cole called.

She chattered like a hopped-up chipmunk the whole walk to the horse barn two hundred yards to the south of the office. Had he ridden before working here? Did he already have a favorite horse? She'd always wanted to keep a horse in Denver and had tried for a while, but there'd been no time. She was sorry to be such a goon, but she hadn't had a day off like this in so long, she couldn't remember.

Yes.

No.

That's too bad.

Goon? Who uses the word "goon" anymore?

This is a day off?

He barely kept up with replies, much less her skipping steps. He might as well have been walking beside Lucky. And to his surprise, by the time they reached the barn, he found a smile tugging at his lips.

"How old are you today?" he teased. "You'd think this was your first ride on a merry-go-round."

She giggled with the low, breathy voice that sent ideas of her being young and innocent racing from his head.

"I *am* acting like a ten-year-old, sorry. I'm so grateful to be here instead of wiping down counters and straightening condiment shelves in Denver."

Ty hadn't felt like a ten-year-old on a carefree adventure since long before Lucky had arrived. He'd certainly been on the greatest adventure of his life since he'd been dropped into his world, but "carefree" was not a word in his vocabulary anymore. Still, Grace was infectious as a toddler's smile. If today's task didn't turn out to be a disaster, he supposed it could end up being … fun.

***

"Somebody had a good eye when they picked her out. Good instincts, too."

Grace relaxed into the saddle, trusting the mare beneath her to keep her head now that they'd had twenty minutes to get acquainted. Jess, they called her, short for Jessica Rabbit, and the name was appropriate. Cole had soft-soaped the mare's beauty. For an animal who'd spent five years in the freedom and rough weather of wild Wyoming, she had little of a normal mustang's scrappy, low-to-the-ground physique. In fact, Jess came as close to the uninitiated person's Disney vision of a wild horse—slick and long-haired—as Grace had seen in a long time.

"You have to *ask* who picked her?" Cole laughed.

"Mia." She nodded, certainty making her smile. "We all know horses," she said to Ty. "Dad made sure of that. But Mia has a gift. Great-Grandpa Eli supposedly had it, too. Never failed in his ability to judge a horse with total accuracy, or so Grandma Sadie says."

A choked cough sounded from behind, and she turned in her saddle to Ty. "You okay?"

A slight wrinkle creased his forehead, but other than that he looked normal.

"Bug," he said simply, and spit to the side as if ridding his mouth of the offending pest.

"Oh yuck."

She added sympathy to her voice, but she didn't believe him. Had he really eaten a bug, he would have spit first and then answered.

"You'd think I'd be the one gathering flies. I know I've done nothing but talk since Cole invited me to come along."

"I hadn't noticed," he replied.

His sardonic tone wasn't lost on her, but too much joy that might not last effervesced through her to care. She was on a fun and fancy little horse, in the mountainous terrain that was part of her soul. The restaurant plan marching through her brain hadn't yet been rained on, and their family was soon to add the next generation to the Crockett legacy. One semi-sourpuss of a handsome man wasn't going to ruin her mood.

As long as she kept memories from last night at bay.

Considering the dream that had awoken her early this morning, it would be difficult. The real encounter with Ty had certainly taken on a *much* different ending in the nighttime fantasy.

She rubbed Jess's neck and sifted the heavy, russet-colored mane through her fingers. One thing Grace had learned in years of running the restaurant with her sisters was how to compartmentalize. Worries and problems all had to be handled at appropriate times with proper objectivity, and that lesson applied even to simple problems like Ty Garraway. The rule was to prioritize—deal with what she could control at the moment. Riding a gorgeous horse into the Wyoming mountains was not the time to dwell on half-erotic dreams, to fret over her plans for the cottage in town, or worry about what her sisters would think. *This* was the time to drag crisp spring mountain air into her lungs, refill the well, gather ideas, build the dreams. She pressed her lower legs lightly against Jessica Rabbit's sides and brought her alongside Cole and his horse Marco, effectively shutting out Ty behind them.

"So tell me how things are really going around here, Cole. Dad's been gone two years now and everything seems to be okay. You look happy. Harper is in heaven. Raquel is the numbers person, so she's usually the one to check on all things financial, and last time she returned from visiting here, she said you've done a great job."

"That's nice of her, and I'm relieved she thinks so." He smiled in the engaging way he'd had since they'd all been kids. Because he'd grown up on the neighboring ranch, which was now part of Paradise, he'd always been as comforting as a big brother even before becoming an official big brother-in-law. "We're working hard. A few of our debt collectors actually smile when we come around these days. It takes a while to dig out of a hole the depth Paradise was in."

"I still find it hard to believe Dad let things get that bad. I know this is old, old news, but he was always so exacting."

"Don't blame your dad." Cole shook his head. "The more we looked into the past and his books, the more amazing it became that he kept Paradise afloat at all. You know how the economy broke my dad, and the Double Diamond was smaller and easier to manage than Paradise. It was your dad bailing out my dad that led to some of the problems. No, Sam Crockett was a good man. Hard as hell, but good. We'll be okay—we've learned to tighten belts and not act like we still rule the world. Now it's more about retaining Paradise's reputation. That's not really all that easy, but we're determined. Three generations worked incredibly hard to build it. We might not rule an empire, but we have the community's respect. I hope."

"Have I ever thanked you for taking on this enormous job?"

"No need to thank me. It's truly a family business now. Mia and Gabe run all the non-cattle programs, like the veterans' mustang project, and take care of the house and garden maintenance. Alec and Joely are the animal experts. Joely knows a surprising amount about breeding and maintaining bloodlines for both the cattle and the horses, and Alec is a marketing genius as well as a hell of a cowboy. You, Raquel, and Kel have been involved in every major decision … It's far from being all me."

"But you're so great with people, Cole. You're our maestro." She let the warmth of his reassuring words about the well-being of Paradise fill her with more contentment. Life was good. Coming home had been the right decision—signs kept piling higher.

"With a lot of insight from Bjorn and Leif."

"Aw, how is Leif? I haven't seen him yet." Bjorn's father, the old Norwegian immigrant who'd been foreman at Paradise since the days of Grace's grandfather, Sebastian, was as much an institution on the ranch as the land itself.

"Crazy strong as ever at seventy-five. He still works a full day. Still has an endless stream of good ideas. He's like Sadie—he can never die because we need him."

"The air around here does something to a person, doesn't it?" Grace asked, pulling another draught of intoxicating air, now scented with scrub pine, into her body. "I'm so glad we didn't vote to sell this place. I think we all hope to raise our kids here—maybe with slightly less of an iron fist than Dad did, so they'll want to stay."

Cole chuckled. "Your daddy had his way all right. Nicest bastard I ever knew. I admit, we've changed a few of the more stringent ways things were done—but that's our way. No insult implied."

"For crying out loud, you don't have to be politically correct about Sam Crockett to me." She laughed. "I miss him terribly; he was my dad. But I liked him better when I lived in Denver. We all liked him better when we didn't live here."

"Well, he gave you enough love of the land that you're all willing to come back."

A sliver of guilt pierced through the perfection of the day. She hadn't spoken to Raquel or Kelly in the four days since leaving Denver. Her job there wasn't critical to the business side of the restaurant, of that she was still convinced. Day-to-day, however, she had been part of the routine, and both of her sisters had been stunned by her defection.

"I'm glad to be back." She made herself bask in the words

and shove aside, like a giant boulder, the idea that she should feel any certain way—about her sisters, her decisions, her reactions. Learn to be strong—that had been her mantra when deciding to break away from Triple Bean. She'd never been the strong one.

She turned back to Ty.

Surprised, she took in his features. She hadn't pegged him for a sulker, but his eyes simmered with annoyance, and his sculpted lips turned down in a firm frown.

"You okay back there, Mr. Nevada?"

"Peachy."

She couldn't stop a smile that floated up to counter his scowl. "Sorry to ignore you."

"I have no problem being ignored." His features eased. "Enlightening conversation all about the Crockett legacy. I'm riveted."

There was a faint tinge of disdain in his words, but then she brushed that off as ridiculous. The man was simply a tangle of weirdness—from swaggering over his kid playing poker, to running away from scary old relatives, to making secretive trips into town that he wouldn't explain even over the best ice cream in Wyoming. Their new ranch hand might be a tall, dark dream-making machine, but he was also a head case.

"The ranch has a pretty interesting history. Colorful even," she told him. "In fact, we're heading right into the heart of one of the best parts of the story."

He tensed statue-still on his mount looking far more like a child's plastic soldier than a cowboy. Finally he lifted his eyes. The annoyance had been replaced by a strange intensity.

"Oh? I'm always up for a good story."

Chapter Eight

"YOU KNOW?"

Grace twisted in her saddle and slowed to drop back from Cole's side.

For one second Ty wanted to choose that moment to make her see that what her family had done was take away the Manterville legacy and chart the angry, ne'er-do-well course his family had followed for the past eighty years. The Crocketts' fortune and reputation had been built by a cheater, not a saint.

Ty certainly didn't blame Grace for something her great-grandfather had done to his, but he did know his family had never had the chance to reclaim its honor. When he'd found the fateful letters from Simon Manterville while looking for family info for his daughter, he'd known there was only one way to make sure she grew up prouder and stronger than any ancestor since her great-great-grandfather had lost those seven thousand acres in a fixed poker game. That way was to get back the Manterville land legally and honestly.

But two lawyers had told him now was not the right time to start that confrontation. He needed to wait for a judge to find there was enough evidence to call a hearing.

"It's impossible not to hear things in a small town like Wolf Paw Pass." He shrugged to show the knowledge was no big deal. "Like you both said, your family has quite the reputation. And since Paradise is the largest privately owned spread in the state, I've found that everyone has a story about it. The one I heard is that the most prized piece of land was won in a poker game."

"I guess that's true," Grace said. "We do have a soft spot in our hearts for this area. Eli Crockett owned around thirty-five thousand acres when he played that game. The big mystery is why Simon Manterville, who owned this section we're walking through right now, bet his ranch in the first place. Not that there aren't tons of theories on that, too."

Ty's gut clenched, and he forced himself to relax again. She would learn soon that the reason for the bet was no mystery.

"Sounds like more good stories," he allowed.

"Some people say Simon was so down on his luck he had to find a way to get money fast, and poker was his game of choice. Other stories say that he owed Eli so much money he had no choice but to offer up his land in a last ditch effort to strike some kind of deal, and he lost. The worst for us Crocketts is the last theory—that Eli had always been an honest-to-gosh card sharp who could beat anyone in this area at the time, so he tricked Simon into playing for the land because he wanted to add to his holdings."

Ty rocked back in his saddle as if she'd tossed him a bag of bricks. The last story was so close to the truth, he barely believed he'd heard her tell it. His heart pounded. Maybe he wouldn't have such a terrible time proving his claim after all.

"Nobody really believes that, of course, least of all us Crocketts." She let spill a genuine laugh, rich like a perfectly crafted bell, whose melody drifted back and over him like a cloud of joy. Everything she did seemed based in happiness, along with peace and love—like she was some modern, good-girl version of a hippie. Even when she was annoyed, she didn't seem truly angry. "Eli's reputation in everything else was upstanding," she said. "By all accounts, he was liked and fair in his business dealings. Smart, too." She shrugged. "Who knows? We have a lot of his writings about the first dealings on the ranch but, oddly enough, there's nothing about that card game or the seven thousand acres. So we choose to hold Great-Grandpa in the best light."

He definitely couldn't say the same about most people in *his* family tree, at least his father's branch. Thugs, alcoholics, and one murderer—that was his pedigree.

Suddenly, blaming it all on Eli Crockett, however, didn't bring him pleasure. For years he'd anticipated confronting the Crocketts about the unethical way their ranch had grown. That eagerness sat like acid in his stomach after Grace's history lesson, however.

But why? Grace didn't know Eli Crockett other than from these stories. He didn't expect she would like knowing her family had to give up the land he'd won, but deep down he couldn't feel sorry for the forty-three thousand acres that would be left after he took back what belonged to his family. Nobody would notice the difference out of nearly ninety square miles. How land rich did one family have to be in this day and age?

To his relief, Grace dropped the subject of Eli Crockett, and for the next two miles of their trip out to the broken fence line, Cole pointed out landmarks—a two-story boulder erratic left by an ancient retreating glacier, a wayward grove of dwarf birch trees that had sprung from who-knew-what random planting or carrier bird, and an open meadow he promised would be wild with color in six weeks. The land held its rugged diversity along with its secrets like a perfectly stitched quilt, one square of color and texture blending into the next with balance and planning. The longer he spent time in the wilderness that sprang up all over Paradise Ranch, the more he understood why people would have settled here and want to stay.

They went through a physical gate to get to the old property. Nothing looked immediately different from the low mountain landscape they'd been passing through for the past hour, but then the windswept, bracken-covered hills started to turn jagged with exposed rock as they led the way to the Rockies in the distance. Mountain ash trees, quaking aspen, and willow tree roots along with gnarled tufts of wild grasses made the going challenging for the horses. But then Ty followed Cole up a long rise, and when they reached the top, the world changed completely.

"Wow." Grace voiced the understated sentiment for all three of them. "I haven't been up here in years. How could I forget?"

Before them spread a vista so diverse and filled with wonder it nearly looked fake. The sun hung at its ten o'clock angle, filling a valley below them with short shadows of purple, gray, and gold. Braided across the valley floor ran a sparkling necklace of blue water.

"Grandpa Eli must have been pretty savvy." Grace turned to Ty, her innocent smile aimed directly at his heart. "This kind of is the soul of Paradise—the puzzle piece that turned it into one continuous property with no breaks within the borders and helped the Crocketts maintain their reputations as the best land and cattle stewards in the state. That was Eli's vision."

Ty couldn't deny it. For that first moment, staring down at the land his great-grandfather had lost, he was unworthy.

What would ever give a construction worker who made part of his utility payments with poker winnings the right to own such magnificence? Overwhelmed, he found he couldn't reply to Grace's awe. He simply stared.

"It was a lucky day when this fell into Eli's hands." Cole leaned forward, resting a forearm on his saddle horn.

Lucky.

Ty's frozen thoughts leaped back to life with renewed purpose. People whose last name happened to be Crockett had no more right to own land than Ty or Teagan Garraway did. Beauty aside, mountains' majesty be damned, this was not about greed or number of acres. It was about righting injustice and being a father Lucky could be proud of.

"There!" Grace's call startled him out of his self-righteous musings, and he popped his head up, following her outstretched finger.

"Aha. Sweet," Cole replied, confusing Ty further.

"What are we looking at?" he asked.

"A break in the fence line," Grace said.

Sure enough, fifty yards down the slope, one metal post leaned cockeyed to the north, and wire hung limply to the ground on either side of it.

"Got lucky," Cole said. "We could've ridden ten more miles before finding it. Now we have time to look for escapees, fix the fence, and inspect a little more of the line. Show our greenhorn here what a snap this job is."

Grace made the most unladylike sound Ty had heard from her. She rolled her eyes and grinned. "Do not trust my brother-in-law. I'm just sayin'."

A cadre of shivers hummed through Ty's bloodstream, reminding him of the electricity between them the night before. He honestly didn't want to remember those long, sweet minutes. Aside from the embarrassment caused by his jackassery, he didn't appreciate that his righteous anger over this land dissipated every time he realized he actually liked these people.

Especially Grace. She was out-of-his-league sweet and good, and she was genuine. He didn't want to find her fascinating, but he did, and that was precisely why Drew Metcalf had warned him to stay impersonal.

When they reached the broken section of wire and dismounted, Ty was astounded at the amazing amount of equipment Cole carried in his deep saddlebags, along with the tools and measuring equipment he'd stuffed in Ty's as well. They unloaded the weightiest items: a coil of heavy-gauge wire, a hammer and a fencing maul, two sizes of wire cutters, and a fencing tool that looked like a medieval torture device.

"You extract information from cattle rustlers with that thing?" Ty asked.

Cole snorted. "Looks gruesome, I know. Five tools in one. It's indispensable for fences, but I'll keep it in mind for other purposes."

"So you bring all the other equipment why …?" Ty let the question trail.

"This far away from home, we come prepared." Cole shrugged. "About all I can't stuff into the bags are actual fence posts. If one of those is destroyed, we come up with Plan B."

These tricks were exactly what Ty had hoped to learn about by coming to Wyoming. If he planned to own his own ranch, he'd have to be able to take care of it.

His ass started smarting when they remounted. By the time another ninety minutes had passed roaming the pasture into which the cattle had supposedly escaped had passed, Ty had spent four and a half hours in the saddle with only one break. He doubted he'd ever walk normally again and the learning curve of what he needed to know grew steeper.

"How long do we search?" He drew even with Grace, attempting to sound merely curious.

She studied him from beneath the brim of her cowboy hat with the insightfulness he'd seen in her eyes before. He used all his willpower to keep his gaze steady and, finally, she grinned.

"Is your butt sore, too?"

He sputtered, unable to help himself. The question was the last thing he'd expected. "Put it this way. I have a whole new perspective on the phrase 'pain in the ass.'"

"Yeah." Her mouth twisted. "I kind of forgot this consequence of the trip when I begged to sign on. A person should remember to ease into riding when she hasn't been in a saddle in more than six months."

"You're really telling me your ass hurts, too?"

"I was telling you my *butt* hurts, but if you prefer crude, yeah."

"You're one of those good girls, aren't you?"

"Depends. What are you asking if I'm good at?"

He held in a laugh while he searched her face for any clue the question was serious, but a deep, confident twinkle simmered in her eyes. So—she could be a good girl with a sense of humor. He wasn't quite sure how to deal with the combination. She'd taken offense at his "ten" comment—the verbal equivalent to a wolf whistle—but she'd just walked into innuendo ripe for the picking.

His mouth dared to voice it before his brain could engage.

"Miss Grace, you sit that pony like you have a whole lotta

things you're good at. I'd ask you about any of them."

"Really?" Her eyes went wide in mock amazement. "You can tell from watching me ride that I'm the only one of my sisters who learned how to knit, and I'm very good at it?"

"Knitting." He chewed lightly on his bottom lip, pretending to consider the information. "Nope, that's not what I was talking about."

"Graphic arts? I can design you a logo in mere minutes."

"Not even close." He bit his lip for real, holding back a full-fledged grin.

"Well then, I have a psychology minor. I can analyze you and pretend I know what I'm talking about. My diagnosis is that you really aren't very good at telling anything about me from my riding."

Ty looked up to make sure Cole still rode several lengths ahead of them. "I can tell that you probably get a lot of compliments like the ones I'm bad at giving. That most men find you … an attractive rider."

She laughed, and he released his breath in relief at the lack of a lecture.

"You are determined to dig yourself a nice big hole, aren't you, Mr. Las Vegas?"

"Hey. Holes can be relatively safe places to be—as in fox."

"Fox?"

"You know. Foxholes. Safe from bullets. Shot by women who are modest about being in the two-digit number range."

She shook her head. "Please tell me you use that line all the time, but that it's never worked."

"Nah." He pushed his luck further when he caught the smile still underlying her words. "I have very little occasion to use a line like that, Miss Grace. You're one of a kind."

"If you'd have said ten of a kind, I'd have pushed you right off that horse."

Her smile broke free and with it, so did his heart—its beat fluttering wildly like a bird released from captivity.

"It wouldn't have taken much of a push," he said. "Speaking of sore ... butts; I don't have much of a grip left on this here pony."

"You really sit a horse pretty well. If you were slapping around in the saddle I'd tease you harder about being a tenderfoot. But I think you've earned the right to be saddle sore."

Her compliment took him aback. With two lines, she'd erased his worry that he looked a fool. Sexism be damned, he'd been telling the truth—she looked like a million fantasies come to life sitting astride the pretty horse Cole had given her to ride. The way her gorgeous, rounded ass ... okay, butt, stayed glued to the saddle seat, the way her hips took up the shock and swayed with the motion of the horse, the way her long, long legs draped around the mustang's barrel and her booted feet rested easily in the stirrups—she could ride into any man's dreams and cause all kinds of trouble.

"Thanks." He shook his thoughts free and forced them away. "I rode when I was young but nothing like this."

"What did you do in Las Vegas?"

"Besides gamble?" He flashed a smile, hoping to tease her off track so she wouldn't ask if he'd ever done exactly that. "I worked construction mostly. I did work at a casino for six months about five years ago. It's where I met Lucky's mother, and Lil for that matter. Recently I've tried like hell to learn how to be a father. It might not seem to you that I have respect for women, but I sure as heck do for single mothers."

"She adores you. Lucky, I mean. That says a lot." She hesitated, obviously weighing words. "Can you...would you, tell me about getting Lucky?"

He smiled for real. "Best day of my life when her mother rang my door bell. I'd known her two years earlier and we'd dated for a total of two months. She's the one who left the relationship and I had no clue about a baby. There's not much else to say. Carrie clearly had or has, I have no idea where she is, problems. She literally abandoned our daughter and the only props I can give her is that she made the effort to find me."

"You're definitely her biological father?"

"I am. Got the tests to prove it. Not that any results would have mattered. Lucky's going to have a lot to deal with when she really starts to care about her mother someday. She's smart enough to know that she was abandoned on purpose for no good reason. I figure I have to prove every day it wasn't her fault."

"The kind of dad you are is the only reason I like you at all."

"Well then." He scoffed. "If that's not the definition of a backhanded non-compliment."

"I'm teasing. You are a good dad, I can tell. Don't worry so much about Lucky," she said. "She plays poker better and spits farther than the boys now, but they'll forgive her when they realize they want her for her brains."

"You do love your women's rights, don't you?"

"When you've had vendors, real estate agents, and customers try to take advantage of you because you're a girl and then see them act astounded when they realize you aren't as stupid as they hoped you were, you learn to speak up."

"On behalf of all chauvinists, I am sorry."

"Fair warning—patronizing isn't acceptable either."

"I get that. The apology was sincere."

She allowed a smile of her own. "Maybe I can like you a little more than I did a day ago."

"I'll take whatever I can get."

Cole took that moment to slow his pace and fall back beside them. "I'm thinking those cows are long gone and we need to look for them later by air. You must both be ready for lunch."

They each had part of the trail lunch in their saddlebags—sandwiches, veggies, some leftover homemade soup in a large Thermos, and best of all, the chocolate whiskey cake left over from the meal the evening before. Thinking about it started Ty's mouth watering.

"I've been ready for an hour, you slave driver," Grace said.

"It's all about the power," Cole replied, deadpan. "We can eat here on this side of the fence and then go fix the break. If we want to be home by supper tonight, we'd best call off the search now and find the cattle when we need them."

"I hope they're all right," Grace said.

"They'll be fine. Five hundred acres to roam for maybe a dozen moms and babies? They're in heaven. Look, there's a rock outcropping ahead. Let's use that."

"Great spot," Grace said. "Look at that view!"

"You serious about breaking away and starting a restaurant of your own?" Cole asked. "I mean, that's almost a rhetorical question, and I think it's great, but I can't say it's not a shock."

"To me, too," Grace said. "But I am serious."

"You could build something out here," he said. "I think a restaurant with this view and the history of the ranch would be a gold mine."

"I can almost see it." Grace swept her gaze around them as they made for the rocks. "Can you imagine—we could set aside some of this land for raising organic beef. I know Harper's talked about that, too."

"We have the organic goats." Cole laughed. "They aren't exactly an enormous moneymaker, but there's a small market for the organic milk and cheese in Wolf Paw Pass."

"I kn—"

"Stop! Whoa!"

Cole, his voice firm, held up a hand and reined Marco to a halt. Startled, Ty pulled King up beside him. "What?"

Jessica Rabbit began to dance under Grace's request to halt. "Oh no. Something got a little one." Grace's bright features folded into dismay, and then she had to look away to try and calm Jess, who snorted and backed up, her haunches bunching as if getting ready to buck. "Easy girl."

It took several more steps for Ty to see the slender animal leg protruding from behind one the rocks. Something had killed a calf.

"I don't think it's a cow," Cole said. "The fetlock isn't right. Neither is the dewclaw. I think it's a young mule deer."

They didn't have time to find out. A hiss like the air brakes on a freight train sounded out a warning just before a six-foot-long, caramel-colored blur made a dash from behind the rocks straight toward the closest human.

"Cougar! Grace!" Cole dug his heels into Marco's sides and tried to get between Grace and the large, angry cat making for her like a rocket-propelled grenade.

"Hell, are you *kidding* me?" Ty copied Cole, urging his horse as hard as he could.

Neither man had any luck before the nightmare happened. Jess reared straight in the air, and Grace, grasping mane and clinging like a monkey for long seconds, failed in her attempt to ride it out as Jess's forelegs flailed in front of her.

With a short cry as she fell, Grace landed on the ground back first and didn't move.

Cole literally jumped off his horse, and Ty, not as practiced, still managed to land on his feet just seconds behind him.

"Get to Grace! I'll drive off the cat," Cole shouted.

He didn't turn back to see that Ty obeyed, and Ty couldn't think about Cole getting mauled to shreds by a mountain lion. But just as he reached Grace, Jess gave a spine-chilling scream, and he couldn't help but look up.

Cole had stopped, and the mare was charging, her hooves striking as she ran. Ahead of her, the mountain lion was beating a zig-zagging retreat. With a groan of adrenaline-laced fear, Ty fell to his knees beside Grace.

Chapter Nine

GRACE OPENED ONE eye.

"Is Cole all right? Where's the cougar?"

"Shit, Grace, I thought you were dead."

"Not yet. You don't have to swear."

Ty's heart nearly beat through his chest in relief. The way she lay, with her right arm twisted awkwardly behind her back and her head cocked to one side, spoke of serious injury. But if she was berating him for bad language, maybe she was okay.

"So sorry." He grinned, hiding his concern in the sarcasm. "Cole is fine. Your horse is both the villain and the hero. She dumped you but then chased off the cat. I'm hoping she stops before she hits Idaho."

"Jessica Rabbit ran off a mountain lion?" Grace rose up on her left elbow but yelped when she tried to draw her right arm out from beneath her back.

"Lie back down," Ty ordered. "You could have hurt your back or your neck."

She ignored him and struggled to her seat, grimacing. "It's not my neck or my back." She batted his hands away when he tried to urge her back to the ground. "It's my elbow. Stop hovering, this isn't my first time falling off a horse."

"That's not comforting. Don't be reckless, Grace."

"Don't be a fishwife, Ty." She glared at him. "Help me up."

"Come on. Give a guy a break. My brain watched you die a few seconds ago. I'm still trying to tell if my jockey shorts are clean."

"Ah, so the question of which kind is answered."

He stared, half in shock at her irreverence, and watched her bite her lip against a smile. With a scowl, he took her left hand and pulled her to her feet. She reached gingerly for her right arm as they looked to where, a hundred yards away, Cole approached Jessica Rabbit, his hand outstretched. The horse skittered back a handful of steps but didn't run.

"Horses don't usually chase predators unless it's a herd mentality moment," Grace said, her eyes narrowed into the sun. "Maybe Jess is half donkey."

"Donkey?"

"Donkeys are fantastic guard animals. They'll go after anything they don't think belongs in their space."

"She doesn't look like a donkey. Just a feisty little redhead."

"Good girl," Grace murmured as Cole reached the mare and grasped her reins. Then she gasped. "Aaaahh! Well, that's probably not good."

"What?"

"This elbow feels a little out of whack."

He stepped around to look at her arm and grimaced at the joint's wrong angle. "Jeez, Grace. Out of whack is an understatement. I think you broke it."

"Great. Just what I need."

No whining. No crying. She was plain old mad. "What you need is to get that looked at."

"I don't see anyone's express clinic out here, do you?"

"Can't someone fly out here and pick you up?"

"That's not how it works. Don't be ridiculous."

He held up his hands. "Look. Are you pissed off at me or your arm? I'm just a tenderfoot trying to help here. Forgive the concern."

"Sorry," she grumbled. "It hurts."

"I'm sure it does."

"Gracie." Cole reached them and handed Jess's reins to Ty. "You're okay. Thank God."

"I messed up my elbow, but I'm fine."

"Uh …" Cole inspected the injured arm. "Looks like a dislocation."

"I landed with it stretched out behind me—palm first. I didn't feel it happen, but …"

"How's the feeling in it, aside from excruciating?"

"My fingers are a little numb."

Cole took her hand, cradling it like a newborn kitten, and placed two fingers against her wrist. A moment later he frowned. "Pulse is pretty weak. You probably stretched the nerves."

"You know how to pop the joint back. I saw you do it once when I was a kid," she said.

"Oh I don't know, Gracie … a shoulder maybe. An elbow is much more complicated. What if it's fractured?"

"You aren't seriously asking him to yank on a dislocated elbow?" Ty balked slightly at the thought of something that required such specialized skill.

"It's too long a ride to make with reduced blood flow to my hand. I'd rather have a broken elbow than permanent damage. C'mon, Cole. You did it to your cousin that time he jumped off the hayloft and missed the hay wagon."

Cole chuckled, but it wasn't a confident sound. "We were

just trying to hide the injury from our parents who'd told us to stay out of the barn. I didn't know what I was doing."

"You were sixteen and Kyle ended up being fine." She fixed him with pleading eyes. "My hand is getting cold. Please? I'll be brave, and Ty here is my witness. I'll indemnify you of any responsibility."

"Well that makes everything different." Cole grasped her wrist and her upper arm, his eyes narrowed, clearly not liking what she asked of him. "You know Mia is going to kill us for messing around with doctoring. She's the one who should be here doing—" Without warning he gave a sharp jerk. "This."

Grace shrieked and put a fist to her mouth. Ty watched tears pool in her eyes, and every instinct begged him to grab her and hold her as tightly as he could. But there was no way she'd tolerate that kind of touch, however well meaning, from him. He stayed in place as she gathered her composure, fully expecting her to berate Cole for his sneaky timing.

"Holy flipping macaroni casserole!" She swallowed and bent at her waist, resting her good elbow on her knees. "That sucked. Thank you. I can feel buzzing in my fingers."

"You would have been all tensed up if I'd given you time to brace," Cole said. "Sorry. This was my best hope."

"I know."

Grace found Ty's eyes and straightened, releasing her breath in a slow, measured stream. "That's how it's done, Mr. Las Vegas."

"You're nuts," he said.

"Probably." She winced as she felt around the elbow joint that had been so thoroughly abused. "But there's no cell tower here, so someone would have had to ride back to the road and find service. Then it would have taken a ton of time to get help way out here. This way, look. Good as new."

"It's not," Ty said. "You can't self-diagnose everything."

"I'll have it checked, Mr. T-for-Tenderfoot." She patted his arm. "I'm nuts but not stupid. You have to understand that on a ranch this size, you need to be able to deal with crises immediately. Sometimes there's no time to do otherwise. This wasn't life-threatening, but having a lot of self-diagnosing skills, be they aimed at humans or animals or machines, is a necessity."

Ty's vision for the future took another ding to its shiny finish. The things he found himself learning were sobering.

"I think you're a tougher girl than I gave you credit for."

"Why, Ty. I think that's the nicest compliment you've given me."

Go figure.

"Speaking of self-diagnosing, let's talk about getting ourselves out of here," Cole said. "It's extremely unusual for a mountain lion to come after humans in the open like that. This one was feeding, but more importantly, she had a cub with her—maybe three months old or so. She was protecting the baby as much as she was her kill, so I don't think she'll come back right away, but I've decided this isn't the best lunch spot for us."

"You think?" Ty asked.

"Let's go back to the break in the fence," Grace said. "It's only a half-hour ride if we head straight for it. Then we can eat, get the fence repaired and head out."

"You're going to ride?"

"Unless you want to take me piggyback." Grace smiled beatifically.

He'd love to give her a piggyback ride, he thought.

"How does it feel now?" Cole asked.

"So much better."

"I have a flexible cold pack around the sodas, and a roll of gauze in the first-aid bag. Let's wrap the joint for now."

She allowed those ministrations, and once Cole had Grace's elbow wrapped as securely as possible, she astounded Ty once more by gathering Jess's reins, making a huge fuss over the horse with pats and kisses and thanks for saving them from the mountain lion, and then mounting one-armed with the ease of a circus performer.

"How'd you do that?"

"Years of misspent youth?" She laughed.

"Years of living on horseback," Cole countered. "When we were kids you couldn't separate us from our horses. She's been riding since she was born."

"True. Remember Brownie, my first big horse?" Grace asked and Cole nodded. She turned to Ty. "Best horse a kid could ever have. Have you ever thought about getting Lucky her own pony?"

"Lucky would personally see to it I got some sort of permanent best father award if that were to happen."

"We'll have to see what we can do. There are other Brownies out there."

"It hasn't been in the budget so far …"

"You're living on a ranch, Ty," she said. "You have to have noticed how many little jobs there are to do. Board is unlimited, and Lucky can do chores to earn a horse's keep just the way we did when we were her age. We'll turn her into a cowgirl while she's here. Never you worry."

Visions of Grace flying off the back of a rearing horse filled his mind. Hell, he was going to worry, all right. The idea of his precious, precocious daughter landing on something much worse than an arm kept him from giving the Best Father award reply Lucky would have wanted.

***

The ride back to where they'd left their pile of tools had been far less painful than getting back up after she'd eaten. Grace hid her discomfort with bright chatter and enthusiastic one-armed help with the fence. Watching Ty helped, too. For as much as they'd dubbed him a tenderfoot, he knew how to wield tools and put in hard work. It took him no time to figure out Cole's procedure when it came to splicing and replacing wires.

Cole asked her frequently how she was doing, but Ty merely watched her like she could shatter any moment. Oddly, his hawk eye gave her comfort. As much as her elbow throbbed, she couldn't make herself resent Ty's vigilance.

"I think that'll do it," Cole said when he and Ty returned from a section far from the original break. "I revise my opinion. I'm pretty sure most of the herd in this pasture plowed through. There are at least fifteen sections down. One little stray break-off group didn't do that. It's fine. Let 'em stay there."

"Are you worried about the cougar?" Ty asked. "Won't she go after the herd?"

"No more than in this pasture. Cougars don't pay attention to fences."

"Duh." Ty shook his head, and Grace smiled.

"We'll let the local DNR officials know we spotted the cat," Cole said. "They might want to try and track or collar her. Somebody's usually studying the behaviors of these guys."

"Who knew there were so many factors to consider when it came to cows," Ty said.

Grace studied his face, thoughtful as he digested Cole's information about the big cat. In truth, the lions didn't like to be found, and she'd only seen them a few times in her life.

"Told you. You have to be a mini-expert in all kinds of weird things around here," she said. "I wish I'd gotten a better look at this girl. Cougar sightings are rare. Less so with a little one. That was actually pretty cool."

"Your encounter was plenty close and not cool at all to watch." Ty frowned. " Especially when the creature knocks you out cold."

She had to smile again. She probably wouldn't have fooled the mama mountain lion had it come to that, but she'd fooled Ty. "I wasn't out, goof. I was playing dead."

"Right."

"I was. Normally you play dead with a bear 'cause they don't want dead meat, but not a cougar because they'll eat anything. This one already had food, though, and since there was no way I could run, my best hope was that she'd think I wasn't going to come after her meal, and she'd leave me alone."

Ty shook his head. "Yup. This is way beyond my pay grade."

"Fortunately, you don't need this knowledge very often."

"Let's pack up and get home," Cole said. "How's that elbow doing?"

It hurt like mad, and the ice pack had warmed so it was more painful than helpful.

"It feels just fantastic." She wrinkled her nose and held out her arm, hiding a wince. "I think I'd rather have the ice pack off. It's pressing on the injury and it's not that cold anymore."

"Done."

Cole unwrapped and rewrapped her elbow, then finished stowing everything in the saddlebags. Ty scoured the construction area for anything left behind. When the horses' cinches had been tightened, Cole offered to help Grace mount.

"I got this," she insisted.

"Okie-doke." Cole stepped up into his saddle, settling in like it was a leather Ferrari seat.

Grace shot a warning look at Ty, who remained standing, waiting for her. "I got this," she repeated.

"I believe you."

He didn't move.

Refraining from rolling her eyes again, she grasped the saddle horn with her left hand, placed her left boot toe deep into the stirrup, and sprang.

Nothing worked the way it had right after the accident. Her left arm gave out, she missed the height she needed and landed chest first against the side of the saddle, and her foot slipped back out of the stirrup. One second later, her butt cheeks smacked dirt for the second time that day.

"Gol *dang* it!" Pain shot down her arm and exploded into her elbow.

"Jeez, Grace, what the f—" Ty swallowed the profanity, but knelt beside her before she could even bend a knee to get back up. "Come on, give us a break and take this slowly. Are you really okay?"

"Yeah. More embarrassed than injured this time."

"Just be smart—let me help."

It was stupid to pretend she wasn't injured just to be prideful. Reluctantly she took his hand. The warm grip sent tingles to mix with the throbbing in her elbow, making her stomach ache with confusion. She tried to shake his fingers loose from hers, but they only tangled more tightly. To top it off, Cole now stood beside her, no longer on his horse.

"You okay?"

Annoyance joined the mash of emotions already assailing her.

"I missed the saddle. Good grief you two; I'm fine."

"I get enough stubbornness from your sister, you know." His eyes crinkled. "Please, will you let us assist you? We're not trying to be condescending."

Guilt slapped her upside the head. She was being purposely difficult, but in truth she was angry at herself and at the timing of the injury. She'd been thinking about spending some time at the little cottage assessing what needed to be done and maybe doing a little polishing to see what lay beneath the layers of dust and ancient grime before going to the bank to ask about a small-business loan for rebuilding. It would be tough to polish anything if she'd mangled her arm.

Not to mention she was here to help Mia. This could wind up being a disaster.

"I never thought that. I'm sorry." She offered Cole a smile of truce. "I'm just ticked off."

"I get that." Cole nodded.

Ty gave Grace's hand a squeeze and guided her until she faced her horse. "I know you won't believe *I'm* not being condescending, but I'm here to help anyway."

She bit back a retort. She'd always liked things done properly and in order. Getting help usually meant doing things inefficiently. With a deep breath, she nodded.

"Thanks."

He released her hand so she could grasp the saddle horn. She jammed her toe back into the stirrup and gave a pleased gasp when Ty's hands splayed around her hips. His touch carried absolute propriety, but it sent skittering pulses of happiness and electricity skipping through her body.

"One … two … three." He lifted and she found herself nestled into the saddle as easily as a feather floating onto a pillow.

He was so *strong*.

She banished the silly-girl thought. "Thanks," she said again.

"You're welcome."

His sincere smile thrilled her a little too much, and she thought of Lil with a stab of guilt. This ridiculous attraction had to stop. Aside from the fact that he was very likely attached, he was also anything but the kind of man she'd ever want: insouciant, slightly crude, and careless in his flirting. He was a great dad, but away from his daughter, Grace would never know he had Lucky or Lil in his life.

She released an impatient breath.

"What's wrong?" he asked.

You. You're all wrong. "Nothing. I think I'm safe to let off the leash now."

"Okay."

"You sure you feel okay to ride? You can always double with me." Cole touched her leg.

"I'm fine. Hanging on to you would be harder than holding the reins. But thanks."

"So I'm guessing you aren't thinking of this as your ideal restaurant spot."

Cole surprised her with the teasing question as they got underway, and although she'd been determined not to bring up her crazy business venture again she had a very big question she hadn't yet wanted to ask. Suddenly, even with Ty just behind them, she needed to know.

"I love this spot," she said. "Can you imagine if diners caught a glimpse of the herd, or of elk moving through, or maybe a mountain lion slinking past? But I don't think it's practical to start out building this far away …"

She trailed off, uncertainty surfacing. This wasn't as small a favor as the simple question would make it sound.

"What?"

"I …" Raquel told her and Kelly every chance she got that running a business wasn't for the faint of heart—or for people pleasers. Grace often saw herself as both.

"I'm going to the bank on Wednesday to talk to Dan Strich. I'm hoping to start the process of getting a small-business loan and take a chance on the new restaurant."

"That's great! I'm impressed at you jumping right in."

"I've been thinking about this far longer than anyone knows." She finally admitted what she hadn't even told her sisters—that this wasn't a spur-of-the-moment thing; her unhappiness at Triple Bean had been growing for more some time. "I know basically what I need; I just don't know for sure how much work the old cottage requires in order to be usable. I also don't have my share of the profits from Triple Bean yet. Rocky and Kel will have to find a way to buy me out. And I don't want to pressure them—they need to be able to keep that business flourishing."

"That's commendable, but if you really want out of the partnership …"

"The stupid thing is, I don't. I love what we all built together, but I'll have to break away eventually because I can't have it both ways. Unfortunately, I do need some kind of collateral for a loan. I can use the restaurant but, again, I absolutely don't want to put Kel or Rocky in financial jeopardy. The other option is—"

"Paradise."

"Paradise," she agreed. "And that sounds awful, because I certainly don't want to put the ranch in jeopardy either. I'll be asking for a lot of money, relatively speaking. What if I default? What if the whole thing is a bust?"

She looked behind one more time. Ty was still studying the landscape as if memorizing it.

"Look." Cole caught and held her eyes with his gaze. "It's not my name on the will that left Paradise Ranch to you six sisters, so it isn't really my blessing you need. But I do more or less manage this place on behalf of you, so I know where it's at financially. Nothing is ever guaranteed—weren't we just talking about how precarious finances can be? But, still, we're here. The land will always be here, and it's priceless. In my opinion, we can weather anything you might come up against."

"Oh, Cole, do you really think so? Despite what you say, your blessing would mean a lot."

"C'mon, Gracie." His look told her she should know better than to question his faith. "You'll have the blessing of me and of all your sisters."

"I don't know. Kelly and Raquel aren't cheering for me to succeed."

"You stunned them, that's all. Eventually they'll be the loudest cheerleaders of all. I watched you three grow up, practically conjoined triplets, and nothing is going to tear you apart. It's simply time you have a shake-up."

Grace had no idea what to do with the rush of emotion that flowed over her at Cole's affirmation. She'd known she'd get support from her family, but pride was an extra-special gift. Then again, Cole Wainwright had always been the Crockett girls' most loyal champion. Sometimes she still found it beyond lucky that he was officially part of their family.

The adrenaline released by her excitement masked the discomfort of her elbow for most of the ride back to the truck and trailer. By the last third of the journey, however, every step Jessica Rabbit took jarred like a mogul hill underneath a skier. When the rig came into sight at last, Grace nearly let tears fall as much from relief as from pain.

"You don't look so great, honey," Cole said.

Grace swallowed and gritted her teeth as she forced herself to dismount on her own.

"It's sore. I think some more ice and a few drugs might be in the immediate future."

"And an X-ray," Cole replied. "We're heading for the clinic in Wolf Paw Pass before we go home."

"That's stupid! It's the opposite way. You've got to get the horses back."

"One of us will stay with you; the other can bring the truck back, pick up your mom or one of the girls, and come back."

Ty, who'd said almost nothing the entire way home, took Jess's reins. "I agree. I'll stay with you since I've never pulled a horse trailer."

"Really, Ty, I honestly think it will be fi—" Once again she stopped herself from contradicting the men. She really did need to have it checked, just to make sure there was no serious damage. "Fine. Better to be smart."

"That's right," Cole said. "C'mon then, let's get the horses loaded."

Chapter Ten

AT FOUR-THIRTY ON a Friday afternoon, the Wolf Paw Pass clinic, small but well-staffed because of the population of military families in town, was halfway between full and overflowing. Ty led Grace to a seat, holding the requisite clipboard and forms for her while she wrote, awkwardly, with the sore arm.

"It had to be the right one," she grumbled.

"Because you tried to catch yourself with your dominant side. It was automatic."

She glared at him. "It was a rhetorical statement."

"Ahhh. Got it."

She wanted to stay indignant and difficult but, truth to tell, Ty made her laugh. "I'm sorry. You're right. I'm not usually so mean. I'm just OCD. I like things to be in their proper places and times. Accidents throw the world out of whack."

He settled into the chair next to hers and propped the clipboard in a better position for her. "Tell me about what's out of whack."

"My list." She met his eyes. The sincere kindness deep in the rain-colored green made her forget her discomfort. She shrugged. "Helping Mia. Drawing up my crazy ideas for a restaurant. Going to check out the cottage in-depth and see what exactly would need to be done. Getting numbers together to meet with a banker."

"That's a long list."

"I guess."

"I'm starting to sense you're not a person who sits around waiting for things to happen."

"Life is short. My father proved that. I'd also planned to try another new recipe tonight, and I promised Mia we'd organize her nursery closet. I'm not happy to miss those things."

"Look. The recipe will keep—eat peanut butter sandwiches tonight, whenever you get home. And the baby isn't due for a month. You have time for the closet. This is about you right now. You'll believe me after you get some drugs." He wrinkled his nose, which for some reason only made him more handsome.

"Do you speak from experience about the drugs?" She tried making her tone judgmental, but his light-hearted caretaking had erased her crankiness.

"I can't lie about going to a pot party or two in high school. But I didn't like that shi—stuff." He rubbed his nose self-consciously. "I do like my beer—the hoppier the better. But, no, I can't actually suggest a helpful pharmaceutical for you."

She stared at him without replying for a thoughtful moment. Every once in a while he used a turn of phrase or a word that suggested he wasn't simply an itinerant carpenter grabbing work where he could find it. His daughter was smart; he couldn't be stupid …

"Good to know." She smiled. "I'm pretty sure there are experts who can do that right here. Come to think of it, Mia could have diagnosed and prescribed something for me."

"Unless she has an X-ray machine in a cupboard at home,

this was a better choice."

"I hate emergency rooms," she said, even though this wasn't a true emergency room.

"I'd worry about anyone who didn't."

She smiled again because he kept making her do it, finished the forms, and then collapsed back in the chair. Ty turned in the clipboard for her and returned.

"You doing okay? Seriously?"

She nodded, but his unexpected sympathy suddenly loosed tears. She wasn't a crier except at sappy movies, but pain had frayed the edges of her composure like the drip-drip of Chinese water torture, and the first fears that this was actually a severe injury were surfacing.

"What would help?" he asked. "Anything right now? Something to drink? Something to eat?"

She wiped the start of tears away and laughed. "You are a true dad."

"Hey, no call for that. I am *not* thinking of you the way I think of my daughter."

"No. No. I just meant you're thinking of everything. You're giving comfort. I hate admitting it, but you're a little bit good at it. And at distraction, too."

"I guess I'll take that as a compliment." He laughed. "Although since you hate admitting it—"

"Don't listen to me. I'm—"

"In pain. Don't worry. I'm a poker player; I'm not thin-skinned. But I'm pretty good at reading faces, and yours isn't hiding the fact that you're hurting."

"You don't have to insult me. I have a little poker-playing blood, too."

"A good girl like you plays poker?"

Why did "good girl" suddenly feel like a something she didn't want to be?

"Poker is a legitimate game. Losing your life savings or having gambling problems aren't requirements for playing."

"That's very true. I've played a lot of poker games in my life. I've never lost my life savings."

"So, do you think you're good at it? Poker?"

"I'm decent enough. How about you?"

"I'll clean you out of every matchstick in your sad pockets." She grinned.

"Was that the sound of a gauntlet?"

"Not at all. Just be warned not to insult me too often about my poker face."

A nurse interrupted their banter, stepping into the lobby from behind a pale oak door. "Grace Crockett?" she called.

Grace shifted to the front of her chair. "Okay, that's the call of fate. I'll be back with the verdict."

He barely raised his brows. "Oh no. I'm coming with you."

"Uh ... You are not."

They barely knew each other. He had no reason or moral authority to be with her. And yet, deep down, part of her was relieved that he'd offered, and prayed he'd go alpha on her and come despite her protests.

He did.

"Don't argue. Pretend I'm your brother if it bothers you."

She did not think of him as a brother any more than he thought of her as a daughter. "You are the most aggravating fake brother in the history of fake brothers. I don't need you. It's just an elbow."

He only shook his head as if dealing with a child. "Look. If they dope you up with painkillers and start giving you instructions you don't understand, my boss will be real angry if I don't know what to tell him."

Grace stood and the room tilted like someone had folded the floor beneath her. Ty grabbed her around the waist before she had time to plunk back down in her seat.

"Whoa there."

"Do you need a wheelchair?" The nurse, too, materialized right beside her.

Grace clutched at Ty's arms and shook her head vehemently. "No. I just stood up too fast. Let me hold on to your arm a second and I'll be fine. I'm fine already."

Her head cleared fully as the nurse led them through the door and into a large space partitioned into six or seven small, curtained examination rooms around three sides with a nurses' station on the fourth.

"I hate hospitals," she whispered. "I don't know how Mia can spend all her time in a place like this."

"It's not a hospital. And we all have things we're good at. I'm guessing your sister is a good doctor, that's all."

"Stop being logical,"

"So the right response was, 'I hear you. Your sister must be an insane ghoul'?"

"That's it." She giggled.

"See why I said I was coming along? You're cray-cray."

"What are you, thirteen?"

"No, I'm a very attentive dad."

She gave it all up then—any need to be strong in front of him, and every thought that he was a terrible choice for her crush. His ridiculous sense of humor had turned into the best medicine for that moment—a moment when control of the situation could leave her hands.

For the next hour he teased her while she waited long, boring minutes for the doctors to check her arm, for radiology techs to fetch her, for the X-rays to get read. He made her laugh. He asked about Triple Bean, and she told him about her sisters. He was perfect company.

In the end, her elbow was not broken, and her nerves were not seriously damaged, just bruised and stretched. They wrapped the joint in an Ace bandage with an ice pack, gave her instructions, and sent her on her way with a prescription for Vicodin and the prediction that she'd feel better within the next week. If not, she should come back.

Anti-climactic was an understatement.

"Well there went two hours of my life I'll never get back." Grace sat on a chair in the lobby, cradling her bandaged and slinged-up arm while Ty, standing in front of her, dug his cell phone out of his back jeans pocket. "I'm sorry we wasted the time—I knew the arm would be fine if I just went straight home and iced it. I was right."

"Come on. You know we'd all have been second-guessing every decision and every moment of pain you were in," he said. "Aren't you glad you know for certain that it's going to heal fine?"

"Yes," she admitted. "I guess. I told you I hate wasting time."

"Stop hating it. It just *is*. And it took a lot less time than we originally told Cole it would." He winked and sat in the chair next to hers. "I'll call him and tell him we're done. Somebody will fetch us and this will all be in the rearview mirror. I know you don't like help—"

"What makes you say that?"

"Every objection you make to somebody taking time out for your benefit. You hate other people being in control."

She shook her head, but a twinge of guilt at the truth kept her from disagreeing. "I don't hate it—"

"You just like being in charge."

"Of my own elbow, yeah, I do." She twisted her mouth into a scowl.

"There's a reason doctors don't treat their own family members, and there's a reason stubborn Crockett girls should not diagnose their own injuries no matter how self-sufficient and smart they are. It's called being too close to the situation. Sometimes, you need to let go of what you think you know and work with whom you're given."

"Like you."

He shrugged. "I'm not your first choice, I know, but yeah. Like me."

She hung her head, tired and sore. "I'm sorry, Ty. People usually think I'm a *nice* person."

"You're very nice. You're just… specific. About what you want."

"I think that was a euphemism for shrew. And it was kind on your part." She offered a small smile.

"Not at all. I don't think you're a shrew. You're a ten, remember?" He held up his hand with a grin. "That's going to be a thing between us now. You have to know this."

"Oh, brother." She muffled a laugh.

"What I'm trying to tell you is there's nothing wrong with asking for help. In fact, based on what little I know about starting your own business, you're going to need to learn to do a lot of asking."

For a second her face burned with embarrassment. Had he overheard her asking Cole for help already?

Then again, what did it matter? So what if he knew her

collateral lay in the land of Paradise Ranch? All of Wyoming knew about the biggest cattle operation in the state. Why would anyone think twice about a Crockett starting a new venture with the ranch behind it?

Her heart lifted. She was going to try this, dang it. Wrecked elbow or no.

"You're right. Thank you," she said. "I guess the first thing I need is someone to remind me to take my own advice and cowboy up."

"I'm irritating enough to do that for you."

He'd softened so much over the past hour he was almost adorable—his eyes impish, his cheekbones high and rounded in a smile, his words sincere behind the teasing. All at once he was the opposite of irritating. Dogged, sure. Cocky, yes. Attached—?

Dang it.

But he could be a friend. An ally. And that was better anyway. He was still everything she didn't want in a romantic interest.

She held out her hand. "Deal. You can be my conscience's official, irritating nag."

He folded her fingers into his grasp, and she immediately forgot how much she didn't want a snarky, poker-playing drifter who lived with his girlfriend in her life. "I'm happy to be your conscience's conscience. Now, how about we get to that pharmacy and get your drug prescription filled?"

"I hate drugs," she sighed.

"It's a wonder you lived this long with all the medical things you hate." He laughed. "I promise you won't hate the drug once you take it. But do you really want to walk five blocks to the drugstore? There's a pharmacy right downstairs here."

"I like Mavis—she's been filling our antibiotic, cough syrup, and painkiller prescriptions since we were toddlers. Until she retires, I'll go there when I'm here at home."

"Tell me if the walking gets to be too much."

"How about if I tell you when you start to fuss too much?" She wrinkled her nose. "I'll be fine, Ty. What are you going to do if I'm not? We haven't called Cole yet, so it'll be at least half an hour before he can get here."

"I'd make you sit down and put your head between your knees."

"Because my elbow hurts?" she sputtered. "Glad you aren't my doctor."

"Hey, it's what my grandma made everybody do whether they were dizzy, ready to hurl, or just whining. It seemed to work."

"What is it with grandmothers? Mine is the same way—it's like a form of tough love."

"You can't possibly be talking about Sadie?"

"Sweet as an Easter Peeps on the outside. Tough as jerky on the inside. Trouble is both sides taste good at any given moment."

"That's a new way to put it." He smiled. "My grandma was okay. A far better matriarch than my mother. She was the jerky."

"Sounds like there's a story in that."

"For a different time. Come on."

They left the clinic, and as Ty made the call to Cole, the sweet May evening started Grace's healing process. She didn't truly hate hospitals or clinics, but she'd spent more than enough time in them after her mother and sister Joely had been in an auto accident nearly three years before. It had been a nerve-racking time filled with trial-and-error surgeries and months of healing. And an atmosphere much better suited to Mia.

Mia.

Some help Grace was going to be to her very pregnant sister. For the next week even tying shoe laces or helping get boots on and off would be dicey activities.

"What's wrong?"

His voice surprised her after nearly a block of walking in silence.

"Nothing."

"If I were an arrow, I could fly miles off of your bowstring tension. That arm hurting so much?"

She hadn't thought about her arm in terms of pain. "It's not. I'm thinking about how limiting this is going to be. I can fetch a glass of water for Mia, but I can't do the dishes or help her with very many chores. And that doesn't touch the surface of what I wanted to start at the cottage."

He thought a moment. "I have an idea. Lucky is pretty talented for a not-quite-six-year-old. I'd be happy to send her up to the house this weekend and before and after school next week. She'd find it fun, since she'd be around grown-ups—her favorite kind of people."

"I wouldn't do that!" Grace had a momentary vision of how she'd spent so much of her childhood—working hard whenever her father cracked the whip. "Lucky needs to be a kid, not be a house helper to two injured women."

"I swear she'd look at it like a game. And tell you what else. Let her play with the cats and dogs and that'll be her double reward."

"She can play with them anytime."

He stopped and took a step to stand in front of her. She

swallowed an unexpected rush of excitement when he dropped his head and nearly touched her forehead with his. "Grace. Grace. What did I just say minutes ago about working with what you're given? Come on. I'm not selling my child into slavery for God's sake. Let her come and sweep the dang floor."

He smelled like left over sunshine, and horses, and a little bit of the alcohol scent in the hand fresheners from the clinic. Her knees went slightly weak.

"You're right. You're kind to offer her help. Will you let me ask her myself? And don't take the Lord's name in vain."

He rolled his eyes. "Fine. But I'm warning her ahead of time that you'll be asking."

"And I'm paying her."

"Hell no. She can learn to be helpful just for the sake of it."

"A dollar fifty a day for the next week."

He opened his mouth but then closed it. His lips were so close she could see every attractive line and crease. She followed their contours with her eyes and swallowed again.

"Absolutely no more than that," he said.

"Deal. She can go shopping with her own money. It's a big thing to a girl."

"She'll put it away, the little business mogul. She has it in her head that if she earns a hundred dollars, she can buy a dog."

"Can she?" Grace sighed with relief when Ty blew his breath out, ruffling the longish bangs that hung to his brows. "I know you said you didn't dare get a dog yet, but having an animal to care for is character building. I think we all had to have an animal when we were kids. And caring for them was part of our chores every day."

"I don't doubt for a minute Lucky would be a good animal owner," he said. "I just need to know we're established first.

Besides, I have yet to talk her out of a giant Alaskan malamute or a Newfoundland or something equally dino-sized. I think she thinks she can double up on dog and pony. Too many big red dog cartoons when she was little."

"Clifford!" Grace let out a little crow. "I loved those books. I guess there is a cartoon now, isn't there?"

"The kid rides the dang dog, and it saves her in every situation. That's what Lucky wants. Some cross between Marmaduke, Clifford, Scooby-Doo, and Lassie."

"Gotta love a kid who knows her mind."

"You gotta love her, but you can't understand her. She's scary sometimes."

"All kids are scary. But they're pretty cool. Anyway—we'll let her meet Alec and Joely's dog Rowan when they get home for the summer. Rowan is an Irish Wolfhound—the biggest dogs in the world. She's flipping enormous, so we'll see if Miss Lucky still wants a dog-moose cross."

"She will."

They reached the drugstore and Mavis Osterholz, a trim, gray-haired woman with glasses and a manner that was half Marie Curie and half Ellen DeGeneres, fussed over Grace and her arm exactly the way her own mother and grandmother were going to do. The way she wasn't about to let Ty do. Mavis took the script and studied it thoroughly.

"Vicodin? Gracie, sweetheart, what did you get yourself into so soon after coming home?"

Grace stuck out her lower lip in a pout. "A stupid cougar."

"A cougar? What? Where?"

Mavis was around her counter five seconds later, wrapping Grace in a familiar hug, completely mindful of the sling around her arm. The warmth only a small town could give enveloped her, along with her old friend's arms.

"On the ranch, fifteen miles or so from the main road."

"That's a little rare, isn't it?" Mavis rocked her for a moment and patted her back. "Not to mention frightening as all get out."

"Yeah, it's unusual to see them. She was protecting a cub; that's why she ran at us. And my horse was more frightened than I was, honestly. I slid off her back and landed on the elbow. So, the cat wasn't directly to blame."

"Thank heavens. Baby, I'm so sorry. I'd heard you were back visiting for a while, but I sure didn't want to see you again while handing out Vicodin. Still …" She bustled back around the counter. "It'll help. Did you break anything or just sprain it?"

"Dislocated the joint. Nothing's damaged; it's just sore."

"Well you give me five minutes, baby, and I'll have you on your way." She looked up at Ty. "Don't believe I've met you before. I'm Mavis Osterholz, the town drugtender. That's a bartender for drugs."

"Nice!" Ty put out his hand with a grin. "Ty Garraway. I recently signed on over at Paradise and I got the long straw— seeing Miss Grace to the emergency room while Cole dealt with driving the horse trailer."

"We're meeting him at Dottie's," Grace added. "Drugs and caffeine while I wait."

"You get yourself one of Dottie's delicious muffins, too," Mavis said. "Some people get nauseated from Vicodin on an empty stomach. A great reason to eat a muffin. Just no alcohol."

"Not a problem." Grace laughed.

"Ah, yes, my little teetotaler."

"Except a good whiskey now and then, right?" Grace

winked.

"Whiskey? *You?*" Ty looked truly astounded.

"My dad taught all of us girls to drink whiskey. I don't love it to death, but I know how to appreciate a good one."

"I wish I'd met your dad."

"I don't know." Grace eyed him with suspicion, and a glint of a smile. "There's been a lot of interest in drugs and alcohol this afternoon."

"Nah. A good whiskey goes great with a serious poker game, that's all. If you know your Glenfiddich from your Jack Daniel's, maybe you're a legit player after all."

"Jack is non-Scottish whiskey with an 'e' and the other is true Scotch whisky without an 'e,' and it tastes a lot better. Like, say, a nice, non-peaty Auchentoshan or a rich Glenlivet."

He shook his head, staring. "I concede. Your knowledge has far surpassed mine. I'm happy with Wild Turkey and a pair of aces."

"Oh good gosh. You *are* a heathen."

They grinned at each other, and Grace felt lighter than she had since deciding that morning she wanted to ride the fence line. Paradise's new ranch hand was fun—if she didn't think too hard about being proper. And he made her want to forget about proper.

As if to punctuate the moment, Mavis chuckled.

"I'm not even going to ask what you two talk about in a conversation when nobody is around." She turned for the locked door behind the counter that led to her pharmacy. "I'll get this filled, Grace. You shop for five minutes."

They were on their way ten minutes later with a huge hug, a long verbal lesson on the use of the Vicodin in Grace's purse, and a phone call apology from Cole that he had an injured cow emergency, and he was looking for Harper or Bella to come and pick them up. A ride was probably still forty minutes away.

"Welcome to the world of ranching," Grace said as they settled into a booth at Dottie's Bistro, which was, next to Ina's, the most iconic place to eat in town. "Ten people, all of them in crisis mode at the same time."

"Even when they know you're hurt and need them?"

"It's a sign of trust," she said. "You should be honored. They believe I'm safe. Am I?"

"I wouldn't take advantage of an injured partner."

"And if I wasn't injured?"

"Hey, you're a ten. What do you think?"

"That isn't funny you know."

"Deal with it."

She made a great show of sighing and removing the bottle of painkillers from her purse. "I have no idea why I like you at all."

"Hey, that's something I didn't expect to hear. You like me?"

"Don't get big-headed about it."

He laughed and picked up a menu from the side of the table. "How 'bout letting me get you that muffin? Better yet, it's nearly seven. How about dinner?"

"We could eat, but I'm treating. You're the one who stuck by me all this boring time. It really was kind of above and beyond."

Countering him, bantering, even arguing with him was so easy. She almost felt like the strong, self-confident woman she wanted him to believe she was. It was different than being with her sisters, where she was loved but considered the eccentric one.

"Choose whatever you want to eat. We'll wrestle over the

check later," he said. "In between, tell me about this cottage you're planning to convert."

"It's been in my family since about 1918. Eli built it after deciding he and my great-grandmother needed a home safe in town for the harsh winters. It needs a *lot* of work to make it anywhere near ready to be a restaurant."

"Can this little town handle another eating place? I'm not criticizing. I'm only asking."

"There are over twelve hundred residents now," she said. "With a VA medical center and the joint fire, police, and military training grounds only twenty minutes away, there's a lot of traffic and a lot of military families always looking for something new in an isolated place like this. My thought is to create more of a specialty place for moms, kids, and special occasions."

She'd shared a few of her general impressions the night before while they'd eaten ice cream at Ina's. But mostly that conversation had been guided by the kids who'd told him about the back garden, the pond, and the swans. Now she gave him more specifics, not really knowing why she opened up to him when she hadn't shared with anyone else.

For the first time since leaving Denver, she didn't miss her sisters with all her heart. Ty listened closely, eyes focused, leaning toward her. He nodded at key moments, asked questions, and her excitement grew.

"You know," she said once their muffins and chocolate shakes had arrived, and she'd swallowed a Vicodin pill with a swig of malted ice cream. "The cottage is only two blocks from here. The easiest way to tell you about it would be to show you."

"You'd let me see it?"

"It's not a secret hiding place." She laughed. "We just maybe won't tell Dottie yet. I plan to ask her advice when I get that far. I want her as an ally, not a competitor."

"You *are* a nice person, aren't you?" he asked.

"Do unto others," she said. "It's not that hard."

For a moment she swore he looked uncomfortable, his eyes narrowed as if in pain. Or thought. Or maybe her drug was kicking in super-fast, and she was loopy. Whatever she'd imagined, his face cleared and he pulled a chunk off his blueberry muffin.

"I'd like to see it," he said. "But you don't have to show me today. That arm should rest."

"It really doesn't hurt. I kind of liked walking around—it was almost easier than sitting. "

"Then if there's time, I'll come take a look at the new restaurant."

Her heart rose with a first flush of real anticipation. "I like your optimism."

Back outside, stuffed with Dottie's scrumptious baking and sent on her way with more concerned wishes and hugs, Grace lifted her eyes to a robin's-egg sky dotted with pinkening clouds. It was pushing seven-thirty, and the temperature had dipped a degree or two since they'd left the clinic. Lightness lifted her spirits and seemed to carry her toward a mission that was blessed.

The Vicodin was clearly working.

They'd barely gone half a block when she saw him. For a long moment, she didn't believe her eyes, and while she contemplated the figure strolling toward them from the corner up ahead, she barely noticed that Ty had stopped dead. He grasped her good arm and stopped her, too.

"Uh, I'm sorry," he said. "I completely forgot something I've been promising to pick up at the drugstore for Lil. As long as we're right here, can we take a quick detour?"

She peered into his eyes, confused by what looked slightly like terror. She glanced around, searching for danger, but all she saw was the elderly man coming closer. "Sure, but hang on. I think there's somebody I know coming this way. If it's him, you should meet him."

"You go ahead. I'll be right back."

She turned from him, distracted, and with a glad start, made a positive I.D.: Trampas Manterville!

"It's a very old friend of my grandmother's," she began. "He lived here in town for a while but has been away for a couple of years. I …"

Ty was gone.

She stared a moment in confusion but had to turn back yet again when a deep, strong voice hailed her.

"Grace? Grace Crockett, my dear girl. Is that really you?"

Chapter Eleven

"MAYBERRY?" GRACE USED the nickname Trampas had been given when he'd first arrived in Wolf Paw Pass two years before. "I can't believe you're here. What are you doing back in Wyoming?"

He wrapped her in a bear hug. The man had a wild life story that connected with Grace's own past in a way that felt more than a little cosmic, now that she'd been back to one of the original pieces of Paradise property. Trampas was the last surviving son of the man who'd lost the poker game to Eli.

"I had some family things to check on, my dear," the old man said. "I arrived just yesterday and haven't had time to call on your grandmother yet. How is she?"

"Feisty as ever. How have you been?"

"Very well." He stepped back and looked her up and down. "And you? Are you visiting from Denver? How is the restaurant?"

"The restaurant is doing well, but I'm considering moving back here. I can't believe you remember all these details."

"I was a teacher for many, many years. I developed lots of tricks for remembering important things."

"Where have you been the past couple of years? Have you continued to travel?"

Trampas had created a most unique way of living for a man in his late eighties, an itinerant lifestyle that took him to any part of the country he wished to see. Since retiring from his professorship in English literature at Oberlin College and moving from Ohio after the passing of his wife, he'd lived in retirement communities or in small apartments, he'd camped in parks and rest areas or bunked with relatives. He'd even, for a time, lived the life of an old-fashioned hobo. And he'd worked as everything from a shoeshine man to a Walmart greeter during times he wanted to conserve his pension. It was his attempt, he'd told her family, of finally seeing the country, and he wouldn't have it any other way. He'd come close to putting down roots again in Wyoming, where he'd spent the first five years of his life, but even a reunion with his old childhood friend Sadie Crockett hadn't convinced him to stay in one place.

"I spent some time back in the Midwest with my daughter," he told her. "Ohio and Minnesota. I hopped a bus to Arizona for the freezing winters. Right now I'm following up on the details of an old letter belonging to my family that was found a while ago. I knew it would be good to see Sadie and her family one more time. Perhaps I'll stay for part of the summer."

Something about his story was familiar. Hadn't Ty said something about family papers?

"Where are you staying right now?"

"A small studio apartment a local soldier is subleasing for one month."

"You should come and stay at the ranch." Grace put her good hand on his arm. "Grandma would love to have you there, and my sisters are big into history. I'm sure they'd help you track down anything you're looking to find."

"That's a generous offer, dear Grace. You're so kind. I hope I might invite myself to visit soon?"

Grace took her turn to offer a hug, one-handed though it was. "Anytime. Pick a night right now, and I'll tell them all you're coming and arrange for a ride to get you out to us."

Trampas accepted her hug. "I'm free any evening after tonight. But I'll call." He pushed her away. "Now tell me what's happened to your shoulder?"

"Elbow." She dismissed his concern with a wave. "Just happened today; a little slip off a horse. It's not broken and it doesn't hurt much. I'm on my way home—if my ride and my babysitter show up again." She looked around.

"You aren't stranded?" Trampas asked, concern still warm in his eyes.

"No. No. I have someone with me but he ducked back into a store. One of our new ranch hands. Nice guy."

If a little odd, she thought.

"You're sure?"

"I am. If you have a minute I'll introduce you to him."

"Grace, I would love to, but if I'm honest, I have a meeting scheduled in about ten minutes with the latest curator of the little Wolf Paw Pass museum. That letter, you see. Let me give you my address. You can always leave messages for me there or at the post office."

"No cell phone yet? Didn't we tell you to jump into the modern era?"

"I had one for a while," he said. "It's not reliable when you live as I do. And I'm happy enough being slightly untraceable."

"Well I will track you down, Mr. Manterville. You are the best storyteller we've had since my grandfather was alive. I didn't get to spend as much time with you as my older sisters did, but I remember."

He grasped her hand tightly and gave it a strong squeeze. "I was meant to run into you, I think," he said. "Tell your grandmama I'll see her soon. I always did love older women."

Sadie was ten years his senior and had, nearly eighty years earlier, been his babysitter. Life was hilarious sometimes, Grace thought.

"I promise." She winked. "Maybe I can make a cougar out of Sadie Crockett. Never know."

He walked away with one last laugh, moving brightly but unhurriedly down the sidewalk and turning the corner a block away. Grace frowned and looked for any sign of Ty. When she saw nothing, she headed back toward the drugstore, only to meet him coming out the door with a paper bag and two candy bars.

"Where's your friend?" he asked.

"Okay, what gives?" She ignored his question and grasped the strap of her purse, waiting.

"What do you mean?"

"You vanished like a spooked deer."

"I'm sorry," he said easily. "I got two storefronts past the diner and remembered I told Lil I'd pick up calamine lotion and some other supplies for her first-aid kit. One of the kids got into some stinging nettles the other day, and she didn't have anything to treat it with. I figured you didn't need a stranger to be there for some reunion."

She eyed him carefully. His excuse sounded genuine and completely plausible. In fact, she couldn't think of any other reason he'd have turned tail so quickly. And, since her brain was feeling lovely and slightly floaty, she decided she'd imagined the true speed of his disappearance.

***

Ty's only sign that Grace wasn't seeing right through his cheerful facade was the ghost of a smile on her lips and the very faint glaze flecking the blue of her eyes. Maybe her drugs were kicking in and she wouldn't analyze his words or his behavior too closely.

"The man you missed is a friend of my grandmother's from over eighty years ago. He was born here and came back two years ago, looking for some family member and telling us some tale about the Mantervilles wanting their part of the ranch back. Kind of weird, considering we were talking about that today."

Panic, acid-like and painful, rose into his throat. Trampas had been here before? The panic swelled and nearly convinced him Grace knew exactly who he was. Maybe his great-uncle had recognized him before he'd escaped to the drugstore on his bogus mission. The story of the poker game that had lost the Mantervilles their legacy was infamous in his family, but nobody had ever cared enough to pursue the convoluted mystery. If Trampas thought he could step in now on behalf of his own daughter …

But that wasn't like him. His great-uncle was nothing if not a decent man.

"You'd like Mayberry, I think." Grace pulled him back to the moment. "He looks eighty but acts forty and seems to have a positive view of everything. I didn't get to know him well but my sisters all rave about him and his stories. You strike me as a guy with a lot of stories, too. Like you could swap a few tales with a man like Mayberry."

Ty could barely focus on the bizarreness of her words, but he did breathe slightly easier. She genuinely didn't seem to know how close to home she was hitting and just how many stories he could swap with …

"Mayberry?"

She laughed. "A nickname the locals gave him when he first arrived. He lived like a homeless man for the first month or so. He's unique—a professional drifter."

A professional weirdo, Ty thought. His uncle was a do-gooder, but he was also the family oddball. So smart he was beyond eccentric.

"So people named him after the town drunk in Mayberry from the TV show," Grace continued. "His real name is Trampas Manterville, but I always kind of liked the nickname. I was so surprised to see him that I didn't concentrate on keeping you here an extra minute. I wanted you to meet him."

Thank God for small miracles. Meeting Trampas in front of Grace? Ty shook his head, trying to let a huge breath out and not have her notice. "I'm sure I'll get the chance if he's that big a friend of your family's."

"If you swear not to let on to Sadie, I'll tell you that I used to notice her blushing—at her age!—when Mayberry came around. I thought I was making it up, but Harper said she saw it too. I guess there's no age limit on romantic crushes. I find that hopeful."

Her bright chatter convinced Ty that Grace hadn't connected him to Trampas. All he had to do now was figure out how to avoid the old man until all the pieces of the plan were in place. It wasn't going to take him long to find out where Ty had landed.

"Guys hate the word crush, you know. Crushes cause no end of grief to a man who doesn't have any intention of falling for a girl or leading her on."

"Well good thing there's no crush going on here, then." She grinned at him. Clearly she felt better. Maybe a little too much better.

"Damn good thing."

"Don't say 'damn.'"

He took her uninjured arm and started them down the street. "You are no fun at all, are you? Come on. If you want me to see this amazing property of yours before our ride shows up, we should head over there. Did you tell Cole the new pickup spot?"

"No, sorry. I got sidetracked."

"It's okay. I'll call him. I don't think you should be texting right now." He laughed at her indignant glare.

"I feel lovely, but because of relief, not the fact that I'm stoned."

"Okay, sweetheart. If you say so."

"You're really awful, you know that?"

"It's a reputation I work very hard to maintain. All right, Miss Crockett. You claim you're not high, so you should be a crackerjack navigator. Lead on."

Ty's first thought gazing at the old building was that any banker should think twice about lending money to rehab a place that needed so much work. But as he prowled the structure, and Grace pointed out some of her ideas, he changed his mind. The bones were solid. Over the years, the little cottage had been maintained despite its outward appearance. The walls were true, and the foundation, expertly stacked fieldstone, had no cracks or sunken corners that he could see. It would cost her, but renovation was certainly feasible.

She came alive as she gave him the tour, and as much as

the old handiwork in the cottage intrigued him—and he was surprised at how much it did—Grace intrigued him more. Even with her arm trussed in its sling, she poked and prodded through old cupboards, moved some small bookcases to look for any outlets or conveniences that might have been added through the years, and brushed dust off of tables to see what they looked like. At every turn, her features lit with delight that made her look like a bright fairy discovering her own magical forest.

Ty made discoveries, too. At the same time he found an expanse of old, decorative plaster work behind a strip of decrepit wallpaper, he discovered how Grace's cheekbones rounded into high, softly pink spheres when she grinned. When he yanked up a hunk of stained carpeting in a bedroom to find rough-sawn pine planks still flat and strong making up the floor, he was charmed by a rich alto laugh that pierced him like a siren song.

She was beautiful as an old time film star but, at the blink of an eye, she could shed the cultured starlet and turn cute as an elf. But what got him in the gut were her words—the ideas for the spaces that spilled from her as easily as breath. They weren't defined or complete, and most of the time she was simply throwing general concepts out to see what resonated. He could see why she'd been a success at such a young age.

She imagined stainless steel appliances and new bathrooms, open concepts and burnished wood. To him, the whole idea of turning the amazing craftsmanship from a hundred years earlier into a slick and modern restaurant was more than sad. Why move so quickly to destroy what a man without benefit of power tools or backhoes had created with his back and his hands?

"I want to have a fun space where the kids can be in their own little restaurant, but the moms, or dads," she added with a nod and a smile to acknowledge him, "will be here in the bigger space and know the little ones are perfectly safe."

"You know? That's a great idea."

"Wow. Your eyes aren't glazed over. I've seen Cole's and Gabe's start to roll back in their sockets when I go on like this. I didn't expect you to find it fascinating."

"I've never worked on anything this old before," he said. "I spent several years on and off with a decent-sized construction company. We did framing and structural work and some remodeling, but there were always plenty of guys with more experience to do the important stuff. I could demo, measure, pound, and frame cabinets with the best of them, but it was always new construction. This kind of workmanship is … frankly," he looked around, "impressive."

"You think so?"

"It would be nice to save some of it."

"Oh no!" Her eyes went enormous. "It would be nice to save *all* of it. I wish I knew right now what was sound and what wasn't so I could plan around what was original."

He stared for a moment, not sure what he'd missed. How had they gone from open concept and all new to keeping the original?

"Really? You mean you aren't talking about gutting this and tearing down all the walls?"

She shook her head. "I was all excited about making something modern with a throwback to the cottage's origins, but now that I'm really looking around, I think it would be way more awesome to do it opposite of that. Leave as much original as I can while still making it look fresh and welcoming.

A couple of interior walls will have to come down for space's sake, but I still think I can make it look close to original."

Flutters of excitement grew in his stomach, as if it were his own project.

"Not that you need it, but you have my approval. I have to admit—the idea of turning this into a modern fairy tale froo-froo place was kind of sad."

"Oh my gosh. You care!"

"You're showing me a potential project and you're excited. I don't *care*." He mimicked the high-pitched surprise in her voice and shook his head.

"Come on. What do you really think of all this?"

"I think you're smart, and brave, to see potential in a hundred-year-old house. I'm all for it."

"What do *you* see?"

A little piece of his heart shifted slightly. Nobody but Lucky and players around a poker table ever needed to know what he thought about something. Bosses told him what he should do, and one ex-lover had shown him very graphically what he was going to do with the rest of his life by dropping off his kid. Lil told him what that kid needed for food and clothing, and lists told him what she needed for school. But here came Grace. Grace wanted to know the most insignificant little thing, and it felt like she'd asked him his ideas for finding world peace.

He really was insane.

"You barely know me," he hedged, still uncertain she genuinely cared what he thought. "What does my opinion matter?"

"I know you always say exactly what you think. I know you're pretty smart—you can use real words, big words sometimes, in a sentence. I know you're a guy's guy trying not to show his soft side for his little girl every other minute. I just think you'd be a good person to tell me if you think this is a stupid idea or one that could work."

"Fun," he said, without hesitation. "I think it looks like a whole lot of fun to turn this into the place you've described. And that's an opinion based on zero knowledge of the economy in town, the number of restaurants already here, the ability to get staff and make decent food. It's based only on …" His eye drifted to the wall in the small bedroom where they stood. "On things like this. Look."

Without ceremony, he tugged on another piece of faded, green-striped wallpaper. It fell away like a dry leaf. Two more strips of the old covering followed.

"Weird," Grace said. "Wallpaper shouldn't come down this easily. What gives?"

"I don't think it was ever properly glued. It looks like it might have been tacked there in a hurry, temporarily. Check this out. The wall here isn't plaster, it's modern sheetrock."

"It wasn't put up with any more care than the wallpaper."

Grace pointed to a seam that was barely taped where sheets of wallboard were warping and pulling free of nails. A turkey-tail-shaped brown stain hinted at water damage. Ty gave the corner of the sheetrock a pull and a chunk three feet square broke off like limestone and powdered the floor. The space behind the hole was empty.

"Curiouser and curiouser," said Grace.

"Yeah. What do you think, Alice, do you want to see what's behind here? A portal to Wonderland? Maybe a doorway to Narnia?"

"You know about Narnia?"

He scowled. "I have a kid, remember? Who reads already

and likes to listen to books above her age level. I've probably read more children's stories than you have."

She nodded in concession. "That's pretty likely true. But I have read *The Lion, The Witch, and the Wardrobe* and *Alice in Wonderland*, so at least I got the references."

He smiled, warmed by the easy camaraderie they suddenly shared. It shouldn't be that surprising, he supposed. They were searching for treasure together after all. "Well, we're more like the Goonies than like Peter and Susan," he said, turning back to the wall and grasping another edge of sheet rock.

"Or Alice, for that matter," she replied. "Because I'm telling you, if we find something with a tag on it that reads 'Drink Me,' it isn't going to be me who tries it."

"Why does that not surprise me in the least?" He swiveled his head slightly to glance back and wrinkle his nose. "Grace Crockett, try an unknown substance?"

"Unless it's a good Scotch."

A grunting laugh burst from him as he won the battle with another chunk of wallboard. "I think I like you, Miss Grace. You don't take yourself too seriously."

This time the snorting laughter came from her. "You'll never ever convince my sisters of that. And, I admit, one of the reasons I'm okay with pulling this down is that I could never leave that hole in the wall. It would bother me in my sleep."

"Seriously?"

Another piece of sheetrock hit the floor.

"Think *Big Bang Theory.*"

"You're telling me you're *that* OCD?"

"I like no mess."

"Aha. That totally explains why you want to clean this place before you get bids on remodeling."

"I guess."

She used her good hand to join him in the demolition. After fifteen minutes, they'd cleared a section of wall about ten feet square. Ty held up his hand to stop them and stepped back.

"Look at that," he said.

"A second fireplace!" Grace bent and craned her neck to look into the brick firebox. "Somebody covered it up, and really quickly, too."

"A quick guess is that it was old and drafty, and this was a stopgap to warm up the room."

Ty swept the chunks and dust away from the exposed hole with his shoe, and knelt at the hearth. Grace joined him, and he had to laugh again at her wrinkled nose.

"Good for you," he said. "Practice for the real dirty work."

"Yeah, well, this feels like some kind of weird immersion therapy."

They both rocked forward at the same time and stuck their heads into the fireplace. As if they'd choreographed it, Ty turned his head right and Grace turned hers left so they could look up the flue. It was black as a well.

A gentle waft of flowery scent filled his nostrils. Without warning his heartbeat accelerated and he turned slowly back, shocked to meet her eyes just inches from his. Her nose nearly brushed his cheek. He could have kissed her. She didn't move.

"I think it's blocked." Her breath feathered his lips. He couldn't take his eyes off the action of her mouth as she swallowed.

"Yup."

"What's this, some kind of new voodoo ceremony?"

The bright, southern-accented voice from behind them made Ty flinch as if he'd been stun gunned. When his forehead crashed into Grace's she collapsed onto her side, hit her elbow and let out a yelp that ended in a choked sob.

"God, Grace!" Ty was out of the fireplace and had Grace in his arms before he could even rub the sore spot on his own head. "I'm sorry. So sorry. Your elbow—"

"I only bumped it. I'm fine, Ty." Her forced half smile couldn't hide the pain in her eyes.

He didn't look toward the door; he'd recognized the voice. Instead, he bent his head closer to Grace. "We should go have it checked again."

"Oh for crying out loud. No we should not."

Grace was first to look at their guests. Ty continued to hold her, unwilling to trust her balance, not wanting to let her go. She felt right and safe in his embrace.

But before he could ask once more if she really was okay, she gasped and wrenched free of his arms.

"Lil!" she said.

In full-fledged annoyance, Ty turned, too, and met a pair of sparkling brown eyes.

"That looked like it hurt, baby," Lil said.

"What the hell are you doing here?" Ty shot back.

Grace popped him on the shoulder with a deep scowl and gave the slightest incline of her head toward the door. He looked more carefully. Lucky stepped away from Lil's side and gave a suspicious little wave.

"Hi, Daddy."

Chapter Twelve

GRACE'S HEAD THROBBED, not as much from knocking it against Ty's as from mortification. Her face heated by levels: neck, chin, cheeks, eyebrows, hairline. As she and Lil locked gazes, all Grace wanted to do was explain and apologize for the questions in Lil's mocha-brown eyes. Lucky, too, eyed her with skeptical curiosity. But apologizing felt incredibly insincere when the sparks she and Ty had nearly ignited in the old, cold fireplace must have been obvious.

"Hi, Nougat," Ty replied to his daughter. "Didn't expect to see either of you two."

Grace frowned as the odd scene started to register. What man snapped at his girlfriend with "what the hell?" when he was caught in a compromising position? And what partner only laughed when she caught her man embracing another woman?

Without planning, Grace's eyes slipped to Lil's hands. Her arms crisscrossed her chest, but the fingers of her left hand were visible. They sported no rings of any kind. She lifted her gaze again and Lil winked.

Winked?

"I got home from picking the Luckster here up at school, and Cole practically accosted me in the driveway. He and

Bjorn have a million and one cow crises, he can't reach Harper or Bella, and Melanie has her kids off on a field trip. So, I'm your taxi service. Better late than never."

"Sorry I jumped on you." Ty ran a hand through his hair and Grace winced when he lingered momentarily over a spot on his forehead. "You guys scared the hair off us."

"It was kind of fun." Lil cocked her brows. "You two moved like freaked-out deer."

"Very funny."

"Curiouser and curiouser," Grace whispered again.

"Huh?" Ty frowned.

"You two are very strange," she said, truly confused.

Ty took her by the upper arms again and spun her gently to face him. He peered closely at her forehead and reached to touch precisely in the middle of the sorest spot.

"Ow."

"I think we'll be comparing goose eggs in the morning."

"We didn't hit that hard," she scoffed.

"I don't know. I think we heard a definite clunk, don't you?" Lil and Lucky exchanged grins.

Ty smoothed Grace's bangs over her forehead, then trailed his palm carefully down her right arm until it rested just above the bandage on her elbow. "Are you really okay? That can't have been good for your arm."

She couldn't answer. His touch both thrilled and disturbed her—the same lethal combo that had plagued her all day. Only now Lil stood right there. Grace twisted away again and glared at him.

"It's already fine."

Confusion clouded his eyes.

"I'm sorry you hurt your arm, Grace," Lucky said. "Cole

told us you got attacked by a mountain lion. I wish I could have seen the mountain lion, but not you falling off the horse."

How could anyone resist such a sweet, sincere, perfect little voice? Grace's smile came easily for the first time since the girl had arrived. "She was pretty awesome. I kind of wish I'd gotten a better look, too, but I played dead."

"You did?"

"I hoped she wouldn't bother me if she thought something else had already gotten me."

"That's awesome!"

"Lucky," Ty warned. "It wasn't awesome. She got hurt."

"But she was smart." Lucky turned to Grace. "That was smart."

"Thanks. When you grow up around here, you learn things like that."

"Does your elbow hurt a lot?"

Her genuine caring made Grace want to hug her. "Not a lot," she said. "But it's sore."

"You should kiss her owie for her, Dad."

At that, Grace took an involuntary step back. No kissing, she thought, panicking even though she knew it was unreasonable over such an innocuous situation.

"You think so?" Ty's voice, humor-filled, drew her eyes reluctantly back to him.

"Yeah, Daddy. Your kisses are magical."

"Well then." Ty didn't even laugh. "How can you argue with magic? Want me to kiss your owie, Miss Grace?"

The air in the wrecked room swirled around her, superheated and close. She *did* want him to kiss her. More than anything. And she almost let the weird, suffocating atmosphere convince her to tell him so. Until she gave herself a mental slap. This was so completely ridiculous.

Yet Lil was grinning. Grace swore the older woman gave Lucky a tiny elbow to the shoulder.

It had to be a joke.

Ty lifted her arm again, and placed a kiss on top of the Ace bandage. She couldn't honestly feel it and yet her stomach slid to her toes.

"Now the bump on the head," he said.

"Oh, for the love …" She pushed him away. "Next thing you know, I'll have to reciprocate."

"Would that be so bad?" His green-forest eyes twinkled.

"You're horrible!" She stepped back and took all three of them into her gaze. "Your young daughter and your girlfriend are right here. What's wrong with this picture?"

"My what?" Incredulous, Ty furrowed his brow and swiveled his head from her to Lil. "What did you tell her about us?"

Lil's laughter filled the room, rich, throaty, somehow deeply sexy. "Me? You blockhead. You're the one who hasn't told her anything." She turned to Grace and stepped forward. With a sweet, gentle motion, she lifted a strand of Grace's long hair and then smoothed it back into place. "Honey," she said. "If I were jealous at all, it would be because Ty got to you first. Very sadly, you are on the wrong team for me. And so's *this* big goof."

"You …?" Grace's first reaction was utter relief. Still she stuttered her reply. "I just assumed … I …"

"I know you're big on … traditional family life," Ty said, his mouth twisted in apology. "That seems pretty important to everyone here. You move from a place like Las Vegas to a place like Wyoming and … I didn't want to rock anyone's religious boat so…"

Wow, stereotype much? she thought, moving past the ruse. Did he think she didn't know any gay people? Didn't have any gay friends? And yet, Ty's caution for her feelings, despite being wrong, were so different from the sanctimonious reaction she'd gotten from Micah two weeks before over music …

"Look, I was surprised because I made an assumption that makes me look ridiculous. But other than that, so what if I have a personal faith? That doesn't mean I'm a *jerk*." She frowned. "In fact, I like to think no one in my family is judgmental."

"I told you people would understand," Lil said.

"Lil has a crush on Kate McKinnon," Lucky said matter-of-factly.

"Well who doesn't?" Lil asked.

"I do," Ty agreed, and grinned at Grace. "I'm really sorry. I wasn't purposely trying to hide anything. It's often easier to let people assume what they want. I forgot I hadn't cleared this up with you. I should have—you definitely are not a jerk."

The whole nonchalant atmosphere broke Grace's reserve. If a five-year-old could discuss this as if she were discussing the weather, and Ty could show a progressive side with such insouciance, then she could get past a little discombobulation.

"Can I kiss your head boo-boo now?" he asked.

Just like that, he flustered her again.

"Leave her alone, you Neanderthal." Lil took Grace by the uninjured arm and led her away. "Come on, sweetie. He doesn't get to kiss you again until he grows up. Let's get you home."

"Kiss me again?"

"Hasn't he yet? Other than the elbow, I mean."

"No!"

"I'm sorry. We'll work on that." She winked and Grace followed blindly. The whole conversation had gone off the rails of normal and into the magical forest of bizarre.

And yet, there was a weird flutter in her stomach at Lil's words. It wasn't like Grace hadn't noticed in Ty Garraway's lips the potential for a pretty decent kiss.

She definitely needed sleep.

The next evening, Friday, Ty brought Lucky up to Rosecroft immediately after dinner. Grandma Sadie led her into the kitchen, where Harper, Mia, Grace, and their mother still sat around the table gathering energy to start cleaning up.

"Look who I found!" Grandma Sadie said, her signature black cane with its bright red poppies tapping cozily along the pine floor. Lucky literally skipped ahead of her and entered the room like a little strobe flash, brightening everything in front of her.

"Hey, sweetheart!" Harper opened her arms and let the child skip into them.

"Hi, Harper. I'm here to help."

Grace stood from her place at the table and watched the family embrace Lucky with a mix of warmth and envy. The others had already known her for a couple of weeks. Grace wanted to know her, to bond with her, too.

And then she looked up. Ty stood behind Grandma Sadie, quietly watching the scene, an easy smile taking the place of words. Grace's heart banged against her ribcage. Her brain reminded her with glee that he was *not* attached, and that was enough to make her temporary, pulse-raising fascination with him less inappropriate.

"Hi," he said.

"Hey."

"How's the arm today?"

"Perfect."

He shook his head and laughed. "You're a tough little ten, Miss Crockett. I hope for the sake of your honesty record, you are fine. A lie could come back to haunt you when you reach St. Peter some day long from now."

He was horrible. And funny. And knew exactly how to push her buttons. The scary thing was she'd stopped reacting badly to his teasing. All the way home from Wolf Paw Pass yesterday evening, he'd needled her with absurd humor.

Are you sure we didn't bump harder?

I can't believe a straight woman actually found me attractive.

Is it me or is it the Vicodin?

"St. Peter won't hold one little lie against me."

"Especially since it's drug-induced." He waggled his brows. "Are you still on the good stuff?"

She'd taken a minimum dose of Vicodin—it had worked like magic.

"It is good stuff," she agreed.

"Glad you're being smart about keeping the pain under control. So … I can come get the Lucky charm in a couple of hours?"

"Yes, anytime you want her. Since there's no school tomorrow, she can stay as long as you're okay with her being up." Grace turned to Lucky. "It's really nice of you to come and help out, kiddo."

The little girl's cheeks chipmunked into a precious smile, and the freckles across her nose shone like cinnamon sprinkles. She left Harper and reached for Grace's hand. With strong steps, like a hiker with a definite destination, she led her two steps back to her chair.

"You can sit back down, Miss Grace. And Grandma Sadie,

too. I can carry the dishes to the dishwasher, and I can wash pots. Lil taught me how to scrub. Daddy taught me how to make sure there are no spots left."

"I don't know." Bella stood. "You'd best be careful, sweetie. You'll make yourself indispensable around here and we'll have to adopt you."

"Could I have a dog if you adopt me?"

The room burst into laughter, and Grace hugged her. "If you know how to scrub pots, you can have whatever you like living here. I'm not beyond bribing your daddy."

"Is that right? With what?" His query came low and deep, sexy and almost threatening. Still, the glint in his eye gave him away.

"I'm a ten. I'll think of something."

"Um ..." Ty choked on a cough. "I'd be careful making offers like that. You have no idea what kind of person you're baiting."

"A person who can dish it out but not take it?"

"Me?" He placed a hand on his chest and backed up as if struck. "I would never dish out anything."

All eyes were on them, but she suddenly didn't care. A sense of confidence and freedom loosed a wide grin at the realization that she could and would handle him—line for line, jibe for jibe.

"You won't ever get to heaven telling lies like that." She gave him a haughty sniff.

"You are all just a little crazy, you know that?" Ty turned with a grin. "I'll be back. Lucky, behave yourself and don't let them brainwash you. I'm not giving you up for adoption."

"But then I'll never get a dog."

"Haven't I always said life ain't fair?"

Father and daughter grinned at each other.

"Yes," said Lucky. "But sometimes I win anyway."

At that moment a loud "meow" filled the kitchen and Lucky squealed. "Jack!"

Deeper in the house, Rory and Gabe were engrossed in the nightly video game Rory was allowed once his homework was done. Grace supposed the gorgeous cat felt ignored and also like life wasn't fair.

"Can I hold him?" Lucky asked, no longer looking like a little professor, but like a starry-eyed little kid who loved animals.

"Hey, you can't do dishes if you're holding a cat. Work before play, remember?" Ty said.

Grace waved him off. "Go home, Dad," she said. "The Crockett women have their own ways of getting things done. Of course you can hold him, Lucky. He's kind of heavy. If you can't lift him, we'll put him in your lap. He's a play-before-work kind of cat."

Lucky beamed at her father, who only growled in defeat. "I'll be back. Enjoy getting your animal fix."

Forty-five minutes later, Harper wiped her hands on a blue dish towel and handed it to Lucky, who'd just finished washing the last of three pots that hadn't fit in the dishwasher. "Do you have to do this all the time at home?" Harper asked gently.

Grace and Mia hadn't been able to tear themselves away from watching the miniature girl handle herself around the kitchen. Her gross motor skills seemed to be as advanced as her intellectual ones, and it begged the question of how much she was asked to do for her dad.

"Two times a week." She shrugged. "I have a different chore every day. Sometimes it's to help with the laundry. Sometimes I have to help dust. Sometimes I help Daddy outside. And some days I just clean up my room. Lil says I don't have to do any more than she does. She hates to clean."

"What do you think of cleaning?" Bella asked.

"Daddy says everyone has to learn how to do things they hate. I don't hate cleaning. But I'd rather practice spitting."

Harper sputtered and took the towel from Lucky once her hands were dry. "You're hilarious, girl. I'm guessing that means you aren't into having your own little kitchen set to play house with. Or dolls to feed and dress."

Lucky wrinkled her nose in distaste, and Grace had to laugh, too. On the surface, the child was the epitome of an angelic girl's girl, with sparkling blue eyes, and her sweet strawberry-blond pageboy held back with a stretchy blue hairband. The only things that gave away her tomboy status were the faded jeans, rolled at the ankles like Huck Finn, and a pair of red Converse tennis shoes. Her T-shirt was pink, but the picture on it was a roaring T-Rex with the words "Fierce Little Girl" beneath it.

"Dolls are creepy," Lucky said. "They have eyes that roll back in their heads. I'd rather have a dog."

"Not all dolls have moving eyes," Grace offered, and Lucky shrugged.

"I like animals better. At least they're cuddly."

"True enough." Grace smiled. "In all honesty most of us girls liked animals better, too. Mia and Kelly liked baby dolls— but they like people in general." She grinned at her sister, who shrugged and adjusted her casted leg on the chair where she had it propped.

"I guess that's why I became a human doctor," Mia said.

"You liked your Barbies, Gracie," Bella added. "I recall going through a phase of making those tiny outfits."

"Oh, man, that's right." Grace laughed. "But that's when I learned to sew and knit. Remember, Grandma? You taught me how to make little scarves on those little needles."

"One of my biggest success stories," Grandma Sadie replied. "You're really the only one who took to the knitting. Which reminds me—I'd like you to take me into town so I can pick up some more yarn. I haven't talked to Wanda at Have You Any Wool for several months now."

"Down to only one closet full of yarn stash, Grandma?" Mia teased.

"Even old ladies have vices," she said simply. "I need to have something to will you girls when I'm gone."

"I'll treasure every skein." Mia blew her a kiss. "And Grace can knit us each a sweater to remember you by."

"It's a deal," Grace agreed. "But I have plenty of time. Grandma's got another ninety years before she's gone."

"Good Lord save me." Grandma Sadie clapped a hand over her chest. "Much as I love you all, and I don't plan to go tomorrow, I think my heavenly Father loves me more than to condemn me to another century down here. Sooner or later you'll have to take over."

"Yeah, yeah," Harper said. "You keep talking, Grams."

"So, Lucky. I'm guessing you don't exactly have a collection of Barbies either. What do you like?" Grace asked.

"I have two Barbies. Lil got them for me. She says they're the only dolls that look like her. Probably because she has giant boobs."

Peals of laughter burst from every one of them. Grace wiped her eyes, holding back tears of mirth. "Oh my gosh. And to think there are some women who believe Barbie is horrible for little girls for exactly that reason."

"Daddy said it was okay for me to have a Barbie as long as I know she's pretend. He says Barbie is like looking at a magazine—she's pretty but so are other kinds of girl shapes. So, Barbie is okay. At least you can make her ride a horse."

"Hear, hear!" Harper said. "I think we had at least four different Barbie horses over the years."

Grace let the conversation swirl on around her, struck dumb by Lucky's nonchalant revelation. Ty? Ty of the "you're a ten and that's now a thing between us" had given his daughter perfect advice about body image? The man was a complete enigma. She had seen precious few moments of seriousness in him, but little by little others were giving her a whole different vision. Now she kind of wanted to kiss him just to apologize for thinking he was an insensitive dude.

Kiss him.

The thought brought on a whole spectrum of inappropriate imaginings and warm flushes. Memories assailed her from the long, dark seconds in the fireplace and the sensation of strength and safety when he'd put his arms around her. She fought them, praying Lucky wasn't clairvoyant as well as brilliant. She shook herself back to the conversation, where the subject had turned from dolls to favorite animals.

"Is yours a dog?" Harper asked.

Lucky shook her head. "No. It's a horse. But I'll never get Daddy to buy me a horse, so I'm working on a dog."

"Why do you think he doesn't want a dog?" Grace asked.

"He says it's hard enough to move without an animal. He doesn't want any dogs or cats until we're settled in our new place."

"New place?"

"We're going to get some land and build our own house and

have plenty of room for a dog. But that'll prob'ly be when I'm a hundred so ..."

So the man had real goals. Grace remembered how Ty had studied the land during their ride yesterday, fascinated by all aspects of ranching, asking questions that had been quite astute, now that she thought about it. It looked more and more as if she'd misjudged the man thoroughly.

"What was your daddy going to do tonight?"

She fixed her darling eyes on Grace and answered without missing a beat. "He was *going* to ask you to a movie. But then he got a phone call and said he had to go back into town and take care of some things. He was kind of distracted, so he prob'ly wouldn't be good company. That's what he says to me all the time—he's not good company when he's distracted."

"Um, this is all well and good," Mia said, fixing Grace with a confused frown. "But doesn't Lil have something to say about Ty asking you on a movie date?"

Grace smiled at the floor, but then looked up, remembering Grandma Sadie's story from days earlier about church.

"I learned something kind of cool about Lil yesterday," she said. "Right, Lucky?"

The little girl looked surprised. "I guess it's cool. Lil is gay, you mean?"

The briefest moment of surprised silence preceded a chirpy chorus of calls and teasing. Harper slapped Grace on the back and then humorously clamped her hands over Lucky's ears. "My gosh, so all this time you could have been flirting with Ty and we never knew it?"

"Don't be ridiculous," Grace said. "Why would I flirt with a man I hardly know?"

"Uh, I would say a near-date experience proves *some* good

stuff went on today."

Lucky shook her head free. "They were in the fireplace together."

"Okay *what*?" Harper asked, as she and Mia broke into high-pitched laughter like grade school girls.

"They were looking in an old Fireplace. Lil and I scared them and they bumped heads. And then Daddy kissed Grace's owie."

"Oh my gosh!" Harper shook her head. "You held out on us, sis. I think this requires a whole story. Out with it."

"Oh stop it," Grace replied, her skin flushing from the soles of her feet to the roots of her hair. "It was nothing. Ty found a hidden fireplace in the cottage and we uncovered part of it. We were looking to see if it was blocked. Lucky told you the rest—except that it was *she* ..." Grace tweaked Lucky's nose, "who was all about kissing owies. Am I right?"

Lucky gave an innocent shrug. "It would be okay with me if you like my dad. He needs a girlfriend. Lil and I both think so."

Grace's flush turned into the outright heat of embarrassment, but she forced herself to stay calm. "Well it was nice of your dad to say he'd ask me to a movie, Lucky. I'm sure we'll talk later."

She shot her sisters warning looks before they could say more, and she scowled at her grandmother. "I'm serious; there's nothing going on, you old matchmaker, so stop smiling."

"Who's smiling?" Grandma Sadie turned to not-so-innocent Lucky. "My girl, I was going to have Grace help me wind some yarn into balls, but with her elbow, she might not find that very comfortable. How would you like to take her place? That would be a big help."

"Okay." She looked a little dubious. "I don't know how,

though."

"Easy as spitting." Grandma Sadie stood from her chair and Lucky broke into a huge grin.

"Okay!" she said again.

Grace's emotions darted between embarrassment for herself and awe over her family. They'd accepted and brushed over the announcement about Lil with barely a blink, but they'd honed in on her possible flirting like an entire flight of heat-seeking missiles.

As much as they mortified her at the moment, they really were an amazing group of women.

Grandma Sadie started toward the doorway to the dining and living rooms.

"Oh, Grandma, wait, I totally forgot." Grace shook off her self-absorption. "I ran into a surprising person today. Did you know Trampas Manterville was in town?"

She barely managed to stifle her giggle at the look on Grandma Sadie's face, because she recognized the breathless shock a little bit too well at the moment. Sadie Crockett, the old sweetheart, had a crush on the fellow. Proof the Crockett women were nothing if not faithful romantics.

"Well, my goodness, child," Sadie said. "Where did you see him?"

"He was coming down Mountain View after I left the clinic, and he saw me first. He said he's only been here a day, and I'm to tell you he's had actual business to attend to so hasn't had time to call. But he's going to."

"Isn't that nice. I'll look forward to that."

"Has he contacted you at all during the last two years?" Grace asked.

Harper moved in to put an arm around their grandmother.

"Sure!" she said. "She and Trampas write now. Keeping the old paper stationery business going. I think it's sweet. A little romantic."

"Romantic. Pah." Grandma Sadie shook her head. "There aren't that many of us from that generation left. We cling to whomever we find."

"Plus, he's handsome in an elderly man kind of way." Grace wrinkled her nose in a smile. "I didn't see him much when he was living here, but from what I do remember, he's pretty nice and very funny."

"He is nice. I used to babysit him, you know. He was this sweet little baby—ten years younger than his brother Oliver. Trampas was sweet right up until he was moved away at age five. I never got along with Oliver who was just like his father—a bully and a braggart."

"I think you should go after him, Grandma," Harper said. "Mia and I agree."

"We do!" Mia said. "One of your last great adventures can be becoming a cougar."

"You three are so disrespectful." Grandma Sadie laughed. "I know what that means, so don't think I have no idea you're teasing me. I can't complain—you all learned it from me. Now go on and leave me alone. Teagan and I have things to do."

Lucky gave her a happy five-year-old's grin.

"Nope! I'm tired of sitting propped on kitchen chairs," Mia said. "Come on, girls. Let's go watch the yarn balling."

To anyone else, that would have been the same as an invitation to watch weeds grow, but with resounding agreement, Grace handed Mia her crutches, Harper grabbed a sketchbook she'd set on a counter earlier, and Bella grabbed a pitcher of lemonade from the refrigerator and six glasses. They trooped after the oldest and the youngest in the group because, in truth, when there was time, everybody loved spending stolen moments like this with Grandma Sadie. She was the most fun youngest-old person on the planet—always ready with a story from the past or a prediction about the future.

They'd barely settled into the cushy, overstuffed chairs and couches in Bella's homey, living room when the landline phone rang. Harper jumped to answer it and several moments later, appeared with the handset and held it out to Sadie.

"Oh, Graaammy," she said, in a high-pitched, teasing whisper. "Time to sharpen your cougar teeth."

Chapter Thirteen

THE NIGHT AIR had chilled enough that Ty could see his breath in the dark. It wasn't unusual, or so he'd been assured, for spring in the Wyoming Rockies to be cold at night. Cole had promised the summer would make up, in beauty and warmth, for the long wait. Ty didn't really care about the weather, but he forced himself to dwell on it rather than what he was about to do.

The four-story apartment building on the outskirts of Wolf Paw Pass looked identical to five others in the complex that housed primarily military and medical families, there because of the VA medical facility and the military training compound twenty miles out of town. Ty entered the airlock-like entry of building number four and stared at a panel of intercoms. His finger hovered over the name Branson—a name and person he didn't know—and he forced himself not to change his mind. This act was likely going to derail his entire plan, but he wasn't usually a coward, and he'd run and hidden, twice now, from Trampas like a middle-schooler avoiding the playground bully. He had to face up to at least one thing in this endeavor.

"Welcome, son, come in."

His great-uncle's disembodied voice, rich, cultured and familiar as if he'd heard it yesterday, preceded a long buzzer granting Ty entrance. He opened the door, took an elevator to the third floor, and searched out apartment 305 in far too short an order.

Trampas, never prone to more than the perfect amount of emotion, gave Ty time for two composing breaths before answering his knock. And then he was there: eighty-six but looking many years younger, built less like a tank than a streamlined Hummer, boxy and sturdy but lithe, of medium height and possessed of a full head of silver-gray hair pulled back into an enviably thick pony tail. His eccentric uncle.

A rush of warmth filled Ty in spite of himself.

"Ty. My boy," he said simply, his eyes shining.

"Hello, Trampas."

The apartment Ty entered was clean, modern, and sparse. Since Trampas was only subleasing it from an enlisted soldier for a matter of weeks, nothing in the space reflected him except a pile of books on a coffee table and a pair of shoes at the side of the door. He always traveled light and lived neatly if a bit on the outdated side of fashion.

"I was surprised you not only found me but were willing to come," Trampas said. "I was fully prepared to play sleuth for as long as it took to find you. Come, sit down. Tell me what you wanted me to know."

Two bottles of Wolfheart, the local craft beer, sat on the coffee table, and Ty raised a brow. "Beer? What happened to tea and crumpets."

"That shows how long it's been since we sat and talked. You're remembering the old college teas with my student advisees. Of course there was no beer then—doesn't mean I didn't like it. This is not bad. Have you had it?"

"Yeah. It's decent."

Small talk—not what Ty wanted. He sat, and Trampas handed him an opener. Ty popped the bottle cap off. Before he needed to jump into the meat of his visit, Trampas did it for him.

"You're working for the Crocketts, you said. Has that been a good thing?"

"No."

The unflappable Trampas paused halfway to a draught from his bottle, his arm poised in midair. "Oh?"

"I never originally intended to take a job at the ranch. Once Cole Wainwright convinced me to come, however, it seemed like providence. I could spend a couple of months, learn the lay of the land, and take care of business. As it turns out, the Crocketts aren't easy to keep at arm's length. They're serially friendly."

"And Grace?"

"My biggest problem."

"What is all of this really about, son?" Trampas took his drink and set the bottle back down.

"This."

From the same folder he'd brought to Drew Metcalf's days before, Ty pulled out a copy of the letter he'd given to the lawyer.

"This was written by your father, Simon. I found it only six months ago."

"I thought you'd found some family documents several years back," Trampas said. "I'd heard you traveled out here back then to stake a claim."

"I had some third-hand journal account written by *my* father, and I came out here for a week about two and a half years ago," Ty admitted. "But the story about Simon and Eli

Crockett was so convoluted and filled with inconsistencies that I couldn't find out anything. Only by digging through Simon's papers in three different places did I find this letter. I've had it authenticated, Trampas. It proves that your father was swindled out of his land."

"And exactly what do you think can be done about it?"

Fifteen minutes later, Ty had introduced Trampas to his plan and told him about Drew Metcalf.

"I have a daughter now," he finished. "I didn't plan her, but she's pretty much the most important thing in the world. I'll be damned if I'm going to let her be raised the way I was. She deserves a good name and the best future I can give her. If that means gambling a little with a family like the Crocketts—good a family as they are—then so be it."

His great uncle sat silently but stared at him as thoughtfully and critically as the Crockett girls did their horses. Ty squirmed but withstood it. Finally Trampas nodded ever so slightly.

"I think you should tell them."

"Of course I should tell them," Ty growled. "But I have two lawyers telling me to wait until I know for sure this whole thing is even going to warrant a court hearing. Why ruffle their feathers if nothing ever happens?"

"But you think something will."

"My lawyer thinks a judge will at least hear the arguments. I had no intention of getting close to the family."

"And Grace?" Trampas asked again.

Ty said nothing for a very long time, tempted to brush her off, tell his uncle she wasn't important, but the man was far too astute for that. Besides, if Ty had any hope of getting Trampas on his side, lying would get him nowhere.

"She's special." He looked to the floor. "And she's the one I'll tell first."

Trampas gave another small nod and almost looked satisfied. "You haven't asked me why I tracked you down," he said.

"Because your kids are so damn near perfect you don't need to butt into *their* lives, you crazy old man."

Trampas's chuckle proved he'd heard Ty's fondness through the words. Whatever the outcome of this meeting, Ty was suddenly glad he'd come.

"You aren't all that far off." The "crazy old man" smiled. "But that's not all. I've kept tabs on you your whole life because you're not like your mother or your father, your grandfather *or* my father—as far as I ever knew him. Your whole life you've tried to break from that mold—to varying degrees of success. But you've never ever slipped into the darkness that Oliver found. Or your mother, who only ever saw men acting badly and so married your father. Thank the Lord he was never able to scar you."

"Oh, I don't know."

"You're a good man. The fact that you're here proves it."

"No." Ty took a nervous breath. "Because I'm here to ask you to lie for me."

"I know."

Ty stared. "What?"

"You're asking for a lie of omission. You want me to keep your secret even though I have my own connection to the Crocketts."

"I ... ah." Ty shrugged, out of justifications. "Yes."

"What's your timeline on this?"

"Within the next week or so I should hear from the lawyer. If there are papers to be served, it'll be time to tell."

More silence followed. Trampas cupped his chin and scratched his lower jaw thoughtfully. Finally he straightened.

"Here's the deal. I don't believe you need this land you're after, but I understand why you think you do. Truth to tell, it would be interesting to solve the old mystery. So. I won't *tell* anyone that I know you—but if they ask for any reason I won't lie directly. The day you hear from that lawyer about court papers, I'll give you a full day to figure out how to tell them. If you don't, then I will help you."

"By that you mean do it for me?"

"Oh no. It's your job, Ty. But I will make sure you do it. They're good people."

"Yeah." Ty's heart sat lighter in his chest. "They are."

Ty walked up Paradise's main driveway from the barn and looked into the cold, brilliant sky. He'd heard descriptions of feeling alone and insignificant in the universe, but he'd chalked up such existential nonsense to the whining of philosophers and malcontents. Now he knew different. He was a mere ant trudging beneath the stars, insignificant to anyone but himself.

After talking to Trampas it felt as though shit had suddenly gotten real, and all he could think was how hurt Grace was going to be once she learned the truth. Ty stopped at the top of the driveway and once more looked up. He needed to let Grace go. It had to be strictly about Lucky from now on. In two years he'd gone from being the universe's most clueless father to one of the most obsessed, and he would have adored his kid even without the genetic testing. The fact that their DNA matched only made his love and sense of responsibility stronger than tempered steel.

He continued to the front porch, hoping Lucky wouldn't

mind walking home instead of driving. After tonight, he simply wanted to spend the extra time with her.

"I understand you stood me up for a date tonight."

Ty jumped three inches and stumbled on a porch stair. Grace's soft, kind laugh floated through the chill air, and she came into view, standing tucked into a far corner, a quilt wrapped around her shoulders.

"Sorry. Thought you saw me."

"Nope." His pulse took its sweet time slowing. "You're no more than a ghostly little shadow."

He reached the top step, and she moved from the corner. "I'd have gone. Just so you know."

"Gone?"

"To a movie. Even a brilliant five-year-old can't keep anything secret."

"Brother," he mumbled. "Sorry. Not very classy to hear it through the kid."

"You're a dad. It's hard to be classy."

"Well that's disheartening."

She giggled again. "You are handsome, though."

"Are you still on those drugs?"

"I like these drugs," she said. "Effective but I'm in perfect control of my faculties."

"I doubt that." He put an arm gently around her shoulders and led her to an oversized wooden swing. "You don't seem to know who you're talking to."

"Of course I do. I was waiting for you."

He stared, dumbstruck.

She ducked from his hold and sat, but then pulled him down beside her. Once he settled against her uninjured side, the seat cradled him, it had been crafted so well.

"Nice swing." He raised his brows, looking for any clue as to what was going on in her Vicodin-laced brain.

"My dad made it for his and Mom's thirtieth anniversary. He didn't have a lot of time to work with his hands, but when he did, he did it well."

In her quilt she looked like a cozy pup wrapped up by a loving owner. He wanted to pick her up and wrap her tighter.

"Everything I hear says your father was an impressive man."

"He was. Hard as a brick wall, but fair."

"Cole's impressive as well. And fair as a boss."

"He is. I take nothing away from him. But if you want to know how this ranch really got turned around after my father died, just spend a few days with Harper. She's the one who's turned an entire section of the southwest corner into a successful wind farm. She picked the acreage that's almost ready to be certified as organic pasture for beef, goats, and, poultry. She's the one who has liaisoned with the town and turned the Crockett name back into a trendsetting, innovative brand. Then there's Mia. The mustangs for veterans program was her idea. It's got a waiting list and has been written up in the national press. Like we were saying yesterday morning, this is the legacy Great-Grandpa Eli left us."

Legacy.

He'd been about to start feeling guilty again, but the word fortified him. He'd been truthful with Trampas: He had nothing against this generation of the family, but the way they revered their flimflam man of an ancestor galled. With grim determination, he changed the subject.

"Why were you waiting for me?"

She hesitated thoughtfully. When she placed her hand on his thigh, he nearly shivered out of his skin. All vestiges of annoyance fled, and heat shot straight up the muscle and fanned out through his groin, his belly, and into his chest.

"I wanted a chance to get you alone one more time before you picked up Lucky." She didn't *sound* fuzzy. "I never thanked you for yesterday at the clinic. I know you went above and beyond for me even though I was a terrible patient. You never got ruffled or frustrated, and because of that I was fine. To be honest?" She quirked a cute little smile at him. "I had a pretty good time—despite the lump on my forehead." She touched a spot just below her hairline. "How's yours?"

"I haven't thought about it once since it happened." He touched his own forehead and felt no tenderness. "Nothing. The perks of having a hard head."

"Maybe. But it protects a guy who, I think, is actually pretty soft inside. I see you with your daughter—I see your daughter, in fact. A kid doesn't turn out nice if her parent is a jerk."

"Even if he's taught her how to gamble?" He lifted his brows.

She searched his face and, as with Trampas, he withstood the scrutiny. She shocked his system once more by leaning in and placing a soft kiss on the corner of his mouth. "My grandmother played poker." She shrugged. "I realize I was too judgmental, and I'd rather go to a movie with a poker player than anywhere with a sanctimonious religious fanatic."

"Uhh, okay. You can't tell me there isn't a story in that."

This time the Vicodin clearly giggled. "I have this reputation."

"I've heard."

"Yeah, everybody's heard. 'Grace is nice.' 'Grace wants a good Christian man.' 'Don't tell Grace *that* joke.' It all translated during college into setting me up with the most rigid guys anyone could find. The last guy was a real doozy."

"So it's not true that you want a perfect religious man?"

She sighed. "I'd like a man of faith and conviction—but not a judgmental fanatic. Then I met you. Everything about you is the opposite of what I thought I wanted. But I like you."

Ty scratched the back of his head with a laughing snort. "I have no idea how to take that."

"Why don't you just take me to a movie, and not analyze it?" She batted her lashes. He had to laugh outright.

"Now?"

"It's maybe a *little* late now."

"Tomorrow it is, then."

"Perfect. Why don't you come and watch Lucky take a riding lesson in the afternoon, and we could go after that?"

"Whoa. A riding lesson?"

"Subject to her father's approval." Grace offered a smile. "She's dying to ride, but since she didn't grow up around horses, we think we should see what her comfort and skill levels are before tossing her on a pony out in the open. She's going to ask you tonight."

"The little con artist. Told you, she knows exactly when to play her cards." He colored slightly, still wary of a poker reference that included Lucky, but Grace only shook her head.

"She loves animals, that's all. We understand because we grew up with animals around us every minute and were slapped on horses from the time we were two. We knew as babes how to push away a jumpy dog or cuddle a barn kitten. I'm afraid you don't have any allies in the no-animals department."

"I like animals fine." Ty relaxed back into the seat. Normally tension rose through his spine whenever Lucky started in on the dogs, cats or, recently, horses. But Grace made the subject nonthreatening. "I think animals need to come into a stable home, though. I want Lucky to learn exactly how to care for a pet, and it's hard to do when she's not settled herself and having to move all the time."

"Are you planning to go somewhere soon?"

He shifted and gazed over the porch rail to the yard. Like it or not, this woman was becoming more special than any other he'd ever known. He might be learning a lot about ranching, but he was being a gigantic ass in the process. He'd promised Trampas he'd tell her soon. He dreaded "soon."

"I have dreams of owning my own place," he said carefully. "I'd like to give Lucky something more permanent than an apartment in Vegas or a ranch hand's quarters." He turned back to Grace who nodded slowly in understanding. "I get close to being able to make that happen and then things go south. I lose a job, or a chance at a tournament, or I have to use savings to pay for a car repair—three times in the last two years, by the way."

"But you're trying. And you know you can stay here and work until you've got what you need. I happen to know Cole thinks you're a great hand."

The compliment meant to assure him only made him feel worse.

"Good to know. Thanks."

"So what's wrong?" She peered at him and he straightened abruptly, giving her as easy a smile as he could muster.

"Nothing. Sometimes I'm like a damn girl, getting lost in daydreams."

"And ..." She stared at him. "Why are girls equated with daydreams?"

He huffed out a breath. He couldn't win. "C'mon, give me a break. It's a stupid guy thing. Men live by stereotypes, not generally by dreams; girls not only know how to dream, they can turn them into reality. That's all I meant."

"I call that a very nice save."

"Yeah. Well it's time to change to a different very nice subject before I dig myself deeper. How's your elbow?"

"It's not bad, really. The Vicodin does help."

"And you think you'll be up for helping Lucky *ride* tomorrow?"

"Harper will be there, too, if you okay the lesson. We might cart Mia down to the barn on the four-wheeler and make an outing of it. She's completely stir-crazy—used to going a mile a minute. I'm not planning to be drugged up tomorrow anyhow, so I think I'll be able to keep an eye on all my charges."

"Unfair. How am I supposed to ruin the dreams of three sisters and my five-year-old daughter by saying no?"

"I can't answer that question for you, Mr. Garraway." She batted her eyelashes. "Seriously. If you have any objections to your daughter getting on a horse, we'll figure something else out."

"My only concern is that I don't want her falling off and getting hurt."

"Valid—especially after you watched me do exactly that, but I promise we make all our kids wear helmets," she said. "And I have a feeling *your* kid isn't going to fall off very easily."

"I'd like her to ride." He felt lighter after saying the simple words. In a funny way, it felt as if he was giving Lucky a first little root hold in the mountains of Wyoming. "I'd love her to have ponies and dogs and cats of her own someday. We both have a lot to learn first."

"Then we'll start tomorrow."

"All right. And after that—dinner and movie."

"The perfect traditional date." She pulled her blanket tighter again. "But …" Thoughtful wrinkles creased her forehead. "Does it have to be a blood-and-guts movie?"

"*Have* to be?" He grinned into her suddenly earnest face. "No, it doesn't *have* to be bloody. But in the interest of fairness, does it have to be a sappy romance?"

"Oh, funny. Violence for the boy versus romance for the girl; I do like a good cliché." She shook her head. "I guess we can find a compromise between bloody and sappy."

Innocent happiness filled her face like a warm, beckoning light. She really was a good girl, he thought, way better than he deserved. But he couldn't resist her. One minute she was lecturing him, the next she was a flower he wanted to save. She didn't accept any form of alpha play-acting from him, but he had the feeling that if he charged up on a white horse, she'd swing behind him and let him gallop her to safety—wherever she imagined that was.

So much for letting her go.

"Personally?" He reached for her hand and squeezed it, loving the feel of its delicate strength in his palm. "I don't think there's been a single cliché thing about how we've gotten to know each other. From poker, to a mountain lion attack, to finding you completely attractive in a hidden fireplace …"

"Attractive?" The innocence remained, now coupled with a hint of surprise.

"Very … attractive."

He didn't plan the kiss, but he dropped her hand and found his clasped gently to the sides of her head, his mouth locked with hers. Before he could think better of his actions and pull away, her lips yielded like soft, grassy ground beneath two lovers.

Every single thing they did not have in common evaporated in the exploration Grace not only allowed but invited. Pleasure rolled through Ty's body like thunder, and his fingers wove through her hair. His tongue slipped between her lips, and the taste of mocha and sweet mint met him. She tasted him back, gentle suction fleeting, tempting. Shivers coursed into his stomach and tugged lower and deeper until he shifted in in response to his timeless male reaction.

A groan escaped him when Grace's hand floated to his cheek, and she stroked the corner of his mouth with a thumb, riding his jaw with her fingertips. Desire flared so hot and hard, he had to pull away.

"Do I need to apologize?" he murmured.

"Hardly." Her words barely rose above a whisper. "I'm afraid I used you."

"For what?" He brushed her long, caramel-blonde hair behind her ear.

"To erase the memory of a really unattractive kiss I got a couple of weeks ago. Sorry, my turn to be the opposite of classy."

"Well at least tell me it worked."

"Oh." She licked her bottom lip lightly. "It worked."

He swallowed. "Another point for the bad boy?"

She stood without a reply, smiled a little shyly, and took his hand. "I think it would be safer if we go in and get your daughter now."

"*I* think it will be safer if you go in first. Although mentioning my daughter after what just happened will take care of at least one growing problem."

A quizzical furrow creased her brow again, and then her eyes opened into full moons. She muffled a squeak of laughter.

"I can't tell you how proud my sisters would be that *I* got you to say that. And that last date I mentioned? He would start a prayer chain for my soul."

"You know what? I don't even know this guy's name and he annoys the shit out of me. You gave me a hard-on when I kissed you—if you kissed him and he *didn't* get one, he has more problems than religion can fix."

Even in the pale porch light, he could see pink rise in her cheeks. For one moment he thought he'd gone too far, despite intending to shock her a little. But she only closed her eyes briefly and took a visible deep breath.

"Heaven help me—that's about fifty points for the bad boy."

"Oh? And how do I redeem my points?"

Unreleased laughter sparkled in her eyes. "Since we're not mincing words, I'll say it outright. Hard-on or no, I don't do sex before marriage. But I'll come up with a list you *can* choose from." She turned for the door. "Come in when you can."

He stared in utter discombobulation. Who in the world was this woman? No sex before marriage? Honestly a virginal throwback to an unremembered age? No. She'd kissed like a fantasy and countered his innuendo with bravado. She couldn't be completely innocent.

He sat on the swing for a solid five minutes, finding it very difficult to calm his confused body when all he could think about was the taste of her on his lips. Finally, he stood and hauled in a deep, fortifying breath.

No sex?

Let her say what she wanted—he didn't need to sleep with her, intoxicating as the thought was, to know that one more powerful kiss with Grace Crockett was enough to desire for the moment.

***

When she entered the living room, Grace knew everyone could see the heat in her face and the desire that had to be shining in her eyes. Her heart still raced, and her pulse pounded through her limbs despite the calm she'd faked for Ty.

She wasn't a child. She wasn't naive or ignorant or sheltered. But she'd never been with anyone who talked the way Ty Garraway had just done. He hadn't shocked her, but her reaction to his kiss and those blunt, hotly stimulating words had. Shocked her because, if she'd followed her heart, she would have dived straight back into his arms.

"Well, hello there." Her mother looked up from a magazine, her reading glasses perched on the bridge of her nose. "Thought we'd lost you."

"Ty's here. He'll be in in a second. I was just … telling him about Lucky's evening."

The fib almost stuck in her throat, but no way was she divulging the truth. Lucky looked up, and her hands stilled, the short metal knitting needles in her hands poised in midair. Grandma Sadie sat beside her.

"Look, Grace!" Lucky held up an inch and a half of a dark orange, garter-stitch mini scarf hanging between her needles. Grandma had, once again, succeeded in teaching a new generation to knit.

"Oh, Lucky, how fantastic! You got that far so fast?"

"She's a natural, like you were." Grandma Sadie nodded contentedly.

"A natural what?"

Ty strode into the room and Grace's breath hitched. He brushed his fingers lightly over the shoulder of her injured arm and gave her a smile fueled by a secret smolder in his eyes.

"Good as new." She offered a tiny smile that only fanned the smolder into a dancing spark.

He passed her and approached his daughter, staring at the knitting. "Pardon me for being ignorant, but what did you do with Teagan Garraway?"

She giggled. "I *am* Teagan Garraway, Daddy."

"No. No, I don't think so. Teagan is interested in cars and spittin' and ice cream and poker. By her own insistence, she does not do girlie activities. This looks suspiciously girlie."

"Grandma says anybody can knit. And Grace can knit anything, even socks and mittens and lace. I'm knitting a scarf for Walter."

"Walter your bear?"

She nodded and went back to the needles, her tongue poking from between her lips in concentration. Ty looked around the room at the five women, and Grace led the gentle laughter.

"She saw me working on a pair of fingerless gloves," she said. "And she wanted to know how the needles worked. I can knit, but Grandma Sadie is the master teacher."

"And you ... *like* this?" Ty asked, the end of his question lifted in a hopeful note.

"It's easy," Lucky said. "It's pretty fun."

"There is one other thing," Ty said. "This ..." He pointed at Lucky's head with a forefinger and made a circle like a halo above her hair, pulled back into a tidy French braid. "Teagan Ann Garraway has this pretty but wild hair that she'll barely wear in a ponytail. And she likes baseball hats. I think I'm seeing a hair band?"

Lucky stopped knitting and sighed, looking up at her father

with long-suffering patience. "Grace told me that a braid would make the hats stick on better and the hair band would keep in the ends of hair and make it look like I'm a soccer player or a girl baseball player. Or a dressage rider. Can I take a riding lesson tomorrow?"

Ty ran a hand across his cheeks and laughed. "I don't know what the devil a dressage rider is, but if it wears a pretty braid, I'm all for it." He caught Grace's eye and made a helpless plea. "She was supposed to be working for you all, not attending charm school. What the heck did you do to my kid?"

Chapter Fourteen

"USE YOUR LEGS to get him trotting again," Mia called.

Mounted on Aiden Thorson's lithe little pinto pony Panda, Lucky obeyed and gave a kick with her heels. Panda hopped into his trot, and Lucky laughed as her seat bounced an inch sideways off the saddle. "Remember how Grace showed you how to rock like on a rocking horse? There! Super good job. Now give him another little kick."

Lucky gave a squeal of delight as Panda surged gently forward into a lope. "Look! Daddy, look! Grace, look!"

Panda, the perfect lesson pony, loped along the fence. Lucky grabbed the saddle horn for balance.

"Woo-hoo!" Ty cheered from outside the round pen where he stood with Harper.

"Panda should feel smooth as a real rocking horse now," Mia said.

Lucky sat several strides in perfect rhythm with the pony and giggled. "It's fun!"

"You look like a real cowgirl, sweetie," Grace added. "Give him another little nudge with your left foot. Remind him to keep going."

Lucky, with her little safety helmet and shiny boots less than a month old, her Paw Patrol sweatshirt and purple jeans, definitely made a mishmashed cowgirl picture, but the grin on her face was that of a genuine horse-lover. After just under an hour in the saddle, Grace knew the girl was irrevocably hooked.

Mia had her lope the opposite direction and then stop and walk to the middle of the ring. Grace took the pony's bridle while Mia gathered her crutches and stood.

"Hey, you," Grace said. "That was awesome. What do you think, Mia? She could probably go on a trail ride pretty soon."

"I definitely think so. Maybe another lesson or two until Grace can go along with you when her elbow is better."

"Couldn't I go now?" Lucky's eyes begged.

"I think maybe your legs and Panda's need a little rest after this," Grace said. "We'll show you how to take care of a pony after you're done riding. There's lots more to being a cowgirl than just having fun galloping around. It's fun to hang out with your horse, too. Come on and ride out to your dad. See what he thought."

Lucky had the steering part of riding at the walk almost mastered. She guided Panda expertly around the outside of the fence and halted in front of Ty and Harper.

"Wow," Harper said. "Have you really never ridden a horse before?"

"Just those fake ones at stores where you put in a quarter and they go back and forth."

"Well you're a natural."

"Hey, kid." Ty held his palm high where she could easily smack it with hers. "You done good, Luckster."

"It was awesome!"

"So were your teachers." Ty found Grace's eyes with his and nodded. "Thanks. You were great with her."

"Well, you're welcome. But you can see why I had Mia do most of the lesson. She's a natural with new riders. I'm too technical."

It was true. Good riding was far more than kicking a horse in the sides and asking it to go faster, but the subtleties of leg cues and shifting seat bones were far beyond what a beginner needed to know. Grace's OCD was better suited to tweaking advanced skills. Still, she was a good cheerleader.

"I appreciate both of the teachers. Thanks."

She could read the honest gratitude in his eyes. The same eyes that had seared her with blazing attraction the night before now captured hers with soft pleasure over the excitement of a child. It was no wonder she found him so confusing. From gambler to lover to father.

An otherworldly techno-tune from her rear pocket filled the air and Harper started to laugh.

"What's *that?*" Ty asked.

"The theme from *Doctor Who*," Harper said. "Raquel's favorite show in the entire world. Sounds like the triplets are finally checking up on each other."

Grace's heart double-thumped. She didn't want to talk to her sister yet. She'd wanted to wait until after she'd spoken to the banker and had more definite plans. Everything Grace did now would affect Raquel and Kelly personally and financially, and presenting her plans in the best light and kindest way was her top priority. But she couldn't ignore this call—Raquel would hound her all weekend out of worry if nothing else.

Grace sent Mia an uncertain glance and pulled her phone from her pocket.

"Rocky!" she answered in her best fake cheery voice.

"Hey, Gracie Pat." Raquel's voice smiled at her through the

magic of technology. "I missed you so much this morning I had to call. How's life in Paradise?"

Grace scanned the excited little grouping around her, and compared the contentment of the moment to the tracings of tension that sprouted from the thought of a morning at Triple Bean. "You know? It's really good," she said. "Everyone is great."

"Are you making Mia behave herself? Stay off that foot? Take care of our niece or nephew?"

"Uh..." Grace laughed. "Well, I'm letting her teach a riding lesson. Baby is big and Mia's beautiful and gets around pretty well on a four-wheeler. I needed her help because of the sling on my arm."

"Jiminy Christmas, Grace. This is your definition of great? What's going on?"

"It's fine, really," she said. "I went out mending fences with Cole, got charged by a mama mountain lion, and dislocated my elbow when I fell off the horse. She was young and she spooked. No big deal."

"Oh my God! What is wrong with you?" Raquel started to laugh as well.

While Harper helped Lucky dismount, and Ty helped Mia onto the four-wheeler so they could head back to the barn, Grace followed behind, explaining the accident to her triplet and making light of the adventure. By the time she caught up with the group, she at least had Raquel convinced that in a day or two the elbow would be fine and there was no crisis.

"So, the real question is, how are you feeling otherwise?" Raquel asked. "We're worried about you in general, you know. Mountain lions aside."

Under any other circumstances, Grace would have wrapped her sister's warm words around herself like a comforting blanket. How she was going tell them she missed them, too, but wasn't coming back, however, made the next words all but impossible.

"I miss you guys," she began, and headed away from the barn for privacy. "I planned to call you with an update very soon. I have an appointment with a banker to talk about an idea I've got. Do you want to hear it?"

Hesitation on the other end of the call gave Grace the first inkling of how this was going to go.

"I don't know, Gracie. *Do* I want to hear it?"

"I hope so. I know it will affect you, but I think you'll be interested and I do want your input. And Kel's, too. I need you both."

"Okay …"

"Do you remember the old cabin in Wolf Paw Pass that Great-Grandpa built back in 1918? The one that's been twenty different things through the years?"

"Yeah?"

"Well, it's empty, and it's got so much more character than I remembered." She paused for courage. "I think it would make a wonderful specialty restaurant, and I think I can use the ranch as collateral to get a loan and not have to have you guys buy me out or put out any money to take away from Triple Bean."

More silence.

"I see," Raquel said quietly. "So it's official. You're leaving."

"Rocky, listen. You know how much I want to try some ideas that just won't work at Triple Bean. I don't want to change that perfect formula, and I don't want to jeopardize the business, so I'd like to see if I can make it work without costing you two anything. It's time for me to see if I can be a leader or if I'm really best at being a first mate."

"I wasn't aware we had ever designated rankings, Grace. Since when are you an unequal partner? That's the part of this I don't understand." Raquel's voice squeezed around the words like a fist.

"That's not what I mean," Grace said. "I don't want to hurt you; not at all. I would really, really love your blessing to try a wacky idea."

Her sister's voice tightened another turn. "I didn't think you were serious about never coming back. I feel a little blindsided."

"C'mon, Rocky. We had this discussion before I left. I made suggestions all along and they were never implemented. I did feel like second or third in succession to the top. You knew what I came here to do."

"I understand you wanting to take time to regroup and rethink some of your ideas. But striking out on your own? That's close to traitorous, isn't it?"

Grace's confidence began its inexorable slide downward.

"You know what, Raquel? I'm trying hard to make sure this doesn't get personal. I completely understand why my ideas didn't work in our business model, and I understand why I have the position I do in our company. I'd like to remain part of that company, but if you think I've turned traitor or I'm doing this purposely to hurt you, then you can buy me out at whatever you think is fair. For all I care at the moment, it can be one dollar and I'll call it good. You let me know what you'd like me to do. I've got to get back to Mia. We'll talk later."

"Grace, for crying out loud. This isn't like you."

"Maybe that's a good thing for a change. Look, say hi to Kel."

She'd never hung up on anybody in her life, and though this first time was a gentle push of the button done without anger, her mortification once Raquel was gone made her numb with disbelief.

How could she have left a conversation hanging unresolved? That went against every principle of kindness she claimed to believe in.

Hastily she brought up Raquel's number and stared at her sister's face. At her own face—with a nose wider by centimeters, cheeks rounder to those who knew the triplets best, and eyes one shade of brown darker than Grace's. She and her sisters were so closely attached that this fight ripped at Grace's heart. Still, her finger hovered over the call button and refused to press it.

Tears rolled down her cheeks, hot, regretful, and angry. She shut off her phone screen, sank to a squat out of sight of the barn door and covered her face with quivering fingers. Why wouldn't Raquel just wish her well? Why wasn't Kelly jumping in to keep them together? They'd been through too much for a change, however major it seemed, to split them apart.

"Hey, hey? What in the world?" Two solid hands gripped her shoulders unexpectedly, and Ty's worried voice sent a warm, feathery whisper into her ears. "Grace?"

She let herself fall unceremoniously onto her rear end and sat heavily in the grass, resting her elbow on her thighs and continuing to cover her face with her good hand.

"I can't do this."

"What? C'mon, honey, what happened?"

"I can't start this restaurant on my own. It's hurting my sisters, and everything is such a mess. I can't stand messes."

"I know. I know." He chuckled and sat beside her, stretching his long legs out while he put both arms around her shoulders and hugged. "Listen to me. I don't know your sisters except by reputation, and I get that they're wonderful and they're your best friends. That's great—but it doesn't mean they have anything to say about *your* dreams. Did you stiff them for money?" He nudged her for an answer.

"No. Of course not."

"Did you do anything to defame their restaurant?"

"No."

"Did you murder anyone they care about?"

"What the heck, Ty?"

He laughed. "I'm just trying to tell you that you don't owe them anything. I know you'll say 'loyalty,' but you can give them that and still start your own restaurant."

"We've never been apart like this."

"'Bout time you tried it."

She stared at the ground.

"I was about to give in. Tell Raquel I'd come back and work things out. And then, I just got pissed off. I always apologize to her. I always go back and see her point. It's a power she has over all of us—and she doesn't honestly know she wields it."

"You don't think outside the box easily, do you?"

She shook her head. "I like order, and I like things to be arranged and to make sense. I'm not spontaneous. What in heaven's name possessed me to start this insane process?"

"Stop right there. Don't start talking like that."

"But if I can't stop falling apart every time I talk to my sisters, this won't be worth it. I need their support."

"No. You don't. What you need is to learn how to live with a little chaos. You need to start stepping out of your comfort zone."

"Sure," she mumbled and wiped her eyes. "Clearly a very easy thing for me to do."

"You just need a guide." He placed a finger beneath her chin and lifted her face to his. Gently, once again with no warning, he kissed her. No hot invitation followed. No tongue beckoned for hers to come play. No moves on either of their parts took them beyond sweet and comforting, but when he pulled away, she reeled as if he'd beaned her in the forehead again. "I've changed my mind. We'll go out tonight, but we aren't going to a movie."

"Where are we going?" She sniffed the last of her tears away and bent her knees so she could lean forward.

"Practice your poker face." He smiled.

"My po—"

He pressed his finger against her lips, which made her shiver as much as the kiss had.

"Poker face," he repeated. "Five o'clock tonight."

Chapter Fifteen

GRACE STARED INTO the slightly smoky room at the large, round wooden table. On it stood several stacks of poker chips and four unopened boxes of playing cards. Behind it sat a man with a hearty grin, a yellow polo shirt, and the girth of a Volkswagen Beetle.

"Are you kidding me?" She turned to Ty clutching his upper arm. "Not in a million years did I imagine you meant a literal poker face."

"Welcome to life outside the box. Told you you'd dressed perfectly. Beautifully, I might add."

She looked down at the full skirt of her favorite lavender sundress and the fancy cowboy boots she'd paired with it. She shrugged her jean jacket closer. Confidence-building purple, cowboy boots, and denim. She could handle anything—and maybe turn a few heads away from her lack of gambling prowess.

The room in the basement of Dottie's Bistro was a well-known space for large parties and receptions. It wasn't fancy, but the plush navy-blue carpet and freshly painted neutral-colored walls could be dressed up for any event. It was the one spot in town Grace would compete with if her crazy restaurant idea ever came to life.

She'd had no idea Dottie's party room also served as Poker Tourney Central.

"What is it you think I'm going to do here?" she asked.

"Play poker." He grinned. "I'm staking you for a hundred bucks, and you're going to break even. If you do, I'll cook you dinner tomorrow night. If not ..." He shrugged. "You can decide my prize."

She stared in disbelief. "You aren't serious."

"Sure I am. But, I'm not going to force you to do anything. You can turn right around, and I'll chalk this up to a missed opportunity to teach you my poker tricks."

"You have tricks?"

"Like I said—I'm a decent enough player."

"But a hundred dollars? I won't let you do that. If I *was* going to do something this nuts, I can stake my own game."

"You can't. You're saving every penny to put into your new restaurant. This was my idea. And I have faith I won't lose any money."

At that she had to laugh. "So you have this all figured out."

He held up both hands. "I brought you to a poker game. After that I have nothing figured out. Based on your reaction to Lucky's game, and despite what you said yesterday about being able to clean me out of all my matchsticks, I thought playing for real money might be an activity contrary to your personality."

"I might have exaggerated the matchstick brag in the throes of pain," she mumbled, and glanced at the floor.

"Ahhh. See? Lies can trip you up."

She ignored him. "How come I didn't know about this den of iniquity? Dottie's the last person I'd think would allow this." She looked around the mostly empty room, nerves setting in as the heavy-set dealer winked at her, and two other middle-aged men across the room assessed her with skeptical but not unfriendly thoroughness.

"The only people who know about the poker games are people who ask the right questions. Or know somebody. You know me. Dottie has her secrets. She likes a little Texas Hold 'Em action herself now and then. Mind you, she's pretty strict on the rules—no high stakes, which means no buy-ins over a hundred and fifty. No tournaments except small, friendly rivalries. No fighting. No betting anything but the currency agreed upon at the beginning of the game. So no ranches or land or Rolex watches."

"I don't believe this. You're crazy."

"Better than being something worse. A murderer. A liar. An alcoholic."

She stared quizzically at the oddly specific examples, but when he held out his hand she decided her suspicion was merely nervousness. When she laced her fingers through his, calm humor returned.

Twenty minutes later, seven players started the game. From the start, nobody gave Grace a single easy pass or helpful hint. Clearly Ty was still a brand-new member of the group, although they all seemed to like him, and although Grace knew a couple of the men—one of whom was the father of an old school friend, which was more than weird—she would live or die on her own.

It took more effort during the first two hands to keep from showing her nervous shaking than it did to concentrate on the game. After two pots were claimed, Grace was down twenty dollars, Ty had won one hand and Rick the dealer had won the other. Her hyperbole to Ty the day before came home to roost—she did know how to play poker, but she wasn't and never had been the best in the family. She wished with all her heart that Kelly—the only one who'd been able to beat their father when he'd been alive—could have been standing behind her whispering pointers in her ear. But once the game had started, even Ty wasn't allowed to give her hints.

Grace folded the next hand when the best she could do was a pair of fives. She began to plan some kind of prize for when she lost to Ty. His one hundred dollar stake for her was fading fast. She reached for her remaining poker chips and started straightening the short columns.

To her surprise, Ty reached across the table and popped his fingers over her hand.

"Leave them." He winked.

"Excuse me?"

"We're outside the box, remember? Leave them uneven— just the way things in the cottage are going to be once you start ripping the insides apart. Chaos."

"They're poker chips for crying out loud." She scowled.

"Try it. If they start to drive you nuts, just kick my shoe under the table."

"I swear to gosh, you *are* insane."

"Maybe. Trust me anyway—this is good for you."

She growled under her breath and turned back to watch the new dealer, Burnsie, deal out the hole cards. She peered under the corners and for the first time her pulse danced. A pair of queens. Ty started the bidding and threw in a ten chip. Grace saw the bet and raised it five. Everyone stayed in play, and Burnsie laid down the flop. Nothing really helped her, but there were two jacks. That raised the odds that someone would already have three of a kind. Still, with her two pair, she kept the faith and stayed in. The turn card was a four of spades. No good at all. She held her breath when the river card was played and got a lesson in keeping a poker face when a third queen showed her face.

Full house.

Not the highest of hands—there'd been two straight flushes and a four of a kind already tonight. But this was more than good enough to bluff with.

Four players folded when the betting went around, leaving her to face a showdown with Ty and jolly-but-shrewd, tank-sized Rick. Ty started humming an ancient Beatles song, "Can't Buy Me Love." He'd done the same thing each time he'd stayed in the last round, and although Grace had zero experience with tells, she was suspiciously certain this was a purposely false one. Something he did so every one of his final hands looked and sounded the same.

"You aren't fooling me," she whispered. "You've got nothing."

"No table talk," he zipped back, and she kicked the sole of his shoe, which made him sputter and garnered sharp looks from the other players.

She forked her index and middle fingers, pointed them at her eyes and then his. Ty only snorted with laughter again, shook his head, and turned back to his cards.

"Raise you five," he said.

She didn't hesitate, just pushed another chip to the middle, along with a second.

"I'm out." Rick laid his cards face down on the table.

"So how good *is* that hand?" Grace forced herself to sit back with a nonchalance she didn't feel.

"Pretty good. How 'bout yours?"

"*Very* good."

She grinned to sell the idea that she couldn't keep her hand a secret. With luck he'd think she was such a newbie that her excitement over a good hand was overtaking her poker face. He rubbed his chin and ran his gaze over her. She warmed beneath his scrutiny.

"I know what I have …" Finally he shook his head. "Nope. I think you're playing me. I call."

She laid down her queens and jacks. "Read 'em and weep." She grinned. "I've always wanted to say that."

"Hmmmpf." He snorted and laid down three eights. "It's all yours, sweetheart. I officially admit I can't read your game yet."

There was mild clapping and a few guffaws from their table mates.

"Told you I could take all your matchsticks."

"Yeah, well, it's way too early for bragging. Let's deal."

She'd won a hundred and seventy dollars in the hand. Unfortunately, it was the only time in the game the cards really fell in her favor. She won a few more smaller hands, but in truth she bet low and lost often. To make matters worse, Ty refused to let her keep exact count of her chips, so her only clue as to whether she was up or down lay in the size of her piles. By the time the game was declared over, she guessed she was close to even, but she really didn't know. Only then did Ty, who had several decent stacks of other players' chips in front him, let her start organizing her winnings.

She counted—twenties, tens, fives, and ones.

"No way," she cried in disbelief. "Recounting."

It came out the same.

"So?" he asked, his eyes sparkling.

"Ninety-nine dollars."

Laughter rolled from him like beer out of a spilled keg.

"You're kidding," he gasped. "I won this little gamble by one dollar? Grace, you are priceless."

"Oh laugh it up, Ace. You're the only one who thinks you're funny."

"Come on. It's hilarious. You played phenomenally for a beginner—a beginner to backroom street poker, I mean—and you basically broke even. It's as good as a win."

"Nice words, but I bet you don't spot me that dollar. You seem like too serious a player for charity."

He shrugged. "Dem's da rules. You'll get me next time. By the way, what's my prize going to be?"

"Holy cow. Mercenary much? I have to think—something worthy of a dollar you can be sure."

Ty pushed his chair back. "Okay, Poker Girl. Time to cash out and go. Thank the nice people for letting you play."

He ducked away laughing when she flicked at his arm with a finger. Then, after doing exactly what he'd suggested but on her own terms, and getting a warm hug from her friend's father, Grace handed her money to Ty.

"You should keep it," he said. "A stipend for putting up with this."

"You need to know one thing about me," she said. "If I don't want to do something, I don't. If I hadn't wanted to play poker, I would have walked away a long time ago. Thanks for staking me; next time—assuming there ever is a next time—I will lose my own dollar."

He nodded. "You're welcome, and it's a deal—losing your own dollar. Although where's the fun of a side wager in that?"

"Maybe I'll stake *you* then."

"Well all right. I'll look forward to it."

"Why, Mr. Garraway. What a perfectly liberated thing for

you to say."

He took her hand without fanfare, led her out a back door and up a short flight of stairs to the street behind Dottie's. Grace looked at all the shop backs facing this rear street and shook her head in disbelief. "An honest-to-goodness secret poker game. At my favorite restaurant. My world as I know it is ending."

"Soon to be second-favorite restaurant." He squeezed her hand.

She cocked her head and eyed him. "Why are you so intent on talking up this restaurant plan? It's like a constant cheerleading assault, but you don't know anything about me."

"Sure I do. I know you're very smart but only have the minimum amount of self-confidence you need to pull this off. I have a definite soft spot for an underdog with a great plan. And your plan is great."

"And I'm an underdog."

"Ah, but you don't have to be. Look at you tonight. You worry too much about what others think. Take a chance. Make a leap. You're afraid of your sisters' reactions, but let me tell you what else I know. You have one of the strongest families I've ever seen. You don't just abandon each other because you're angry. You stick up for each other. Your sisters aren't going to stay mad at you for trying this."

"You gleaned all that after knowing my family for a month and me for a week?"

"Yes, because you're also not a secretive family. And I don't mean that in a bad way. It's made it easy to get to know you despite our rough start. You all look for the truth in people and in situations. I'll be honest—I didn't want to come and work here. For a lot of reasons. But now I think it's one of the best places I could have fallen into not just for me but for my daughter."

The sincerity in his voice touched her. He'd moved from teasing to serious in the space of moments. There was even a touch of vulnerability in his tone.

"That's high praise. My family is far from perfect, and it keeps morphing in the weirdest ways—adding in an old childhood friend, a therapist who brought a whole flow of wounded veterans with him, and a one-legged rodeo champion."

"Alec." Ty laughed. "I'm looking forward to meeting your other brother-in-law. He sounds like a force."

"That's an understatement. He can do things most people with two legs wouldn't try, all while charming the socks off a horse. That's what I mean. We're weird, but we're strong together. That's why fighting with my sisters is hard."

"You don't know what family fighting is, believe me." Again he squeezed her hand, and she returned it—loving the warmth of his touch but concerned with the tinge of bitterness that filtered through his words.

"There's a story in that," she said gently.

"The story is that your family helps make you. The non-support in my family goes back as many generations as the support in yours does. My own identity stems from a long legacy of poker players, alcoholics, absentee dads and people who don't fight for what's right. Mind you, the only one of those things I appreciate at all is what you saw tonight—I like to play poker. But since Lucky arrived, I'm determined to be the end of the negative part of the cycle."

"I think you've succeeded, Ty."

"Oh not yet. It's a work in progress." The seriousness disappeared at last, and he grinned. "A good woman who'll tell you when you're being a chauvinistic idiot is not a bad thing to add to *my* mix."

She rested her head jokingly on his shoulder as they walked. "Aw shucks, Mr. Garraway. I ain't all that, nor a bag of chips neither."

Ty stopped without warning and pulled her to him so quickly and firmly, he took her breath away. His mouth came down on hers, hot, searching, immediately deep and thrilling. She had no time to decide whether she wanted the assault on her senses or not—the desire that blew over her like an unexpected thunderstorm decided for her. She sought his tongue, pressed to stretch her length against his, worked hard and failed to keep a moan of pleasure from escaping. He pulled his kiss from hers slowly, lingering to grasp her lower lip in his teeth and softly worry it before pressing last light little kisses along its contour.

"Sorry," he said. "But you are definitely the bag of chips. You're the box of donuts a guy should say no to but can't. Salty, sweet—by your own declaration, forbidden. I've been wanting to do that again ever since we did it the first time. To see if it was a fluke."

"It wasn't, was it?"

"Do I need to repeat out loud what you do to me?"

"No," she whispered. "It's too hard. To hear, I mean."

"God, Grace, for a good girl, you say awfully nice bad things. I like it. A lot." He slipped another kiss onto her lips—quick and light.

"I'm not good. I'm …" She hesitated only a second—but this was Ty, so she shrugged. "I'm not even a virgin. Sometimes, though, things happen that cause a person to make big decisions for sanity. For safety. Just because."

"The no-sex decision."

She shrugged again in agreement. "Yeah. That."

His next words came out slowly, carefully, and he ran one thumb from the corner of her mouth to her cheek. "What happened, Grace? Who hurt you and how? Is he still around to be pounded into a pulp?"

"Oh no, no, that's not it. Thank God." She lifted her good arm and placed her forefinger on his lips, warmed by the depth of concern in his eyes. "It wasn't me who had a bad experience; it was Raquel."

"Was she—?"

"Raped? No. Although only because she has two sisters who can all but read her mind. Weird things happen when you're a triplet. Raquel had dated a guy her senior year of high school who came to visit her during our first year of college. She trusted him, but Kelly and I never liked him much. He took her out after gushing all over in front of us how much he'd missed her, how much he needed her and wanted her and what a great time they were going to have. Long story short, Kel and I let them go, but then we both knew without a doubt something was going to go very wrong. So, we played Rizzoli and Isles and tracked them down. We found her fighting him off in the car outside a motel about ten miles from campus. He'd locked her in and was in the process of undressing her. Suffice it to say, we used a tire iron to smash his window and, big as he was, he couldn't fight off three angry Crocketts."

A combination of admiration and astonishment filled Ty's eyes. "Crazy! But good for you. Thank heavens it all worked out. I hope the guy got reported."

"He did. When Dad found out, he made sure Raquel pressed charges. The guy never bothered her again."

"But that swore you off of sex?"

"No. My own boyfriend at the time—a guy I'd dated almost a year and a half—one night started teasing me and flirting and making it clear he wanted to have sex. We'd slept together already, but that night, thinking about what had happened to Raquel when she'd said no, I wasn't interested. He got angry and wouldn't stop pushing. I was done. In solidarity, we three sisters made a pact. We were never going to give up control to a man again, and there would be no sex until we found the men we were willing to trust with our whole lives."

"Wow," he said. "Don't get me wrong—I think I understand. But that's a drastic life choice based on one or two guys."

Grace laughed softly. "Of course it is. I admit that vow only lasted a year or so for Kelly and Raquel. And I'm not clinging to a vow either—that was the act of three idealistic, freshmen girls. But, over the years, I found that the decision works for me. It's no longer at all about anger at one or two guys—it's about the gift of choosing to give myself to someone. It's also a little about my faith but even that isn't a 'rule' to me. Mostly it's about looking for the man who gets me and who I can trust, not just with sex but with every part of my life. And someone who trusts me the same way.

"What I will say, is that whatever it is holding me to this desire—to wait—has caused a lot, and I mean a *lot* of teasing over the past five years. There've been too many one-time dates to count, dates with very judgmental men, and one three-month relationship that ended because he didn't want to make it a celibate four."

"This explains a lot, Grace. It makes you unique. It makes you … a little inspiring." He sighed. "It's also mildly depressing since I really did like our two kisses."

Heat flushed her cheeks.

"Clearly I have nothing against kisses." She half-laughed. "In fact, I don't do *that* as much as …" She stopped. It was one thing to talk openly about academic thoughts sex. It was another to delve into her complicated inner desires.

"As much as you'd like?" His brows went up in a hopeful question.

"As much as I'd like," she agreed.

"Sex can mean a lot of different things, you know. What *is* the strict letter of your personal law? I assume it starts with no traditional tab A in slot B?

"Wha—what? Oh my gosh—you're serious." Her eyes widened.

"C'mon." He chided. "It's a euphemism, that's all. But, yeah, I'm serious. What's the line you don't want us guys to cross? No breast touching? No heavy petting? Just kissing? I'm not criticizing, I swear. I want to know how a guy could prove you can trust him."

Her insides scrambled for something logical to say, but there was nothing. "I truly believe I'll know."

"By some kind of magical sign?"

She stopped short. That was precisely what Raquel and Kelly accused her of looking for.

"There's nothing magical. I have faith about that part of things."

"Ah, faith that you'll know Mr. Perfect when and if he comes along? A guy who won't stop you from putting your poker chips in neat stacks."

"Maybe. Is that so wrong?"

"Nope. A little boring maybe."

Boring like a guy who critiqued your iPod playlists and

found them wanting? She had to admit there'd been nothing boring about coming up a dollar short in a poker match with a guy who wouldn't let her keep her poker chips tidy. And, oddly enough, it had stopped bothering her three-fourths of the way through the game.

Before she could tell him so, he lowered his head again to kiss her deeply and thoroughly, until her legs quivered and he pulled away with a groan of his own.

"That might have been a little too dangerous in light of the conversation we just had," he said.

"And we should go home anyway." She set her forehead against his chest until she caught her uneven breath. "It's nine-thirty and we promised Lucky we'd come home for dessert."

"You've given me a lot to think about," he said. "I should probably take Lucky home and forget about these kisses for tonight."

Before she could reply, the phone in his jacket pocket went off, his eyes lit. "That could be the Luckster herself. Or Lil."

"Yeah, I want to know about Lil, too."

"An honest-to-goodness Las Vegas showgirl."

He glanced at his phone, and the lightness in his expression turned dark and concerned in half a heartbeat. He held up one finger and answered the call, turning away. Grace frowned at the few words that followed.

"That's, uh, good news ...I can meet this week ...The seventh? That should be fine. As long as I have time to let them know."

"We'll talk Wednesday then," Ty finished, and a moment later he faced her.

"Everything all right?" She waited for his reply, but he looked, strangely, as if he wanted to sink through the sidewalk concrete.

"Remember the crazy family I told you I have?" he asked at last. "That was a lawyer I'm working with. There's some unfinished probate business one of them left when he died. It's … highly aggravating."

"Ah. Big pain."

"More than you'd believe." He nearly mumbled the words. "A mess of ancient paperwork I just want to be done with."

She nodded and let it go without quizzing him further. When she took his arm he relaxed visibly, but for the first time in two days, she had the old feeling he wasn't quite telling her the whole truth.

Chapter Sixteen

THE LIGHTS WERE on at the ranch house when he and Grace returned, and Ty pointed out the ugly orange Kia Lil drove in the driveway, indicating both Lucky and Lil were still inside.

"Guess you'll have to come in and eat after all." Grace met his eyes with her humor-filled gaze. "Otherwise you'll disappoint two people. We don't have to kiss." She leaned in, squeezing the hand she'd held tightly for the entire drive home, and kissed the side of his mouth. "I'll be good."

"That's too bad. But it does make things less—"

"Don't say 'hard.'"

"Difficult." He turned his head so their lips met and she buzzed a laugh against his mouth.

She was unbelievably different from the tough, earthy women he'd been drawn to in Vegas. How could a woman be smart, independent, and worldly, and yet soft and naïve at the same time? So naïve she claimed she'd recognize a man she could trust when she met him.

God knew *he* was not that man. But that didn't mean he wanted her to think any worse of him than she would once the truth came out. She'd certainly been nothing but honest with him.

"I'll come in. I can't abandon my kid now. But you have to stop treating this as if I'm part of the family. I'm a hired hand dating the boss's sister."

"But that means you are part of the family. The Paradise family, as hokey as that sounds. It's the way hands here have always been treated. Why Bjorn's dad, Leif, never left. He feels ownership in the ranch, too, and passed it down the generations. Something this big can't be run without a lot of family."

As if God's own lightning bolt had nailed him, he felt worse than ever. He wasn't a bad person. He wasn't out to hurt anyone. In his heart he believed he'd landed where he'd been guided to land, and in that sense he'd told Grace the truth. The bend in his branch of the Manterville family tree needed pruning and redirecting, and while he might not be the best representative, he was miles ahead in character from his worthless father.

Ty had his faults—he generally kept jobs no longer than a couple of years because he was always looking for the big chance, and he'd learned to lean on poker for extra income— probably for the same reason. His net winnings tonight, for example, in excess of two hundred dollars, wouldn't hurt when it came to paying Drew Metcalf. But despite looking for easier ways to help himself and now Lucky out, he couldn't fathom ever hurting a woman like Charles Garraway had done.

"Grace!"

His daughter's lithe little body flew through the living room once he and Grace were inside. Lucky threw her arms around Grace's waist and wriggled close. Ty, amused, folded his arms over his chest.

"I see how it is now," he said.

"Hey, sweetie." Grace hugged her back with her good arm.

"This is a lovely greeting. What's up?"

"I finished my scarf, and I learned how to purl. Grandma says I'm ready to make a bigger one, and you can teach me how to do one of the fancy stitches you use."

"Wow. I am totally impressed," Grace said. "You are a fast learner."

"I know," Lucky said in the forthright way it took most people a long time to realize wasn't intentional arrogance. "I like to keep learning new things. It's not boring then."

"Let me see this scarf."

Ty cleared his throat. "Hello to you, too, daughter."

Lucky giggled. "I was getting to you, Daddy."

"Darn good thing." He lifted her off the ground when she came for her hug, and when he wriggled his fingers in her side, she screeched.

"Put me down, put me down!"

He did. Lucky grabbed his hand and then Grace's. "Come on! I want to show you. Oh, and Grandma said, too, I could go to the yarn shop sometime and pick out something fun."

"Oooh, fun! I haven't been there yet this trip. Maybe we can find you some yarn made out of alpaca fiber. It's so soft."

Ty barely heard the exchange. In the throes of combined joy and guilt, he thought he'd gladly spend every penny he'd won tonight on whatever yarn Lucky wanted. Maybe he'd buy her a real alpaca. Maybe then she'd forgive him when all the shit hit the fan. He followed his skipping daughter into the living room where Sadie and Bella sat, their own knitting needles clicking softly.

"Hi, Mom. Grandma," Grace said. "I hear there's an award-winning scarf in here somewhere."

"Hi, honey. Ty. Welcome back," Bella replied. "It's definitely award-winning. Your grandmother has nurtured yet another protégé."

"I heard. 'Grandma Sadie said …' and 'Grandma Sadie told me …' I remember when that was all I could say." She bent and kissed her grandmother. "You're a wonder."

"Look, Grace, look!"

Lucky held up her work, a mini scarf complete with fringes on both ends. It measured about three and half inches wide by two feet long—perfect for a stuffed animal. It was an eclectic mix of knitting and purling, delightful in its randomness and slightly warped edges. Grace made a show of inspecting it with an expert's eye.

"I'm impressed, Lucky," she said. "Hard to believe this is only your first finished piece. It's really good—and totally fun."

Lucky beamed. "I want to make a purple one for Lil."

"Oh! Where is Lil?" Grace looked around.

Ty had all but forgotten her.

"Lil is eating again," Lil said, emerging from the kitchen with three bowls. "About all I can say for myself is that I left enough to share with you two."

"Cottage pudding," Mia said, her voice a sigh. "We were supposed to have company tonight, but he canceled last minute. We'd planned something special."

"Oh?" Grace asked.

"Trampas called again this morning while you all were out with the horses," Grandma Sadie said. "I invited him to dinner even though he said he was coming down with a cold. He called back later and said he really didn't want to spread it. We rescheduled for next weekend."

"I'm sorry," Grace said. "He's okay?"

"He sounded coldish, but he said he went to the clinic and

he's fine."

Once Ty's heartbeat evened out again after its surge when he'd heard Trampas's name, he swore Sadie looked disappointed. But then his mind raced. This was getting too close to real. Was his uncle really sick? Or was he simply putting off having to lie to this family? And if he did have a cold—what had Ty been exposed to and given to Grace?

His life was losing focus.

Lil handed him a bowl and the scent allowed him to forget his worries. He stared at a generous square of pound cake swimming in a pool of chocolate sauce.

"You have to have two pieces," Lil said firmly. "There's also a vanilla version, and no way can you decide which is best without a comparison test."

"I like how you think, Lil." Grace took the other bowl. "This is a family tradition—made on all kinds of special occasions. Which is silly, because it's not elegant and it's not difficult. It's just delicious."

Ty sank into a chair and scooped a spoonful of the saturated cake. It melted in his mouth like decadent candy. "Oh my God," he moaned, sinking to the floor in front of the couch where Lucky and Sadie sat. "What's *in* this?"

"Sugar and vanilla and chocolate," Mia said. "Like she said—it's not fancy."

"You have to serve this at your restaurant," he replied. "It tastes plenty elegant to me."

"Excellent idea," Bella said.

"You really are ahead of yourself with this project." Grace wrinkled her nose at Ty. "Maybe I don't want to share the family specialty."

"Oh pshaw. It came from an old cookbook." Grandma Sadie

waved her hand in the air. "I think it's time to share it. So, speaking of that possibility—you're still going ahead with your plans this week?"

"Yes, I'm meeting with the banker Wednesday," Grace replied. "I'll apply for the small-business loan since you all were so great about using Paradise as collateral." She looked at her sister.

"Of course we were! We're excited for you."

"Then I'm hopeful they'll think this is a good idea," Grace said. "I also have a call into Kevin DeMars about construction. I'll talk to him after I talk to Dan at the bank."

"So, you're serious about this?" Bella asked.

"Crazy or not, yeah. I have to know what will happen if I try. And I really want to get in to the cabin and declutter as much as possible on my own to save money. I want this to be as practical an investment as possible."

"Your first steps have been impressive already," Bella said. "We'll help all we can."

Grace's eyes lit with warm joy, and she reached impulsively for Lucky sitting beside her on the couch, to give her another squeeze. "It's a good night all around, wouldn't you say, Miss Teagan?"

"Yup!"

"You could even say it's a *Lucky* night," Grace teased her.

"That's my name, don't wear it out."

The room responded to her quip with bright laughter.

"Hey, you stole my line, you little mynah bird," Ty said. "It's only for when you say 'Daaa-ad' a million times a night."

His daughter lifted her chin. "Mynahs come from Ceylon, Indonesia, and India. They can learn up to a hundred words but mostly not after they're two. So I'm not a mynah bird. You should call me a little African gray parrot."

Ty snorted and grasped Lucky's ankle. He set his bowl on the floor and tugged his daughter off the couch and into his lap, wrapping her in a hug before covering her mouth with his hand and wriggling his fingers in her side again. She howled and struggled, but not hard enough to get away.

"What animal talks too much?" he asked. "Whatever it is, that's what you are."

"Stop, Daddy! I *like* to talk." Her muffled words filtered through his fingers.

He stopped tickling her but kept his hand over her mouth. Grinning, he looked up to Grace still on the couch. "What can I say? She can surf the web. It's kind of scary."

"Oh, Ty, she's delightful."

"Well, I guess she is that, too." He released her and plopped a kiss on her forehead before letting her up. "But what I planned to say before I was distracted by human African gray parrots, is that if you could use an extra pair of hands when you start your clean-up, I'm available any night once your brother-in-law lets me off for the day."

He caught her eyes and tried not to give away the shimmy of desire that danced through him at her smile. He wanted more of that sunshine, pressed against his lips, laughing into his kiss, breathing lightness into his heart. Something about knowing her feelings on sex made kissing her all the more exciting. She was a taste of something special. Something unique in these days of jaded, common relationships.

On the other hand, she should be considered off-limits, totally forbidden, and he should recant his offer of help, take his daughter and nanny and go home. He needed to sit there until his own meeting Wednesday. According to the phone call earlier, Metcalf had papers for him to sign and a court date. Telling Grace and her family the truth would happen soon.

Wednesday turned out to be a top-ten beautiful mid-spring day. Ty almost regretted having to leave the ranch, since working outside repairing an outbuilding roof had been a warm and sunny treat.

He'd managed to keep his contact with Grace to a minimum for two days—bringing Lucky to the house and leaving without staying to chat. Not that it had been easy. How he could feel so needy for a woman after only eight days was beyond him, and how he could worry about losing her when he didn't even have her made less sense. He went over scenario after scenario of how he would deal with revealing his plan to claim seven thousand acres of her family's land, but everything that sounded logical and fair in his mind, no longer did.

The Crocketts revered their heritage and loved the land passionately. They would fight for their legacy tooth and nail just as he was willing to fight for his. His very faint hope was that the Crocketts' code of ethics was as unwavering as it seemed. Cole ran the business with a fair hand. Grace was a throwback to days of integrity. If he could make them see past the last month to the inherent fairness in his quest, maybe they'd look on the loss of a tiny sliver of property as insignificant.

And maybe trout would fly and birds would make nests in the waters of the Kwinaa River that ran through Paradise Ranch adjacent to "his" land.

No. He would make enemies out of his future neighbors.

Still, he believed the outcome would be worth it: redemption for his family name, a future for his daughter, and a new life. People had to sacrifice for those things—just because it was the twenty-first century and not the early twentieth didn't mean he couldn't start now.

He rang Andrew Metcalf's doorbell at 9:30 a.m., and the Metcalf who greeted him this time was much less buttoned-up and lawyerly than he had been previously—more like a college professor on his weekend off than a smartly groomed man out to impress a client. His blue and green checked dress shirt was rolled at the sleeves, and the tails hung untucked from worn jeans. It made him much more approachable, and Ty, in his own jeans and boots, relaxed.

"Hey, Ty," Metcalf said. "Glad you could make it this morning. Sorry for the casual dress. I'm taking a couple of days off, but I wanted to be sure you got this information right away. I know you're anxious to get this going. Come on in. Let me show you where we are."

Seated in front of Metcalf's desk, Ty's nerves returned. The moment he'd planned for the past two years seemed simple and anticlimactic on the surface, but in reality he was about to trigger an earthquake.

"I've followed up on the letter you gave me and on all the timelines and information on record with the county. It looks like what you understand is true. Eli Crockett filed a homestead claim on November 7, 1935, but there is no record of a deed, a transfer of a deed, or any handwritten grant deed. Since that homestead claim, the Crocketts have renewed the homestead every time it was required, so there's been no question as to the validity of ownership. Given the lack of a deed, and no indication from the Crockett side that the land was officially deeded to them, the letters from your great-grandfather and your father, both containing specifics about the nature of the poker game and the presence of threats of bodily harm, there were grounds to file your letter and claim of wrongful possession with the court. Now I have to say, this is basically two against one—your relatives' written account against a legally filed homestead. I don't know how the deed transfer got overlooked, but the fact that it doesn't appear to exist will be, in part, our argument."

"What are my chances?" Ty asked.

"I have to be honest," replied Metcalf. "The Crocketts will fight this, and they are smart. They'll point to the eighty-plus years that land has belonged to their family and the fact that nobody has ever contested the homestead. They'll bring in statutes of limitation, and they'll contend that your letter is no more than desperation from a regretful loser—Simon's word against Eli's. They'll say that however unfair a way poker is to win land, this was the way things happened back then. And," his brows knotted, "logic will be on their side. That being said, you have proof your letters are genuine, and while they represent merely two men's opinions, they make a case that your great-grandfather was swindled and run off his land— that goes to sympathy. Our biggest job will be proving that the deed was never filed so the land was never legally transferred. As for the eighty years, we'll argue that you acted on this information as soon as you learned of it."

"Well, as soon as I could verify the letter," Ty amended.

"Exactly. Due diligence. Your chances? I'd guess fifty-fifty, possibly a little less. If the Crocketts can't come up with an actual deed, you're in good shape."

The odds were worse than Ty had originally thought. He could go through the exercise, make enemies out of Grace and her family members, and end up with nothing. Still, he had to see this through as a matter of pride and so he could tell Lucky one day that he'd tried his best.

"I trust you know what you're doing," he said simply.

"We were fortunate to get that quick court date of June seventh—that's only two and a half weeks away. I can send the papers whenever you wish, but now I think it's finally time to lay the cards on the table, if you'll forgive the reference. The family should have time to get themselves counsel."

Ty rocked back in his chair as if blasted in the chest by a cannon. Real. It was all going to happen. He looked around the room at the bookcases, the table suitable for poker, the worn, burnished desk, and the friendly man he now found more than competent. With a shaky breath he nodded. "Mail the papers on Friday. That will give me time to tell the family first. It's only fair. I'll talk to Cole Wainwright, the ranch's manager, this weekend."

"I know Cole. It's your choice You can tell him or let the papers do the talking."

"Cole is a fair man. He won't like this, but I owe him this much honesty."

"All right. Then I just need your signature on a couple of documents and we'll be set to see where all this goes."

He knew where it was going—to a place of no return. Win or lose, he wouldn't be able to undo the damage to a relationship he'd never had any intention of making much less nurturing. Regret filled him, but he sucked it up and took the pen Metcalf offered him.

Sacrifice. No gains without sacrifice.

Cole hadn't asked Ty too many questions about his mid-morning trip into town, but he had added one task to the time off, so Ty headed into the hardware store on Second Street to pick up the order of roofing nails that had come in for his boss. He walked in a surreal bubble as he made his way to the back of the store. The world felt different, both exhilarating and oppressive, and his head and heart fluctuated between the two emotions.

He didn't see Grace until he literally ran into her in the middle of an aisle filled with cleaning tools and supplies. When he focused on her, she placed her hands on her hips and met him with laughing eyes.

"Did you get attacked by zombies and turned into one of the walking dead?"

"Huh?"

"You are so completely zoned out it's a little weird. I said hello twice when you turned down this aisle."

"You did?" He scowled. "Jeez, I'm sorry. I just finished—"

"At the lawyer's. Cole told me, and I remembered from Sunday night. Everything's okay?"

"Sure. It's going to take a few days to get stuff filed, so I guess I'm just going over everything to make sure it's straight in my mind. I didn't see a single zombie on my way here."

"What a relief." The humor in her eyes deepened. "So we both have good news this morning."

"Yeah? You met with your banker?"

"I did!" The humor turned to sparkles, and her grin made her look like a kid at her birthday party. "The loan is pre-approved. With the ranch backing me, he doesn't see any problems. So—I get to start working on my plan." To Ty's shock she pressed up against him and planted a quick kiss on his lips. "Thank you!"

He encircled her with his arms and automatically tightened them. Her nearness, her pretty citrus-and-flower scent, calmed and cleared his mind, made him feel ridiculously safe. "What are you thanking me for?"

"For telling me more than once this wasn't just a pipe dream. You've made me believe all along that this was going to happen. I was so nervous last night I barely slept, but finally, this morning, I thought about how you told me I had every right to dream, and that I had to believe in myself. I'm always going on and on about how I trust in my prayers and their answers. In a way, you were reminding me to put my money where my mouth is." She kissed him again. "So, yeah. Thank you."

"I didn't do it for thanks, but tell you what. You can thank me for the heck of it anytime you want."

"I missed you yesterday at Lucky's riding lesson. She did great."

"I heard. I'm sorry. I wanted to finish a couple of things so I could be gone this morning. I was pretty sure there'd be more lessons."

"Yeah. The next one might be an actual trail ride. I should be ready to get on a horse in a day or two. Isn't Lucky done with school soon?"

"Friday."

"Maybe that would make a nice start-of-summer present—a trail ride on Saturday or Sunday. Wanna plan to come along?"

His stomach dropped. By sometime on Sunday he needed to have told them his plan. Once he did that there'd be no more trail rides.

"Sounds like fun," he said vaguely. "But for right now, I have to ask, what's a newly minted restaurateur doing in a hardware store just before lunch?"

She laughed and pulled away, then pointed at a push broom

next to a bucket filled with cleaning supplies.

"Stocking up to get started on my cottage cleaning. I've actually had *two* meetings already this morning. I also went to see the best contractor in town—Kevin DeMars. He's more than happy to take on the remodeling, but his crews are booked for the next month. It'll be July before he can really get going. I was a little bummed about that—but I don't officially have the money until next week anyway, so there's no point in being overeager."

"You wanted him to join you this afternoon and get started right away." He smiled, understanding both the excitement and the disappointment.

"I did. But I didn't expect it. I still need to consult with a designer anyhow. Kevin suggested a lady in Jackson who sounds really talented, and he gave me some ideas for getting things rolling if I want to save some money. If the whole cabin is emptied, and basic demolition is done, I don't have to pay his men to do it. I figure I know a lot of big strong guys I can bribe to help. And saving money would be a good thing—the loan won't be gigantic, just enough."

"Do you know what you're going to ask the designer to do?"

"I'm going over to the cabin when I'm done here to study it in more detail. I'd at least like to know all the features I want and then make a rough sketch of the current layout."

Ty hesitated, weighing his options and his words. Pure selfishness made him want to be with her though it was unquestionably a stupid—in a way a cruel—thing to do.

"Would you like some company? Or would you rather work the ideas out on your own?"

"You?"

"Don't act *that* surprised."

She shook her head. "No, no, it's not that. I'm just amazed you'd want to go back there after I dragged you top to bottom through the gross old place last week—and injured you in the process."

"True." He nodded, feigning thoughtfulness. "But I do like old buildings. Maybe we'll find another fireplace."

"We shouldn't be allowed in fireplaces."

"Oh, I don't know …"

He left the line hanging with a hint of innuendo, and she blushed just enough to prove she remembered those seconds before Lil had scared them into butting heads.

"You have time?" she asked.

"I can fudge another hour or ninety minutes. Cole has a soft spot for this project, too, in case you didn't know. If I tell him I was helping you when you were, you know, all alone, he'll be fine with it."

"Well aren't I special?"

She had no idea *how* special she was becoming.

"More like beloved. Anyone in your family would lie down in front of a speeding truck for you."

For a long moment she didn't speak, nor did she look at him. When she finally did, her eyes shone. "That's nice of you, but it isn't just me. It's anyone in the family. We can fight like mad cats but if push comes to shove …"

"And don't you lose sight of that when you start to worry about what you're doing. Right now what you're doing is starting to take advantage of any help offered, anytime."

"Hey, I never turned down your offer. I'm not going to look you in the mouth, gift horse. I don't care *why* you offered."

"I'll tell you anyway. It's so I can take a chance that you'll neck with me by that fireplace we found."

She grabbed the broom and thrust it into his hand. "Incorrigible. Is that your middle name?"

"No. Tyrone is my middle name." Her mouth opened and then snapped shut. "You didn't expect that did you? Nobody expects 'Ty' to be 'Tyrone' anymore."

"I guess. You don't strike me as a retro kind of guy, that's all."

"The retro is thanks to my mother. I don't remember the last time I signed the whole name."

"So what's your first name?"

When had he last uttered it? He hated the ostentatious thing—a name from somewhere in ancient ancestry. Since grade school, the moment anyone found out about it, the result was merciless teasing. His official signature, from credit card purchases to check signing to the signing of the papers this morning in Metcalf's office, was simply T. Garraway. That he was willing to trust her with it surprised him—but only a little. She made him carefree and careless.

"It's Alastair."

"Really? That's so cool." A pleased grin lit her face. "I love those old British names."

He was dumbfounded. Nobody except his mother had ever complimented the name. His father had taken gleeful pleasure in mocking it with a faked British accent when he was angry.

"Cool?" he asked, when he could say anything.

"I see you wouldn't want the nickname 'Al' but the whole name is so unique. Just like you, so it fits. Yeah. Kinda cool. Alastair Tyrone."

"Okay. Never ever call me that again. But ..." He leaned forward and kissed her quickly. "You just made me hate that a little less."

"You're so weird, Ty."

"Never said I wasn't. Come on. Let's go and you can fully explain why we're cleaning a cabin that's going to be torn apart as soon as we're done."

Chapter Seventeen

"I'D *LOVE* TO tear out this wall. Can you tell if it's load-bearing?"

Grace stood, hands on hips, and stared at the ceiling of the cabin's living room as if doing so could magically give her the answer to the question. More importantly, it kept her from staring at Ty, who stood on a folding stool Grace had picked up at the last second before leaving the hardware store, reaching over his head to probe along the junction of the ceiling and the wall between them and the north-side bedroom.

A smooth crescent of skin showed between his belt and his T-shirt hem, not enough to give her the smallest hint of his physique, but it didn't matter. His "so I can take a chance that you'll neck with me by that fireplace we found" line from the store played through her mind. And skin was skin, after all.

Fortunately they hadn't gotten as far as the hidden fireplace yet, and better yet for putting a needed damper on her imagination was the fact that Ty had taken to the structural analysis of the building like he'd found his mother ship. Not that she wasn't also attracted to the rapt expression on his face as he checked walls, looked at the wiring that had been added piecemeal throughout the years, and hmmpf-ed over the plumbing. He knew an impressive amount about construction.

A sexy skill for a man—like knowing how to play a guitar, or throw a perfect curve ball, or hold a newborn baby.

"I'd need to go into the foundation or up into the roof to make sure, but I doubt it's load-bearing." He made a few more taps with his fingers and then pounded once with his fist before twisting over his shoulder to look at her. "Some of these are the weirdest walls. The outer ones sound almost hollow, and the joints here between wall and ceiling feel like I could poke through them with a kid's plastic hammer."

"What does that mean?"

"I don't know, but I sure am curious. The place was built in, what, 1918 you said? I'm no expert in historical construction techniques, but people used to use all kinds of things for insulation, since obviously neither fiberglass batt or spray-in foam was around then."

"What should I do about the wall? I definitely want this space bigger."

"Depends on what you're willing to do regardless of what you find. If the wall is coming out whether or not you have to spend money on a beam or header to span the space, then we can rip into the wall anytime. I'll check the attic—such as it is. If money is a huge deal, then don't do anything until a structural engineer looks at everything."

Decisions. Reality hit like a brick to the head. This was no longer a fantasy—nobody was going to make even simple decisions like this for her, and she'd asked for it. With sudden fierceness, she wished Raquel were at her side. She'd know the exact next logical step.

No.

With a deep breath, she consciously straightened. She didn't want to do what Raquel envisioned; she wanted to implement the visions in her own head. Ty had already proven he'd give an honest opinion about anything if asked—but he hadn't once acted like he knew it all. Raquel would have been sketching madly, inspired if completely unartistic, and she would have had a plan that made sense within minutes. And Grace would have gone along with them—

Sketching.

Grace sketched all the time when it came to determining color, furniture placement, and ambiance. Why hadn't she thought to use that skill on layout of the restaurant as a whole?

"Paper," she said. "I need paper."

"There's some in the bathroom ..."

"Very funny. No, there's a kids' drawing pad in my car. Rory left it there the other night, and I keep forgetting to grab it and return it. Be right back."

She grabbed the cheap tablet from her car and rushed back to Ty. Digging in her purse, she found a pen and then plopped herself down in the middle of the floor.

"Oh boy, a picnic." Ty sat beside her, folding his legs tailor fashion and leaning into her.

"Huh, I forgot all about lunch."

"We'll eat when we're done. What's the plan?"

"To make a plan." She grinned. "I need a rough sketch of the cabin's footprint. I do this all the time when I'm figuring out decorating; I don't know why I haven't done it before now."

"Is it okay if I watch?"

She normally didn't like people to witness the creative process—she preferred showing off a finished product. But she shrugged. "This is going to be so rough and so general, but maybe I'll learn what I don't know."

She looked around the living room for a few minutes and

then set the pen on the paper. With sure strokes, she drafted a square with a porch in the front and an extension room off the back. Then she roughed in the current wall placement.

"Look close to right?" she asked.

"Yeah. I think the current kitchen area is more …" He leaned around her. "Could I draw on your drawing?"

She handed him the pen, surprised at her willingness to take his help. He changed the positions of three walls and the floor plan suddenly looked perfect.

"Oh my gosh—the proportions are dead-on."

"I have an eye for spacial stuff," he said.

She turned her head toward him leaning over her shoulder. He smelled good and slightly spicy—dark chocolate and musk. It turned her on and reassured her at the same time. "Impressive. You could come in very handy."

"At your service." He handed back the pen. "Now, what do you want to change?"

She X'd out two walls, pushed a third back so the future dining room would be an evened-off rectangle and bent to the kitchen.

"Makes the kitchen tight," she said, musing over her drawing.

"Here, let me have the pen again."

Once more his strokes were unhesitating. "What if you leave the dining room irregular—give it a few nooks and crannies, maybe one secluded corner? Then you don't lose the kitchen space and if you want to use this addition out back, you can build in the freezer/refrigerator. Perfect size, I'd think."

"That's brilliant."

He drew the correct lines, and Grace could see the uniqueness and the charm although it warred with her need for symmetry.

"I like it."

"What's on this side—in the new fireplace room?"

"My kids-only restaurant."

"Oh yeah, you mentioned that. Great idea. And if you expose the whole fireplace, think of how you can decorate it in kid stuff for all the holidays. They'll love it."

"You think so?"

"A place where they can order their own food?"

"From a mom-approved menu, of course." She laughed.

"See *that's* cool. My kid will be in there every day."

She laughed as a wave of optimism washed over her. He made her feel happy without any dramatic gestures; it had been that way from the first moment she'd seen him striding up the driveway with amusement in his eyes over her holier-than-thou sermonizing.

Why did he like her? So often lately she acted like the very men she hated dating. And yet, here Ty was, smelling like a Greek god had to have smelled and discussing her dream as if it were his as well.

A second wave, this one closer to a tsunami, crashed into her, filling her with an insistent longing. Turning to the side she fit her lips to his before she could talk herself out of the boldness. Immediately their tongues met in a waltz of surprise and pleasure.

Long minutes of sluicing pleasure into the kiss, Ty pulled his lips away but set his forehead against hers.

"We're in the wrong room," he said.

"I decided something. I don't think any room would be the wrong one with you."

It was true. She wanted him in a way she'd promised herself

not to want a man until he'd undergone a lot of scrutiny. She'd barely known this one two weeks.

"We could try them all and test that theory."

She sputtered but managed to contain her laughter. "You know I'm not that kind of girl."

"So you say." His eyes glittered with fun, but he spoke seriously. "Look. I wasn't raised by a great role model of a father, but my mother made very clear what I should to do when a girl says no. Whatever room I'm ever in I will respect that. Now, if the girl says yes ..." The glitter in his eyes began to smolder.

"Do a lot of girls say yes?" she asked quietly.

He took a moment to consider then he squeezed her hands.

"In the past, maybe. But I have a child now, and even though I don't regret for one moment the accident that gave her to me—it was an accident. So, lots of girls? Not so much anymore."

"Sorry again. See, that's really none of my business."

"I disagree, Grace. You have the right to know if I'm just playing games."

The man could knock her socks off with surprise every time he opened his mouth if he wanted to.

"And are you?"

"I'm having fun getting to know you, so I guess it's a little like a game. But not the way you think, I promise. And if you don't pull away and we can go back to being okay with stealing kisses when the mood strikes, I promise, too, I'll never push for anything that isn't mutually enjoyable."

Grace placed a hand on his chest. "You talk a smooth game, mister. I'm not proud that I'm so wary by nature, but with you I'm less so. Maybe it's because you don't talk like the neglected kid you say you were. You're smart, and I like smart."

"Sweetheart, I'm so rarely smart. But I did go to college—for three years until there were no more loans to be had and I couldn't win enough poker matches to pay tuition. My mother wanted me to be book-learned."

"Wait. You really tried to gamble your way through school?"

"Desperate times …"

"What was your major?"

"For the first two years, Earth science and history. I found out pretty quickly I'd make a terrible teacher. I'm not mature enough. True, the money ran out, but I'd already messed up enough to make the third year a flop. Poker and seasonal work—those were my fortes. I didn't start growing up until much later."

His honesty struck her again. He neither bragged nor apologized, and he didn't sugarcoat anything. He was what he was, and she loved the lack of game playing. Even she and her sisters pulled punches sometimes to avoid hurting each other's feelings. Knowing Ty stood on little political correctness was liberating.

"You must have picked up some character along the way. "You're a nice guy, although you try to hide it sometimes. I guess I can trust you alone in an abandoned house—smooth talker or not."

Surprisingly his eyes dulled, and he grasped the hand she still held against his heart, pulling it away and turning toward the side bedroom that housed the half-exposed fireplace. "No more of this good-guy, nice-guy schmaltz. Bring your paper. Show me what you have in mind for this room."

To her great disappointment, he didn't try to kiss her again—not by the fireplace and not in any other room of the cabin. She wanted to make a move again herself, but Ty had clearly taken her putting-on-the-brakes request to heart, and she found no opportunities to show him she really had changed her mind.

What they did share were surprising discussions about function and design, and close looks at what elements of original charm had been left and what had been remodeled over the years. The two fireplaces were definitely focal points, and several sections of barn wood walls clearly needed to be refinished and kept. Other features needed to go.

An hour passed like mere minutes, and when they'd scoured every inch of the cabin, Grace's detailed drawings, enhanced by Ty, were good enough to bring to any designer or architect.

"You have a talent for this," he said, when they stood outside the cabin.

"Thanks. But look who's talking. You made this a lot easier."

He touched the brim of his hat and the familiar ring of his cell phone floated from his pocket. She chuckled. "There seems to be something about me standing next to you and phone calls coming in."

He checked the phone, and his forehead creased in concern just as it had the last time.

"It's Lucky," he said. "It's way too early for her to be home … Lucky?"

The girl's excited, high-pitched voice came loud and clear through the phone. "Daddy, Daddy you have to come home!"

"Lucky?" The start of panic crept into his voice. "Are you all right? Why aren't you at school?"

"Because it's so awesome! A water pipe broke in the school, and they can't fix it by Friday, so school's done early for summer! Isn't that cool? But you have to come home now, because I have to ask you about the dogs."

"What dogs?" The panic dissipated, replaced by sagging-shoulder relief, and then skepticism. Ty frowned at Grace, and she bit back a smile. Whatever this was, Ty was about to get hit with the unavoidable curse—or as some people saw it, a blessing—of being on a ranch where animals were key.

"The dogs Miss Joely brought home."

"Joely's back?" Grace asked. "She's early! We didn't expect her and Alec for another week."

Ty ignored her. "Again I ask, what dogs?"

"Eight dogs. She found them on the road."

Ty nearly dropped the phone.

Grace couldn't stop a full belly laugh, and reached for his arm, about to go lax at his side with the phone in his hand. She pushed it back up until he held the phone tightly against his ear again. "Oh come on, Ty, it's not like she said she found eight wanted fugitives."

"Eight?" he asked into the phone. "Don't you dare say you told anyone you'd ask your dad about eight dogs."

"No, just one or two."

"Lucky ..." His voice lowered to a warning growl.

Grace put her fingers against his lips and took the phone. "Lucky, sweetie, I think you shocked your dad. We'll be home in about twenty minutes, okay?"

"Okay! They're so, so cute, Grace."

"I'm sure they are. Where are they all now?

"In a fence by your house."

"Okay, that's good. Is Lil there with you?"

"Yup. She likes the brown and black one."

Oh boy. You're out of luck, Ty.

"Grace, can I help you by helping the puppies?"

"Oooh, sweetheart, it's way too early to tell about that. I'm sure for tonight, there'll be plenty to do."

"Grace? I like the mostly yellow and brown ones."

"I can't wait to see them," she replied. "Just don't get too excited until we know more, okay? You have to be careful living on a ranch. It's easy for animals to get lost from their real owners, and it's really easy for them to get sick, too."

"That's what Miss Joely said. I like her. She's funny and nice. But not as fun as you."

"You're my favorite little girl, you know." Grace smiled at Ty. "I have to go now so we can get there."

She hung up and handed the phone back to Ty. "I'm sorry, but I think you're about to become a daddy to a puppy. Brown and yellow, if I understood correctly."

"Oh-ho, no." He stuffed the cell unceremoniously back into his pocket. "There comes a time when you just have to put your foot down."

"And sometimes it lands in puppy doo-doo."

"Exactly why I'm watching very closely where I'm walkin.'"

***

Ty watched the two sisters hug like they'd thought the other dead and just learned differently. Joely Crockett Morrissey was stunning, just as Grace had told him she'd be. A former beauty queen who'd been in a serious car accident and now walked with a limp, Joely carried herself with an almost regal bearing but with the personality of a best friend. Once she and Grace let each other go, Joely offered a handshake to Ty.

"I've heard so much about you," she said. "It sounds like Cole was beyond fortunate to find you."

He shook his head. "I'm the fortunate one. Happy to meet you—everyone here has been counting the days until you got back."

She eyed him with amusement and winked at Grace. "They're right. He's good."

"Good?" Ty asked.

"Silver-tongued," she said. "In a good way. Things girls love to hear."

"You're ahead of the game, bro." Joely's husband, Alec, shook his hand, too. He was the most cowboy-looking man of any of them, with an easy, swinging gait and clothes—jeans, boots and T-shirt—that looked as comfortable as if he'd been born in them. "It was scary how much I didn't know when I started."

"It's the poker playing," Grace said. "He's learned how to bluff into anything."

"Yeah, sure, that's it." Ty snorted. "Nice to meet you, Alec."

"Poker, 'eh?" Alec asked. "Used to play on the circuit all the time. You a pro?"

"Not at all. There was a time when I thought I wanted that, but the game lost its fun. Now I just play for truck payments."

"We'll play a game sometime, just so I can polish the old skills. Not that I was ever much good."

"He's good," Grace said, patting Ty's arm. "Just be warned."

Ty swallowed. He was getting in deeper the more Crocketts there were.

"Daddy!" Lucky danced around him once the intros were past. "You *have* to come and see them. You *have to!*"

"Oh yeah," Grace said. "I heard some crazy story about eight dogs?"

Ty grimaced while Joely linked arms with Grace and nodded toward the back door. "It's the kind of story only an insane person could have to tell."

"She's not insane," Alec said. "She's just crazy." He brushed a kiss on her temple as she passed him.

The whole family was one big sappy love fest, Ty thought, suddenly and thoroughly cranky over the prospect of being badgered by his child into considering a dog. Every flippin' sister on the place, his own Grace included, would side with the girl, too.

His own Grace?

His mood slipped further. He was losing it.

The puppies weren't what he expected. Instead of being tiny, new creatures, they were boisterous, bounding, fifteen-pound baby dogs that Joely said were at least two months old. The mother—an emaciated golden retriever—had clearly been abandoned. Her dark yellow coat was brushed but far from lustrous, and her eyes were pathetically friendly but nervous and hungry.

She wagged her tail from a grassy spot outside a portable fence enclosure about eight feet square. Inside, the pups tumbled joyously over each other and three kids, Rory, Aiden, and Aiden's sixteen-year-old sister Skylar.

As Ty approached, Lucky dashed away and let herself into the little pen, immediately grabbing up one puppy and plopping to her butt. The pups were on the thin side, although shinier and far bubblier than the bitch, and they ranged in color from brown and black short-hairs that looked like little Rottweilers, to muddy-gold, long-haired mutts with dark faces and paws, like the one Lucky held. Gathered around the outside of the fence appeared to be the rest of Paradise Ranch's human population. Adults who beamed and laughed as if they'd never seen dogs before.

In truth, it was mostly women—Bella, Mia, Sadie, Lil and

Melanie Thorson—and Leif, the patriarch of Paradise's ranch workers. One other man stood by as well, a square-jawed, big-muscled guy Ty had never seen before.

"Seriously?" he asked Grace. "There's a party over a bunch of stray dogs?"

"It's really a party for Joely and Alec. Think of the puppies as the clowns they hired for entertainment."

"And they definitely are clowns," Joely said as they stopped beside the fence. "We left Fort Collins and were headed on our cross-country vacation to Alec's aunt and uncle's in Minnesota, when we saw mama over there wandering along the side of the highway. Normally we wouldn't have paid any attention, but we weren't anywhere a pet would have been taking herself for a walk. Plus, she kept looking over her shoulder, almost as if she was hoping we'd see her and stop."

"Didn't you already have Rowan in the car with you?" Mia asked.

"We did." Joely shook her head. "I told you, this was insane."

"Rowan is Alec and Joely's Irish wolfhound," Grace explained. "You haven't seen a big dog until you've met Rowan."

"We talked about getting her a horse trailer," Alec said. "It would almost make more sense than stuffing her into the car."

"So you stopped for this dog," Grace prompted.

"We did, and she came right up to us. But then she pulled away and headed off into the woods. She still kept looking back, making sure we were following. When she stopped in front of a shallow cave, that's when we found these eight. I wouldn't have believed it if I hadn't been there, but this girl kept her babes alive like wolves do. I doubt she really knows how to hunt, so I don't know what they ate. And I doubt they were there longer than a couple of weeks. Still, it's very impressive.

How could we just leave them?"

"So you drove over a thousand miles with ten dogs in a Subaru Forester?" Grace raised her brows appreciatively.

Ty stared in wonder. "You're right," he said, laughing. "I don't know you well yet, but I declare you certifiable."

Joely grinned at him. "Long story short, we hauled them all to Aunt Chris and Uncle Rick's farm, stayed for two days and left about eleven o'clock last night. We wanted to do the whole eight hundred miles in one stretch, and we wanted to drive overnight so the dang dogs would sleep. Ta-da! We're here. And once we get the all-clear from Sheila in town, we'll be finding homes." Joely glanced around the mini crowd. "I already have leads on several."

"Can you tell what breeds might be mixed in?" Grace asked.

"Mom is definitely a golden," Joely said. "I think Dad was a Rottweiler or maybe a Rottweiler-shepherd mix? They don't remotely look like litter mates, do they?"

Ty knew basic dog breeds, but not enough to discern parentage in stray puppies. He could tell some of the dogs had the rounded, squat builds of a Rottweiler and others had pointier, intelligent faces like a German shepherd. The one Lucky held looked like a retriever with Rottweiler coloring that had been smudged by the artist. He had to admit it was cute. But all puppies were cute.

"We've decided to keep the mom and that little girl over there." Joely pointed to one of the shaggier pups.

"I've been thinking about getting a dog." The unidentified man spoke for the first time.

"You *need* a dog, Damien," Mia said, and clapped him on the back. "This is a perfect way to get one! Pan needs a sibling."

"Damien Finney is one of Mia and Gabe's original veterans,"

Grace whispered. "He keeps his horse Panacea here. The horse has helped him make huge strides in overcoming his diagnosis of PTSD. What's more impressive is he recently signed up for firefighter training at the base west of here. He wants to fight wild fires as a smokejumper. A pretty awesome guy."

The tiniest flutter of jealousy sparked at her praise, but died when Ty reminded himself firmly that Grace hadn't lived here for years. She had no attachment to this man. The way Ty should have no attachment to her.

"Dad, come on! Look."

Lucky stood, her bundle of puppy in her arms. "You have to hold him. He's so cute. His name is Rupert."

Beside him, Grace sputtered. "What a great name," she said.

"You can't name him, honey." Ty firmed his lips. "We can't get a dog right now."

"But they need to have homes. I can't just abandon him; someone already did that."

"I don't think there'll be any shortage of people willing to take care of these guys."

"But we live on a ranch now." Lucky's little face squeezed into firm determination. "You always said we didn't have the room, but you can't say that now. Lil wants one, too, don't you?"

Lil, who'd been uncharacteristically quiet, nodded to Skylar in the pen, who scooped up a black and brown pup with long, silky hair and placed it in Lil's arms.

"This one." Lil stared at him as if daring him to defy *her* choice.

For the first time in months, Ty's temper got the better of him. To his credit, he kept his outward cool in front of so many strangers, but he glared back at Lil, his face heating. "We'll talk.

As for you …" He turned to Lucky. "You can play with these dogs as long as you want to. But this is not the right time and we won't be taking one home. Understand?"

For the first time in longer than he could remember, tears filled his daughter's eyes. She was not a crier. His heart fell to his boots.

"We only do what *you* want. You made us move here. I didn't want to but now I like it. You want to do everything so you can get land to live on. I only want a dog. That's all."

She turned away from him, her logic irrefutable even though he was the dad, the decision-maker.

"I need to get back to work," he said gruffly to Grace. "Cole is going to wonder where the hell I got to. Lil will take Lucky home when they're done here. Do you still want Lucky to help tonight?"

"We agreed on a week," Grace said. "She can come."

"Fine."

He started away but Grace didn't let him go alone. He scowled. "Do not try to talk me into a fool dog, Grace."

"Hey, you're the father. I can't make the decisions for your family. It doesn't make any sense, though. You say you like dogs. She's so ready for one. What really gives?"

At first he'd been serious about not wanting a dog to be part of moving from pillar to post. But now? The truth hit him like a blast of frozen air. Now that he was so close to implementing this plan, he'd begun to realize it could fail.

He'd never considered the possibility in his single-minded pursuit of this dream. But now that he knew the Crocketts, he also knew they would fight him with every bit of power they had. And if it all went belly up—he didn't want a single thing around him to remind him of what he'd lost.

"It's my life, Grace. Nothing gives."

"Okay." Her frown was skeptical at best. "Just wanted to make sure you're okay."

"I'm fine."

He felt rather than saw her slow and fall a step behind him. He rounded the deck heading for the front of the house, and they met a woman hurrying toward them.

"Grace!" she cried. "I found you! You haven't been answering your cell."

"Marni? My gosh, what's going on? I'm sorry, I left it in my purse in the house."

"Time-sensitive stuff! Hi, I'm Marni Dressler, Grace's real estate agent." She held out a hand to Ty.

"Ty Garraway." He shook, tamping down the petulant anger that had driven him here.

"Garraway …" Marni assessed him. "Sounds familiar. Oh well, I'll think of it when it's least convenient. Anyway, I just got a call from Kevin DeMars. He's been trying to reach you, too. He had a major contract cancellation, and despite having another client contact him, he was intrigued by your project. He said if you're in any position to move forward next week, he'd be happy to look at the plans. But he needs to know almost immediately. It's a lucky break."

Grace jumped in place. "Yes! Yes, I would love him to start. I'll go call him now. You made a trip all the way here just to tell me? That was awfully nice of you."

"No trouble. I'm excited about this project, too."

Grace hugged her and turned to Ty, grasping for his hand.

"You're a big part of this now," she said. "Come on. Let's go ask Mia when it would work for me to throw a demolition party at the old cabin."

Chapter Eighteen

THE MESS IN the cottage threatened to drive Grace right out the door and into the Basecamp's bar for a neat whiskey. Ty had already told her to concentrate beyond the mess on the people who'd come to help and the quick work they were making of demolition. But excited and grateful though she was, the urge to sweep things was fueling the need for alcohol.

For the moment, she sat on a step stool in the smaller of the two bedrooms, alone with the sketches she and Ty had made, studying them for the hundredth time and taking a breather from the amazing chaos in the room next door.

Her crew of enthusiastic family and friends had volunteered without hesitation when offered the chance to swing sledgehammers, eat pizza, and drink beer. And they'd done an amazing job. It was seven o'clock on Friday night, and since four they'd torn out fifties-era kitchen cabinets, pulled up ugly tile in the little bathroom to expose original pine floor planks, removed all the stained and frayed carpeting that had been added throughout the last fifty years, and were now taking down the second of three walls. They'd nearly filled a Dumpster sitting in the front yard, and reality had struck with its heaviest punch yet.

Now that she was having a family treasure gutted for her

pleasure, Grace wondered if she really had the slightest clue what she was doing.

A whoop that could have come from a football stadium of crazed fans sent her doubts into hiding and brought her to her feet. She didn't have time to turn around before a pair of warm, long-fingered hands popped over her eyes from behind.

"Here you are." Ty leaned in and kissed her on the earlobe—the first kiss he'd given her since she'd put him off earlier in the week. "Is everything okay?"

She tried to pry his fingers from her eyes but he refused to let loose. The heat from his hands melted her insides into quivers. "Absolutely fine," she said. "What is this weird game?"

"It's called come with me; I'm making sure you don't peek."

"Oh boy! Is all the remodeling magically done and this is my big reveal?"

"Exactly right—how did you know?"

He guided her to the living room, where the voices of her other volunteer crew members—Harper, Cole, Joely, Alec, Lil, the unexpected Marni, and Gabe, who'd left his injured wife home with the cell phone nearly glued to her hand, now that her due date was only two weeks away—mingled in loud laughter and self-congratulations.

Ty pulled his hands away, and she blinked at a room transformed. Piles of wood, shards of wallboard, and coatings of dust still created chaos, but the huge open space left by the walls' deconstruction gave Grace the first inkling of what her new space was going to look like.

But when she saw the sweaty, dust-plastered faces of her friends and family members, tears beaded in her eyes without warning.

Ty peered at her, concerned. "Well okay, I lied a little. It's not actually completely done," he said.

"Oh. No, no, it's fantastic!" She cleared her throat, embarrassed. "You guys are amazing."

"We are that, but mostly we're all crazy-good with sledgehammers." Alec grinned. "This was great. Got any more walls we can knock down?"

"Yeah, wonderful aggression therapy," added Lil, standing tellingly close to Marni.

The two had met the day Marni brought the news that construction could start. The way the pair hadn't left each other's sides was proof that you never knew what you didn't know about a person. Grace hadn't known Marni was gay, but she and Lil made a gorgeous couple, if absolutely the most unexpected pair of volunteers. She wiped at more tears, and Ty grasped her hands.

"Grace. What?"

"I'm overwhelmed, that's all. I've only been home a short time and I expected to be doing no more than looking around for an idea, or actually helping my sister and mother like I came to do. This is happening at lightning speed. I'm blown away by all of you being so willing to help."

"Hey, there's nothing better than heavy labor after a long day in unseasonable heat." Cole laughed.

"That assuaged zero guilt, you know." Grace narrowed her eyes.

"It wasn't meant to, because there should be none to start with," he replied. "We're excited for you. There hasn't been something this new since we put up the wind farm—and for that, we didn't get the perk of bustin' down solid walls."

"Okay then," Grace replied.

"So you're not weeping over the mess?" Ty asked.

"Nope."

"That's my girl."

She heard the possessive but said nothing. In fact, she hugged it to her heart, making the generic endearment far more important than it was. Ty made her believe she had a cheerleader who honestly thought she could pull off this scheme. And for some foolish reason, she trusted him—maybe because of the way he never pulled punches, or maybe because she always saw sincerity in his eyes.

"What's next?" Lil asked.

Grace surveyed the room. "Eventually that short outside wall in the kitchen will come down to make room for the expansion, but not until construction can start. There's more work on the fireplace wall in the big bedroom. And, of course, cleanup. But I think we should call this a fantastic day's work, order pizza, and then let you all go home and clean up."

"Quit already?" Harper said. "When there are piles of junk lying around? Who are you and what did you do with Grace?"

"Grace is learning to deal," Grace said. "You all have gone above and beyond, and it's so hot in here."

"Then I say we skip pizza delivery, head over to the Basecamp Grill and cool off where they have cold beer," Harper said. "I'll tell you all about who I've got booked to do a couple of workshops at the center. Afterward, we'll come back to work on the fireplace room and clearing out the biggest chunks. It's Friday—who cares how late we're out, and Grandma and Mom will put Lucky and Rory down."

"Hear, hear," Joely said. "We haven't been out to eat in town since we got back. Who's coming to town, Harpo?"

"Just one Gray Covey."

"The *singer*?" Joely crowed.

Gray Covey, one of the biggest heartthrob singers of late eighties, still filled concert arenas worldwide. He lived in the oddest of places for a superstar—Minnesota. And he had the reputation of being a nice guy but very protective of his privacy.

"The very one." Harper puffed her chest in pride. "He's coming between Thanksgiving and Christmas. Come on. I'll tell you all about it."

"Oh, yay." Alec rolled his eyes and made smooching noises at his wife. "We can talk about Joely's music boyfriend all night."

"You can drink beer and talk about Shania Twain." Harper batted her lashes and kissed Alec on the cheek.

"That's all right then."

"It is! Who wants to go home early on a Friday anyhow?" Marni grinned at Lil, who gave a cute little smile in return, her face prettily flushed.

Grace nudged Ty surreptitiously. She didn't know Lil that well, but she'd always struck Grace as a big personality—not the one who'd be the blusher in a relationship. "A match?" she whispered.

"About damn time," he replied. "I've been telling her all along to stop using Lucky as an excuse for staying home."

"Sometimes you just have to let fate take her time. They're cute."

"Then it's agreed," Gabe said. "Let's go eat. I'll check and see if maybe Mia wants to come hang out here afterward, now that the biggest, dustiest demo is done."

"Great idea!" Harper brushed at her arms and jeans legs. "Will they let us into the Basecamp looking like this?"

"They will because we're Crocketts." Joely laughed. "I never pull rank, but tonight we will if we have to."

"As if there's any rank to pull." Grace snorted in laughter. "But I'm all for trying. Tell you what. I'd like to check the dock out back by the pond while it's still light out. I want to know what to tell Kevin about work on that, too. You all head over and I'll meet you in a few minutes."

"I'll stay," Ty said. "You can't go poking around the water all alone."

"I'm not five, Ty." Grace made a face at him.

"Tease me all you want, but water can be lethal."

"Fine," Grace said. "But I'm not doing anything dangerous, so you're signing on for a boring job."

"That's my fervent hope."

She loved the way he talked—the bad boy with big words.

Once the others had headed for the restaurant, Grace led Ty out the back door, the slightly cooler temperature outdoors drying the sweat on her forehead.

"What are you thinking about for this area?" Ty asked. "We never came out here with your notebook."

"I know. I've been obsessed with the inside, but this is such a gorgeous space. I can see an outdoor eating patio in the summer, game areas, maybe a hike around the pond—if you can get all the way around—it's fairly large, maybe two or three acres."

"Does the land all belong to your family?"

"Yes, ten acres. Pretty prime, right? Eli thought of everything."

She knew him well enough to recognize when he purposely went silent. Glancing back, she saw a mini storm of emotion in his eyes.

"What?" It was her turn to ask.

His features cleared immediately. "This is a mesmerizing spot. You'll have a great place here."

They stood at the small dock and stared together over the pond. The sun still stood high in the sky and turned the clear water into diamond glass with smoky edges, where trees and brush threw dramatic shadows onto the surface.

"It really doesn't look that far around," Grace mused. "Want to see if there's any way to cut a path through the trees? Will it take too long?"

"Do you care?"

"Only that they'll all come looking for drowned bodies if we don't show up."

He shrugged and held out his hand. "We'll turn around if it's too tangled. You should be able to call someone if we get held up."

"So practical," she teased, and took his hand.

More peace stole into her soul as Grace picked through the woods with Ty. The trees weren't as thick as they'd appeared from the dock, and despite rolling terrain and no path, it wouldn't be difficult for a construction or excavation company to create one. Ty navigated, sure-footed and nimble. Grace hadn't been hiking for years, but she'd grown up in these foothills and she felt as though she was walking back to simpler, happier days.

They spoke little except to toss out ideas about the space in general terms, and they easily stayed within view of the pond until a spot about five hundred yards from the start. The ground rose sharply, and dense growth blocked their straight path.

"This way." Ty squeezed her hand and angled toward more open ground.

They found themselves climbing a shallower side of the rise, and when they reached the top, both of them caught audible breaths.

"Man alive." Ty let his breath out in awe.

The little rise was high enough so the view cleared the treetops and left nothing obstructing the sight line to the Grand Teton massif and its guardian peaks. To the left stretched the undulating landscape of Paradise Ranch and Wolf Paw Peak, the only actual mountain on Crockett land.

"This is unbelievable," Grace said. "I never knew this was here."

"Quite a picnic spot."

The idea flashed into her head. "What a perfect place for romantic outdoor dining. If it wasn't quite so far away …"

"Well." From behind Ty wrapped his arms around her waist and leaned his chin on her head. "What if it was an exclusive hike-to spot people could reserve? Your chef staff could have a packable menu they could send along in a backpack—including wine and dessert and specialty dinners."

"We could build an environmentally friendly shelter," Grace continued. "Make it romantic but not something to obstruct the view or be out of place." She bounced in excitement, turning herself around in Ty's arms. "You're a genius!"

"Of course."

His smile, inches from hers, lit her up inside. His scent, a mix of pine and cedar and warm outdoors, sent her head spinning. "I'm serious." Her voice rasped to a near whisper.

"So'm I."

He lowered his lips and she raised hers. The kiss did not start out gentle or chaste. He plundered her mouth like a man who'd just discovered the intoxicating properties of wine, and she pressed back, letting her grip on any reality but the sweet, wet kiss fall away. They twisted and searched, played with pressures and tastes. He suckled her lip; she explored the soft contours in his mouth. Her limbs weakened and she let him hold her upright, clinging to his strength, drawing from it, loving the idea that she could play but let him be the haven for any care that threatened.

In the middle of the dance, he lowered them to the ground and they sat on a soft carpet of pine needles and sparse grass. His fingers dove into her hair and massaged her scalp, sending fire through her body and tingles to the end of every finger and every toe. She grasped the back of his head and pressed closer. Before she could stop herself, she straddled his lap and he groaned—pulling her tight to his body and lifting his hips to show her clearly what she did to his self-control.

"You could build a private little room where people could come to do this," he said.

"More genius. Keep on talking … all these ideas are …" She hesitated, her natural awkwardness at intimacy kicking in a little.

"Turning you on?" he asked, nuzzling a spot between her ear and her shoulder. "Turning you on a lot?"

"Yes." She laughed softly at his ticklish assault, now heading down the side of her neck, across the front of her throat, and to the other earlobe. "I am not this kind of girl."

But she wanted to be. Suddenly and swiftly, she wanted to take this to the next level. Nothing about this felt wrong or uncomfortable. Nothing in her wanted to say no.

"I *am* that kind of guy, though," he whispered into the ear he was nibbling on. "The kind who wouldn't have any trouble seeing how far we can take this right here and now, when we're supposed to be somewhere else."

He slipped one hand beneath her, grasped her butt cheek and pulled her closer to him. "See?" He pressed his hard length against her. "You do this every time."

"Sorry."

She rocked her hips, driving heat straight into her core and through her entire body.

"Grace?"

"Hmmm."

"Don't stop yourself. Trust me to do it."

She pulled back enough to find his eyes. Beautiful. Liquid. Sincere. "To stop me?"

"To stop *me*."

He lifted them up together and spun so she stretched beneath him on the soft ground. Resting over her on his elbows, he smoothed back her hair with long, slow strokes, promised heaven with his eyes, and kissed her. She shifted for him when he searched for the hem of her T-shirt and granted a pathway to her breast, which he reached and touched with a sibilant hiss of breath. When he pushed the fabric out of his way and grazed his thumb softly over her nipple, Grace moaned with pleasure.

"Yeah?" he asked. "It's okay?"

"Boy is it." She closed her eyes and smiled.

It took no time for him to ratchet up the tension in her body. Expert touches, smooth trails of kisses that led him across the sensitive skin of her stomach, up her torso to her breasts, left her feeling both wanted and incredibly inept at returning the feelings. For most of her adulthood, sex had been about protecting herself. Tonight it was about wanting to share equally and being as mindful of Ty's pleasure as she was of her own. But after so long, she simply didn't know how to give back to him.

She explored his hard planes and male beauty with eager hands, but it felt like giving herself presents. The contours of his back, curving in and then swelling into his glutes, the bunching of his triceps as he held himself over her and then lowered to kiss her, the sexiness of his jaw, working as he played with her tongue and lips, all combined to raise her desire to fever pitch. She barely paid mind to it until she understood how close she was to letting all her inhibitions go.

"You are something else." His voice broke the spell and she drifted down a little from the stratosphere.

"It's not me," she said. "I have no idea what I'm doing for you—this is selfish."

The laughter he released into her ear rang as genuinely happy. "You're not paying attention then. You know what you're doing so well that it's time to stop."

"Now?" She traced his jaw with a finger, pouting impishly. "That hardly seems fair."

"Tell me the truth. If I asked you to keep going, would you do it?"

"Yes." She three-quarters meant it.

"You answered way too quickly. That tells me it's the electricity talking."

"This is absolutely not electricity. It's something I haven't wanted in a long, long time. But you are different from any man I've ever known. I don't quite have a handle on everything in your life, but there's something true and faithful and honest about you. I know it's silly to say after such a short time—but you might just be the guy who could change my mind about guys."

She started to laugh, but Ty's face changed so abruptly it caught in her throat.

The light in his eyes flipped to shadow, and his mouth, so soft and sensual on hers moments before, thinned into a wounded line. He rolled away from her, lay one moment on his back, pushing his hair away from his forehead, and then sat. He held out a hand and pulled her up as well.

"What did I say?" she asked. "I'm sorry, I didn't mean to force you—"

"Stop. Grace. It wasn't that. You didn't say anything wrong. I feel the same way about you. But we can't. There are too many things you don't know—just as you said."

"Then tell me."

"Okay. Tonight when we have plenty of time. No matter how late we work on the cabin, promise me you'll come with me and we'll talk."

"A guy who says 'we'll talk'?" She grinned at him although her stomach no longer fluttered with desire but churned with worry at his somber tone. "This can't be good."

"Believe me, there is the possibility that you're exactly right."

They withstood the razzing at dinner for being forty minutes late, and Ty seemed to relax once he was back with the group. Grace, however, never lost a growing sense of impending doom. She tried to analyze it. Was it because she'd been ready to trade in her moral stance for pleasure?

No. She wasn't a prude and neither was the God of her faith.

Was it because she'd moved too fast? Made Ty think she was too serious about him?

No. He was a grown man, and she knew from watching him with his daughter and on the job that he could handle his feelings without running away. It was one of the things that made him so attractive.

But something was wrong. When the crew returned to the cabin, Ty couldn't seem to get fully back into the crazy fun. He joked. He teased. He looked at her with desire that was easy to read. But he wasn't all there—as if part of his brain was working on a plan to escape. How she could know that, she had no idea—except that a connection had grown between them that felt as real as their physical touch had been. She knew. And she dreaded.

"This is looking pretty good."

Cole arched his back and stepped away from the wall in the bedroom about an hour after everyone but Gabe had returned to the cabin. He, Alec, Ty, and Grace had pulled down the last of the sheetrock in front of the fireplace and the room looked massive.

"Looks as if we can finish this tonight," Cole said. "After that I think you'll be in good shape, Gracie."

"I'm astounded. Thank you!" She looked around and tried to gauge Ty's reaction. He was studying the fireplace with a keen eye. "There's so much character in every space." She moved to his side. "Why do you think they covered this up?"

"Not a clue. No more idea than when we first found it," he replied. At long last he met her eyes with an authentic smile. "But I'm glad it's been found."

A resounding knock on the front door was followed immediately by the door swinging open on its squeaking hinges.

"Mia! Gabe!" From the living room, Harper's voice identified the knockers.

"We brought a visitor." Mia's voice sounded strangely flat.

Grace glanced back at Ty and shrugged. They both entered the opened-up middle room of the cabin and stopped in their tracks.

Trampas Manterville stood between Mia on her crutches and Gabe. All three looked like somber heralds. Trampas gazed past Grace directly at Ty.

"Hello, son. I apologize. They found me first."

Grace could almost hear dust settling in the seconds that ticked past after that. Her heart lurched, her stomach took a terrified nosedive. Trampas knew Ty? She looked at Ty's profile. The color had leeched from his skin.

"Ty?" She touched his arm.

He gently took her hand and let it drop, shaking his head sorrowfully, then turned to the old man at the door. "Uncle Trampas," he said. "It's all right."

"Uncle?" Cole came up behind Grace.

"Uncle?" Harper said at the same time.

"Great-Uncle," Trampas said. "I really am sorry, Ty."

"What is he talking about?" Grace grasped Ty's arm again.

"These." Gabe held out a legal-sized manila envelope. "I was in town this afternoon and Bev at the post office handed me tomorrow's mail—perks of living where everyone knows you. Seems our newest ranch hand is not who he says he is."

"That's not true," Ty answered quietly. "I'm exactly who I said I am. I simply didn't tell you who my relatives are. Trampas is my grandfather's brother—thirteen years younger. Simon Manterville's son."

The truth rained down like a roof caving in. Grace stared, open-mouthed, as the sparse facts sorted themselves, and she understood.

"Dear God, Ty. You're a Manterville?"

Chapter Nineteen

NOT MUCH GOT the Crockett family to call an all-hands meeting, much less caused a true uproar. The last time Grace remembered such a gathering had been the day of her father's funeral, when they'd learned of Paradise Ranch's financial straits. There'd been disagreements about what to do, but there hadn't been the kind of hot anger that permeated Sam Crockett's old study this time.

The study hadn't been changed much in the three years since her father's death. A few pictures had been swapped out and the room no longer smelled like Sam's pipe tobacco, but the dark blue and burgundy color scheme and the classic leather furniture remained, along with pictures of the Crocketts who'd run the ranch from one generation to the next—Eli, Sebastian, Samuel, and now Harper and Cole and Mia and Gabe. The room served as a business office and quiet haven for thinking or reading, but it wasn't a shrine. Today it served as the equivalent to a courtroom.

Sitting in a corner of her father's favorite leather sofa, Grace felt like the lowest bug at the bottom of a well. Her world had closed in on her, dark, angry, and confused. Her heart, trampled and unsteady, beat painfully in her chest. Everyone around her had one united opinion, but hers was confused and slightly dissenting. Grandma Sadie sat beside her, her ancient fingers wrapped around Grace's, but she and Grace's mother beside her were as stunned as everyone else.

For the moment, they all hated him.

Alastair Tyrone Garraway, only son of Clarissa Manterville Garraway, grandson of Oliver Manterville, great-grandson of Simon Manterville, who'd lost seven thousand acres to Eli Crockett in 1935. Traitor, liar, schemer, opportunist.

Anger burned in her, too, but Grace couldn't detest him the way her family did, although she wished she could. She still remembered his eyes once the truth had come out three nights before; eyes she could read like a book written just for her—green and filled, not with regret at getting caught, but with anguish over hurting people he'd come to admire. Yes, he'd lied—colossally. He'd taken advantage of the family. Used them. And, yes, she'd told him to go away. But she believed with her whole being Ty was doing what he thought had to do.

The papers that had been served naming all six Crockett heiresses in a land dispute case, to be heard in front of the Lincoln County court on June the seventh, were official and tightly drawn up by a skilled attorney, according to the lawyer who'd been in charge of Paradise's legal affairs for two decades. Ty's plan might have been a long shot, but he'd executed it with forethought and precision. He was not an opportunist—he'd been planning this for a long time.

Mitchell Radcliffe, Paradise's attorney and a long-standing family friend, stood behind the desk in the study, chatting with, of all people, Trampas, waiting for the last people to arrive. Grace dreaded the moment they would. She already felt like the family traitor for not jumping fully onto the anti-Ty Garraway bandwagon. She didn't need to be reminded of when her mutiny had started.

Kelly entered first, Raquel second, and Grace's heart immediately stopped hurting. Her sisters sought her out with barely a glance at anyone else in the room. When Kelly leaned over and took her into an enormous hug, Grace knew something missing had been replaced. Tears she'd refused to cry flowed in a healing stream.

"I am so happy to see you," she wept.

"I can't tell you how much I've missed you," Kelly replied.

"It's true." Raquel held herself slightly more stiffly, but still she embraced Grace and held her for long seconds. "Don't think we're reconciled or anything, but you *were* missed."

"We have a lot to work out, I know, Rocky. It's okay if you're angry with me."

"Kelly's not. But I am." Still, she offered a smile.

Grace smiled, too, for the first time in three days. "Thanks for the warning. At least I got a hug."

"Bah, it's not important right now anyway," Raquel said. "What's this moron Garraway really up to? He must be an idiot. I heard he tried to get in good with you to further his plan. Are you okay?"

"He didn't use me, Rocky. Dumb as it sounds, he's a nice guy. A great father. Smart. Caring."

"For the love, Gracie." Raquel rolled her eyes. "We set you up with the purest guys on the planet, and you hate them. You meet a poker-playing con artist, hang out with him for three weeks, and you're ga-ga for him. When did you get knocked on the head and forget who you are?"

"I haven't forgotten anything." Grace sighed. "I've learned that moral character is not easily pigeonholed and everything is relative. I trusted Ty. About many things, I still do. It's just that, this is a biggie, you know?"

"Would we be here if we didn't?" Kelly pulled her up from the sofa. "Come on. Let's show some solidarity. We're here to help make a plan."

Bella stood with them and hugged her youngest daughters gratefully. "Thank you for coming home," she said. "We need everyone's wisdom right now."

"All right, let's get started." Mitchell Radcliffe, with his silver temples and towering stature, stopped all conversation with a precise voice. "You asked me here to go over these papers with all of you and to help formulate a response. The charge claims, in effect, that Eli Crockett willfully set out to steal land from Simon Manterville, and he did so by forcing him into a poker game at knifepoint and by holding his wife, Lydia, hostage in an undisclosed location as an added threat until the game was played. It also contends that Mr. Crockett was a professional card player but Mr. Manterville was only a small-time player who got himself in trouble by bragging—his only crime. Further, there is no record of the land transfer ever having been officially filed by Mr. Crockett.

"Therefore, even though the statute of limitations has passed, because the evidence—a letter written by Simon Manterville and another by his son, Oliver—were lost and only recently found and then verified as authentic by Mr. Manterville's great-grandson, this is the first possible time the illegal land transfer can be contested. Mr. Alastair Garraway is suing for seven thousand acres to be returned to the heirs of the Manterville family."

"What's the deal with these letters?" Mia asked. "We have the one from Oliver Manterville but not the one in Simon's hand. It sounds like a lot hinges on that."

"It's highly unusual that all the evidence wasn't disclosed at one time, but after speaking with Mr. Garraway's attorney, I understand we'll have the letter next week. It's not clear exactly why it was kept separate. But they are not planning to withhold evidence, so I don't think we need to make an issue unless something changes."

Harper sighed. "The whole deal sounds frivolous to me. It's been over eighty years. How can this possibly be a thing?"

Their lawyer chuckled. "Any suit, if it's not thrown out, is a 'thing,' Harper. And the judge didn't throw this request out. So, do I think it's going anywhere? No. But do I know for certain? I do not. My advice is not to dismiss this out of hand. The very best thing would be to find some kind of proof from Eli's records that the land was legally and willingly transferred. Barring that, we'll take our chances with the judge. I know him. He's a pretty by-the-book, law-and-order man. But he also has been known to make some controversial decisions that favor the underdog. This is a classic underdog story."

"How did I not see this guy's game?" Cole muttered. "Looking back, it's clear. He was inordinately interested in the history of the ranch. He asked a million questions about those seven thousand acres."

It was true. Ty had not only been hyper-interested, but he'd frozen up like a Popsicle whenever Eli's name had been mentioned. None of them had figured it out.

"Worst of all," Cole continued. "Trampas here warned us about him two years ago. He even told us his name—Tyrone." Cole looked at Trampas, who hadn't said a word. "You thought then he was after part of Paradise, right?"

The old man nodded slowly. "I'd been told he'd found the letter from my father that had been a legend in the family. Ty's mother, my niece, also said he'd started talking about reclaiming the family legacy. When he disappeared for six months, I came looking for him. When he wasn't here I convinced myself he'd come to his senses."

"He charmed us all," Bella said. "I found him to be a lovely man. And little Teagan is delightful, too."

"Too bad he's an unscrupulous a-hole," Alec piped up, old rodeo cowboy crudeness surfacing in his anger.

At the name-calling, Grace's heart pounded in anger, too, but she forced herself to speak calmly.

"What if he isn't?" All eyes turned to her and she stood up to stare out at her family. "Seriously. I love the romantic stories about this ranch as much as anybody. Remember, Joely, how much it hurt two years ago to think our heritage wasn't as pristine as we'd been taught? We got over it. We've even turned it into our own mythology—Eli was a young, talented go-getter who outwitted a guy defaulting on his land. Adds a little color to a bland history. So—my question is, what if Ty is right? What if there's more to the story and Eli truly did threaten Simon? What if, God forbid, Eli wasn't the saint we keep putting up on a pedestal? What if the land really should go back to Trampas's family?"

Rumbling complaints grew from every quarter.

"What kind of a spell did he put on you, sis?" Raquel asked. "I knew you liked him—but sticking up for him at a time like this?"

"There was no spell," Grace said. "I don't like this any more than any of us does, and I'm plenty angry with Ty Garraway. But one thing I truly believe is that this isn't revenge. It's a legitimate action in his mind."

"I have to say, I think Grace is right about that," Trampas

said. "Not that I condone it."

"Then why did he agree to work here knowing he planned to turn on us?" Joely asked.

Grace shook her head. "You know it was to use us for information—about the land, about what really happened all those years ago. But there are always two sides to a story. How do we know Eli's side wasn't the darker one?"

"Because." Grandma Sadie spoke for the first time. Trampas sat beside her and patted her hand gently. "Eli Crockett didn't have a mean bone in his body. A manipulative one, perhaps, but not a mean one. He wouldn't have kidnapped a woman or threatened a man with a knife."

"What do you know about that time, Miss Sadie?" asked Radcliffe. "Do you have information that will shed some light?"

"I'm not a born-and-raised Crockett. You all know that. I married in. When I first met Eli I was maybe ten and he was in his late forties—a good-looking, funny, very persuasive man. He loved his wife and his sons, and this land meant the world to him. Paradise Ranch consisted of thirty-one thousand acres then, and Eli bought another four thousand during the first five years of my marriage to Sebastian. I never knew him to be anything but fair. Now, I'm not saying he wasn't a firebrand when he was in his twenties and just starting out—he was always ambitious, and smart. But a cheater? Cruel? I don't believe it. We're missing something here."

Silence followed her short speech and Grace swallowed. Ty believed with all his being that his great-grandfather had been threatened and cheated. Sadie believed her father-in-law had been a good and decent human. Sadie had to be right—there *was* something missing.

Trampas cleared his throat. "I'm not much help. I barely

remember my father. He had lived on his land for six or seven years as a bachelor and he was thirteen years older than my mother. They married because my brother Oliver came along. There were two babies who didn't live after that and my father was fifty years old when I surprised them in 1930. I was only five when this poker game supposedly happened so I didn't know Eli. I remember Sadie because she was just a year younger than my brother and Sebastian Crockett, and she took care of me once in a while. My mother never spoke ill of Eli, but she often said that Oliver followed in our father's footsteps. My brother drank too much, smoked too much, and married because he got his girlfriend pregnant—just as my father had. I'm not saying my father wasn't cheated—he might have been. I don't think he was a good man—but there are a few who followed who've tried to do better. I think, whether he's misguided or not, Ty is one of those. Still, if any of my story could serve as a character witness for Eli—I am not shy about sharing it."

Just like that, Trampas was part of the family. Her sisters hugged him, Sadie beamed at him, Bella kissed him on his gray, grizzled cheek. Grace was grateful, but part of her wished he'd stood up for Ty even more.

Radcliffe held up his hands for attention and the hubbub died down. "If you have more questions I'll answer them, and I'll dig further into the county files myself. If you find any papers in your family records that could be of help, please let me know. Any of you who can be present for this hearing, plan on attending. I'll go after this from the legal aspect—the land has been in the Crockett family for eighty years and that establishes ownership. The only proof they are offering are handwritten letters from a man and his son, both of whom we can contend were of weak moral character."

"We'll get what we need," Harper said, among murmurs of full agreement, and the official meeting broke up slowly.

Lunch was a strangely boisterous affair, with every Crockett sibling and the three spouses around the huge dining room table that could seat twenty. Everyone's mood was upbeat; everyone agreed that although the lawsuit was credible, it was not likely to succeed. Grace believed she was the only one who knew how smart and determined Ty was. She'd listened to all his hopes for the land he wanted for his daughter's future. She simply hadn't realized he'd already picked the land out. He saw this as a chance to redeem his family and secure Lucky's future. He wouldn't have started this if he didn't think he could finish it.

On the other hand, he was a gambler, however small time. He wasn't averse to trying to win a month's groceries with a good poker hand. Maybe this was simply another big gamble.

Once everyone had gone back to jobs and, in the case of Mia and Grandma Sadie, naps, Grace sat alone in the living room with Kelly. Raquel had gone to visit the horses. She definitely was not happy with Grace, her new project, or her stance on Ty versus Eli.

"She'll get over it," Kelly assured her. "She misses you, and she's afraid this is personal because she's the one who decided to close the second restaurant in Denver."

"That's the thing," Grace said. "This *is* partly because of the second restaurant. But that's not the only thing. I needed to start finding my own confidence. I love you both so much, but this has been an incredible experience, Kel. And if you could meet Ty, you'd see why I think better of him than everyone else does. He's been supportive, strong, full of ideas, insistent that I not give up ... I've grown to need him. It kills me that he's doing this."

"Were you falling in love with him?"

"That might be too strong. But I was certainly starting to know I *could* fall in love with him."

Kelly tapped a finger thoughtfully against her lips. "I know you. You wouldn't say that lightly."

Grace had no time to reply. A rapping at the back door brought both girls' heads up. Grace frowned as Kelly hurried through the kitchen. She followed and heard a little voice that made her heart sink even as she smiled.

"Grace, Grace, I—"

"Sweetie, hold on. I'm not Grace, I'm Kelly. I'm sorry."

"Kel—?"

Grace peeked over Kelly's shoulder and grinned. "Hey, Lucky. Remember I told you I had two sisters who look just like me? This is one of them. Was I right?"

For the first time since Grace had met her, Lucky looked nonplussed. She swiveled her head back and forth between the sisters several times. Finally she nodded. "You're right. But your mouth is a little different and your nose doesn't go like this the same way." She put a finger to her own nose and pushed the tip up about half a centimeter. "But your hair is the same color and your eyes, too. You're both pretty."

"My word, who is this child. I like her. A lot." Kelly laughed.

"This is Teagan Garraway," Grace said. "Better known as Lucky. She's very smart and very sweet. We *all* like her a lot. And behind her, getting entirely ignored, is Lil Wagner. She's mostly a friend, but she acts as Lucky's nanny."

"No, mostly she acts as *my* nanny," Lil said. The smile she offered shone through miserable eyes. "Nice to meet you,

Kelly."

"Nice to meet you, Kelly." Lucky stuck her hand out, too, and Kelly shook it vigorously.

"Come on in, you two," Grace said. "It's just us at the moment."

"I was a little afraid to come," Lil said. "But I really needed to."

Tears filled Lil's eyes, and Grace's heart broke as she understood. These two lives were affected maybe more than anyone else's.

"You're always welcome. Both of you."

Lucky, took two steps and threw herself into Grace's embrace. "Everyone is mad at Daddy. Aiden and Rory won't play with me. And Lil's new friend Marni won't see her either."

"Oh, sweetheart. I'm so sorry. That's not right. Come on. Let's get some lemonade and a cookie and we'll talk about it. Lil, what on Earth?"

They settled into the comfortable living room with its soaring windows and sunset-colored accents. Lucky sat on Grace's lap—highly unusual. Lil held a cup of coffee, insisting she was cold enough inside to enjoy the warmth.

"Where's Ty?" Grace asked.

"I don't know. Cole let him go with two weeks' severance pay and as much time as he needs to find a new place to live. He left about nine this morning and said he'd be back for Lucky's bedtime. I'm not really worried. He might have gone to Jackson to find a game."

"I'm sure you're right."

"I called … Marni." Lil hesitated, then shrugged. "You all know about us anyhow—I don't know why I keep being so coy about it. It's been a very long time since I'd found anyone to connect with like I did with her. But this morning, she just said she didn't think it would be a good idea for us to see each other right now." Lil's voice caught. "This definitely is a Crockett-centric town. You all have loyal friends."

"We do. But if that's what one of them is saying, then I'm ashamed of her. Of them. You have nothing to do with any of this, Lil. I know that."

"That means a lot, Grace. Not everyone feels that way. Melanie told us Aiden was busy all day today." Lil sighed. "And Rory went to work with his dad, I guess."

Grace exchanged a steamed glance with Kelly. "Honestly, I don't know what's wrong with my family."

"I was supposed to go on a trail ride with everyone today," Lucky said against Grace's chest. "And I almost had Daddy talked into the last puppy—I know it. Now he won't talk to me about them. He said this was exactly why he said no in the first place. What would we do with a puppy if we move to an apartment? Or back to Las Vegas."

"Oh, darling, be patient about the puppy. I have a feeling Rupert will wait for you. We'll keep working on your dad. As for the trail ride—we'll still do that, too. Maybe tomorrow when everyone is feeling a little better, okay?"

"Okay. Can I go play with the puppy?"

"Of course. I have an idea. How about we take Rupert for his first outing? I'd like to go to the cabin in town and finish something. I'll show you how we can walk around the pond."

"Really? He can come?" Lucky jumped off her lap.

"He can."

"Puppies?" Kelly asked.

"Joely and Alec found an abandoned mom and her litter while driving home. They're adorable. Go ahead with Lucky, and she'll introduce you."

"Yeah, I think I'd like that. C'mon Lucky," Kelly said.

"We'll be right there," Grace added, with a grateful thank-you in her voice.

When they were gone, Grace set her hands on Lil's shoulders and looked her straight in the eyes. The misery there went further than sadness about Marni.

"We haven't had a lot of time to really get to know each other," Grace said, "but you are amazing. You're wonderful with Lucky, you keep Ty in line, you cook, you stay gorgeous, and you're brave. We're going to fix all of this, Lil. Don't give up."

Tears ran freely down Lil's cheeks and she hugged Grace tightly.

"Just so you know, I've kept Rupert and the black-and-tan pup you like, but they're Lucky's and yours. They can live here until we knock some sense into Ty's head. You and Lucky each *need* a dog. Trust me, I know for a fact what good therapy they are."

"Why?" Lil snuffled and wiped her nose and eyes. Grace found her a tissue. "Why are you being so good to us? Aren't you mad at Ty, too?"

"I'm furious," Grace admitted. "But I know he believes what he's doing is right. He hurt us, but he's not a con-artist who set out to do it on purpose. His actions don't have anything to do with you. Can we still be friends?"

"You have no idea what a gift that is. I'm pissed as hell at him, but I love the guy, Grace, and even though it's only been a few weeks, you're the best thing that's happened to Ty in a long time. I'm sorry he screwed it up."

"I am, too." Grace let her go and gave a sad smile. "There are two puppy collars and leashes hanging by the back door. We'll bring your little girl to town, too. Help Lucky put Rupert's on, and I'll be out in a minute. I have one thing to do before we go."

"Okay." Lil started off, then turned back and hugged Grace again. "I think you might have just saved a little girl's day, maybe her future, by showing her what true charity looks like. A big girl's, too."

Grace shook her head, too emotional to argue. She'd done automatically what her entire family, and her faith, taught her to do. How had everyone else forgotten it all of a sudden? When Lil was out the door, Grace picked up her cell phone. It took only seconds to find the number she wanted, and when her old friend answered, Grace spoke kindly but with no room for argument.

"Marni? You and I have to talk."

Chapter Twenty

TY LEANED AGAINST the side of the cottage, amusement momentarily overshadowing piercing unhappiness. He'd accomplished nothing today and come to no terms with what he'd done to the Crocketts—which was send them into a frenzy of wagon circling, war preparations, and anger. The only person who'd spent any time talking to him had been Cole. And that was simply to tell him, in his reasonable and managerial way, that it wouldn't be a good idea for Ty to continue working.

He'd expected as much. What he hadn't expected was how deeply he'd feel the hurt. Still, he'd done it to himself. He'd taken the advice to be dishonest and known the consequences, and although falling in love with Grace had been beyond stupid, he'd allowed himself to keep falling. He deserved this.

He stared at the four people playing with the puppies in the cottage's back yard. Cole had told him Grace and her triplet siblings were of the truly rare variety—genuinely identical. Whichever sister was with her, proved it was true. The two were so alike physically they could have been made on God's copy machine and then animated. It didn't matter; Ty knew his Grace without question. She was the one who moved like a gazelle—sure and strong but graceful and lovely. She was the one who bent to show Lucky how to kindly stop a puppy from chewing; she was the one whose laughter shimmered rather than rang; she was the one who shone with the quality in her name.

He wanted her. Clearly it had nothing to do with her looks or he'd have been attracted to her sister as well. But the brasher, louder, more athletic second triplet looked like fun but not like love embodied. After three nights, Ty sensed how empty his world was going to be without Grace in it.

Lucky and the puppy bounded closer to Ty's hiding place, and he ducked into the shadows.

"Grace! He knows his name!"

"He's learning it."

"Do you think Rupert will help Rory and Aiden like me again? I think boys maybe like puppies."

Grace squatted in front of her. "Rory and Aiden don't need anything to help them like you, sweetheart. You've been friends for a while now with no puppies at all."

"But they told me I was a traitor, so I don't think we're friends anymore."

"Listen. Rory and Aiden are little boys. They don't really understand what's going on; they only know that their parents are upset. You have to show them you understand and you have to let them be mad at your dad if they want. Your dad is big enough to handle it. If you're patient and if you don't stoop to treating them the same way they treated you, they'll come around. Pretty soon they'll miss their friend. Rupert is just another toy—it's you they like."

They wandered back to the main yard again and their conversation faded from earshot. Ty slumped against the side of the cottage. Grace had just done something for his daughter he never would have done—turn a negative into a positive. Aiden and Rory were no longer bad guys, and she'd managed to guide Lucky into being nice, all the while telling her she was special. She'd even upheld *him* in his daughter's eyes.

There was no denying Grace was the sexiest woman he'd ever known. But the sexy came from something more powerful than beauty. And he'd royally screwed up any good thing they'd had a chance to create together.

"What are you doing here?"

He looked into Lil's eyes and hung his head. "She's taken you under her wing, too, I see."

"She's an amazing person. Why are you hurting her? Hurting her family?"

"Lil, I planned this long before I met any of them. My mistake was getting to know them."

"Really? That's your excuse? Honestly, Ty, I feel like I don't know you."

Lil had been one of his best friends for five years. Her barb stung. But he had no energy to discuss his real feelings with her.

"I need to talk to her. Just for a minute. Can you ask her?"

She pursed her lips and studied him. "I will. But it's because of her, not out of any great loyalty to you today. See Marni over there?"

He nodded.

"An hour ago she refused to speak to me. Grace got her to come. Because of that kindness, I think the first girl I've found in years that I really would like to spend time with, is going to stick around for a while. So, I'll pass on the kindness and do you a favor. She'll come because that's who she is, but you'd better be nice to her."

He couldn't watch while Lil made the request. He waited, half nervous, half excited, with his back literally against the wall of her cottage, eyes on the ground, mind racing.

"I should kick you off my property for trespassing."

He lifted his head and reveled in the sensation of his heart slamming into his throat. He was alive, painful as it was this moment.

"I'm sure from where you stand it would be fitting."

"What do you want, Ty?" Her features gave away no emotion—not anger, not sadness, definitely not attraction.

He reached into his back pocket and retrieved a business-sized envelope. "To give you this." He held it out. "Your family's lawyer has a copy as of this morning. I wanted to hand one right to you. Apologize in person."

"What is it?"

"A letter Simon Manterville wrote to the county commissioner in 1935. I think if you read it, you'll at least understand why I have to try and reestablish a little honor for my family. I'd like Lucky to know that sometimes stories passed down through generations are not completely true as told."

"But eighty years, Ty. How can you possibly think you still have a right to that land?"

"This information was buried in a weird place it didn't get to accidentally. I don't know why but I think it was hidden. I'd have brought it to light sooner if I could."

She hesitated but then took a breath and opened the envelope.

As she read, her cheeks blossomed with bright spots of color, and she worried her bottom lip. When she finished, she looked up, anger bright in her eyes.

"This is what the whole case hinges on?"

"It explains a lot, don't you think?"

"This is no more than the desperate plea of a man who realized he'd gambled away his home. Of course he's going to try to get it back by calling foul. There's no proof any of this is real."

"I think my lawyer has put together some convincing facts and a timeline that fits everything in that letter."

With an angry snap, Grace folded the papers and shoved them unceremoniously back into the envelope. "So that's it. You're really going through with it."

"I have to."

"That's a load of bull crap, Ty. You don't have to do anything." She looked around desperately, as if searching for words that failed her. "After all this time, you don't need that particular piece of land; you just want it. You keep saying this is all to restore family honor but what does that mean? From what I can tell, you didn't even like your family. Why make this all live on?"

"You think this is all about the past? It's not. It's about the future. My father was just like Simon. To my dad I was nothing more than a tool, something he'd made himself, to be used whenever, wherever and however he wanted. I used to tell him all the time I wished to hell I'd been born in Trampas's family. I got angrier and angrier, and it started to show in all kinds of ways—bad friends, bad clothing, bad habits. I was defined by the genetics of that branch on the family tree. Even poker playing, which I liked and was good at, identified me as Simon's progeny. My father finally threw me out when I was fifteen. He sent me to Trampas. God knows, that saved me. He's a good man, Trampas Manterville.

"But his side of the family has lived with Simon's black mark, too. This is a chance to clear the record a little. There may be bad seeds in the family, but the land belonged to good people, too, and they got cheated out of it. I want that clear record for Lucky. Can you understand that?"

"Of course. We all want our histories to be perfect. My family is gnashing its teeth and tearing through old boxes looking for proof that Eli wasn't the kind of man who'd do what this letter accuses him of doing. How do you think national and international history gets whitewashed? We want pristine answers to hard questions."

She tried to hand the letter back, but he shook his head. "Keep it. It's a copy. The original is now filed with the court documents."

"I'm sorry you feel you have to do this," she said. "I wish you could be happy with the person you are deep down. Lucky doesn't need anything more than the dad she has—the wonderful person I was getting to know."

Heartsick, Ty ignored the implied compliment. "I understand why this changes everything, Grace. I wish it didn't have to."

"I'm sure you do. Oddly enough, I believe you're a hundred percent sincere. I even defended you this morning. But that's not enough for my family at the moment; this is personal. So I'm stuck in the middle. That's my choice, my problem. We'll duke it out in court and a judge will decide. Seven thousand acres isn't going to make or break Paradise Ranch, but you stirred up strong, protective instincts. It won't be pretty."

"I know what I'm getting into. I lose no matter what. If a judge gives me the land, I'll be ostracized as the ass who stole the property. If I lose, I'll leave Wyoming, and good riddance."

"So why?"

"Principle."

"You know? I can respect that, even though I think you're kind of an ass for the way this turned out."

"Remember the other night, I told you I wanted to talk to you no matter what time it was? I was going to give you this envelope and tell you everything. Your family wasn't supposed to get the court papers until this week."

"Is that true?"

"I swear. If my word means anything anymore."

"Just tell me one thing. Why? Why did you come to work for us even though you knew you were going to stab us in the back?"

He shook his head sorrowfully.

"You're right, Grace, I believe in what I'm doing. I believe my family has a right to that piece of land. I was focused only on that—on the future for Lucky. But I was scared, too. What do I know about *living* on a ranch much less starting one? Who better to learn from than the best of the experts? I planned to watch from afar, but then Cole offered me the job. Was it assholery to take it? I guess it was. Was it malicious? Not intentionally. And you? You were never part of the plan. You just happened to me because of who you are—good and smart and the embodiment of the kind of family I wish Lucky could have."

He stopped, finally, almost out of breath at the long, uncharacteristic speech. He looked away.

For the first time, Grace softened. She kicked at a clod of dirt and gazed wistfully at his averted face. "There is another solution."

"Oh?" His eyes found hers again.

"I could give you the land, free and clear."

"You don't have that authority."

"I do if I'm giving it to a husband. I could marry you and request that land for my own—we each get to choose our own piece of Paradise, you know. We could skip this whole ugly trial, I'd section off the seven thousand acres you want and give it to you as a wedding present. I could make sure it was a hundred percent legal before we divorce and each go our happy way. Done."

He stared at her. "Do you know, I think you'd really do that. Just to stop your family from going through this."

"Or maybe I think the land *should* be yours."

"But you don't. And I don't want you to wimp out because of any words I just said."

"I don't know *how* I feel, Ty." She turned away, frustrated again.

"I'd never marry you to get an easy ride into this."

"Oh? Why not? You're looking for an easy way as it is. Land just sitting there for you to jump in and claim? What sweat equity did you put into it? What tears did you shed over people who died making it viable and useable?"

"The modern kind of sweat—and tears." His voice tensed in frustration now, too. "Fought through the legal system instead of a poker match, but still legitimate."

"Then so be it. Fight your way in, Ty. But you're right. It won't be the gold at the end of the rainbow you think it is."

"I'm not looking for gold."

"Good. Then I hope you find exactly what you *are* looking for."

Grandma Sadie lifted the letter again, adjusted her glasses

and caught Grace's eye over the top of the paper.

"You're right. It's quite the literary work," she said, before beginning to read where she'd left off.

"'I got to admit that on the night I met Eli for the poker game, I downed a whiskey or two. I was plenty nervous. It's a well-known fact Eli is pretty near a professional poker player. He's won money off of almost everyone in town. I am only pretty good—when Eli isn't around. So I tried one last time to get out of it and make a deal for a different way to pay off my debt to him. I said I could spend some time workin' for him along with my boys. I told him my wife was willing to take in laundry or watch their little Sebastian anytime they needed since he was the same age as my Oliver. That's when Eli pulled the knife and told me to shut up about my wife. This was between men.

"'I asked him again where was my wife and he said I would find all that out when we was done. What he said exactly was he was in control of Lydia and if I wanted her to come back, I had to grow up and act like a man. He said I'd promised to play him for the deed to my land and by God I was gonna keep my word. If I won, he'd clear up all the bank loans and what I owed him and we'd be done. He'd send Lydia back home. If I lost, he got the land and I would have to beg my own wife to come back to me.

"'It was a forgone decision that I would lose that game and I did. At first I won some chickens and a couple head of cattle off him. But he was just toying. He shut me down faster than river water slides over a wet rock and before I knew it, he was polishing up that knife again and I was signing the note that turned over my land to him.

"'I tried to protest but he sent me on my way, saying he'd

tell Lydia what happened and she could come back to a loser like me if she wanted. There was no call for that, but I went home, I admit, like a whupped dog, and the worse part was, by the time I got there, my older boy had been scared off and my young son was gone, too. I got a note from Lydia sayin' she couldn't live with a man who lost his farm in a gambling game.

"'I take full responsibility for bein' hotheaded enough to agree to the poker game. But I ask you to look at the circumstance. I was threatened and bullied. I thought I had no choice if I wanted to stay alive. Please look into reversing what happened. I believe I was cheated purposely and that Eli Crockett has no right to my land.

"'Most sincerely yours,

"'Simon W. Manterville, Lincoln County, Wyoming'"

"Well if that isn't heartrending." Sarcasm dripped from Bella's words, and Grace looked at her mother in shock. Bella never said anything negative about anyone. Her pique was telling.

The whole family had gathered again, but the room was quiet.

"What do think, Grandma?" Grace asked.

"I think he got somebody to dictate a calm and coherent letter to him. He didn't speak this well on his own. What about you?" Grandma Sadie turned to Trampas, the only non-family member present.

"I don't recall anything about the poker game except that after it my mother and I went to her sister's. Oliver ran off and I didn't see him until I was a teenager. My mother died of tuberculosis when I was ten. I never saw my father again. I think Ollie did."

"I'm so sorry, Trampas. It's kind of a sad story," Mia said.

"I had a good life," he replied. "I had a wonderful wife, my daughter is lovely as is my grandson, and there's Ty. I think he needs to see this through for his own sake—we've all got to learn in this life. I would hope you'd remember that he isn't a bad boy."

"Maybe you're right." Mia spoke as compassionately about Ty as anyone had to that point. "The bottom line is, however, that the letter *sounds* coherent, logical and plausible. It's going to be his word against ours—basically, Grandma, it's you against a ghost that can't defend itself."

"I'm starting to worry that this is not a slam dunk," Harper said. "We have to keep digging."

"We could just give him the land."

Grace tried one more time. Her head ached from trying to figure out exactly how she felt.

"Why would you suggest such a thing?" Harper asked.

"All we have are our own stories. Even you two," she looked at Grandma Sadie and Trampas, "only have perceptions of Eli. You don't know what he was like in town after a few beers. Maybe, even though Simon was a drunk and a mean man, the story is true."

She stopped for a moment and took in her family—so united in their loyalty to Paradise.

"Think about it," she said, her voice rising slightly. "Ty is fighting for his future, for his family, for what he truly believes is his, just like we are. In some ways, that's the kind of dedication and conviction I'd want in a man. Someone who'll go as far as he needs to for his family." She caught Raquel's eye and stared steadily. "Not a religious freak who sacrifices my feelings in the name of his own beliefs." She took in the room again. "Look. What difference does seven thousand acres make out of fifty thousand? We could be done with this in a day, go back to being friends, and life goes on."

A very long minute of silence reigned after her lecture, but she didn't look away or back down.

"It's just a bad precedent, Gracie," Cole said at last. "You girls get to decide this, of course, but you know how hard it's been to plot the future of Paradise after your dad died. We laid out plans for every inch of space for now and the future. True; those relatively few acres won't impact a lot, but if they're to be sold, then they should be sold, not given away. What happens when the next guy comes along and wants a piece?"

"Oh, who's going to come along?" Mia sighed and placed a hand on her swollen belly. "Other than this child, very soon I hope. And then we have a whole new generation to provide for. I vote we see this through. If a judge gives Ty the land then I say we all agree to abide by it and treat Ty fairly. Same if we win."

"We're going to win," Harper said.

"Then we'd better hope this judge does not have a soft spot for sob stories." Cole kissed his wife and smiled. "Or ghosts."

Chapter Twenty-One

GRACE MISSED TY.

After nearly four weeks of spending time with him every day and two weeks not seeing him at all, she could no longer deny she had feelings, strong ones, for the traitor of Paradise Ranch. He had disappeared into a part-time job in Wolf Paw Pass, and the only way Grace knew he was all right was from Lil's and Lucky's reports. They all remained in the house on the ranch while Ty looked for a new place he could afford. Having precious Lucky around was Grace's only solace

Grace loved the precocious little girl and spent every minute she wasn't at the cottage or helping Mia with Ty's daughter. They knitted together, they trained Rupert and Flora, the name Lil had given the other pup. And Grace, Harper, and Kelly took Lucky and the boys on Lucky's first trail ride. Ty gave his permission but nobody expected him to come along. It was sad, Grace thought. If ever an angel on Earth looked like she'd found her way back to heaven, it was Lucky trotting Panda on the trail toward Wolf Paw Peak, and her father missed it.

Lil claimed Ty didn't say much about the impending court hearing, and she didn't ask him. Nobody talked about the doom-like heaviness that hung over the ranch. Now that the hearing date was a mere two days away, everyone had exhausted all speculation on what could happen, and nobody knew *what* to say, so they lived silently with the gloom. The only joyous things were the children who, just as Grace had promised, were once again fast friends.

The call from Kevin DeMars at the cottage reached her on Tuesday afternoon while she was going through Mia's hospital suitcase for the third time in a week. Since baby was due on the hearing date, prepping for his or her arrival also claimed high status as one of very few cheery activities, even though Mia was no longer a calm and patient mother-to-be. Since she normally thrived on being healthy and perpetually active, the forced inactivity because of her broken foot had taken its toll and made her alternately cranky and depressed.

She let Grace talk her out of funks, and Rory was always a balm for her nerves, but her mother, her grandmother, and Harper were too close, and she barked at them the way she did at her rock of a husband, Saint Gabe. The wonderful man never took a word of his wife's irritation personally, and Grace tried to follow his example.

Nonetheless, the urgent request from the construction crew came as a welcome respite. Grace set Mia up in front of a good romantic comedy, set a plate of cookies and lemonade beside her and told her not to go into labor for the next two hours.

"I wish I were the kind of person who flipped anyone the bird," Mia groused. "I'd flip you a giant emu."

Grace left, laughing at the funniest thing anyone had said in ten days.

"We finally got into the back of the kitchen here because we have time to frame in the addition today." Kevin DeMars, a short, slender man in his forties with the upper body of a gymnast and a voice like Tom Waits with a head cold, led her to a section of wall bearing the unmistakable outline of a door that had been caulked shut. "We found this underneath several layers of wallpaper."

"Based on all the shoddy walls and covered up features, my father and grandfather definitely gave renters of this place free rein," Grace said. "Wonder if this leads to anything."

"If it does, it's not a very big space," Kevin replied. "But I didn't want to demolish the wall without checking."

"I appreciate it." She looked around at the progress Kevin and his crew had made. Much of the new framing needed for her dining room and new restrooms was finished. Two original outer walls had been sanded and prepped for new stain. Insulation had gone into the roof and the roof itself had been replaced with light-colored, eco-friendly metal— something Ty had read about and suggested.

She longed to call him now and have him help check out this secret surprise door.

"You guys are doing an amazing job. I hate to set back your timeline, but could we take the time to open this properly? I want to keep as much of this place original as I can. I doubt it'll amount to anything but I'd still like to look."

"Your wish is my command," he laughed in his rasping voice. "It shouldn't really take any time. We'll do it this afternoon. Why don't you go inspect the little dining room you're putting in—see what Casey did with the fireplace." He gave a little wink to tell her he knew she'd be pleased.

The once-hidden fireplace in the small dining room brought tears to her eyes. The beautifully crafted stacked stone had been sandblasted and looked like it had just been set. The firebox had been replaced with a safer gas insert. The thick, uneven beam used as a mantel had a fresh, light coat of varnish. The multiple colors of the fieldstone hearth almost sparkled in earth tones from gray to black to deep maroon. All she could think about was coming so close to kissing Ty while trying to see up the flue. He would love the refurbishment. He would have ideas about the door.

His ideas were everywhere.

"I thought you'd like this." Kevin caught her wiping away tears, and she grasped his arm quickly.

"I do. Oh I do. It's stunning—almost prettier than the big one in the main room. I'm just … totally blown away that this is all happening. Forgive the tears."

He nodded with a slightly embarrassed grin. "That's what I wanted to hear. All right, then, I'm off to pull some wires for electrical in the other little room and the bathrooms. I'll open that door after everyone gets back from lunch and I can grab another guy to help handle it properly. You can be here with us, or I'll call you. Whichever."

Oh, she was going to be here, all right. She just didn't want to be here alone. But who would she ask? Mia wasn't an option. Grandma wasn't either. Her mother was still working at the art center with Harper, and although Kelly had visited once, Raquel hadn't ever been here. In their defense, each had flown back and forth to Denver to keep tabs on Triple Bean. They were both back so they could attend the hearing, but Grace knew Raquel was still deeply hurt.

She pressed Joely's number, hoping maybe she was in town at the vet clinic where she worked during the summer. But when she reached her sister, she was twenty miles away on a call with Dr. Ackerman, the town's only vet until Joely finished in a year.

Sighing, Grace resigned herself to figuring out whatever came of the door alone. Looking around the future restaurant gave her thrills of anticipation. It also scared and saddened her. What good was a dream if you lived it all alone? Her mother and most of her sisters supported her, but the two she loved most deeply barely acknowledged she *had* a dream, and the person who'd encouraged her above everyone else? He was as good as dead from her life.

The truth overwhelmed her and tears dripped once more. She'd only come this far at such lightning speed because of one person. He'd never allowed her to let doubt seep in. He'd never given her anything but sound opinions and had forced her to keep moving, keep making decisions and keep fulfilling her dreams. She might have let herself get overwhelmed and quit had it not been for Ty.

She looked at her phone and anger hit.

She couldn't and wouldn't call him, but there was no reason under heaven she shouldn't have the next best choice for support. She was letting Raquel mold her feelings again. It was time to become the leader.

"Rocky?" she said when Raquel answered her call. "You and Kelly need to come to the cottage. Now."

"We're going to—"

"No." Grace firmed her voice and took the step into her new character. "Short of picking up lottery winnings that you're going to share with me anyway, or taking Mia to the hospital to have the child, you are out of excuses."

A moment of shocked silence almost made her laugh. She gave it no time to grow.

"I *need* you. Both. I need your ideas, your expertise, your support. And now there's something kind of big happening, so get your butts over here by one o'clock."

She didn't wait for a reply; she ended the call and stuck her phone back in her purse. It didn't ring back, and Grace's spirit soared for the first time in days. She'd taken the lead and, in the process, shown herself she was an equal triplet. And she loved the other two more than ever.

Forty-five minutes later, Kelly grabbed Grace's upper arm and Raquel stood behind, embracing them both, her chin on Grace's shoulder. Her sisters had not only come, they'd brought the gift of acceptance. "You need us?" Raquel had asked. "We kind of thought you didn't want us."

"Dork," Grace told her.

And now they waited the last seconds before the old door was completely off its rusted, filed-down hinges.

"This is a lot of anticipation for what's going to be nothing," Grace said.

"Like that thing with Al Capone." Kelly laughed. "What is it Mom always says? Don't get too excited—it could be Al Capone's empty vault."

"Well I never saw that so I don't care," Raquel said. "I choose to go with buried treasure."

They laughed, together, and two workers pulled the door away. It took another minute for one of them to hang a utility light. "There you go," he said. "It's a room of some sort."

The girls crowded to the door.

The size of the windowless space surprised them all. It was narrow and long—about seven feet wide by half the length of the cottage—twelve or fourteen feet. Neatly fitted wood planking lined all four walls and the ceiling

"It's like a … a … I don't know what the heck this would

have been?" Raquel said.

"Look at this!" Kelly cried. "There's furniture."

"An old writing desk." Grace ran her hand over the piece, its slanted front closed for who knew how long.

"Here's a trunk and two wooden chairs," Kelly said.

"And a pile of old blankets." Raquel lifted a folded quilt from the top and shook it open. "Oh my gosh, this is beautiful. It's really worn, but it must be handwork from decades ago."

There wasn't much else except dust, but Grace felt like they'd found a little treasure anyway. She tugged on the desk door and it dropped down easily. The inside was lined with delightful little cubbies, and she discovered two old pencils, a bottle of dried ink, and a beautiful blue and red cloisonné hair clip.

"Somebody used this for an office or a little hideaway," Grace said. "It's so cool—I wish I knew what it really means."

"Whatever it was, let's make sure and take the quilt and blankets home and let Grandma look at them. The desk would be a cute accent piece for your restaurant." Raquel smiled.

Grace wrapped her arms around her sister and held her tightly. "Thank you, Rocky."

"I'm so sorry," Raquel said. "I love you, Gracie. I don't want you to leave Denver, and I've been so angry about it because I can't imagine working there without you. But if I'm honest, I always knew you'd be the first to find your own way. This is good for you, and we'll figure out how to help you long distance."

Kelly placed a hand on Grace's shoulder. "Ditto. I think … hey, what's this?"

She peered at the inside of the desk and pointed. Grace saw the tiny indentation in the writing surface and touched it. It proved to be a small trapdoor leading to a space behind the drawers. Once she lifted it, another surprise awaited in the indentation—a black bound book, just five by seven inches and an inch and a half thick. The cover leather bore a faded, gold-leaf scrollwork border with the letter "L" in the middle. She stared at her sisters and opened the book slowly. Pages of clear, beautiful, feminine handwriting greeted her.

"Oh my gosh," she said, almost reverently. "This is somebody's journal."

They brought the book out into the light of the kitchen, sent the two construction crew members back to whatever they'd been doing before, and all sat, oblivious to the dust on the floor. It took only seconds to find the name inscribed inside the cover.

"Lydia Canby Manterville." Grace's mouth dropped open and stayed there.

"You found Lydia Manterville's journal?" Kelly asked. "This is unbelievable."

Randomly, Grace opened to a page near the middle. "This is from July of 1935."

"'Times are getting tougher every month,'" she read. "'Another big cattle operation opened between us and Sheridan last week. Simon refuses to allow that he can't compete anymore with our little herd of three hundred head when operations like the new place have three thousand. Folks like Eli Crockett will do fine because he knows how to properly manage his business. Simon just gets more stubborn and meaner. He hasn't paid our grocery bill nor the doctor nor the banker for the new addition on the barn for near four months now. And Oliver and I are having a hard time keeping the place going what with Simon gone playing cards in town most nights. Little Trampas is just plain scared of his daddy's anger. I wish Simon would sell before he loses everything.'"

"What?" Kelly's eyes were big as moons.

Grace flipped more pages, and the girls took turns reading random entries, each one more and more heartbreaking than the last. The Manterville ranch was falling apart. Simon was rarely sober anymore. Oliver was seventeen and getting wilder. Worst of all, Lydia was taking the brunt of Simon's anger—in two entries, she wrote that he'd hit her.

"Spousal abuse back then, too," Raquel whispered, her face pale. "This is awful."

"'August thirteenth,'" Grace read quietly. "'Of course Brigitta came over today. She only comes every few weeks and I usually look forward to her visits with all my heart. But today my arm was twisted and bruised and my cheek had a mark on it I couldn't hide with what little powder I have left from Jackson. I know Brigitta doesn't believe my stories about falling or running into walls, but she never says a word.'"

"Great-Grandma!" Kelly said.

"Here's the rest," Grace said. "'This morning, though, she took one look at me and just pulled me into her arms. She rocked me like I was her baby and I'm ashamed to say I cried like one. She said I have to think about leaving because I'm too far away to get help if Simon really hurts me. I tried to deny he did, but she wouldn't hear it. She put cold compresses on my cheek, and she wrapped my sore arm and made me a sling. I'll have to hide that when Simon gets home, but it feels better for now. It would be a sin to leave my husband, I know this. But I am scared. Mostly for the boys. If he hurt one of them, I would never forgive myself. I don't know what to do. But thank God for Brigitta. She and Eli are a wonder. If they were a different kind of people, the whole town should know about my problems—but they don't.'"

They read entry after entry, engrossed and horrified as the saga unfolded in Lydia's perfect, beautiful penmanship. It was nearly an hour after they'd first found the diary when Grace came to the last two entries.

"I'm afraid to read these," she said. "This next one is dated September fifteenth—it's almost ten days after the last one."

"You have to," Raquel urged.

Grace nodded and took a breath. "'I am going to hell, I'm sure, even though I've asked God's forgiveness for abandoning my husband and oldest son. I have no choice but to give them up to God's mercy and Eli's strength. Eli is my only hope. Now that I am safely hidden in Brigitta's house in town, I will write it. Simon Manterville is a dangerous man. Eli Crockett is the only one who can handle him. He came to the house for the poker game, and Brigitta was with him. Eli had to threaten Simon with a knife to get him out to the barn, where he said they were going to play cards like men. He did it so Brigitta could get me away. I could barely walk but she helped me to hurry. I am sick to be abandoning my vows, but I have not felt this safe for as long as I can remember.

"'Simon doesn't know this room in the town house is here. If he were to come looking, he can't find me. I don't know how it will turn out. I hope Trampas will get to my sister's safely. I know Oliver won't come—he's partial to his daddy. I do pray Eli will be all right. Simon was drunk and cursing when he got hauled to the barn for the game. Eli will win—he's a far better poker player than Simon. Brigitta always laughs that it's his one vice. She does love him so. It's the only thing I'm ever envious of. I don't deserve such a friend.'"

"Oh my God," Raquel swore for one of the rare times in her life. "It's all true, just like the letter said, but this twists it around completely."

"Read the last one," Kelly begged.

"'It's done,'" Grace read. "'Simon signed over the land to Eli and good riddance, and now Simon has gone. They've been looking for him since the end of the game but he's run off. I think he's all right because they say he packed a case. Eli threatened to tell how he hurt me. Simon always believes Eli so I think he just ran away. I am more worried about my boys. Trampas is on his way to Anna's in Illinois, so Brigitta says. I believe her, but I have no word from Oliver. I'll stay hidden for several more days and then travel to my sister and son. I only hope Oliver, wherever he is, will forgive me for what I did. I should miss Simon and feel bad, but I'd rather burn for breaking my vows than have Simon hurt one more hair on our heads. Oliver is already acting too much like his father … At least Trampas is safe thanks to the Crocketts. A bigger sin is my gratitude, even a little bit of love in my heart for Eli. He has saved my life, whether it was worth saving or not. I refused to let him pay me full market value for the land, but he insisted on giving me half—ten dollars an acre. I talked him down to five, which is still thirty-five thousand dollars. I'll put it in savings for the boys, otherwise, whatever am I going to do with so much money?'"

The girls sat together in stunned silence.

"That's it?" Kelly asked.

"She must have left in a hurry and forgotten this." Grace stared at the last page, willing words to appear and finish the story.

More silence followed and she made the mistake of looking

up at her sisters. Both of them wiped tears from their eyes. Grace began to cry as well, but just as quickly as her silent tears began, she was choked with simultaneous laughter.

"You do know what this means, right?" she asked. "Lydia Manterville just gave us an out to our problem."

"I wish it hadn't come at such a cost," Raquel said.

"A huge cost—" Grace was cut off by her phone. She found her purse and answered.

"Gracie?" Mia's voice held controlled panic. "You need to come home."

"Is it the baby? Are you ready?"

"No. No. Not that. It's the kids. Rory, Lucky and Aiden. They're missing. It's an all-hands search. You don't by chance know where Rocky and Kel are?"

"They're here, they're both here. What happened?"

"Don't know. Lil said they were going out to play with the dogs and that was two hours ago. They didn't come back for lunch and we've searched all the buildings."

For a pregnant lady who had to be worried sick, she maintained her cool well. What else could go wrong? Grace wondered, her own heart beginning to pound.

"We'll be right there. Don't worry. We'll find them."

"I know. Kids wander off all the time around here." Mia paused. "Hurry?"

Chapter Twenty-Two

"TY, HONEY, STOP your pacing." Bella touched his arm and gently forced him to stop. "This won't be the last time kids go temporarily missing on this place. I swear I used to lose one or more of the girls every other day."

"I wish that helped," he said, and Bella chuckled.

"I know. And I'm not making light. We never take for granted they're okay until they're home. But Aiden knows Paradise as well as he knows his own room, and Rory does, too. Ah! There are the rest of my girls."

He hadn't seen Grace in nearly two weeks, and the sight of her now was like salve on a burn. He'd also never seen all three triplets together. It made him want to stare in wonder, and at the same time laugh at the bizarre sight of three Graces. He still knew her immediately—from the way she walked to the light in her eyes. To him she was as different from Kelly and Raquel as Mia and Harper were from each other and Joely. He tried to smile, knowing she wasn't here for him. Even missing children didn't absolve him of his crimes.

It shocked him to his core when she approached nearly at a run and grabbed him into an embrace. At first he couldn't even hold her. Then, as her warmth and scent enveloped him, his body let go of its painful tension and he squeezed as hard as he could.

"Are you okay?" she asked.

"Hardly."

"She's fine, Ty. I guarantee it. She's brilliant and resourceful, and the boys know all about the dangers of going too far."

"But it's been more than two hours since anyone has seen them." His heart slid to his stomach for the hundredth time. "And I wasn't here. I should have been here. She's five years old."

"Don't start. You're working. It's a crap time for everyone. This is not your fault. My sisters and I used to go hide for hours. Three's a safe number."

"So they keep telling me."

They released each other, but he stayed close to her for the next forty-five minutes, amazed at the calm, choreographed production taking place while he went useless inside. He wanted to go search, but he had no clue where to look. Bella and Bjorn insisted he was better off waiting for Lucky right where he was, along with Mia and Melanie—both missing their kids, but both a lot calmer than he was. Cole, Gabe, Alec, Joely, and Bjorn's daughter Skylar were out on horseback. Gabe's father, Russ, a local pilot, even had his plane in the air. Neighbors, the sheriff and everybody was on the lookout, no matter that the kids weren't officially considered missing yet.

Most amazing of all was that everyone seemed to have forgotten he was the enemy. He was plied with coffee and back pats. Nobody mentioned the court hearing. He didn't understand, but he was grateful.

The top of the fourth hour approached and Ty's stomach was in such a knot he could barely breathe, when the first whoop came up from outside the barn.

Grace, seated next to him on a hay bale outside the barn's lounge, gave his back a quick rub and nodded. "It's good news," she said. "Go."

He ran to the door in time to see Leif, cowboy hat pushed back on his head and mustache twitched over a grin, marching toward him, each hand holding onto a different boy's ear like in a movie from the fifties. Ahead of them strode Lucky, her head high, narrowed eyes trying to mask the fear that she was in deep trouble.

"Here you go, Ty. Mia. Melanie. They tried to make it to Mexico, but we nabbed 'em at the Rio Grande just shy of the border."

"Grandpa!" Aiden complained. "That's dumb. And you're hurting my ear."

"Sorry, boy," Leif replied. "Your mama might be gentler when she grabs it from me." He let Aiden go, bent and gave him a kiss on the head and pushed him toward Melanie, who grabbed him into a hug. "You're in a whole lotta trouble."

"But I wasn't doing anything wrong."

Mia crutched her way to Rory, who was also now free of the old Norwegian's ear hold. Like Melanie, Mia hugged her son the best she could around the baby bump and then pulled back. "Where were you guys? We called. We looked for over three hours."

"We …" Rory shot a glance at Lucky, who simply shrugged. "We walked all the way down to the river bend by the fourth bungalow and were playing in Aiden's fort."

"Aiden has a fort?"

"He just built it last week. It's cool."

Ty heard no more. He picked up his own child and held her as if she'd been gone a month. Lil was right behind him. "Crap on a Cheez-It, Lucky! I thought you'd been swept off by the river or buried alive in a rock slide. What made you wander off like that?"

"We were just playing."

He knew the look of guilt she could never hide when she was in trouble.

"You were not. What's going on?"

She struggled out of his arms. "We were playing poker, okay? I'm only trying to help you."

He was at a loss, but his adrenaline still pumped so hard he couldn't yet be angry at her. "I don't understand that logic. Feel free to explain."

"I know you're in trouble because of what's going on with the court and the land and moving to our own place. I've been saving as much money as I can to put into your account so maybe we can just buy someplace. I know I'm only supposed to play for buttons and gum—but you can't use those things if you're really trying to buy something."

If he hadn't felt like a heel before, he certainly felt like the squashed bug beneath one now. "Aww, shoot, Lucky. I …" He turned away, unable to finish, only to find Grace waiting, her eyes shining with tears about to fall.

"That's quite a kid you've got there."

"I don't know what to say or do," he said. "Everyone went above and beyond. What happens next?"

"We tell everyone the kids are back. You take Teagan home and hold her tight. And we see you in court day after tomorrow."

With that she hesitated, looked almost like she was going to kiss him, but then patted his arm, bent to give Lucky a hug, and walked away.

He watched her retreating figure a long time, knowing she was everything that could be right with his world, if he hadn't taken a very wrong turn somewhere before he'd ever met her.

***

The Lincoln County Courthouse in Kemmerer was only a forty-minute drive from the southern boundary of Paradise Ranch. It took three vehicles to get all the Crocketts who came to lend their support to the county seat, including Mia, who would not be dissuaded. Grace had to laugh when the clerk looked askance at the Paradise entourage settling in half an hour early outside the courtroom. She looked around for Ty and his lawyer, but they hadn't arrived.

They were ushered into the courtroom at quarter to ten. Grandma Sadie and Trampas were surrounded as if they were fragile treasures, but Grace knew the two elders weren't nervous. In fact, nobody was nervous about losing the land anymore, not since they'd heard Lydia's journal entries. What set Grace's nerves quivering was imagining Ty's reaction to the disturbing, and damning, journal.

The Crocketts had voted to do their own relatively dishonest thing—to refrain from revealing the journal's existence to Ty's lawyer. There could be legal consequences, and the family would accept them if it came to that. But there was one mitigating factor: a final, unanimous family vote—at Mia and Harper's suggestion.

But by ten after ten, Ty still hadn't arrived.

The judge checked in with them, asked several questions, and announced Mr. Garraway had until ten-thirty before forfeiting the time. He'd have to resubmit for a new hearing date.

The minutes ticked past. Grace worried—it wasn't like Ty

to be careless. Finally she tried to call, but got no answer. She looked up Drew Metcalf's number and called him as well, but had no luck there either. Car trouble? Illness? Something wrong with Lucky? Concern led to restlessness for the entire family.

Their wait didn't end until time was almost up, when Metcalf finally appeared, red-faced and harried with a much calmer, but quiet, Ty in tow. The lawyer smiled at the assembled Crockett family and stepped in front of the judge. Ty stood to his side and made no eye contact with anyone. Grace's stomach churned.

"Is everything all right, Mr. Metcalf," the judge asked.

"I sincerely apologize to the court," Drew said. "My client and I had some emergency information to deal with. At this time Mr. Garraway asks permission to speak to Your Honor and the Crockett family."

"Mr. Garraway?" The judge turned to Ty. "You're free to talk."

Grace had never seen the demeanor Ty presented as he turned to face them all at last. Quiet and certain, he nonetheless wiped his palms on his thighs and cleared his throat.

"First of all, I'm here to apologize publicly to the whole Crockett family for hiding like the fox in the chicken coop and withholding my intentions so long that you all had to find out my plans from someone other than me. That was never my intention. What I wanted was to get my bearings here in Wyoming and, I admit, learn from working with you before I became the enemy. In hindsight it probably wasn't right, but I did it for my family, and I take responsibility.

"Secondly, I learned far more from you than I ever knew I would. You are the kind of family I wish I could give to my daughter—so, I've decided that rather than fight you, I'd prefer to concentrate on Teagan. I've given Mr. Metcalf here permission to ask the judge to rescind all the claims I've made on the seven thousand acres of Paradise land. That's all I want to say. I'll leave the legal details up to my lawyer."

He stopped, and Grace could hear birds chirp all the way through windows and walls. When Ty's gaze found her, she caught her breath at the sincerity—and the sorrow—clearly written in his liquid, green-gold eyes.

Before she could say anything, he nodded, exchanged one look with Metcalf, and left the room. Grace leaped to her feet, but Mia stopped her.

"Give him a minute," she said, gently. "Let him process this and get ready to talk to you."

Grace nodded reluctantly. The courtroom door closed and latched.

"If there are no questions, Your Honor, I have nothing further." Drew Metcalf's voice drew her attention back.

"Well, I have nothing to add," the judge replied. "Does anyone from the family have questions?"

Grace saw nothing but astonishment on the faces around her. Finally Mia stood and faced Metcalf.

"That's it? He really wants nothing from us?"

"Nothing," the lawyer agreed.

Harper shrugged, glanced through the crowd of silent Crocketts. Shock ruled the moment.

"Then I dismiss this case and our session is adjourned," said the judge.

The buzz through the family grew slowly into celebratory laughter as they stood, and hugs began to fill the courtroom. Grace didn't linger, however. As soon as she disentangled herself from the family knot, she left the room and searched the empty hallway, then ran for the outer doors.

Ty was nowhere to be seen.

"He's gone. He drove separately." Drew Metcalf moved in beside her, looking not like a man who'd just lost his case, but exactly the opposite. He smiled. "He did ask me to give you this." He handed her a small envelope. "And, just so you know, I told Ty this was absolutely the right decision."

Harper, Kelly and Joely joined them and Grace had no time to ask why the lawyer would be on their side. "Drew," Harper asked. "I do have a question. Did you hear about the journal?"

"Journal?"

They explained briefly about Lydia's evidence—all but proving Simon hadn't been swindled. Evidence that might very well have lost the case for Drew had it gone ahead.

"I certainly knew nothing about it," he said. "I'm pretty sure Ty doesn't either. He would have mentioned that as a reason for giving up. As it is, he gave me no reason. He just said he wouldn't go through with it. I was glad. I think he wanted the land for all the right reasons. I don't think it would have made him happy. He seems to have figured that out."

Grace's heart soared at the news. Ty had let the suit drop of his own free will, not because he thought he'd been beaten.

"We all need to go out and eat. In relief." Kelly laughed.

"I'm totally in for that," Harper added.

"I think I need to get back." Grace looked at the envelope in her hand.

"And I'm sorry, but I'm afraid I need to go home and pick up a well-packed overnight bag." Mia swung up to them on her crutches, her face sporting a wide smile.

"Really?" Kelly grabbed Mia's cheeks between her palms

and squealed. "The baby?"

On its due date?"

"Well we've a ways to go, but, yeah, I think contractions started on the way down here."

"What? You didn't tell us? Are you *crazy*?" Grace put her hands lovingly around Mia's neck. "You're a frickin' *doctor*."

"That's right. And this is my first, so it's not going to go that fast. The contractions were so mild I wasn't sure that's what they are, but now I am. And I'm fine. Grace, you can come home with Gabe and me. Everyone else is going out to eat."

"Eat now? No way!" Raquel shook her head adamantly.

"Look, we're not going to have the entire Crockett family waiting for hours at the hospital. Gabe will call when something happens. Meanwhile, Grace has someone she has to find."

"Yeah," she held the envelope tightly, "I do."

She found him several hours later where his note had said he'd be, on the stoop of his house at the ranch with Rupert in his arms. He leaned against the porch railing, gazing toward Wolf Paw Peak, stroking the puppy absently so that the dog lay in limp ecstasy.

"You left awfully fast this morning," she said.

"It seemed the better part of valor—let you all figure out how you want to feel about what I said. I'll talk to everyone again before I leave—but I wanted to talk to you first."

A smile toyed with the corners of his mouth. Grace wanted to grab Rupert out of Ty's embrace and take the pup's place so she could smother the smile with kisses. She pushed away the impulse and let the doggy's back rub continue for the moment.

"You dropped the lawsuit."

He nodded and finally looked at her. She read his eyes

perfectly: contentment. "I feel pretty good about that, actually."

"You surprised us, I will admit. I'm not sure I understand. Why?"

"You. Uncle Trampas. You both said the same thing—I don't need land or possessions to pass down to Lucky. I love her. That's all she needs. Yesterday when she was lost, *I* was lost. I panicked because I had no frame of reference for organizing a search. But you all did. Every one of you came running, and you stayed calm for me and turned the world upside down for a little girl you'd taken in as your own. Didn't matter that you hated her father; that was put aside."

"Nobody hates you."

He shrugged. "We could argue, but the point is, for the past six weeks, I've been seeing the way a real legacy works. Nobody cared about the ranch at that moment—they only cared about the people on it. That's all my daughter needs from me. It's what Trampas gave his family, why he'll go running from anywhere if his daughter needs him. It's why he came after me. His daughter doesn't care that her great-grandpa lost a bunch of land in Wyoming."

"It's all true." She moved closer to the stairs.

"So." He set Rupert on the porch and dusted his palms together. "I'm not going after the land. I don't need it. What I need is you. What Lucky needs is you. Your kindness, your example of how to be a decent human being. I want to be that guy—the one you can trust your life with. The one you'll make love to because you no longer have to keep a vow to protect yourself. But ..."

"But?" She barely got the word out—her heartbeat nearly choked her with surprise, with desire. With happiness.

"That's asking too much. I think it might sound a little like same old Ty Garraway selfishness. I gave up the land but only so I could have you in return."

"I never thought that for a second."

"Your family might."

"I can prove to you right now that they won't. Do you know the story *The Gift of the Magi*?"

"The woman sells her hair to buy a gold watch chain for her husband, who sold the watch to buy her combs for her hair? Yeah. Always thought that was kind of depressing."

"Well, that version maybe. But today is like *The Gift of the Magi*, only nobody lost anything."

"I don't know about that. You lost me."

"You skipped out too quickly, so you don't know that we likely would have won, without question." She handed him the diary. "Read the paragraph marked with the ribbon."

Moments later he looked up, his eyes hard. "Simon, that bastard."

"Yeah. But your great-grandmother? That was one brave lady for her time. A woman simply didn't leave a man back then. Not without gaining a big scarlet letter. She saved her boys the best she could, saved herself, and punished a dangerous man without harming a hair on his head. That's some legacy for your daughter right there. But, you also don't know that we were going to turn down the judge's award if he gave it to us. The land is yours—our unanimous choice."

His gaze bored into hers; his jaw worked soundlessly, trying to form words.

"You see," she continued, "we had an epiphany after Lucky went lost, too. Same as yours. The land isn't important. What's important is caring for the people because without the people, the land doesn't matter. So—we got off our high horses and the choice was simple. But …"

He waited.

"You ruined our plan." She smiled. "So I'm here to tell you that nobody won or lost. We just did what makes perfect sense. As for some kind of *quid pro quo*, me for the land, you didn't need the journal you're holding to convince you to drop your suit; you just did it. What more proof does anyone need that you aren't looking for something in return?"

"I want you. I want you because you teach me how to be a better man."

"That's a crock. You're willing to sacrifice anything for your family. Nothing needs to be better than that. As for me? I'm an OCD girl living in limbo—that would *not* be easy."

He brought his hands to either side of her face and brushed her hair behind both ears. "I would be honored to be in limbo with you. Besides, we wouldn't be there long. You're barely getting started and your restaurant is going to be a big success, so that's exciting, not scary. And if you go too OCD on me— we'll play poker with messy chip piles. The question is, are you willing to start over with us? I'll find a job."

"You have a job."

"Cole won't want—"

"Cole absolutely wants you. And that's a quote. You're a great hand, Ty. And you'll need the experience if you ever want to get your own place up and running."

He let out an exasperated breath. "Come here," he demanded.

"Are you ordering me around? I thought we'd covered this."

"Just come here."

Her heart flew as she laughed and took the three porch steps in one leap. A second leap took her into his arms, and he lifted her so she wrapped her legs around his hips. Classic, cliché, a stereotype of budding love. She didn't care. It felt wonderful. He felt like home.

"How many times do I have to say this? I don't want the land. Not just in my name, anyway. I don't need it. I'd rather live here. If Paradise will have me. If you'll have me."

"Can I show you my answer rather than tell you? There's nobody in the house, right?"

"Right."

"Then you come on. I decided a while ago that you're The Guy."

"I want you, Grace. I love you."

"And I not only want you, I think I fell in love the moment you told me you'd taught your daughter how to play poker. For buttons, gum, or rocks. I was so self-righteous, but underneath, you reminded me of my dad, teaching his girls to play cards and know good Scotch. But with rules."

"Rules are necessary."

"I just have one rule for what we're about to do." She nuzzled his neck while electricity from his strong hands on her back and beneath her seat zapped every nerve ending in her body with desire.

They were interrupted by Grace's phone.

"Oh, yeah." She kissed him. "Sorry. We have to take this. Mia went to the hospital four hours ago."

"What? Why are you apologizing? Babies beat out sex."

"*That's* interesting to know." She grinned and answered the phone

A minute later she knew the news but Ty didn't, and he poked at her arm continuously, like an annoying five-year-old. She batted him away, grinning.

"Oh, Gabe, I'm so thrilled. I'll be there as soon as I can. Might be an hour or so …"

She looked up at Ty and batted her eyes. "Come on, come on," he urged, ignoring the tease.

"What?" she asked into the phone. "I did find him. I will invite him. See you."

"All right. All right," he said. "What's the news?"

"They want you to come up with me."

"I can't process that right now. Your family is—"

"It's a girl." She placed a finger against his lip. "Sadie Isabella."

"Your family is a made-up fairy tale." He kissed her slowly and pulled away. "Damn, though, there's an awful lot of estrogen on this place. Rory has a lot on his shoulders. When was the last male heir born?"

"Nineteen forty-seven. My father."

"Something needs to be done about this."

"You didn't win the baby pool you know. Gram did—which is sad; she'll only use the winnings to buy yarn. But—" Grace pushed closer to him, torso pressed hard to torso. "Want to bet you and I could take on the baby gender problem? In a year or so?"

Wide eyes of surprise melted quickly into a grin that could have powered all of Paradise.

"Grace Crockett, I'll see that wager. And I'll raise you this …"

He lowered his mouth and, moments later, they were both all in—forever.

The End

Acknowledgments

It takes a village to nurture almost everything in life, and getting a book to its published stage and into the hands of people who want to read it is no exception.

First and foremost thank you to Cat Schield, who started me on this journey with the self-publishing equivalent of baby formula and then spoon fed me every nourishing morsel to help grow my idea into a full-fledged, finished novel. Thanks for spur-of-the-moment graphics, fielding late night questions, and convincing me, despite stubborn resistance, to try new ideas.

Ellen Lindseth—thank you for being the best writing buddy, psychologist, whipping boy, debate partner, movie date, and inspiration I could ask for. I don't know if I would keep going without you on this roller coaster beside me. Nancy Holland and Laramie Sasseville—you are and always will be the best critique partners. No matter whether we meet often or infrequently, you're always there to inspire. I treasure you, your smart ideas, your willing help, and your friendship.

Jennifer Bernard—thank you for phenomenal beta reading and making my stories better—like WAY better—every single time. Also for all your insight into writing and taking new paths. You are my friend, my hero, and one of the authors I admire most. Someday I'm collaborating with you, dang it, and becoming famous following in your footsteps.

Thank you to my savvy editor Kelli Collins. The cool things you found to fix in this book astounded me—plus I really like the LOLs and the smiley faces and the memes you added to your track changes. They made me feel smart even though I can't do math and one of my characters would have had to be 118 if I'd left the numbers as I originally had them. I can't tell you how glad I am you caught that!

I first got to work with my cover artist Dana Lamothe when I wrote a novella for Kindle Worlds and she found a perfect cover photo after I'd had no luck at all. She did it again for this book. Dana I think you're a wizard!

To my uber-talented daughter Jennifer Van Vranken, thank you for copy editing above and beyond. Thank heaven you remember my previous books better than I do and caught on to commas and semi-colons faster than any kid needed to (or did) way back when you were revising stories in grade school.

Finally, thank you to my sister-in-law Robin Selvig—the greatest cheerleader of all time. And most of all to my amazing husband, Jan, who simply is the best romance model—the best man—I know. Thank you for putting up with so much crazy writer crap. I love you!

About The Author

Award-winning author Lizbeth Selvig writes fun, sexy-sweet contemporary romance. She is a winner of the Romance Writers of America Golden Heart® award, and a nominee for RWA's prestigious RITA® award. She turned to fiction writing after working as a newspaper journalist and magazine editor, and raising an equine veterinarian daughter and a talented musician son. Lizbeth shares life in Minnesota with her best friend (aka her husband, Jan), an under-ridden gray Arabian gelding named Jedi, two human grandchildren, and her four-legged grandkids of which there are over twenty, including a wallaby, two alpacas, a large goat, a mammoth-eared donkey, a miniature horse, a pig, and many dogs, cats and regular-sized horses (pics of all appear on her website). In her spare time she loves to hike, quilt, read, and horseback ride. She also loves connecting with readers—so contact her any time!

www.lizbethselvig.com